THE

BLACK BAND

OR, THE

MYSTERIES OF MIDNIGHT

BY

M. E. BRADDON.

I0607384

ILLUSTRATED BY GUSTAVE DORÉ, JANET LANGE,
BERTAL, AND OTHER ARTISTS

"There are the Secret Societies, an element which we must take into
account, and which at the last moment may baffle all our arrangements;
Societies which have regular agents everywhere, which countenance assassin-
ation, and which, if necessary, could produce a massacre."—LORD BEACONS-
FIELD, *speaking as Prime Minister of England at Aylesbury, Sept. 20th, 1876.*

LONDON: GEORGE VICKERS, ANGEL COURT, STRAND

MDCCCLXXVII.

CONTENTS

CHAPTER								PAGE
I.	Midnight at the Masked Ball	...	...	...	...	...		1
II.	The Central Office	...	...	...	...	...		5
III.	Ellen Clavering	...	...	...	...	...		7
IV.	The Midnight Marriage	...	...	...	...	...		9
V.	Midnight in Belgravia	...	...	...	...	...		11
VI.	Midnight in the Gaming-house	...	...	...	...	...		15
VII.	The Duel on the Seashore	...	...	...	...	...		20
VIII.	The Dead Reveal no Secrets	...	...	...	...	...		21
IX.	Uncle and Nephew	...	...	...	...	...		26
X.	The Millionaire's Resolve	...	...	...	...	...		28
XI.	Samuel Crank's Agency	...	...	...	...	...		32
XII.	The Star of the Ballet	...	...	...	...	...		35
XIII.	Too Late!	...	...	...	...	...	...	40
XIV.	The Tempter	...	...	...	...	...	...	45
XV.	The Spaniard's Love	...	...	...	...	...		48
XVI.	The Poisoner is Defeated	...	...	...	...	...		50
XVII.	On the Watch	...	...	...	...	...		52
XVIII.	The Midnight Encounter	...	...	...	...	...		57
XIX.	A Merited Reward	...	...	...	...	...		59
XX.	Maclomond Castle	...	...	...	...	...		61
XXI.	The Abduction of Clara Melville	...	...	...	...		67
XXII.	Help at Hand in the Hour of Peril	...	...	...	...		69
XXIII.	A Dark Story	...	...	...	...	...	...	74
XXIV.	The Lady in the Scarlet Jacket	...	...	...	...		77
XXV.	The Ghost Appears to Donald, the Shepherd	...	...	...		81
XXVI.	Poor Clara	...	...	...	...	...	...	85
XXVII.	The Grand Master at Work	...	...	...	...	...		88
XXVIII.	The Secrets of the Association	...	...	...	...		90
XXIX.	The Robbery at the Sham Hotel	...	...	...	...		94
XXX.	Cast Off	...	...	...	...	...	...	95
XXXI.	The Winding Ways of Life	...	...	...	...	...		99
XXXII.	The Two Detectives	...	...	...	...	...		103
XXXIII.	The Missing Gold	...	...	...	...	...		108
XXXIV.	In the Toils	...	...	...	...	...		111
XXXV.	Still Waters Run Deep	...	...	...	...	...		117
XXXVI.	Mr. Rupert de Lancy Receives a Visitor	...	...	...		119
XXXVII.	Clara's Promise	...	...	...	...	...		128
XXXVIII.	The Vaults below Clavering Abbey	...	...	...	...		131
XXXIX.	The Hidden Dagger	...	...	...	...	...		136
XL.	The Secret Interview in the Albany	...	...	...	...		140.
XXLI.	Dark Deeds Brought to Light	...	...	...	...	...		143
XLII.	The Lawyer's Hack	...	...	...	...	...		148

ii.

CONTENTS—*Continued.*

CHAPTER		PAGE
XLIII.	The Star of Hope Shines on a Dark Horizon	150
XLIV.	The Strange Travellers at the Duke of Atholl	153
XLV.	The Plotters at Work	156
XLVI.	The Midnight Flight	159
XLVII.	The Secrets of the Darkness	162
XLVIII.	The Secret Mission	163
XLIX.	Antonio Vecchi Reveals the Plot	165
L.	The Funeral of the Murdered Chief	168
LI.	Lolota's Midnight Guest	169
LII.	The Warning	171
LIII.	The First Act in Lady Edith's Revenge	174
LIV.	The Legend of the Dead Hand	179
LV.	The Fever-stricken City	181
LVI.	Is He Too Late?	182
LVII.	The Second Marriage	184
LVIII.	The Compact	187
LIX.	The Clue to the Secret	189
LX.	The Perfume in the Golden Bottle	192
LXI.	The Rock of Terror	193
LXII.	The Dark Journey	196
LXIII.	The Burial of the Living	201
LXIV.	The Meeting in the Valley	205

THE BLACK BAND

OR, THE

MYSTERIES OF MIDNIGHT

THE STRANGER IN THE RUINED ABBEY

CHAPTER I.

MIDNIGHT AT THE MASKED BALL

As the clock of St. Clement Danes chimed the three-quarters after eleven on the night of December 20th, 1852, a tall man, dressed in a loose overcoat, and wearing an opera-hat slouched over his eyes, hailed a cab from the stand by the church, and, jumping into it, told the man to drive to the door of Drury Lane Theatre.

In less than five minutes the cab dashed up to the box entrance of the theatre, the approach to which was crowded with carriages, masque-

raders, and noisy, drunken spectators. The young man sprang out of the cab, paid and dismissed the driver, and passing rapidly up the steps and across the crowded portico, made his way into the lobby of the theatre, surrendered his ticket and his overcoat, and hurried on to the stage, where the dancing was going forward. He wore a plain evening dress and a small velvet mask, and he carried an opera-glass in his hand. He was tall and slender; his hair, which he wore rather long, was of a reddish auburn; but the eyes, flashing under the velvet mask, were as black as night. On reaching the stage his manner altogether changed; he no longer walked rapidly, but loitered about, mingling with the dancers, and every now and then raising his opera-glass with an air of foppish languor, looked lazily round at the crowded scene.

There was only one peculiarity about his simple but fashionably-made black dress. This one peculiarity was a narrow strip of black crape tied round his left wrist, and fastened with a slip knot.

He did not dance, but, after making the round of the stage, placed himself against one of the pillars of the side boxes, drew out an elegant gold watch of the smallest size, and looked at the time: it wanted five minutes to twelve.

The close observer might have remarked that as the man with the red hair did this, two other men, on the opposite side of the theatre, watched him closely. One of these men was dressed as a clown—the other as an English sailor, and both the clown and the sailor wore a strip of black crape tied round the left wrist with a slip knot. At the same time with these two men, a third, a fourth, and a fifth masquerader stopped at a little distance from the red-haired man, and appeared to watch him closely; while in another part of the vast assembly two of the dancers abandoned their partners—a Scotch peasant and a Swiss flower girl—and walked away in the direction of the pillar against which the mysterious red-haired stranger was standing.

As the clock struck twelve, the clown, the sailor, and the five other men, each of whom was differently dressed, but all of whom wore the same badge of black crape round the left wrist, threaded their way through the crowd of dancers, and congregated round the man with the red hair.

They were all closely masked, and they all appeared young.

"Good," said the red-haired man; "there are seven of you, I see."

"You said seven," one of the masqueraders answered, in a gruff voice.

"I said seven, but I shall only want three—Captain Davis, Lieutenant Morrison, and Corporal Pierce; the rest may go."

At these words four of the men dropped slowly off from the little group, and mingled once more with the dancers. The other three remained standing close to the red-haired man.

"I have nothing to tell you yet," he said; "disperse now, and meet at the central office at two o'clock this morning."

The three masqueraders walked away without having uttered a word, and the red-haired man was left alone. He unfastened the strip of crape from his left wrist, put it into his pocket, and raising his opera-glass, examined the house with a deliberate and piercing gaze.

The stage was crowded with noisy, reckless masqueraders — sailors, smugglers, chimney-sweeps, Charles the Seconds, clowns, Lady Jane Greys, charity girls, Mary Queen of Scots, and Henry the Eighths.

Presently the stranger lowered his glass, and said, shrugging his shoulders, "They are not here; perhaps my information was incorrect."

As he spoke a quadrille ended; the dancers walked away from the centre of the stage, leaving it comparatively clear; and out of the crowd a man slowly advanced, with a lady leaning on his arm, in the direction of the boxes against which the stranger was standing. The man wore the dress of a Greek bravo; an immense scarf, of the richest materials and the most gorgeous hues, crossed his chest and fell over one shoulder, the deep fringe nearly reaching to his feet. The lady was dressed in a Venetian costume of a far more costly character than the dresses of any of the other masqueraders. Neither of them was masked, and they seemed so utterly absorbed in conversation as to be utterly indifferent to anything passing around them.

The red-haired man concealed himself behind the pillar as they approached. "My information was correct, then," he said; "they are here."

The face of the young man in the brigand's dress was marvellously handsome. There was something of a foreign character in the dark, olive complexion and the dreamy grey eyes, shrouded by long black lashes; but the masquerader and his companion were both English. The face of the woman was scarcely less perfect than that of the man upon whose arm she leant, though there was something repellent in the cold, clearly-cut, aquiline features, the determined expression of the mouth, and the strongly-marked black eyebrows.

"Edith," said the young man, in suppressed but impassioned accents, "once more, and for the last time, do you love me?"

"Once more, and for the last time—yes," she answered, with a scornful laugh.

They were close to the pillar behind which the masked stranger stood—so close that he could hear every word they uttered.

"And yet you refuse to marry me," said the Greek bravo bitterly.

The lady lifted her haughty white eyelids, and raising her flashing eyes to his face, said defiantly—

"Lionel Montfort, I refuse to marry you because you are a ruined man; because you are fettered with debts which you cannot pay; because you are hourly in danger of disgrace and a prison; because you are, in short, a penniless younger son, with no chance of ever becoming anything better, unless——" She stopped suddenly, never taking her eyes from his face; their burning glance seemed to scorch his inmost soul. He almost shuddered as he took up her unfinished sentence—

"Unless my brother Angus, one of the noblest-hearted fellows in England, were to die in the prime of life."

She shrugged her shoulders with an action of graceful contempt. "Poor Angus has an excellent constitution," she said, replacing her velvet mask, the lace border of which entirely concealed her face; " I am not afraid of seeing you wear crape round your hat for him."

"And this is your final answer, Edith Vandeleur? All my mad love and passionate folly end in this—you reject me?"

"Dear Lionel, be reasonable," she said, with the same scornful laugh. "I was not born to marry a poor man. You are young—you ought to be ambitious; the world is all before you. Conquer the world, win wealth, and then come to me and ask for the hand which I refuse you to-night."

"Edith," he exclaimed, "you have never loved me."

"Have I not? Is my coming here to-night no proof of my love? Think what would the world say did it learn that the Lady Edith Vandeleur had come alone and secretly from Hampshire to London, on the 20th of December, to meet her lover at a masked ball at Drury Lane Theatre? Have I made no sacrifice in this?"

"A small one, Edith, compared to the sacrifices I would willingly make for you. I had several reasons for asking you to meet me in this crowded place. To-night, Edith, is a turning point in my life. For your sake, and blessed with your love, I would have become a better man. The small income which my brother allows me would have enabled me to lead a quiet country life; that life would have been one of unalloyed happiness had it been shared by you. One word, then, my beloved. Will you accept the hand of a poor but an honest man? One word, Edith, and remember that the future career, for good or evil, of the man who loves you hangs upon that word. Will you accept me—yes or no?"

"Once more, then, Lionel—no. Never until you are a rich man will Edith Vandeleur marry you."

The man behind the pillar laughed softly to himself as the lady uttered the words. "Piti-

less demon!" he muttered; "hers, and not mine, is the hand that drives him to his fate. So be it."

"Edith, you are as heartless as you are lovely," said Lionel Montfort; "but angel or demon, you alone have power over my soul. Let me lead you back to your carriage. Your maid is waiting for you?"

"Yes, she is in the secret; I pay her well. I have little faith in her fidelity, or, indeed, in the fidelity of any one to anything except their own interest. I make it her interest to serve me, and she serves me well. Come, Lionel."

He looked at her with a sigh. "Edith," he said, bitterly, "you should always wear a mask."

"Indeed!"

"If you could wear it over your heart."

They disappeared amongst the crowd in the direction of the doors leading out of the theatre. The red-haired man emerged from behind the pillar, and looked after them earnestly. "I think he will join us to-night. My information was perfectly correct. Poor Lady Edith! she pays her maid well, no doubt; fortunately, I can afford to pay her better."

He crossed the stage in the direction taken by the lovers, and remained near the door, watching for the young man's return.

The Greek bravo was masked when he re-entered the ball-room. The red-haired man allowed him to pass, and then following him, tapped him lightly on the shoulder.

The masquerader turned, and as the other raised his mask, exclaimed—"Colonel Bertrand!"

"Lord Lionel Montfort! So you have been beguiled by the delights of a masked ball? I thought you had exhausted all such amusements."

The young man removed his mask, and turning his gloomy face to the Colonel, said with indifference, "All the masked balls in London and Paris could not amuse me for half an hour. I had a motive in coming here."

"Ah, precisely; an appointment."

"No matter what; but allow me to ask what has brought the elegant and fashionable Colonel in this direction?"

"I suppose the elegant and fashionable Colonel has come here because he has very little else to do. Or, Lord Lionel Montfort, suppose I am candid, and confess my motive in coming here?"

"As you please."

"How if I came here to meet you?"

"What! you knew of my coming here?"

"I knew of your coming here; more, I knew your motive in coming here, the person you cause to meet, and I also know the result of that meeting."

"Colonel Bertrand, you are insolent."

"Lord Lionel Montfort, it is in my power to be your friend—to help you to the object of your ambition, to unite you to the woman whom you love. Will you accept my friendship?"

"Not until I know who you are, and what you are."

"That you will never know. It never yet has been known to mortal man, and while I have life it never shall. Accept my services if you will; serve me if you please. Let it suffice you to know that I can be useful to you, and you to me; but ask to know no more."

"Colonel Bertrand, you are a mystery."

"Young man, great cities have their mysteries. I am one of the mysteries of great cities. Mention my name in London, Paris, Vienna, Rome, St. Petersburg, Constantinople, and they will tell you of my reckless expenditure, my horses, my carriages, my inexhaustible wealth, my fabulous generosity. Go a step farther, and ask them if they know the sources of that wealth, the secret of that luxury! They will shrug their shoulders, but they can tell you nothing. Calumny has never assailed my name, no traducer has ever dared to tarnish my escutcheon."

"I have no wish to insinuate a doubt," said Lord Lionel.

"You are in debt; you are penniless; you love and are beloved by an ambitious woman; and you would be rich. That is your history in a sentence, is it not?"

"It is."

"Are you scrupulous as to the means by which you would become rich?"

As the Colonel asked this question, his piercing black eyes met those of Lord Lionel. The two men seemed as if they would read each other's thoughts.

"From to-night I am not," answered Lord Lionel, passionately; "the woman I love urges me on upon a terrible road. Show me any means, honourable or dishonourable, by which I may become rich before my hair is grey and my youth departed, and I will adopt those means, whatever they may be."

"A brave answer, Lord Lionel. Now listen to me. I am the centre of a system so vast in its operations, that it extends over the greater part of civilized Europe. I am the captain of a company so large that there are men in it upon whose faces I have never looked, and never expect to look. It is a company which, though continually at war with society, can yet—secure in its internal strength and the unfailing produce of its operations—afford to defy society year after year. Recall to your recollection some of those gigantic robberies which have startled the wealthiest cities of Europe—robberies in which a skill has been displayed partaking almost of the supernatural—robberies which have defied the determination and perseverance of the cleverest police in Europe, and which have remained undiscovered until this hour. Remember these, and you may form some idea of the resources of the mysterious company of which I speak."

The Colonel had led Lord Lionel into a deserted corner of one of the refreshment rooms; they had seated themselves opposite to each other at a small marble table. The face of the young nobleman grew ghastly white at the Colonel's last words.

"And you ask me to join a band of robbers," he said.

"I ask you to do what better men have done before you," said Colonel Bertrand, coldly. "Members of the company have been the inhabitants of palaces before to-day. From the highest to the lowest—the strength of the band lies in that. Wherever there is genius, courage, endurance and patience; a hand that can strike, or withhold from striking; a tongue that can be silent, and a head that can think,—wherever there are these, there is a worthy member. High or low, let him enter the band. He will never leave it."

"Your words appal me," said Lord Lionel, gloomily.

"Will you join us—yes or no?" asked the Colonel.

"What do you promise me if I do join you."

"The wealth you desire, and the hand of Lady Edith Vandeleur before the next year is out."

"On those terms I am yours," said the young man recklessly, grasping the hand of Colonel Bertrand.

The Colonel looked at his watch. "Half-past one," he said. "Lord Lionel, I shall want you to come at once to one of our meeting-places."

"You have more meeting-places than one then?"

"We have more than a hundred. Put on your mask and follow me."

The Colonel left the theatre with the young nobleman. At the doors Lord Lionel threw a loose coat over his conspicuous costume. The Colonel and his companion sprang into one of the cabs waiting in Brydges Street. The Colonel whispered a direction to the driver, and the cab drove off in the direction of Leicester Square.

As they entered the square, the Colonel, taking a black silk scarf from his pocket, said to Lord Lionel—

"You will have no objection, I suppose, to being blindfolded? It is one of our first conditions."

"I have promised to join you," answered Lord Lionel, with the indifference of desperation: "I am entirely in your hands."

The Colonel bowed; and as the young man bent his head, Bertrand fastened the scarf with considerable dexterity over his eyes.

"Of the twenty or forty men whom you may see to-night," said the Colonel, as they drove slowly along, "not one knows the name or the face of the other. They meet masked, and they do their work masked. They may encounter each other in the streets, and pass as strangers. They may be brothers, and yet not recognise each other. Silence is one of the conditions of the order: if they have anything to say, they say it to me. They can have nothing to say to each other. Their work is planned for them; they have only to execute it in silence. I know their names, their occupations, the names of their friends, and the uses to which they may be put. I am the supreme ruler and commander of the order."

"By Heaven!" exclaimed Lord Lionel, "you must be something more or less than human."

Colonel Bertrand laughed softly to himself at the young man's words.

"I am a colonel in the Austrian army," he said; "at least, so the world thinks. Shall I tell you what I really am, Lord Lionel."

"Yes," exclaimed the young man, eagerly.

"I am Captain of the Black Band—the Companions of Midnight!"

CHAPTER II.

THE CENTRAL OFFICE

It seemed to Lord Lionel to be upwards of half an hour from the time of the cab entering Leicester Square, when the driver suddenly stopped, and the door of the vehicle was immediately opened. He was lifted by two men out of the cab, and then conducted by them up a flight of steps, across a hall, and through several passages, which seemed of almost endless length. Just as he was beginning to wonder when this journey would end, he felt himself released from the men who had been leading him, and he heard the voice of the Colonel, at apparently a considerable distance, ordering some one to remove the bandage from his eyes.

The order was obeyed, and a blaze of light burst upon the dazzled eyes of the young nobleman.

He found himself standing in the centre of an immense amphitheatre, brilliantly illuminated with gas. All round the sides of this amphitheatre were ranged tiers of benches, upon which were seated upwards of a hundred men, differently dressed, and of widely varying appearance, but each wearing a closely-fitting black mask and a narrow band of black crape tied round the left wrist.

Exactly opposite to him, upon a raised platform, he perceived a desk hung with black velvet, and a high-backed arm-chair, with cushions of the same sombre material. In this chair a man was seated, who alone of all the assembly wore no mask. His hair, which was raven black, was cut close to his head, giving a sinister character to his pale face and burning black eyes. For a moment Lord Lionel recoiled, thinking he beheld in this man a stranger; but a second glance convinced him that he was looking at Colonel Bertrand, the Austrian. The red hair, for which he had become celebrated in society, was, then, a wig.

As Lord Lionel scanned the strange apartment, and its still more remarkable occupants, he was bewildered by perceiving there was no visible mode of egress or ingress. The walls were hung with black, and he looked in vain for any indication of a door by which he could have entered. While this was passing through his mind the Colonel spoke.

"Brothers," he said, in a strange and solemn voice, entirely unlike his ordinary tones, "I bring you a brother."

There was a death-like silence, during which the masked assembly solemnly bent their heads, as if in assent.

"You are willing to receive him, although, according to the inviolable rules of the society, you will never see his face, you will never know his name, you will, perhaps, never hear his voice. Are you willing to accept him because I think him a fitting assistant in our work, and because I believe that he may be trusted?"

The masked assembly bowed again, and, as before, in utter silence.

"You hear, brother," said the Colonel, "you are accepted by the Companions of Midnight. Is it not so, brothers?"

The masked company raised their hands simultaneously. Lord Lionel noticed that while many of the hands elevated were coarse and large, others were small, white, and delicate, and adorned with costly rings.

"Executioners of the order, advance!" said the Colonel.

Two men rose, and advanced from opposite sides of the amphitheatre. They were both dressed in black from head to foot, and Lord Lionel perceived that they each wore a long slender knife, fastened to a belt which went round their waists.

Each of them silently took one of Lord Lionel's hands, which he held while the Colonel uttered the following words—

"Executioners of the Order of the Companions of Midnight, the brother whose hand you now clasp will be never harmed by you, while faithful to the society which he this night swears to serve. If unfaithful to that society, he will become yours to strike when you can, and how you can. Mercy is unknown to you—you are the blind and pitiless instruments of the order to which you belong. If the new brother is too weak to take the oath of the order, let him release your hands as I speak these words. If he holds your hands after these words, he is supposed to have taken the oath. Silence is the rule of the order. If he refuse to join, let him drop the hands of the executioners."

A deadly shiver agitated the frame of the young nobleman, but his hands tightened upon those of the executioners, which he grasped with a convulsive strength.

"The new brother does not draw back from the oath of the order," said the Colonel, after a long pause. "He is one of us. Brothers, accept him and receive him."

The executioners retired.

One after another the masked brothers descended from their seats, and advancing to Lord Lionel, severally grasped him by the hand, and then returned to the benches. He could feel, in those strange greetings, sometimes the rough horny hand of labour, sometimes the soft touch of a palm as delicate as his own.

Then the Colonel, descending from the platform, advanced to him, holding a strip of black crape in his hand.

"Brother," he said, "it is my task to fasten round your left wrist the badge of the Order of the Black Band. It is tied with a slipknot, and represents the noose which the law employs for the execution of those who offend against it. The brethren of the Black Band defy the law and its executioners, and the noose of crape which they wear, they wear in mockery of the law, and its engines of punishment. They wear it also as a badge by which they may recognize each other, when it is to the interest of the society that they should meet and act in unison. Now, brother, I must blindfold you once more, and then I will give you your instructions."

The Colonel fastened the scarf round Lord Lionel's eyes. He had scarcely done so when, to his astonishment, the young man perceived himself to be sinking through the floor of the assembly. He seemed slowly, and almost imperceptibly, to descend for about five minutes; and at the expiration of that time he felt a hand unfastening the bandage, and looking round, found himself alone with the Colonel, in a small, but luxurious apartment, lighted by a pair of large wax candles and a blazing fire.

Three sides of this apartment were covered by shelves, upon which were ranged rows of volumes, bound alike, numbered and dated. Beneath the books the space was occupied by innumerable pigeon-holes, into which papers were thrust. At one side of the fire-place there was an elegant little desk of walnut wood, covered with scarlet morocco; on the other side, a cabinet, also of walnut wood, furnished with numerous drawers, each of which was fastened by a steel lock of peculiar construction. In this apartment, as in the amphitheatre, Lord Lionel was utterly unable to discover any door or window.

The Colonel stood with his back to the fire, and his hands in his pockets.

"This, my dear Lord Lionel," he said, re-assuming his natural manner, which was celebrated for its vivacity, ease, and polish, "this is my snuggery. Pray sit down and help yourself to a glass of wine," he added, pointing to an exquisitely cut crystal jug, which was filled with claret. "You can make yourself perfectly at home here. We shall not be disturbed by any of the brotherhood; those who have work to-night know their task, and will do it."

"Are we in your house?" asked Lord Lionel, looking round the room.

"In my house!" said Colonel Bertrand, laughing. "I am too much a citizen of the world to possess such an incumbrance as a house of my own. I have chambers in the Albany, an apartment in the Boulevard des Italiens, and other apartments at Vienna, St. Petersburg, Rome, Florence, Naples, Homburg, and Baden-Baden. But this, my dear Lord Lionel, is the central office of the English Brethren of the Black Band. Every city has its chief office; this is the chief office for the city of London. Look round at the rows of volumes upon those shelves. Those volumes contain the reports of the society—the names and addresses of the members, the personal and secret histories of their acquaintance, whenever those histories are likely to be of use to the community. You are now in the most sacred chamber of the office. This apartment is filled from floor to ceiling with the secrets of the brotherhood, known only to me, and kept by me alone."

"Strange," said Lord Lionel, thoughtfully. "You tell me this, and we are here, two men of the same height, the same size, both unarmed. What if I were a scoundrel, and were inclined to take advantage of my position, and possess myself of some of the secrets of your order?"

The Colonel laughed long and loudly, and looking at Lord Lionel with a smile of consummate scorn, he said, pointing to the books,— "Those volumes are written in a cipher, not one character of which is known to any creature but myself. Again, you are now in an apartment from which it would be impossible for you to escape without my aid. You might rot here before you would ever discover the secret means of ingress and egress. If my word does not satisfy you, look at yonder cabinet."

They were seated opposite to each other at the table, some paces from the cabinet of which the Colonel spoke. Lord Lionel fixed his eyes upon the mysterious article of furniture. As he did so Colonel Bertrand leaned with his elbow rather heavily upon the table; the several drawers of the cabinet burst open with a metallic sound, and at each of the openings there appeared the muzzles of a row of pistols. At the same moment the cabinet slightly revolved, in such a manner as to place the muzzles of the pistols exactly opposite to Lord Lionel Montfort.

"You said I was unarmed, Lord Lionel," said the Colonel, still smiling; "you were rather hasty in your conclusion. Now, my lord, listen to me while I reveal to you the services which I shall expect you to render to the brotherhood."

CHAPTER III.

ELLEN CLAVERING

IN a lovely little village hidden amongst the woodland scenery of Hampshire lived an old man, whose ancestors had been squires of the place. The rustics would show to the inquiring traveller an old mansion which, fifty years before, had been occupied by Squire Hugh Clavering, the father of Lucas, the old man, but which had long been suffered to fall into a state of hopeless ruin and decay. Clavering Abbey was situated at some distance from the village, and the honest rustics would walk a mile out of their way rather than pass the old building after dark. The decayed and tenantless rooms were supposed by many to be haunted; but others declared that Clavering Abbey was a meeting-place for all the thieves and ruffians of the neighbourhood. In one of the ivy-grown lodges attached to the deserted mansion Lucas Clavering and his only daughter had taken up their abode. Lucas was a man of nearly seventy years of age. After a youth spent in riot and debauchery, and having wasted a noble fortune upon the turf and in the gambling-houses of London, he had returned, at the age of fifty, a broken-down invalid, to the village of Clavering. He found the Abbey falling into decay; he was too poor, he said, to live in it, and the bats and owls were welcome to riot beneath the roof under which his infancy had been passed. He brought with him a young wife, a fair and delicate-looking woman, and an infant daughter. Mrs. Clavering did not live long to endure the poverty and wretchedness which were her fate; three years after her arrival at Clavering Abbey she died, leaving her helpless child to the care of the ruined gambler. From that hour Lucas Clavering changed. He swore that his child should live to restore the Abbey to its former splendour, and that Ellen Clavering's children should enjoy the home of her ancestors. With his infant daughter he occupied the little rustic lodge at one of the gates of Clavering Park. It was very rarely that any human creature, except the old man and his daughter, entered the humble abode. Lucas watched over his little girl with the care of the tenderest of mothers, and Ellen was never so happy as when sitting on the knees of her grey-haired father, listening to some child-like stories. But as years advanced, the little girl began to perceive that there were times when she was left alone in the cottage. After she had gone to bed she would hear her father quietly creep out of the house, to which he did not return till late on the following morning. When she grew older still, and was able to wait on herself, Lucas Clavering would often leave her for days and nights together, merely telling her he had business in London, and that she was not to be uneasy if he should be delayed longer than he expected.

Once when she had reached her fifteenth year, he spoke to her more seriously than usual before starting on one of these journeys.

"Ellen," he said, "you never go into the village in my absence?"

"Never, father; Goody Brown brings me all that I require in the morning, and if I want fresh air, I walk in the dear old avenues of the Park. I never go beyond its gates."

"My good girl, my noble Ellen!" said her father, tenderly; "but Goody Brown is a chattering old woman. Has she never asked you anything about me?"

"Yes, she has sometimes seemed rather inquisitive about your absences; but I always told her that you were away on business, and would soon be back."

"Now, Ellen," said the old man, earnestly, "listen to me : it is best in all cases to be prepared for the worst that can possibly happen. If I ever chance to stay away more than a month without either sending or writing to you, you may conclude that something serious has occurred."

"My dearest father !"

"In that case, Ellen, look into the desk in my room. You have the keys. You will find in that desk a sealed packet, in which are written my instructions for your conduct. Should your father never return to you, my poor child, you will find he has not left you penniless."

This was the only occasion upon which the old man ever alluded to his journeys in his daughter's presence. He would quietly depart, and as quietly return. The villagers felt little curiosity as to the actions of the ruined gentleman. Some thought him merely eccentric; others openly called him mad. They pitied his pretty daughter, immured within the boundaries of Clavering Park ; but none dared offer any civility to the only child of Lucas Clavering. Poor as he was supposed to be, he had all the pride of his ancient race ; and resented any intrusion on his privacy with haughty words, and cold, angry looks. Meanwhile, Ellen Clavering grew every day more beautiful. Hers was a delicate beauty, scarcely calculated, perhaps, to charm the vulgar eye. With complexion pale as marble, her hair was of a golden brown, falling in heavy waving masses about her oval face. Her eyes were of the darkest shade of hazel ; her features small and delicately shaped. The crimson of her pouting lips contrasted vividly with the unvarying pallor of her complexion, and gave a peculiar charm to her beauty. She was a creature for a painter to dream of as the model for a Madonna. Pensive, gentle, timid, she seemed made to be the object of one of those soul-absorbing passions, which shed their fatal influence over a life-time.

In the December during which Lord Lionel Montfort and Lady Edith Vandeleur met at the masked ball, Ellen Clavering had attained her eighteenth year. She passed a dreary Christmas alone in the little cottage in Clavering Park, for on the 19th of December her father had left her for an absence of a fortnight. But her solitude was startlingly broken ere the day fixed for her father's return had arrived. To explain how this happened, however, we must go back to the preceding summer, and narrate an event which, although apparently accidental, served to turn the whole current of Ellen Clavering's life.

One evening in July, as she was slowly returning homewards from a long ramble in the Park, she was startled by hearing the hoofs of a horse in the shady avenue behind her. On turning round she saw that the rider of the animal was a man about five-and-thirty years of age. He was tall and slender. His eyes were black, and his hair of a golden auburn. His hat was slouched over his face, as if he wished to avoid recognition. Ellen blushed as she met his eyes, for she felt that her scrutiny of him must have attracted his attention ; but as Clavering Park was so seldom entered by strangers, she could not help feeling some slight curiosity about this handsome horseman. To her surprise he bent over his horse's neck to speak to her.

"Will you be so good as to tell me," he said, "whether I am right in supposing that a gentleman of the name of Clavering lives near here ?"

"Mr. Clavering's cottage is at the other end of this avenue," Ellen answered ; "I can show you the way if you will follow me. Mr. Clavering is my father."

"Your father !" exclaimed the stranger ; "I had no idea that Lucas Clavering had a daughter —still less that he had so lovely a daughter," he added, looking admiringly at the young girl.

Ellen hurried on ; and the horseman had no time to engage her in conversation before they reached the cottage in which Lucas and his daughter lived. As Ellen entered the ivy-grown door, the stranger sprang from his horse, and having fastened the bridle to a neighbouring tree, followed her into the little sitting-room.

The old man was seated at his desk, writing. He had lighted a lamp, which shed a feeble glimmer over the worm-eaten oak furniture of the humble apartment.

Lucas started from his seat at the sight of the stranger, and an angry frown darkened his still handsome face.

"What is the meaning of this visit ?" he cried, fiercely ; "I thought my home was sacred."

The stranger laughed scornfully. "*You* thought !" he said, with a sneer ; "I tell you, Lucas Clavering, no place is sacred, however lofty, or however lowly. From the palace to the pauper's workhouse, wherever there is *one of us*, the place is open to *all of us*. I have come on business."

"Ellen," said the old man sternly, "leave us ; this is no fit place for you."

The young girl looked from her father to the stranger with a glance of alarm, and then stole quietly from the room. Lucas walked to the door as she closed it behind her, and turned the key in the lock.

"You hide your jewel carefully, Clavering," said the stranger; "who could have dreamt that you had so lovely a daughter?"

"Your business, Captain," said the old man, coldly.

"You do not like me to speak of your daughter. So be it, then; we will change the subject. You are wanted in London."

"Again?"

"Yes, again. You have talents that are peculiarly your own. They are useful to us, and they are ours to command when we need them."

The old man sighed heavily, but did not answer. He leaned his elbows on the desk by which he was seated, and hid his face in his hand.

"You are a strange man, Lucas Clavering," said the stranger, looking round the dingy little apartment; "there are few in your position who could live in such a place as this."

"It is for *her* sake," replied the old man, "only for her sake. She will be rich when I am rotting in my grave."

"She is worthy to be a duchess," said the stranger, with enthusiasm. The old man looked at him from under his lowering grey eyebrows.

"What have you seen of her?" he said, suspiciously; "what is she to you?"

"She is only what every lovely woman is to me, Lucas Clavering, an object of admiration and respect. I am no profligate. Go and ask in the gay world to which I belong. You will hear no dark stories against my character."

The old man took no notice of this speech.

"When do you want me?" he asked.

"To-morrow night. At the old place. At twelve o'clock we shall be assembled."

"I will be there," answered Lucas. The stranger bade him good night, and leaving the cottage, mounted his horse and galloped through the broken gates of the Park.

CHAPTER IV.

THE MIDNIGHT MARRIAGE

THE next day Lucas Clavering set out for London, and Ellen was left alone once more. The old man was away for upwards of a fortnight, and during this time Ellen constantly met the stranger in Clavering Park. He would dismount from his horse and wander for hours with her under the spreading branches of the stately oaks. She struggled hard against the fascination of his rich, deep voice, his handsome face, his flashing black eyes, and brilliant powers of conversation. She was utterly without even ordinary feminine vanity, for beautiful as she was, she had very rarely been told of her beauty; but it was impossible long to remain ignorant of the stranger's ardent admiration of her. One day, when the fortnight of the old man's absence was drawing to a close, the stranger fell on his knees on the mossy, flower-bespangled ground, and told her of his love. "And you will be mine, Ellen," he said, "will you not? I dare not ask for your father's consent, and our love must be kept a secret from him, until I can carry you away from this dreary home and make you my wife, for my life is enveloped in a cloud of mystery, and the rules that apply to other men can never apply to me. My name is Darcy—Philip Darcy. I have wealth enough to surround you with every luxury, to anticipate your wildest wish. Ellen, say you will be mine."

In vain the young girl pleaded her dislike to deceiving her father, her horror of concealing even a thought from the old man. The flashing eyes were fixed upon her flushing face, and seemed to penetrate to her very soul. The pleading tones of the rich, deep, imploring voice stole into her heart, and she consented to breathe the vow which marked her as the future wife of Philip Darcy. "Before these oaks bear the green leaves of another summer, I shall have claimed my bride, Ellen," said Philip as they parted.

From that hour life to Ellen Clavering wore a new aspect. The influence which Philip Darcy exercised over her innocent mind, rapidly as it had arisen, was deep and lasting. Every feature of the handsome face seemed engraven upon her heart. She saw him seldom, and only in the absence of her father; but their meetings were the bright and starry moments in the lives of both.

"I am older than you, Ellen," Philip once said to her, "by nearly twenty years. Can you remember this and love me?"

"Mine is not love, Philip," she answered, her long eyelashes drooping upon her blushing cheek; "it is worship."

One circumstance was always a grief to Ellen. Philip, although he would come sometimes two or three hundred miles for the sake of a brief interview with his promised bride, would never consent to write to her.

"I am so unhappy when you are away from me, dearest," she would say to him; "I fancy you ill, or even in danger, and when I am troubled by these dark thoughts, a few brief lines in your dear hand-writing would give me so much happiness. Tell me, why is it that you never write?"

"Ellen," he answered gravely, "do not question me. I have told you long ere this that my life is not like the lives of other men."

The snow covered the woodland paths of Clavering Park during the Christmas week which Ellen spent in the little cottage by the gates. She heard the merry peals of the bells from the distant spire of the village, and she knew as she sat by her solitary hearth that there was rejoicing and festivity in the little village—festivities in which from her childhood she had never shared. "My life has been very dreary," she thought, as she watched the red embers dropping through the bars of the little grate; "but Philip loves me, and the future must be a happy one since it is to be shared with him."

On the night of the 13th of January, any wayfarer passing within sight of Clavering Abbey would have been astonished, and no doubt alarmed, by perceiving a light shining through the apertures of the thick oaken shutters of one of the disused rooms. But when this light first gleamed through the wintry darkness it had already struck eleven by the Clavering clocks, and there was not a creature abroad in the inclement night. Let us enter the old and ruined mansion, and following the intricacies of several dark and winding passages, make our way into the apartment where the light is burning. It is a large oak-panelled chamber, with a wide, open chimney and a broad hearth, upon which there are iron dogs. A blazing log sends a shower of sparks upwards through the black mouth of the chimney, and before the fire, in a worm-eaten oaken chair, a man is seated with his elbows resting on his knees, and his flashing black eyes gazing thoughtfully into the red flames. This man is Philip Darcy. He is evidently thinking deeply, and at the same time there is an expression in his face that shows that he is listening.

Presently he hears footsteps in the corridor without, the door is thrown open, and a man, dressed shabbily in rough and common garments, enters the room.

"Will she consent?" asked Philip, turning to him eagerly.

"She will," answered the new comer; "she hesitated at first, but when I told her that you were too ill to stir from this place she consented."

"Good!" exclaimed Philip Darcy; "wheel yonder couch over to the hearth."

The man obeyed, and with some difficulty dragged a heavy oaken sofa from the other end of the room. Philip flung himself upon this couch, while the man threw a heavy cloak over his recumbent form. This was scarcely done when a light hand tapped at the window.

"It is she," said the man; "I told her she had better tap at the window. It opens to the ground, and I can easily admit her."

He crossed the room as he spoke, and opening the window, admitted Ellen Clavering, wrapped in a grey cloak, and with the snow hanging about her hair and garments. She was pale and agitated, and rushed at once to the couch on which her lover lay.

"Philip," she cried, "you are ill.—" She knelt by his side and looked anxiously into his face.

"I have been ill, Ellen," he answered; "but I am better now. Tell me, dearest, would it grieve you if I were to die?"

"Philip! Philip!" she cried, the tears starting to her lovely hazel eyes.

"If that is so then, Ellen—if your heart is indeed mine alone, you will not refuse to consent to what I have to propose."

"And that is?" she asked, eagerly.

"That you will be mine this night. I have brought a clergyman with me, who is my best and oldest friend. I am provided with a special licence, and he will unite us in this room, this very hour, if you consent, Ellen, my beloved!"

"My father; my dear and devoted father," she murmured.

"I have told you, Ellen, that I could never ask your father's consent. When we are married he will forgive us freely, for he will be happy in beholding the happiness of his child. Ellen, I have suffered much since we last met; your love is the only star of a dark and troubled life. Say that you will be mine."

"I am powerless to refuse you," she whispered; "your happiness is dearer to me than my own."

"You are the angel of my life, Ellen," he exclaimed with rapture. "Morris," he added, turning to the man who had retired to the other end of the room, "summon Mortimer; you will be the witness of the marriage."

The man left the room.

Philip Darcy rose from the couch and clasped the pale and agitated girl to his breast. She was sobbing violently. He uttered a few consoling words, and she tried to dry her tears, when the man re-entered, bringing with him a gentleman, who looked like a clergyman of the Church of England. The man Morris placed a lamp upon a table, at one end of the large chamber. The clergyman opened a prayer-book, and when Philip and Ellen had taken their places before the table, began to read the marriage service. His voice echoed amongst the rafters of the oaken roof, and had a strangely solemn sound, as it broke the stillness of the desolate building.

There was something ominous and sinister in this midnight and secret marriage.

When the clergyman had concluded the service, Philip whispered some order to Morris, who left the room again.

"Allow me to congratulate you, Mrs. Darcy," said the clergyman.

Ellen started at the sound of her new name. At this moment the wheels of a carriage and the hoofs of a pair of horses were heard, in the court-yard of the Abbey.

"Now, Ellen, dearest, come with me," said Philip, drawing his arm round her waist, and leading her towards the door; "bid adieu for ever to this dreary place, and come with me to scenes more fitted to your youth and beauty."

"But my father," exclaimed the sobbing girl, "who will tell him? He will think that I have abandoned him. Philip, remember my father!"

"I do, dearest," replied her husband; "you shall write and tell him all when we have reached our destination." Before she could make any further remonstrance, he hurried her through the long passages leading into the court-yard of the Abbey. He opened the door of the post-chaise, and lifting her in his arms, placed her in the carriage, and seated himself by her side. He gave some directions to the postillion, and the horses galloped away, the wheels of the chaise crashing through the snow that lay in the avenue. Away they sped! Whither, Ellen knew not.

CHAPTER V.

MIDNIGHT IN BELGRAVIA

THREE months after the December night upon which Ellen Clavering had given her hand to Philip Darcy, the fashionable quarter of London was beginning to fill with its aristocratic inhabitants. The Houses of Parliament were opened, and the Earl of Horton, the father of Lady Edith Vandeleur, had taken possession of his superb mansion in Belgrave Square. Lady Edith Vandeleur was the youngest of several sisters, each of whom had married well. In personal attractions she was superior to all of them. Her ambition was, however, boundless; and she disdainfully refused offer after offer. Lord Lionel Montfort, younger brother of the Marquis of Willoughby, had long loved her. She returned his affection, loving him as much as it was in the power of her haughty nature to love any human being; but she could not sacrifice the wealth and luxury which seemed necessary to her very existence at the shrine of affection. She pursued her own dark course,

shining like a star in the fashionable hemisphere; brilliant and unhappy, weary of the gaudy scenes to which she sacrificed her life, but too proud to abandon her pursuit, or to let it be said that the beautiful Lady Edith Vandeleur had made a worse match than her far less-attractive sisters.

To inaugurate the commencement of the season, Lord Horton gave a magnificent entertainment, at which upwards of six hundred people were present.

Lady Edith was the belle of the evening.

She wore a dress of cloud-like white crape, which floated round her in voluminous folds, only relieved here and there by large water-lilies, from which hung clusters of diamonds clear as the drops of falling water which they were intended to represent. Round her thick, raven hair she wore a wreath of these large water-lilies mingled with a profusion of diamonds, and forming a crown which set off her queen-like beauty with a gorgeous and regal grace. She had never looked lovelier, and it was whispered amongst the guests that this ball was partly given to celebrate the fact of Lady Edith's approaching marriage with a gigantic railway speculator and millionaire; a man whom the proud daughter of the Earl of Horton would, had he been poor, have scarcely tolerated in her presence, but who, being rich as the prince in a fairy tale, she consented to honour with her hand.

"It is quite a new affair, this marriage, is it not?" asked a young guardsman of his neighbour, as Mr. Merton, the millionaire, led Lady Edith to her seat after having been her partner in a quadrille.

"I believe it is. There was some talk of her marrying Lionel Montfort; but I suppose it was only a flirtation. Montfort's as poor as Job."

"But his brother, the Marquis, is a single man, with a superb fortune," said the young officer; "and if anything were to happen to him, Lord Lionel would tumble into a good thing."

Rumour was not altogether correct in pronouncing Lady Edith to be positively engaged to Robert Merton, the rich railway director. Mr. Merton had been one of the lady's numerous admirers for some months, but he had never, as yet, proposed marriage to the haughty daughter of one of the proudest noblemen in the peerage.

Robert Merton had begun life as an errand-boy in a small house of business at Manchester.

His parents were working people, who, for their honesty and straightforward conduct, unflinching industry, and unchanging truth, were respected by all who knew them.

LORD LIONEL MEETS LADY EDITH AT THE MIDNIGHT MASQUERADE.

Robert inherited the good qualities of his father and mother, joined to talents which very soon made him so useful to his employer, as to cause his advancement from errand-boy to clerk, from clerk to junior partner, from junior partner to sole proprietorship of several great houses of business and prosperous manufactories.

His next step was to invest a portion of his capital in railway shares, and his good fortune in this, as well as in every other speculation, was unfailing.

At the age of five and thirty, therefore, Robert Merton the errand-boy had become Robert Merton the millionaire, and the noblest houses at the West End of London opened their doors to receive him. He was feasted at the tables of Dukes and Marquises, and the loveliest women in Belgravia were anxious to captivate one of the wealthiest men in England.

Amongst others the Lady Edith Vandeleur tried the power of charms which had seldom failed to please.

This proud girl worshipped wealth as a means, rather than an end. She looked to Robert Merton's thousands to make her queen over the fashionable world; for she knew that in that false and hollow circle nothing but wealth and power was really respected.

"Goodness, virtue, truth!" she cried, with a sneer ."will those win me admiration or respect? No! I must be able to outdo them all in pomp and splendour, and then, though they may hate me, they will bow down to me, and lick the dust under my feet."

If anybody who beheld this lovely creature (crowned with snow-white flowers, emblems of the purity which was a stranger to her scheming soul) could have known the secrets of her wicked heart, how loathsome would her grandeur and beauty have appeared!

How far before her the poorest cottage girl, walking barefoot over her native heath, whose heart could glow with a sincere affection, and whose soul could scorn a falsehood!

The ball was the most brilliant of the season.

As the hour advanced the gorgeous rooms became every moment more crowded. Diamonds sparkled on every side. Rich silks and satins, laces, feathers, and jewels, glittered and shone wherever the eye could look. Late in the evening Robert Merton led Lady Edith away from the crowded ball-room into a conservatory at one end of the noble range of apartments. The conservatory was lighted by lamps subdued by rose-coloured shades, and placed here and there amongst clusters of orange-trees, whose golden fruit contrasted with the dark green of the polished leaves, and the pure white of the

N°. 2.

scented blossoms. In the centre of the conservatory, which was paved with different coloured marbles, a fountain played into an alabaster basin, ornamented with cupids of frosted silver, which clung about the border and seemed to disport themselves in the crystal water of the fountain. Here and there, amongst the shrubs and flowers which bloomed in china vases, there were sofas covered with the palest blue satin, bordered with fringes of silver.

To one of these sofas Robert Merton led his lovely partner.

"Lady Edith Vandeleur," he said, with sudden energy, "do you hear what people say of us to-night in your father's crowded ball-room?"

"What they say of us!" Edith answered, raising her arched eyebrows; "what can they say of us, Mr. Merton?"

Robert Merton was of a reserved and quiet disposition. Very few men could fathom the mind of the Manchester merchant. His manners were gentlemanly, though grave; but he said little, and to the people around him he was a perfect mystery.

"He is going to propose," thought Lady Edith. "Poor fellow! he fears me, and dreads a refusal."

"Lady Edith Vandeleur," said Robert Merton, "I have overheard the whispers of your father's guests. Those whispers have coupled your name with name. Nay, more, it is openly reported, that before the season is over the fashionable world will have witnessed the marriage of the wealty merchant with the daughter of an Earl. Shall it be so, Lady Edith? Can you forget that the man who now speaks to you owes all his wealth to honest industry? I know that that alone is a sin in the eyes of your haughty circle; but I know, too, that money is power, and that, without it, even you, Lady Vandeleur, lovely, accomplished, high-born, though you may be, are less than I, the Manchester trader—I offer you, then, a fair exchange. I will not speak of the deep and passionate love which lurks beneath this seeming coldness. I am not skilled in romantic expressions. I *do* love you. How deeply you may never know; but wrong me, and you will learn how deeply I can hate! Edith, will you be mine?"

The artful girl dropped her heavy eyelids till the long dark lashes swept her rounded cheek.

"Edith," cried the millionaire, "do you consent?"

She allowed her beautiful head to sink upon her lover's shoulder, as she murmured softly—

"Yes, Robert, yes."

At this moment the boughs of some lofty

tropical plants which formed a thick screen at the other end of the conservatory, were suddenly parted, and a young man strode towards the sofa upon which Robert Merton and Lady Edith Vandeleur were seated.

The intruder was Lord Lionel Montfort, who, although he wore an evening dress, had not been present at the ball.

He was not alone; for another man, also in evening dress, remained concealed by the shade of the foliage, while Lord Lionel advanced to Lady Edith.

The haughty girl rose, pale and trembling, from the sofa. She dreaded an outburst of rage from her old lover, which might cost her the hand of the millionaire.

She had no occasion for this alarm. Lord Lionel bowed, and said, with studied courtesy,

"I come just as the festival is concluding, I fear, Lady Edith; but though I have been to half a dozen balls to-night, I could not resist the temptation of the chance of a waltz with you."

He offered her his arm as he spoke.

She hesitated for a moment, cast one uneasy glance at her newly-accepted lover, and putting her little gloved hand through Lord Lionel's arm, left the conservatory, in the direction of the ball-room.

Robert Merton looked after her with admiring eyes.

"She is very lovely," he said to himself. "I ought surely to be the proudest and happiest of men. But will she be true? I tremble when I remember that she is one of the queens of this false and hollow world of fashion. How can she ever love the rough man of business—the child of the people? Robert Merton, what have you done in trusting your heart to such a woman?"

As he was thinking thus, the stranger who had entered the conservatory with Lord Lionel Montfort advanced from amongst the shrubs, and walked to the fountain near which Robert Merton was standing. His tall, elegant figure, reddish auburn hair, and piercing black eyes, proclaimed him to be the Austrian officer whose eccentricity and wealth had made him to be one of the most fashionable men in London.

"Colonel Bertrand!" exclaimed Robert Merton, who had met the Austrian frequently at the houses of the great, "I did not know that you were here to-night."

"I have only just dropped in for half-an-hour with Lord Lionel Montfort," said the Colonel; "the young man and I have been together all the evening, and from some silly whim or other he insisted upon coming here, late as it is. I fancy he must have some love affair upon hand, for I cannot get a word out of him."

Robert Merton looked intently at the Austrian officer. The merchant was a man who, beneath a quiet outward seeming, nourished strong emotions, and his love for Lady Edith Vandeleur was a deep and powerful feeling.

"Colonel Bertrand," he said, "I know very little of this fashionable world; I am but a rough manufacturer, who was never guilty of a dishonest action, and who is no great hand at picking and choosing his words. I hear a great deal of the senseless chatter of these splendid assemblies; and, amongst other things, I hear that there was once a strong attachment between Lady Edith and Lord Lionel. Is that true?"

The Colonel shrugged his shoulders.

"I am Lord Lionel Montfort's friend, Mr. Merton," he said, haughtily, "but I am not a spy. I know nothing of his sentiments with regard to the lady you name. If you wish to ascertain the truth," he added, "you had better judge for yourself."

He pointed as he spoke to the open door of the conservatory, through which Robert Merton looked into the room beyond.

This room was merely an ante-chamber to the ball-room, and there were not many people in it at this time, for it was nearly the close of the entertainment.

In the deep recess of a window, half-hidden by the sweeping folds of the amber satin curtains, stood Lord Lionel and Lady Edith in close conversation.

Colonel Bertrand laughed maliciously.

"You must judge for yourself—you must judge for yourself, my friend," he said, as he left the conservatory.

Robert Merton flung himself upon the sofa upon which he and Lady Edith had been seated, and, hiding his face in his hands, abandoned himself to bitter and deep reflection.

"Edith," said Lord Lionel, as he stood with the lovely girl's hand clasped in his, which clutched her slender fingers with an iron force, "Edith, why were you and that man seated side by side just now? Why did you start and turn pale when I saw you."

She laughed scornfully. "My dear Lionel," she said, carelessly, "I thought that, upon the twentieth of December last, when you and I met at the masked ball in Drury Lane, the question was settled once and for ever. I told you then, that, however much I may have loved you, however much I may love you still, I will never marry a poor man."

"I remember every word you said upon that fatal night, Edith Vandeleur," answered her companion. "From that night I took my course. It is now three months ago. Some men waste years, others a life-time, in gaining a fortune. Mine will be won in a day. "Not only a fortune, Edith, but a title—honours—an estate. Before this week is out I will lay all these at your feet. Then you will not reject me."

He raised her hand to his lips, kissed it passionately, and hurried away.

"Lionel," she cried, following him towards the door of the ball-room, "Lionel, listen to me! You do not know—you—Lionel—"

She wished to tell him of her intended marriage with the wealthy merchant.

False as she was, she had no motive for concealing that.

Just at this moment a set of quadrilles had finished in the ball-room, and the dancers came crowding into the ante-chamber. In this crowd Lord Lionel Montfort disappeared, and she tried in vain to overtake him before he left the house.

How often the happiness or misery of a life-time may hang upon the utterance of one word! Had Lady Edith Vandeleur told Lord Lionel what she wished to tell him, these two people might have been spared a long career of dark guilt and splendid wretchedness.

Lady Edith returned to the conservatory, where she found Robert Merton seated in the same attitude into which he had fallen after his brief conversation with Colonel Bertrand.

She was alarmed for a moment, thinking that he might have overheard the dialogue between herself and Lord Lionel.

"Robert," she said, in her sweetest tones, "what is the matter, dearest?"

The merchant started to his feet. He was as pale as death, and there was a strange calmness in his manner. "Edith," he said, "I have reason to think that you are deceiving me. I will not ask you whether I am right or wrong. I only say to you this: think twice before you betray a man whose brain and energies have been strengthened by a life of honest labour. Think twice before you deceive a man who never told a lie in his life, and who never forgave one in another. Think of this, and decide this night whether you will be mine or not."

They were quite alone in the conservatory. She fell on her knees at the rich speculator's feet, and, clasping her jewelled hands, exclaimed solemnly—

"Robert Merton, I have never, and shall never, deceive you. As there is a Heaven above me, I will be your true and loving wife."

If her lover could have read the depths of her soul, he would have shrunk with a shudder from the false and perjured creature,

But he could only look into her beautiful face, which was the lovely mask which covered all her guilt, and he lifted her from the ground, and clasped her fondly in his arms.

"My loveliest and dearest," he cried, passionately, "you have sealed the vow which makes you my wife in the happy future. All that devoted love and boundless wealth can do to make your lot a bright one shall be done. I live only to be your slave."

When Lady Edith retired to her room that night, she cast off her diamonds with feverish impatience.

"So I have reached the height of my ambition," she said. "Sold, sold, for gems and gold, for fine houses and carriages, horses, lands, and jewels! Surely I ought to be happy. Poor Lionel! how handsome he looked to-night; and what could he mean by that wild talk of being a rich man in a few days? Poor fellow, I fear love has driven him half mad. That Manchester man is a horrible creature; but a million—a million of money—the words seem written in letters of gold, and dancing before my aching eyes."

CHAPTER VI.

MIDNIGHT IN THE GAMING-HOUSE

THE evening after that on which the events above described took place in the house of Lord Horton was wet and gloomy.

The rain poured down in torrents, and the streets at the West End of London were deserted by foot-passengers, except when now and then some wretched woman, dressed in gaudy silks, which were splashed and dripping with the mud and wet from the overflowing gutters, hurried shivering by, on her way to some of the haunts of vice and dissipation.

Now and then, too, a solitary man, wrapped in a great coat, crossed the street, struggling to hold up an umbrella, in spite of the wind, which made the task a hard one.

As the clocks of the churches in the neighbourhood of Piccadilly were striking eleven, an elegantly-appointed cabriolet drove from the neighbourhood of the Albany into St. James's Street, where it drew up at the corner of one of the smaller streets leading out of that thoroughfare.

A tall man, whose figure was quite disguised by the heavy loose overcoat which he wore, sprang from the vehicle and handed the reins to the groom.

"Return here at one o'clock, Jarvis," he said, "and wait at this corner till I come to you."

The groom bowed, and the gentleman turned

into the bye-street, leaving the servant standing in the rain, looking after his master with considerable curiosity.

"This is a rummy start," muttered the man; "what, in the name of all that's dangerous, does the Colonel want that way? Mischief, I should think." And the groom mounted into the driver's seat and rattled homewards.

The owner of the cabriolet walked nearly to the end of the street, looked about him to see whether he was observed, and then knocked at the door of a respectable-looking house at the corner of a bye-street.

It was to be noticed that there was not one spark of light to be seen in any of the numerous windows of this house, nor in the fan-light over the street door. It seemed as if the inhabitants must every one have retired to rest, for there were no shutters to the windows, and the white blinds were visible through the glass.

This, however, did not discourage the stranger, who knocked a gentle double knock.

The street door was immediately opened by a young man out of livery, who seemed, however, a servant, as he made no remark to the visitor. Neither did the latter ask any questions, but walked straight to the further end of the hall, which was very dimly lighted.

Another man, seated in a porter's chair, half asleep, looked up at the sound of the stranger's approach.

"Who is it?" he asked.

"The Grand Master," replied the stranger, who was no other than the Austrian officer, Colonel Bertrand.

"Pass on, Captain," answered the man, with grave respect.

As he spoke he pulled a cord, and a green baize door, exactly opposite to that leading into the street, revolved with a metallic clank, revealing, as it did so, an inner hall, into which the Colonel passed.

This inner hall was of much smaller dimensions than the outer one, and a stranger would have been surprised at perceiving that there was no staircase. Looking up, you could see straight to the roof of the house, the different storeys being marked by narrow iron galleries running round the four sides of the hall.

But how were these galleries to be reached?

The Colonel did not stop long to consider. He pulled one of a row of brass knobs, each numbered and lettered differently, and a bell rang in the gallery on the first floor.

Scarcely had it done sounding when a light iron ladder lowered itself as if by magic from one end of the iron gallery, in the railings of which a little gate opened.

The Colonel stepped lightly up the ladder, sprang into the gallery, and, pushing open the door facing him, walked into a large room in which a number of men were seated at a table covered with green cloth, and scattered with cards, dice, and heaps of gold and silver money.

Colonel Bertrand was in one of the most secret and yet most noted "hells" of London—a place marked out by the police for destruction, and which yet defied the police—those at least whom it could not bribe, for there were some of the force who would accept a five-pound note from the owners of this infamous resort.

The house was lined with iron, like a fortress. Its appearance on the outside was always the same, the front rooms being kept solely for show; and it was supposed to be inhabited by a respectable retired tradesman, who had saved enough money to live in his own house, but the state of whose health prevented his seeing much company.

The Colonel looked with his searching black eyes into every corner of the crowded room.

He advanced to the table, still looking about him; and taking a seat amongst a group of noisy and excited players, who were evidently new to the miseries of a gambler's existence, he staked a handful of gold, and while the game proceeded, looked anxiously round at the faces of the players.

A shadow of disappointment spread itself over his face.

Evidently the people he expected had not arrived.

"Can that foolish boy have managed matters badly?" he muttered. "Can he have failed in persuading his brother to come?"

At this very moment the bell which served as a signal to the attendant whose duty it was to lower the iron ladder, rang two distinct times.

"Two new comers," muttered a man seated near the Colonel; "the room is crowded enough as it is."

"This must be they," said the Colonel to himself.

He had scarcely said so when the door was opened, and Lord Lionel Montfort, followed by a man a few years older than himself, entered the room.

This man was Angus, Marquis of Willoughby, Lord Lionel's elder brother.

He was a noble-looking fellow, tall and stout, with a profusion of fair ringlets and a light moustache. He seemed to have been drinking, and was rather inclined to be noisy.

"So this is the place you made such a row about, Lionel," he said, looking about him; "what a prison-like hole it is! I can't think what on earth made you so anxious to drag me here."

Colonel Bertrand looked up from his stake, which had been doubled, and which he still left upon the card.

As he did so, he met the eyes of Lord Lionel Montfort.

The young man burst out laughing, and catching his brother by the arm, exclaimed—

"Angus, do you see this? You remonstrated with me for coming to this haunt of vice, as you call it. What do you think, then, of finding the steady Austrian Colonel, whose conduct, though he is the most fashionable man in London, is held up by our mammas as a model to us wild young men? What do you think, I repeat, of finding Oscar Bertrand in such a place as this?"

The brothers laughed heartily at the meeting, and Colonel Bertrand, who was celebrated for his good temper, rose from his seat and joined them, laughing as loudly as themselves.

"One gets tired of balls and parties, Marquis" he said, when they had finished laughing; "and as to pretty girls, I verily believe pretty girls are all alike nowadays; so for a change I came here to spend an hour or two, little expecting to meet Lord Lionel and yourself in such a place. Will you play *rouge et noir*, Marquis?" he asked; "or shall you and I have a hand at *ecarte* while Lord Lionel looks on to see fair play?"

"A hand at *ecarte* by all means, Colonel," answered the Marquis. "I have played *rouge et noir* half over Europe, and I'm heartily sick of it. I should not have been here to-night, I assure you, but for Lionel. The young scamp dined with me at my club, and after we'd drunk a bottle or two of wine, of which he made me take the best part myself, nothing would satisfy him but our looking in here for half an hour. I did not know the place, and should not have been able to find my way in, but Lionel appears perfectly familiar with everything and everybody about it."

"Lord Lionel keeps some very strange society, I'm afraid, Marquis," said the Colonel, laughing. "But now for the *ecarte*."

As he spoke he led the way into an inner room, handsomely furnished, where there were two or three small tables. This apartment, which was brilliantly lighted with gas, was quite empty. The Colonel rang a bell, which was answered by a well-dressed waiter.

"Bring half a dozen of sparkling moselle," said Colonel Bertrand, "and see that it is well iced."

The Marquis seated himself opposite his opponent. An attendant brought several packs of untouched cards; for it was a rule in this, as well as in all other gaming-houses, that no pack of cards was ever played with twice.

It is scarcely necessary to say that this is a very needful precaution. So many methods are there of cheating, by paring the cards at the sides and ends, clipping them at the corners, and otherwise marking them in different manners.

The waiter brought the wine in silver coolers filled with ice, which he placed by the Colonel's directions on a sideboard close to his elbow. The glittering champagne glasses were put upon the table, but the Colonel pushed them away impatiently.

"Bring us tumblers," he said. "We are not little children; we don't want to take our wine by spoonfuls."

The play had commenced by this time.

Lord Lionel looked over his brother's shoulder; but soon growing weary of this, he retired to an easy chair by the fire, and taking up a newspaper, with which he shaded his face, apparently fell asleep. A close observer might, however, have discovered that the young man was very restless, and that every now and then his dark eyes glanced uneasily over the newspaper in the direction of the Marquis of Willoughby and Colonel Bertrand.

The Colonel was particularly attentive in keeping the Marquis supplied with wine. As often as the nobleman emptied his tumbler, Colonel Bertrand was on the watch and ready to refill it, and all so quietly that Angus scarcely perceived how much he was drinking. He had been by no means too sober on entering the room, and he was every moment growing worse.

He played badly, and lost his temper with his own play, and with his opponent's good fortune.

"You are very lucky, Colonel Bertrand," he said, rather impatiently, as the Colonel won game after game.

"Perhaps I am a pretty good player, my lord," replied the Austrian officer, significantly.

"It is not very difficult to play with such cards as you contrive to get, Colonel Bertrand," the Marquis answered, laying a stress upon his last words.

"Such cards as I *contrive to get*, my lord," said the Colonel.

"As you contrive to get, certainly, Colonel; those were my exact words."

"Then you might have chosen your words better, my lord," answered the Colonel. "*Contrive* is scarcely the word to apply to a game of chance."

"*Ecarté* is not a game of chance," said Angus, curtly; "it is a game of skill."

"But, like all games of cards," replied the Colonel, "the chances have something to do with it."

"Very little, I should think, as you play it, Colonel Bertand; I should call it quite a game of skill."

The door of communication between the smaller and the larger room had been open all this time, and many of the players, some whose purses had been emptied, and others who were growing tired of the gaming-table, had dropped in to watch the *ecarté* players.

Throughout theis dialogue, though the Marquis, excited by what he had drunk, raised his voice considerably, Lord Lionel had remained asleep, the newspaper still covering his face.

"I must trouble you to retract those words, my lord," said the Colonel, who was dealing.

"I never retract my words," his lordship answered; "and if you want to have plainer speaking you shall have it. You have not won one of the eleven games which we have played this night by good play alone, but you have won them by trickery—by cheating. Do you think I can't see? " cried his lordship, growing every moment more and more excited; "do you think I'm blind drunk? Why at this very moment I can see the king concealed in the sleeve of your coat."

It really seemed as if his lordship was right; for as he spoke the king of trumps dropped on to the table.

"A misdeal," said the Colonel, coolly sweeping up the cards. "Lord Willoughby, what you say is a lie."

As he spoke Colonel Bertrand flung half a tumbler of moselle into the face of the Marquis.

"Serve him right," exclaimed one of the lookers-on. "How dared he accuse any gentleman of cheating in this place?"

At this moment Lord Lionel Montfort dropped the newspaper, and opened his eyes.

"What's the matter? What's wrong?" he asked, starting from his chair.

"Very little," answered his brother, wiping his face with a handkerchief. "Colonel Bertrand," he added—addressing himself to the Austrian officer, who had risen from his seat and stood calm and composed as if nothing whatever had happened—"Colonel Bertrand, you must answer to me for this."

"Whenever you please, my lord."

It was to be observed that Angus was perfectly collected, while Lionel's face was as white as the face of a corpse, and he trembled like a leaf.

"The sooner the better, then," answered the Marquis. "There are some insults which nothing but blood can wipe out, and this is one of them. Name your time and place of meeting."

The two men had spoken all this in German, to avoid being understood by the crowd collected about them. The Marquis had travelled a great deal, and spoke the language almost as well as the Austrian officer.

"As to the time, my lord," said Colonel Bertrand, "I perfectly agree with you that it cannot be too soon. Let us say, then, to-morrow morning, at daybreak."

"With all my heart," replied the Marquis.

Lord Lionel tried vainly to interpose, but neither of the men would listen to a word he could say.

"As to the place, I think I could suggest the best place of all others," said Colonel Bertrand.

"Indeed! that place is——?"

"The sands under the Dover Cliffs, a little way out of the town. By choosing such a spot, the survivor, whoever he may be, will have power to escape with ease by the Calais packet, and will gain the opposite shore before the hue and cry can be raised in his pursuit."

"A very good idea, Colonel Bertrand. I have my passport. You, of course, have yours, so we shall both be prepared."

The two men were as cool as if they had been planning a dinner party instead of a duel. But Lord Lionel Montfort looked from his brother to the Colonel with a white haggard face, almost horrible to behold.

"Angus, Angus!" he exclaimed when they had left the gaming-house, and parted with the Colonel—who walked off to look for a friend whom he was to send to Lord Willoughby to make all final arrangements—"Angus, what are you going to do? Desist, I implore you, before it is too late."

"Desist!" exclaimed Angus; "desist, when I have been insulted! Surely, Lionel, you do not know what you are saying."

"You do not know this man," answered Lord Lionel; "you do not know him, Angus! Man! He is something more than a man. He is a demon, gifted with a fatal power over guilty and erring creatures. Walking the earth to tempt and to destroy them. Be warned—be warned, Angus! I dare not say more to you."

"My dear Lionel," said Lord Willoughby, whom the quarrel had sobered, "your love for me blinds you to the state of the case. A man has insulted me. I shall kill him if I can. If I cannot kill him, he must kill me. I cannot live and let him go with impunity."

The Marquis found the Colonel's friend waiting for him when he entered Willoughby House.

There was something almost demoniac in the rapidity of the Austrian's movements.

Where could he have found this man at such an hour, and in so short a time?

The stranger was waiting in the Library into which the servants of the Marquis had shown him. He was a pale-faced, cadaverous-looking man of about forty years of age.

He gave the Marquis his card, upon which was engraved "Lieutenant Saunderson, Mordaunt's Hotel."

The Marquis scarcely looked at the card which Mr. Saunderson had presented to him.

"I think almost everything is arranged," he said; "my brother will serve me as second. If there is anything else to settle, you can settle it with him. In this cabinet," he added—taking a key from his waistcoat pocket, and opening an immense cabinet on one side of the apartment—"in this cabinet you will find several pairs of duelling pistols; be so good as to select suitable ones."

Mr. Saunderson walked to the cabinet, and began to examine the different cases of pistols with great deliberation.

"Our grand point must be to save time," said Lord Willoughby. "The night train for Dover starts from London Bridge at half-past two; it is now past one."

He rang the bell, and ordered his servant to procure a cab.

"You will meet us with Colonel Bertrand at the station?" he said to Mr. Saunderson.

This gentleman, who spoke very little, bowed in reply to the Marquis's question, and left the room after having saluted the two brothers.

When Mr. Saunderson had left the house, Angus looked anxiously at his watch.

"I can spare five minutes," he said, "to run and speak to my mother and Lucy. There has been a party this evening, and I shall be sure to find them still up."

The Lucy whom he spoke of was his cousin, a girl of about eighteen, whose parents had died, leaving her almost entirely dependent upon the Dowager Marchioness of Willoughby.

Angus was right in his conjecture as to his cousin, but his mother had a few minutes before retired to rest. He found Lucy Maldon in a pretty morning room leading out of the drawing-room. She was still dressed in the light robes she had worn for her aunt's party, and she wore a wreath of forget-me-nots in her fair hair.

She was reading by the light of a shaded lamp; but at the sound of her cousin's footstep she started and looked up from her book with a blush.

"Angus," she cried, "is it really you? I fancied you would not return home to-night, but I thought I could not be mistaken in your footstep."

"Lucy," said the Marquis, taking the young girl's hand in his, "I am going out of town for a few days, and as I am starting rather suddenly, I have only two minutes to bid you good-bye."

Something in his manner alarmed her, in spite of his calmness; and she cried in accents of terror—

"Angus! Angus! something is wrong, I know. How pale you are!—as pale as death. Oh, Angus! Angus! I know that something terrible is about to happen."

"No, no," said the young man, violently agitated by the grief of his gentle cousin, whom he had loved from childhood, and whom he had intended before long to have made his wife! "No, Lucy, there is nothing to fear. I have been suddenly summoned to attend the bedside of a sick friend—that is the reason of this hurried journey."

Before she could question him further he had rushed from the room.

Lucy Maldon clasped her slender hands upon her beating breast, as she listened eagerly to her cousin's retreating footsteps.

As the sound of the Marquis's tread upon the stairs died away, the young girl hurried from the room, and running to the apartment in which she slept, rapidly exchanged her ball dress for some dark winter garments, and wrapped herself in a large cloak which quite concealed her figure. She went out on to a landing-place leading to a back staircase used by the servants, down which she hurried, and thence into a hall which led into the street.

The rain still poured in torrents, and the night was pitch dark.

So quickly had the occurrences above described followed each other, that the clocks chimed the half-hour after one as Lucy Maldon slunk into the doorway of the house next to that tenanted by the Marquis of Willoughby.

Her purpose was to watch for her cousin's departure, and, at any risk, to follow him. She had not long to watch.

In less than five minutes he came out of the house, followed by his brother Lionel.

"Lionel with him!" thought Lucy; "then I was right. Something must have happened."

She listened to the direction which the Marquis gave to the cabman, after he had dismissed the servant who had attended him to the door of the vehicle.

"London Bridge Station."

Lucy heard the words with perfect distinctness, and as soon as the cab containing Angus and his brother had driven off, she flew, rather than walked, to a neighbouring stand, where she sprang into a cab, directing the driver to hurry with all possible speed to the same place.

CHAPTER VII.

THE DUEL ON THE SEA SHORE.

The cold grey dawn of the early spring morning was slowly breaking as four men left the station, and walked two and two into the town of Dover.

The four gentlemen walked straight to one of the principal hotels, where they asked for a private room. One of them ordered breakfast; and while it was being prepared, Lord Lionel Montfort and Lieutenant Saunderson seated themselves at a side table, and discussed some trifling arrangements connected with the coming duel.

No nobler heart had ever throbbed in a manly bosom than that which beat in the breast of Angus, Marquis of Willoughby; and in this still and solemn hour, with the mighty works of the Creator arrayed in all their sublime grandeur before his eyes, he could not but feel a keen pang of regret to think that he was perhaps about to trifle away the life which had been given to him by his Maker for a far higher purpose.

Perhaps, too, one thrill of anguish shot through his heart as he thought of his loving cousin, Lucy Maldon.

He little knew that at that moment Lucy herself was standing in a window situated in another part of the hotel, from which she could command a view of the principal door of the house.

She had reached the London Bridge Station in time to see Angus take Dover tickets for himself and his brother. Having contrived to ascertain this without having been herself observed, she had lost no time in taking her own ticket and hurrying to a carriage, in a corner of which she seated herself, after having made sure that the Marquis and Lord Lionel had entered another.

Arrived at Dover, she had acted with the same precaution, and by this means had contrived to follow the four gentlemen at a sufficient distance to avoid being seen by them. She had watched them into the hotel, and about ten minutes afterwards entered it herself. She told the waiter and chamber-maid who attended upon her that she was going to cross to Calais by the eight-o'clock boat, and she had ordered breakfast, not an atom of which was she able to touch.

The four gentlemen had told the same story to the waiters as that which had served Lucy as an excuse for her presence at a Dover hotel at that early hour in the morning.

The people belonging to the inn did not perceive anything singular in the conduct of the travellers, little knowing that the small carpet bag carried so lightly by Lieutenant Saunderson contained duelling pistols.

The Colonel and his second breakfasted at one table, and the two brothers at another.

Neither the Austrian officer nor Mr. Saunderson appeared in the least affected by the terrible scene in which they were so soon to take a part. They ate an excellent breakfast, drank a couple of bottles of claret, and talked a good deal in an under tone, inaudible at the other table.

Angus, on the contrary, was grave and silent, though perfectly calm. He pushed his plate away from him, with an untasted cup of coffee, and resting his elbow upon the table, leaned his head upon his hand, and seemed lost in thought.

Lord Lionel was far more agitated than the Marquis. His hand shook so violently that he could not hold his knife and fork, and was compelled to abandon even the pretence of eating.

"Lionel," said the Marquis, after a long pause, "if I should fall this morning, which is very likely, for the Colonel is ten times a better shot than I am, you will be Marquis of Willoughby."

"Angus, Angus, do not, for pity's sake, speak of that," cried Lord Lionel, with a shudder.

"I must speak of it," answered the Marquis; "for I have a request to make, which I wish you to remember, Lionel, as a brother's dying prayer."

"I will remember it, Angus, whatever it may be," exclaimed his brother.

"It is that, when I am gone, you will supply my place, not only to my mother, but to Lucy Maldon. She is lovely, Lionel, lovely as she is amiable, and the world might deal hardly with one so innocent and beautiful. Had I lived she would have been the Marchioness of Willoughby. Remember this, Lionel, and do not let her want either a friend or a home."

"She shall be my tenderest care, Angus," replied his brother; "but you must not talk so despondently. You may survive this encounter."

"No, Lionel, that I shall never do. Something in my heart tells me that I shall fall; something tells me, too, that you also think so."

The eyes of the two brothers met, and the dark eyelashes of Lord Lionel drooped under the steady gaze of the Marquis.

"There is no time to be lost, gentlemen," said Mr. Saunderson, interrupting this solemn dialogue between the Marquis and his younger brother. "Remember we have half a mile to walk before we reach the spot suggested by Colonel Bertrand."

The Marquis put on his overcoat and hat, and, followed by his brother, left the room; he turned at the foot of the stair, and drawing back, said to the Colonel and his friend—

"You, gentlemen, had better lead the way, as you know it best."

Colonel Bertrand bowed, and the four men left the house, having first paid the bill and told the waiter that they were merely going for a stroll.

Lucy Maldon, who had seen them leave the hotel, rang the bell immediately afterwards, and asked for her bill. While she was paying it the waiter said—

"There are four gentlemen from London going by the same boat as you, miss. They have just breakfasted, and have stepped out for a saunter by the shore."

This intelligence partly re-assured Lucy. Perhaps, after all, Angus had only told her the truth. He might have been summoned to some sick friend on the other side of the channel. But, then, why was he accompanied by Lionel and these two other men who were strangers to her? And why, again, had he been so strangely agitated on coming to bid her farewell? In any case she determined on following them.

She left the hotel, therefore, and keeping the little party in view, followed at some distance till they had left the town behind and were walking along the shore.

There was not a creature about, and she feared the chance of one of the gentlemen turning round and catching sight of her. She kept, therefore, at as great a distance as she could, feeling assured that under the cliffs she was not likely to miss them entirely.

"It must be as the waiter said," she thought. "They are only walking here to beguile the time before the starting of the boat. What would the world think of me if it were known that I had followed my cousin to this place? How I should be ridiculed for my folly!"

The hot blood flushed to her cheeks as she thought of this. She felt utterly ashamed of the devoted affection which had brought her on such a journey in the dead of the stormy night.

The rain had cleared away, and as the sun rose the wind lulled itself to rest, and the sea grew almost calm. Long rippling paths of sunlight gilded the waves and lit the yellow sands as the little party hurried onwards.

They walked every moment more rapidly, and Lucy at last was left so far behind that for a time she lost sight of them altogether.

At that fatal moment they reached the spot which had been chosen by Colonel Bertrand.

The spray dashed into their faces and cooled their fevered brows. The sea foam, pure in the morning light, shone like glistening silver as the waves rose high against the breakers.

Half a mile from the town, and sheltered by the lofty cliff which towered above it, the spot was at this early hour perfectly secure from intrusion.

Mr. Saunderson lost no time in placing his man; Lord Lionel, on the contrary, was so agitated as to be quite useless as a second, and the Marquis of his own accord took his place opposite to his adversary.

At this very moment Lucy Maldon, who had hurried with all her strength, in order to come within sight of the men whom she was watching, approached near enough to behold what was going forward.

She saw Colonel Bertrand and the Marquis standing opposite to each other under the morning sunshine. She saw a white glove flutter as it fell from the hand of Lieutenant Saunderson and dropped softly to the ground. She heard the sharp report of a pair of pistols, the whistling of the bullets, and as that terrible sound vibrated in her ear, sank senseless upon the stony pebbles at her feet.

CHAPTER VIII.

THE DEAD REVEAL NO SECRETS

LET us return to Ellen Clavering, or, rather, Ellen Darcy, whom we last beheld upon the night of her mysterious and secret marriage, in the lonely chamber of the ruined abbey in Clavering Park.

Strange changes have come over the fate of the lovely girl since that eventful night.

She now sits in a splendidly-furnished boudoir, which leads out of the drawing-room of an elegant house situated at about ten miles distance from the West End of London.

Gorgeous pictures and costly gilding adorn the walls of the small apartment. A bright fire burns in the glittering steel grate, for the March night is cold and cheerless. Over the marble chimney-piece hangs a portrait of Philip Darcy, the master of the house.

The piercing black eyes seem to send forth flashes of lightning upon the beholder, and Ellen herself thinks, as she sits in her lonely chamber, that there is surely something more than natural in the picture.

Look which way she will, the eyes always seem to meet her own.

Sometimes she fancies that they assume a

dark and threatening look, and she almost shudders as she glances upwards at the handsome face upon the canvas.

The young girl's life, since her marriage, has not been altogether happy.

All that wealth can do has been done to surround her with beauty and luxury. Her hands glitter with the diamonds and rubies that sparkle upon her slender white fingers. Her costly silk dress sweeps the rich carpet upon which she walks. The tiny watch at her side is covered with gems, and has cost at least a hundred guineas. She has a lady's-maid to attend her, and is waited on by servants in livery. Philip has purchased for her an elegant little brougham, with a pair of superb chestnut horses, and a bay saddle-horse, upon which she sometimes rides, followed by her groom.

He has left nothing undone by which he could add to her happiness, and yet she is not happy.

Her husband, whom she loves with the deep and pure devotion of a noble heart, is as great a mystery to her as upon that first day on which she met him under the shade of the oaks in Clavering Park.

Dearly as he loves her, and in her most fearful moments she cannot doubt his affection, he is not often with her.

When he comes, his visits are hurried; and he often seems so reserved and melancholy that Ellen, at times, almost fears to address him. His visits are sudden and mysterious. She never knows when to expect him, how long he may stay, or when he may leave her.

He has a small room allotted to himself in the lower storey, which he calls his office, and he has rarely been in the house an hour before he is disturbed by the arrival of some messenger, who is shown into this office, and with whom he sometimes remains closeted for hours together.

It is in vain that Ellen questions her husband as to the mystery in which his life appears to be wrapped. He will tell her nothing, but that he has rich and powerful relatives, who would cast him off were they to discover the fact of his marriage with a penniless, though lovely girl. For this reason he is compelled to keep his wife concealed in the quiet neighbourhood in which they live; until the death of a wealthy uncle, from whom he expects to inherit a large fortune, may enable him to reveal his marriage to the world.

"Patience, my Ellen! wait and trust in me, my beloved," he would sometimes say; "the day will come when I can own my lovely bride in the face of the assembled world. Till then, Ellen, be patient, and trust in me."

She did trust. But the long separations from him she so tenderly loved, wearied and tried her gentle heart. Never since the night of her wedding had she been allowed to hold any communication with her father. Philip Darcy assured her that he had written to Lucas Clavering; that all was explained, as far as it could be for the present, and that the old man had no occasion to be uneasy about his beloved daughter. But even this could not quite lull to rest the anxiety which sometimes tortured Ellen's loving heart. She thought of her father, parted for ever from the child he had so tenderly reared, and she wept to think of his sorrow. Did he accuse her of ingratitude? Alas! it was only too probable; and then she would look upwards to the dark eyes that flashed upon her from her husband's pictured face.

"Ah, Philip, Philip," she murmured, "you have need to love me well, for I have sacrificed all for you."

She has cast aside the book which she has been vainly trying to read. She cannot take her eyes from the gilded timepiece over the marble chimney. She watches the hands. How slow they seem to her, and how long it is before the musical tones of the clock chime the weary hours!

Two! Half-past two! Three!

"No, no," she whispers to herself. "He will not come to-night."

At this very moment she hears a cautious knock at the door of the house. The servants have retired to rest. She descends the staircase, and, crossing the hall, opens the door with her own hands.

Two men are standing on the threshold; both so disguised by the loose overcoats in which they are wrapped, that for a moment she trembles lest she may have opened the door to strangers, who may have some evil intention in knocking for admission at so late an hour.

But one glance convinces her that the taller of the two is he for whom she has been so anxiously waiting.

"Philip, Philip!" she exclaimed, with an hysterical cry of delight.

He clasped her in his arms, and drawing her head upon his breast, kissed the fair, uplifted face.

"My Ellen, my darling, did I alarm you by arriving at so late an hour?"

"No, dearest, no! I never can abandon the hope of your coming; and even to-night, though I had almost despaired of seeing you, I was not surprised at hearing you knock. But come upstairs, Philip, it is so cold down here, and there is a blazing fire in my boudoir. Come!"

At this moment she remembered the presence of a stranger, and blushing crimson, she said, hesitating, "But your friend, Philip; he, too, must be cold and tired."

"I've no doubt he is, poor fellow," said Philip Darcy, laughing; "he and I have had a hard day's work, and neither of us have closed our eyes for upwards of four-and-twenty hours. But let me introduce him to you, Ellen. Mr. Montague: my wife," he added carelessly.

The stranger, who had removed his hat immediately upon entering the hall, bowed politely to Ellen Darcy. He was a handsome young man, with dark hair and eyes; but his face was deadly pale, and he seemed labouring under some suppressed agitation.

"Now, lead the way, Ellen," said Philip, "and you shall give us a bottle of wine in your own room."

Philip and his friend followed Ellen Darcy into the luxurious boudoir, where, as she had told them, a blazing fire burned with a cheerful light, which illuminated the gilded mouldings and splendid pictures upon the walls.

Ellen left the apartment to seek for the wine for which her husband had asked.

Philip Darcy flung himself into the velvet-cushioned easy chair by the side of the hearth.

"Come, Montague," he said, "sit down, man, and do not stand there staring into the burning coals with as gloomy a face as if you had committed a murder."

The young man shuddered at the sound of these terrible words.

"There are dark deeds committed in this world," he muttered, "to which men fear to give their right names. This morning's work was one of them."

"This morning's work!" cried Philip Darcy, with a sneer; "one would think you were sorry for what has been done."

"Heaven knows I am!" answered the young man, dropping into a seat by the table, and burying his face in his hands. "Heaven above knows that I am."

Philip Darcy rose suddenly from his chair, and, looking at his companion with flashing black eyes, which seemed to dart forth flames of fire, he said, scornfully,

"Fool! dastard! poor, pitiful craven! You are no fit comrade for me, and I did wrong in choosing such as you for my friend and confidant! You have the courage to plan a work, but not the boldness to go through with it. Your mean spirit quails before the accomplishment of your purpose. Coward! I despise and abjure you!"

The man to whom Philip Darcy had spoken these contemptuous words sprang to his feet, and grasping the chair upon which he had been seated as if he would have hurled it at the speaker, cried, in tones of terrible and unwonted fury,

"This language from you to me! To me—the scion of one of the oldest and grandest houses in the land! Remember who I am, and remember too, what you are."

Philip Darcy laughed scornfully.

"What!" he cried, "you taunt me with your birth, your fortune, your superiority! Bah! Remember that I belong to a set of people who acknowledge no rank, who respect no fortune. Genius and courage, a strong arm, a wise tongue, a bold heart, and a clear head; these alone we bow down to, and if you have not these, you are not worthy to be one of us. Remember this; and remember, too, that I have kept my promise made to you on the 20th of last December."

The speaker was no other than the man known to the reader as the Austrian officer, Colonel Oscar Bertrand. His companion, as may easily be imagined, was Lord Lionel Montfort.

Ellen Darcy returned, carrying a silver salver, upon which there were two crystal decanters and a couple of superbly-cut glasses of a peculiar but beautiful shape.

Philip Darcy (for we will still call him by that name by which he is known to his fair young wife), Philip Darcy poured out a glass of Madeira, and pushing the decanter to Lord Lionel, who had thrown himself once more into a chair, he raised the glass to his lips, and said with a smile,

"Let us drink to the most noble the Marquis of Willoughby."

A convulsive shudder shook the frame of Lionel Montfort.

Yes; the title was indeed his. The noble brother, whose generous heart had never felt one vile or selfish throb, had fallen beneath a murderer's hand, and Lionel, the penniless younger son, the rejected lover of Lady Edith Vandeleur, was now Marquis of Willoughby, the owner of a princely fortune, and a superb estate in one of the richest counties in England.

"Tell me," said Philip Darcy, as he drained a second glass of Madeira, "have I kept my promise, yes or no?"

"You have; you have!" cried Lionel; "you have kept that fatal promise only too well."

Ellen retired to rest, leaving the two men seated by the fire in her boudoir. It was broad daylight before Philip Darcy led his guest to a spare room situated in the storey above. When he had bade Lionel good-night, or rather good-morning, he descended to the room in which his wife slept, and stood silently at her bed-side gazing thoughtfully at the innocent face which was never more beautiful than when in repose.

The curtains of the elegant canopied bedstead were of white watered silk and embroidered muslin, richly trimmed with valuable lace. They fell about the bed in snowy clouds, in the midst of which Ellen Darcy seemed like a sleeping Madonna.

Her long auburn hair fell in rich masses about the pillow upon which she lay. The dark lashes of her closed eyes drooped upon the pale and delicate cheek, and her rosy lips were parted in a half-smile, disclosing the small and pearly teeth. One jewelled hand was lying upon the counterpane.

Philip fell on his knees by the bedside, and pressed his lips to this delicate little hand.

"How pure, how beautiful she is!" he murmured; "how hard that sin and sorrow should ever come near her!"

She awoke while these words yet trembled on her lips.

"Philip! Philip!" she cried; "ah, it is indeed you. I was just dreaming of you, and such a sweet dream, too, dearest."

"Tell me the dream, my beloved," said her husband, seating himself on an ottoman by her pillow, and twisting her auburn tresses round and round his slender fingers.

"I dreamt, Philip, that we had left this place; that you had abandoned the mysterious existence which gives me so much pain, and that we were living together in some quiet country village, where nothing ever happened to part us for an hour. Oh, how happy we were in that dear dream! Your face was always as I see it now, with that tender smile in your large dark eyes, not as I have seen them, sad and thoughtful, as if some terrible secret were consuming your soul! Oh, Philip, why cannot such dreams be realised! I would gladly give up all chance of wealth and luxury to be blessed by your love, to be united to you for ever!"

He clasped her to his heart, and covered her alabaster forehead with passionate kisses.

"My Ellen," he cried, "my beautiful and innocent girl, it can never be. I told you even before I asked you to be mine—I told you that my life was not like the lives of other men, and that the rules which apply to other men could never apply to me. I dare not tell you more."

*　　*　　*　　*　　*　　*　　*

The following day all London was in an uproar at the report which spread through the West End, of the sudden and unaccountable disappearance of the Marquis of Willoughby and his orphan cousin, Lucy Maldon.

The dowager Marchioness, the mother of the missing nobleman, was distracted by grief and fear at the disappearance of her son, but one ray of hope suggested itself to her bewildered mind.

How was she to account for the fact of Lucy Maldon being also missing? The gentle and timid Lucy, who had never been known to quit the house except in the company of her aunt, and whom the Marchioness had herself left in the morning-room on the night of the Marquis's departure.

There was only one answer to this question in the mind of the dowager—namely, that an elopement had been planned and executed by Angus and his cousin.

Yet why an elopement? thought the Marchioness. Angus was of age: his own master, to act as he pleased. Nay, beyond that, Lucy had always been so great a favourite with her aunt that the Marquis could scarcely have feared any difficulty in obtaining his mother's consent to a union with his beautiful cousin.

Neither the servants nor Lord Lionel could throw any light upon the affair. The Marquis's confidential man could only assert that he had admitted a stranger at one o'clock in the morning, who had waited for his master's return, and had been closeted for about a quarter of an hour in the library with the nobleman and his brother, Lord Lionel. He had then fetched a cab for the Marquis, in which he and his brother had driven off at about half-past one.

He had not heard the direction given to the cabman, and could not say which way the vehicle went; but he could positively declare that Miss Lucy Maldon was not with her cousin.

Lord Lionel, who had bachelor's apartments in the neighbourhood of Piccadilly, revealed nothing which tended to clear up the mystery.

He said that he had been with his brother at a gambling-house where the Marquis had had a dispute with some men over *ecarte*. One of these men had challenged Angus; but he (Lord Lionel) had interfered, and the quarrel had gone no further.

On his return with the Marquis to Willoughby House, they had found a stranger waiting for Angus. The Marquis and this man were for about ten minutes engaged in conversation, not one word of which was heard by Lord Lionel. The stranger then left, and the Marquis requested his brother to drive with him in a cab back to the gaming-house, where he said the affair was to be settled amicably.

Lord Lionel had consented to this, and had left his brother at the door of a house in the neighbourhood of St. James's Street; after which he (Lord Lionel) had happened to meet

"THERE IS BLOOD ON THE NOTES!"

his friend Colonel Bertrand, of the Austrian army, whom he had accompanied to his apartments in the Albany, where, on account of the severity of the weather, he stayed all night.

All this only served to make the mystery of the Marquis of Willoughby's disappearance still darker and more alarming.

Had he resembled more closely many other members of the aristocracy, the fact of his absence from home for two nights running would have excited very little alarm among the members of his household. But he was the most domestic of men—never happier than when in the society of his mother and his gentle cousin, and never known to seek those haunts of dissipation which the misguided and foolish mistake for the temples of pleasure.

He would never, the Dowager Marchioness

repeated constantly, as her alarm every hour became stronger—he would never have left London without informing her of his departure.

Lucy Maldon's absence was more extraordinary still.

The detectives were soon at work; that wonderful police, without which there would be safety neither for life nor property in the streets of civilised London, was put in motion, and every step was taken likely to lead to the clearing up of the mystery.

Gambling-houses were broken into by the fearless members of that brave band, who are always ready to encounter danger, and who are unrewarded by glory or honours.

There are medals for the man who cuts down his enemy upon the battle-field; but there is no medal for the policeman who, alone, and in the dead of the night, enters some den of infamy,

No. 3. [Weekly, One Penny.]

and struggles, single handed, with a gang of desperate thieves.

In vain did they question Lord Lionel Montfort as to the exact whereabouts of that gaming-house at the door of which he had parted with the Marquis.

He could not tell the street in which it was situated, much less the number of the house.

Both times that they had been there they had gone in a cab, and his brother had given the direction to the driver without his being able, or even trying, to distinguish what the address was.

The night had been so dark and stormy that, even had the street been familiar to him in the day, he could scarcely have recognised it at such a time. In short, question him how they would, he could give them no clue. He knew nothing, but that the house was somewhere in the neighbourhood of St. James's Street.

In the midst of this distress and confusion came tidings which brought desolation into the noble mansion of the missing Marquis.

An express arrived from Dover, bringing the intelligence that the body of a young man, shot through the heart, had been found by some fishermen in a retired spot under the cliffs, about a mile out of the town.

From the clothes and jewellery in which the corpse was dressed, it had been concluded that the deceased was a person of the highest respectability; if not a man of rank. The body had been removed to an hotel, there to wait the coroner's inquest; and in the meantime, inquiries had been set on foot, with a view to the identification of the deceased.

A clue was soon found by a gentleman from London, who stopped at the Dover hotel on his way to Paris, and who had heard of the disappearance of the Marquis of Willoughby. The landlord of the hotel had shown this gentleman the watch and seals found upon the person of the deceased, and the traveller had immediately recognised the Willoughby arms engraved on the back of the watch.

This was enough. There was little doubt that the unhappy man who had met with an untimely end beneath the cliffs of Dover was no other than the missing Marquis of Willoughby.

The distracted mother hurried to Dover upon receipt of the terrible intelligence, only to recognise in the still features of the corpse the handsome face of her beloved son.

But this was not all.

Late in the evening of the day upon which the body had been found, a young girl had been seen wandering about the cliffs, and gazing thoughtfully down upon the wide ocean beneath her feet.

One or two passers-by had spoken to her, warning her of the height upon which she stood, and of the danger of approaching too near to the edge of the precipice. Their warnings had been in vain; for at day-break the next morning she was found dashed to pieces upon the shingly beach below—her delicate frame cruelly mutilated, but her face in no way disfigured.

Another blow was destined to strike upon the tortured heart of the Dowager Marchioness.

This young girl was her beloved niece, Lucy Maldon.

CHAPTER IX.

UNCLE AND NEPHEW

NEAR a wharf situated upon the banks of the river Thames, a little distance below London Bridge, there stood in the year '51 a tumble-down old house, that had once no doubt belonged to a City merchant of some standing. Long rows of high, narrow windows looked towards the water, and a handsome doorway with a flight of stone steps also faced the river-bank, but the windows, with the exception of one or two of the higher ones, were all walled up, the stone steps were green with moss and damp, and the heavy oaken door was rotting slowly away.

On the morning succeeding the night on which the events described in the preceding chapter had taken place, a young man, dressed in a suit of shabby black, might have been seen entering the old river-side house by means of a key which he inserted in the rusty lock, looking cautiously round as he did so, to see whether he was observed.

He was pale and thin and looked careworn, but his features were regular and his face handsome; though at this moment there was a look of severity and determination about his firmly compressed lips that gave an air of unwonted sternness to his countenance.

The street door opened into a large hall, paved with black and white marble, and leading to a broad staircase, the heavy oaken bannisters of which were crumbling with age, and white with the dust which had perhaps accumulated for years.

The young man ascended the stairs, raising a cloud of dust with every footstep.

"What a vault for any human creature to live in!" he muttered, as he glanced around him.

He continued steadily mounting till he reached the upper floor, when he stopped at the door of a room situated at the back of the house, and listened. The door was slightly ajar, but not a sound issued from the chamber within.

"He is asleep, no doubt," muttered the young man; "I had better enter."

He opened the door as he spoke, and walked softly into the apartment.

It was a large oak-panelled room, the furniture dark, heavy, and gloomy-looking, but still handsome. At the end of the chamber nearest to the door, there was a great oaken book-case, well stocked with heavy volumes; near this there was a table covered with a cloth of green velvet, and scattered with papers and parchments; and opposite this table stood a ponderous bed of black oak, hung with green velvet curtains, and occupied by a very old man, who lay fast asleep upon the pillows.

He was so old that his face was almost disfigured by the wrinkles which lined his parchment-like skin. His attenuated hand clutched nervously at the air, every now and then, while he slept, as though he was agitated by some terrible dream, and ever and anon a low moan or some broken word escaped from his pale and shrivelled lips.

Seated by the side of the bed, with her eyes fixed anxiously upon the sleeper, was a woman of middle age, dressed in shabby black, and whom it was not difficult to recognise as the mother of the young man.

"How has he been all night, mother?" asked the new comer, looking at the invalid.

"Pretty much the same," answered the woman; "restless and feverish, talking in his sleep, and wandering in his mind when awake."

"What did he talk about?"

"Always the same. A secret that has been trusted to him, and that he has been paid for keeping. A secret that weighs upon his mind, and that he wants to reveal before he dies."

As she spoke, the old man suddenly opened his eyes, and starting from the pillow, looked about him with a wild stare.

"Who talked about a secret?" he cried, hoarsely; "who was it dared to talk about the secret? Haven't I been paid to keep it all these long years; paid handsomely, too: no stint, no pinching; money down, and lots of it. Ha! ha! Twenty years; five and twenty years; thirty years! Thirty years I've kept the secret—taken the pay; who says I want to sell it? Who says I am such a fool as to want to sell it?"

"Nobody said anything, uncle," said the woman soothingly. "It is only Antony, who has come to ask after your health."

"Oh, it's only Antony," cried the old man, with a mocking laugh, "it's only Antony, is it, niece? Antony, who has come to ask after my health. Shall I tell you what he has come for, niece? He has come to smell out my gold; to find out where my money is hidden—if I had any, if I had any, which I haven't, for I'm a poor old man, a very poor old man, nephew. He has come to try and wring my secret from me; but he never shall, he never shall! I've kept it thirty years, thirty long years, and I'll keep it till I die. It shall rot with me in my coffin."

"Dear uncle," said the woman gently, "last night, when you were very ill, and uneasy in your mind, you said you could not die happy, with some terrible guilt upon your soul. Has that guilt anything to do with the secret?"

"It has, it has," answered the old man, with wild vehemence. "It is a guilty secret; but it's not mine, it's not mine. It's a secret that keeps rightful heirs out of a princely fortune; it's a secret that does wrong to many for the advantage of one. It's a bad secret; but mind, the guilt is no guilt of mine; I've kept the secret, that's all; I've been paid for that and nothing else."

Antony Verner, for that was the name of the old man's nephew, drew nearer to the bedside, and taking his uncle's attenuated hand in his, said solemnly—

"Dear uncle, for pity's sake, do not die with this sin upon your soul. It may not yet be too late to do reparation, and to restore the innocent to their rights."

"It is too late, it is too late," muttered the old man.

"No, no, uncle, surely not; let us hope not; only confide in me; tell me whom this secret concerns."

"It is the secret of a rich and powerful man, who is strong enough to crush his enemies," answered the invalid, whose mind seemed to be a little more collected.

"But those whom this rich man has wronged?" asked Antony Verner.

"They are those who should have been nearest and dearest to him, but he loved nothing but himself; selfishness was the root of all," murmured the invalid, relapsing into delirium.

"Only tell me the name," urged his nephew.

"Never, never. They were brothers. Brothers! Heaven help them! one so proud and noble, the other so vile and base. How could they be brothers? Strange—strange!"

"But, uncle, if you should die, have you left no record of your secret; no written testimony which might still be used to restore the wronged man to his inheritance?"

The old man looked at his nephew for some moments with a wild and angry stare; then bursting into a fierce laugh, he cried—

"Ha, ha; all alike, all alike—all for themselves. I know what you want, Antony, you pale-faced hypocrite. You want to wring my secret from me, and to sell it; to sell it to the highest bidder. That's what you want. But you shall not. You may try and wring it out of me when I'm dead, but you never shall while I'm alive."

Exhausted by the violence of his emotions, he fell back upon the pillow gasping for breath.

Antony Verner watched quietly by the bedside of the sick man, who soon sank into a fitful doze, which lasted for hours.

With untiring patience the mother and son kept their post by the side of the churlish old man, Mrs. Verner carefully preparing and administering his medicines as the appointed hours came round.

Antony and his mother scarcely once spoke to each other. The young man was grave and silent; the woman sighed heavily now and then as she looked from her son to the sleeping man. They sat so long in their silent watch, that hour after hour struck from the eight-day clock in an adjoining room, and still the old man slept a disturbed and fitful slumber, only waking to a state of half-consciousness when Mrs. Verner administered his medicines. The shades of the spring evening were darkening in, when the invalid suddenly raised himself from the pillows, and grasping his nephew violently by the arm, gasped into the ear of the terrified young man—

"Antony, I can't die with the guilt upon my soul! I've tried hard to do it. I've fought hard with my guilty conscience, but I can't, I can't."

"Speak, dear uncle, I am attending to you."

"Listen, then, to every syllable, as you value your own soul, and as you hope to save mine."

"I am listening, uncle; speak, I implore."

"Behind one of those books," whispered the old man, "you will find my keys; one of them unlocks the door of——there—there—that's where the secret is kept written, written, every word of it—and signed by me—remember!"

"But, uncle," cried Antony, "what door? what door? you have not told me that?"

The old man stared at him with a wild and stony gaze, pointing with his bony finger to his lips, and then with a terrible effort he shrieked rather than said—

"Yes, yes, the door—the door is—"

But he never finished the sentence; for a stream of blood rushed from his lips and dyed the bed-clothes with its sanguine hue. He had broken a blood-vessel. He never spoke again, and three hours afterwards he died in his nephew's arms.

Death set his seal upon the old man's secret: that great mystery, the grave, swallowed up one other mystery in its own black obscurity.

CHAPTER X.

THE MILLIONAIRE'S RESOLVE

ROBERT MERTON, the millionaire, sat alone in the well-furnished library of a handsome house in Park Lane.

From the ceiling to the floor the walls of the large room were covered with books, in plain but expensive bindings. Books which from their character became a key to the mind of the man who had selected them.

Robert Merton, plain and unaffected as were his manners, was neither a fool nor a dunce. He had educated himself from the hour in which he had first begun the world as an errand-boy in that Manchester warehouse. No opportunity had ever been lost by which he could improve his mind or extend his knowledge. Blessed with an intellect far above that of his fellows, he had, at a very early age, cultivated and refined his taste in matters both of science and art.

There were many of the proud aristocrats, amongst whom his lot was now cast, who freely owned him their superior in all those mental attributes which, far more than rank or high-sounding title, serve to make a man truly great.

Let us look at the wealthy merchant as he sits under the light of a green-shaded reading-lamp.

It is that very night upon which the dreadful tidings of the Marquis of Willoughby's untimely death have reached the despairing and sorrow-stricken mother.

Robert Merton is not what the world commonly calls a handsome man. The broad forehead upon which the subdued light of the lamp now falls is the shrine of intellect rather than of mere physical beauty. The bright and fearless blue eyes beam with an expression which reveals a noble and truthful soul. The features, though sufficiently regular, are not strictly beautiful, and the complexion is bronzed by exposure to all varieties of weather, for Robert Merton is a bold rider and a daring sportsman, and his country seat is renowned for its hunting stud, and the princely hospitality of its owner, who is beloved and respected throughout the county to which he belongs.

The book falls from the hand of the millionaire, who relapses into deep and earnest thought.

"If I could only think, if I only dared believe that she loves me," he murmured, "I should be the happiest and proudest of men. But I fear that I am blinded by this mad infatuation. Deluded, perhaps, by an artful woman who sets her loveliness against the wealth which buys it, and glories in the unnatural barter."

He took up his book as he finished speaking, and tried to bury himself in its pages.

He had been reading about half an hour, when the door opened and a footman entered, carrying a silver salver, upon which lay about half a dozen letters, which had just arrived by the last London delivery.

He looked at them with an eager glance as they lay spread upon the salver with the addresses uppermost, and then swept them on to the table with a careless gesture.

He had been able in that one brief glance to discover that neither of the letters came from Lady Edith Vandeleur, and he was perfectly indifferent as to their contents.

He opened one envelope after another, and cast the letters away after reading the first line.

One or two were business letters, three of the others contained cards of invitation; the last was directed in a hand that was unfamiliar to him. He looked at it thoughtfully for a few moments before breaking the seal, and then tearing it open, began to read.

No sooner had he read the first line than a fearful change came over his face.

He read the letter once, twice, three times; gazing at it as if he thought his eyes must deceive him; but after the third line he groaned aloud and exclaimed—

"It is not a dream, my worst fears are realised, and I am indeed the dupe I feared to become."

The letter, which was anonymous, ran thus :—

"You are deceived, and fooled to the top of your bent. Lady Edith Vandeleur is a heartless coquette, who would reject you to-morrow with scorn were you deprived of the wealth for which she alone values you. A rich marriage has been her ambition ever since she left the nursery. The man she really loves is Lord Lionel Montfort, the younger brother of the Marquis of Willoughby. Be warned in time, and withdraw from this ill-omened marriage before it is too late.

"A Rival, but a Sincere Friend."

"Coward !" exclaimed the merchant, rising and throwing the anonymous epistle into a bronze casket which stood upon a side table. "Coward to stab in the dark, and to slander a woman from the shelter of his nameless insignificance. 'A friend, although a rival !' A

rival ! He owns as much. This letter is dictated by the impotent fury of a jealous mind. I will prove myself superior to this infamous insinuation. And yet, and yet—it only confirms my own fears. Lord Lionel Montfort, the very man who surprised us in the conservatory. I noticed her agitation on beholding him, even in that moment of triumph and rapture, when I thought I had won her as my own. Lord Lionel ! The very man with whom I watched her in such close conversation in the ante-chamber of her father's ball-room. The very man to whom Colonel Bertrand, the Austrian, pointed when he told me to judge for myself. By Heaven ! " cried Robert Merton, his teeth clenched together, and his blue eyes flashing with an unwonted light, " I will judge for myself. I will put her to the test. And if I find her true, a life's devotion shall repay her for a moment's doubt."

Early the next morning Lady Edith Vandeleur received a letter from her affianced husband, in which he implored her to go to him immediately, hinting darkly at some terrible calamity under which her love alone could sustain him.

She turned pale as death as she read the epistle which was handed to her at the breakfast-table, where she was seated alone with her father, Lord Horton.

The first thought that flashed through her brain was that the man to whom she was to be married was perhaps ruined. She had heard of the dangers of speculation, and she fancied that Robert Merton's princely fortune might have fallen a prey to some terrible crash in commercial affairs.

But her powerful intellect and strong will did not allow her to be subdued even for a moment. Collecting herself in an instant after the reading of the letter, she said to her father, with seeming indifference—

"Do you know how Mr. Merton is going on, Papa ? He is not hazarding his fortune, I hope, by any silly speculations ? "

Lord Horton looked up from his newspaper, and laughed as he glanced at his daughter's handsome face.

"What, Edith," he exclaimed, "are you beginning to tremble already for the thousands of your future husband ? Do not be alarmed, my dear girl. Though Robert Merton is the most open-hearted and generous of fellows, he is prudence itself. I believe that he has done with speculation, and that he does not intend to risk another penny of his fortune, which is so large that he can have no wish to increase it."

"He'll find a little difference when I begin to spend it for him though, Papa," replied Lady Edith, joining in her father's laugh. "I mean to show the fashionable world what splendour is, when I change the ancient name of Vandeleur for that of a Manchester tradesman."

"Never mind the trade, Edith," answered the Earl. "Robert Merton is a noble fellow, and I shall be very proud of him for a son-in-law: and as to his money, I can tell you that the Bank of England is not more secure than the fortune of your future husband."

Lady Edith glanced contemptuously at her good-natured old father, and soon after retiring from the table, ordered her carriage, and went to her own apartments to assume her out-door costume.

"This is an extraordinary breach of all etiquette," she said to herself, as her elegant clarence drove her from Hanover Square to Park Lane; "but what can be expected from a man who was bred in a merchant's office and educated at a clerk's desk? He asks me to go to him as if something very important depended upon my complying, and I do not like to oppose his silly whim for fear of his taking it into his head that I do not love him. For the country booby has some stupid romantic notion of wishing to be loved by the woman he marries. Heaven help him!"

Arrived at Park Lane, Lady Edith Vandeleur was shown into the library in which Robert Merton had been seated when he received the letter which had given him so much pain.

The lady glanced round the room, and then sinking into an easy chair, prepared to await the coming of the master of the house.

He was rather longer than she had anticipated, and growing weary of waiting, Lady Edith rose and amused herself by looking at the decorations of the room. She was just growing tired of this, when her eye was attracted by the exquisitely carved bronze casket standing on a side table.

This was the very casket into which Robert Merton had thrown the anonymous letter received by him the night before.

Lady Edith approached the side table and examined the carving on the sides and lid of the casket.

"It is very beautiful," she said. "Who would have thought that a Manchester merchant could have had such taste? Now I'd venture to guess that my uncultivated husband—that is to be, keeps nothing better than his cigars in this valuable casket."

As she spoke she carelessly raised the bronze lid. There was nothing in the casket but two or three crumpled papers; the writing upon the uppermost of these was clearly visible, and Lady Edith Vandeleur's piercing glance caught the syllables which formed her own name.

"So," she muttered, "it appears that this concerns me."

She glanced at the door of the library; it was firmly shut. Rapid as lightning in her movements, she snatched the letter from the casket, and ran her eyes hastily over its contents. Having done so, she dropped the paper back into the box, and closing the lid, threw herself into an easy chair to await the entrance of Robert Merton.

"So I have enemies, have I?" she said, with a dangerous fire flashing from her glorious dark eyes. "Enemies who envy me my good fortune, and who wish to destroy my prospects. No matter, we shall see if Edith Vandeleur cannot be a match for those who would injure her. This poor fool loves me. His sending for me this morning; his dark hints at some calamity which has befallen him; all this may be only meant to try me. I shall be upon my guard. How fortunate that I happened to find that letter, for that will give me a clue to his conduct!"

The door opened as she spoke, and Robert Merton entered the room. He was pale and haggard, in consequence of the sleepless night which he had passed. In the long hours of darkness his truthful and honest heart had been cruelly rent with bitter doubts of the woman he loved. But now his blue eyes beamed with a new light—the light of happiness; for he thought that her coming to him in reply to his alarming letter was no small proof of her sincerity.

"Robert," she cried, her whole manner changing as her affianced husband advanced to meet her; "Robert, tell me what has happened; your letter has filled me with alarm; I implore you to keep no secrets from your future wife."

"I will not, Edith," said the merchant, gravely; "resume your seat, I beg, for I have much to say to you. Much that must be said, and on which, perhaps, the happiness or misery of our future lives may depend."

He seated himself opposite to her, and after a few moments' reflection began thus—

"Lady Edith Vandeleur, from the hour in which I first beheld you I have loved you with that mad and blind affection which a man can know but once in a lifetime. My humble origin, my lowly parents, a youth of labour, and a manhood devoted to commerce, all these separated me from that haughty sphere in which you moved, a bright particular star. But lacking high birth and an ancient name, title, and hereditary honours, I had still that which enabled me to take my place among the proudest of you —I had gold, lady! gold! without which I should have been spurned from the doors which now open to welcome me. Gold, the magical key which unlocks all hearts, and admits its owner into the lordliest mansion as a courted and an honoured guest. Presuming perhaps upon my wealth, I ventured to reveal my love, and to implore its return. You swore, Lady Edith Vandeleur, to love me. Forgive me if I allude to these things, but I do it for a solemn purpose. Forgive me when I tell you that there have been times when I have doubted you—when I have thought that, perhaps, had I been poor, you too, like the rest of the world, would have despised and spurned me. Edith, Edith, tell me, I implore you, is this so?"

"Robert, how can you think it?"

She lifted her beautiful eyes, beaming with tenderness, to his face as she spoke.

He must have been more than man if he could have resisted that bewitching glance.

"And you would love me still, Edith, were I a poor man to-morrow?" he asked.

"As dearly as I have ever loved you. As dearly as I love you now."

The heartless and mercenary woman laughed within herself at the double meaning of her studied reply.

"Then, Edith, I am about to test the sincerity of your words. *I am a ruined man!*"

She started, and for a moment her presence of mind forsook her. But the words of her father, the Earl, flashed back upon her memory —those words in which Lord Horton had so positively asserted that Robert Merton had ceased to speculate, and that his fortune was secure as the Bank of England itself.

Remembering this, the mind of Lady Edith Vandeleur was resolved. She knew what course to take.

"If it is so, dearest Robert," she murmured, extending her white hand to the astonished merchant: "if it is indeed so, your changed fortunes shall make no difference in my love. I am not, perhaps, well fitted to become a poor man's wife, for I have been nursed in the lap of splendour and luxury. But I will do my best to make you happy, and whatever your fate may be, I will share that fate without one word of repining."

Robert Merton rose from his seat and clasped her in his arms.

"My beloved," he cried, "how little did I know your pure and noble heart! I have put you to a cruel test, my Edith, and I must implore forgiveness for the unmanly deception. My fortune has never been in any danger. I am as rich as ever."

"What!" exclaimed Lady Edith. "You have indeed wronged me by a doubt which I so

little deserved. But I forgive you for the sin against my love, for, at least, it has enabled me to prove the truth of my affection."

"One more proof, Edith; grant me but one more," urged Robert Merton, pressing his lips to her arched brow. "My love is so intense that I am full of jealous fear: I dread a hundred things which may occur to interfere with my happiness. Grant me one favour?"

"Name it, Robert."

"Our marriage is appointed for this day month, to take place at St. George's, Hanover Square."

"It is."

"Marry me privately to-day. I ask none of the privileges of a husband. I will leave you at the church door, but let me only feel that you are indeed mine, united to me by the sacred tie of the church—mine in life or death. Will you grant this, Edith?"

"It is such a singular request," she said, hesitatingly.

"It is, my darling. But love is full of wayward fancies. Be my wife. Then were I to die to-morrow, to you, and you alone, would I leave my fortune, for who could have so good a right to it as my wedded wife? The licence is procured; an old friend of mine, a banker from Manchester, the truest and most honourable of men, will act as father, and give my fair bride away. Say, Edith, that you will consent."

"I can refuse you nothing, Robert," murmured Lady Edith.

The merchant rang the bell.

"Tell Mr. Danvers that I shall be glad to see him here for a few minutes," he said to the servant who answered the summons, "and order the carriage."

"We will proceed at once to the church, dearest. Your own carriage can wait in the meantime. If you should think it necessary to explain your absence, you can say that we have driven to a jeweller's to order the setting of some diamonds which are preparing for you. I do not ask my beloved to tell a falsehood, for I am about to request you to choose what sets of jewels you would like to see on the toilette table of Lady Edith Merton."

At this juncture Mr. Danvers, the banker, made his appearance, and was introduced by Robert Merton to the lovely bride.

Arthur Danvers was a man of about sixty— tall, stout, and powerfully built, hale and rosy, with iron-grey hair and a handsome face, he was the very model of a country gentleman. Truth and candour beamed in his honest countenance. His sonorous voice rang through the room, his hearty laugh warmed the heart of the listener. He was a bachelor, and pretended to be a woman-hater; but he had half a dozen penniless nieces, the daughters of a deceased and scapegrace brother, living with him at his handsome country house; and there was not one of those six young ladies who would not have declared against all the world that Arthur Danvers was the gentlest-hearted and most amiable of men.

It was not very safe to offend him, though, for he flew in a towering rage in five minutes, and would bluster until those who did not know him were terribly alarmed.

His penetrating glance narrowly observed Lady Edith Vandeleur as his friend introduced him to her.

"My friend Bob, here, couldn't have chosen much better, my lady, if it's beauty he wants," said the blunt old banker; "but beauty is but skin deep, you know, and I hope Robert has secured something that will wear better than the brightest eyes or the loveliest face. Surely there must be goodness and truth below such a fair surface. Eh, Bob?"

Though Mr. Danvers spoke half jestingly, a close observer might have discovered that the worthy banker glanced rather uneasily at Lady Edith's handsome face.

Robert Merton handed his betrothed into the carriage, and then took his place opposite to her. Mr. Danvers seated himself by his friend's side, and abandoned himself to a long and earnest scrutiny of the lady's face.

Arthur Danvers and Robert Merton had been true and sincere friends ever since the latter had begun his career as a junior clerk in the warehouse in which he had once been an errand-boy.

They had been associated in many speculations, all of which had been successful, and the attachment between them was such as might have existed between a father and son.

It was little wonder, then, that the banker looked with some curiosity at the lovely face of the woman who was about to become the wife of his friend. He knew the world, and had been, in the course of a long career, brought into contact with many strange characters.

To him the face was always an index to the mind—a key by which he could often read the secret workings of the heart. The countenance of Lady Edith Vandeleur puzzled him. It seemed all candour and radiance—a little proud, perhaps, but there might be nobleness of soul even in that very pride, and yet he felt restless and uneasy, and was not altogether satisfied with his friend's choice.

The church to which they drove was situated in an obscure corner of the city—a quiet little nook in which the appearance of a lady, bonneted and shawled, attended by two gentlemen in morning costume, attracted no attention.

The service was read; the vows pronounced, which are so often spoken by perjured lips, and Robert Merton and Lady Edith Vandeleur were man and wife.

Did the holy words of the ceremonial awaken no solemn thoughts within the worldly soul of the ambitious woman?

Alas, no! Wealth, splendour, luxury, grandeur, pomp, and pride—these were the things for which she sold herself, and of these alone she thought.

The ceremony over, the carriage drove to a jeweller's at the West End, where Lady Edith selected several sets of jewels, at the request of her generous husband, who valued his wealth only for the power it gave him to gratify every wish of the woman whom he loved.

The jewels were taken to the carriage, upon the back seat of which they lay, glistening and sparkling in their caskets of morocco, lined with purple velvet and snow-white satin.

The lady gazed at them with triumphant eyes as her carriage drove her back to her father's house. It was for such baubles as these she had uttered the false vows which become a blasphemy upon the wicked lips which speak them.

What Eastern slave, purchased by a Sultan's emissaries in an Oriental slave-market, was ever more degraded than the woman of rank who sells herself for the gold of the man whom she despises?

CHAPTER XI.

SAMUEL CRANK'S AGENCY

IN one of the busiest quarters of the City of London there is a narrow court, so hidden away behind thick clusters of warehouses, so shut in by the lofty piles of building which close around it, that a stranger would fail to find it without a guide.

This court is called Kelman's Alley.

The light of the blessed sun rarely penetrated into this dismal spot; the window-panes of the dark house were black and grimed with the accumulated smoke and dirt of years. No children ever came to play upon the narrow pavement between the two rows of dreary buildings. Deserted by the light of Heaven, it seemed as if the place was almost deserted by mankind.

The whole of one side of this court was occupied by the back of some large manufactory; on the other side were half a dozen irregular tumble-down houses, the door-posts half rotting away; the worn-out paint upon the panels of the doors cracked and blistered; the window-panes broken; the entire aspect of the place proclaiming misery and desolation.

Upon the centre panel of the door of Number Two, there was a rusty brass-plate, upon which was engraved, "SAMUEL CRANK, AGENT."

Agent for whom, or for what?

The brass-plate threw no light upon that mystery. Had a stranger asked any of the neighbours—men who had lived half their lives in Kelman's Alley—for information respecting Mr. Samuel Crank, he would have obtained little more than that afforded by the brass-plate.

No one knew anything of Samuel Crank. No one had ever known for certain that they had really seen him. Young men, old men, women, boys, children, had been seen to come from the door of Number Two; but no one had been perceived to go in or out so often as to justify the neighbours in supposing him to be Mr. Crank.

He had lived in Kelman's Alley for some years. Nobody remembered his coming. The residents had seen one morning a brass-plate upon the door with a name that was unfamiliar to them, and that was all.

Whoever he was, he could only use the house as a place of business, for lights were never seen in the shutterless upper windows, nor was any food ever seen to be carried in.

On the morning of the day following that on which the events took place which we have described in the preceding chapter, a dark and quiet-looking brougham drew up in one of the busiest thoroughfares of the East End of London, and a tall, elegant-looking man alighted.

"I am going to my bankers', Carson," he said to his coachman, "and as I may be engaged with him for some time, you had better drive home. I shall return in a Hansom."

The man drove off, and the stranger looked about him thoughtfully.

"Strange," he muttered, "often as I have been here, I always forget the way to the wretched place."

After a few moments' deliberation, however, he appeared to recall the neighbourhood to recollection, and striking into a dismal square, he walked rapidly through several winding and twisting streets, then under an archway that conducted him into Kelman's Alley.

"Our birds have no snugger nest in all Europe than this, I think," he murmured, as his brilliant black eye glanced round the dingy court. "I would defy all the detectives in England to find us here. There is Mr. Crank's office. A sly old dog, a clever old dog, is Samuel

Crank. Takes to his business as a fashionable beauty takes to a rich husband. A useful man, a perfect treasure!"

He knocked at the door of Number Two as he made these reflections.

After some delay, it was opened very cautiously, with a great rattling of chains and bolts, and the stranger entered the dingy passage, at the end of which, though it was but noon, a small oil lamp was burning.

Samuel Crank—for he it was who opened the door—was an elderly man, with white hair, and bushy black eyebrows. He wore the dress of fifty years ago—knee breeches, grey stockings, shoes and shoe-buckles, and a long white flannel dressing-gown.

This old-fashioned costume, and his white hair, made him appear a great deal older than he really was.

He was what many people would have called a benevolent-looking old man. But the close observer might have perceived, in the small and rat-like eyes which twinkled behind his spectacles, a strange and dangerous glitter—something like the glitter of the eyes of a serpent when fixed upon its helpless and fascinated prey.

He bowed very low as the stranger strode into the narrow passage.

"Your humble servant, Captain," he said, with an air of cringing humility; "if I had known it was you who knocked——"

"You would have come a little quicker, eh, my worthy Samuel," said Colonel Oscar Bertrand, the Austrian officer—for he it was who was the visitor of Samuel Crank, agent. "Well, certainly, Kelman's Alley isn't the pleasantest place in the world for a gentleman to kick his heels in. Lead the way upstairs, my good friend, and let us see how business is going on."

Mr. Crank, stopping at almost every step to bow, or to apologise to the Colonel for the wretchedness of the place, led the way up the narrow staircase, and into a room on the first floor.

This room was fitted up much after the fashion of a lawyer's office. A large desk and a high-backed leathern chair occupied the centre of the apartment; there was a book-case against the wall, and other shelves, on which stood one or two rows of heavy vellum-bound volumes, which looked like ledgers. At the back of the high arm-chair there was a narrow recess, which had been occupied by a window, now bricked up, and before this recess hung a shabby chintz curtain.

"Now, most excellent and sagacious Samuel," said the Colonel, flinging himself into the office chair, and deliberately drawing off his delicate primrose-coloured kid gloves, "let us go into our affairs. How is the retail trade going on?"

"Pretty well, pretty well, my honoured Captain," said the old man, chuckling and rubbing his hands. He had not presumed to seat himself in the presence of the Austrian officer, but stood by, as if ready to obey any order he might receive.

"Humph!" muttered Colonel Bertrand, running his ringed fingers through his bright auburn hair. "The money does not drop in quite as fast as I should wish. The society is a rich one, but its expenses are enormous. A midnight robbery, Samuel Crank, is a speculation—a speculation by which the robber, however clever and experienced, sometimes loses. For the last few months nothing great has been done by the society either in England or abroad. We want new members, Samuel—new members for the Black Band, and they do not come to us fast enough."

"But we are on the watch," said the old man, thoughtfully—"always on the watch. To-day a gentleman, to-morrow a ploughboy. We lose no chance of strengthening our resources, and adding to our members. No one is too lofty, no one is too lowly: that is our motto, is it not, master?"

"It is," said the Colonel.

"I expect a member to join this morning, nay, this very hour, for it is past twelve, and he should have been here at twelve."

"Indeed!"

"Yes. He has come from a distance to this great city, and he has ventured a great deal to reach it; but he had not been here an hour before he fell into the hands of one of our scouts. The scout met him at a public-house belonging to the society; played skittles with him; drank with him and made him drunk; got all his secrets from him, every one of them, and then told him to come here this morning to me, Mr. Crank, a worthy man, an honest man, and an agent who will put him in the way of investing a little money he has about him. And he's coming, he's coming, poor lad," repeated the old man, grinning and chuckling with a revolting expression of fiendish glee; "he's coming, poor lad! Hark! he's come!"

At this very moment a bell in the passage below rang with a feeble tinkling noise.

"He's humble, poor lad," chuckled the old man; "he's humble, though he's got his little bit of money to invest; he doesn't give a double knock; he rings the bell."

"He mustn't see me here," said the Colonel, taking up his hat and gloves, "and yet I can't pass him on the staircase. I've a good mind to stay and hear the interview; I know what a

clever fellow you are, Samuel, and I should like to find out how you manage matters."

"Then step into that recess, honoured Captain; the lad will never see you there. Step in; I'll draw the curtain across, and you'll hear how we do it. Ha! ha! ha!" chuckled the old man as the Colonel concealed himself.

He left the room and returned in a few minutes, followed by a young man in a countryman's dress, who looked about him as he entered the room.

"It's a queer place you live in, Mr. Crank," he said.

"Rich people often do live in queer places," said Samuel Crank, with a sly laugh; "queer places are the safest."

"So they are, so they are," answered the young man.

He was a pale-faced, cadaverous-looking youth, of about five and twenty years of age. He had small, cunning black eyes, and he seemed to be very well able to take care of himself.

"So you want to invest a little money, my young friend?" said Mr. Crank.

"Who told you that?" asked the young man, sharply.

"The friend who sent you here, Mr. Timothy Hodge," answered Samuel. "Why not be open and candid now," he added, seating himself in his office chair; "why not be candid, Mr. Hodge, and tell me all about it?"

Mr. Hodge looked rather distrustfully at the old man, and then said with a sulky air—

"Well, then, this is all about it. I've had a lot of money left me by my grandfather, and I want to invest it in some safe concern that will bring me a good interest for my principal. It's—all in notes," he added, hesitating, and turning very white, "and I should like them to be sent abroad."

"Should you?" said Mr. Crank, the agent, with a strange chuckling laugh, "should you really now, my dear young friend? But why?"

"Never you mind why," muttered Mr. Timothy Hodge.

"But I do mind, my dear young man," answered the old agent, fixing his penetrating rats' eyes upon Mr. Hodge's changing countenance. "Shall I tell you why? Because, you know very well that the number of every one of those notes is known, and that payment is stopped at the Bank of England. Because you came by them dishonestly — and because——"

"What, what?" cried Timothy Hodge, his presence of mind wholly deserting him in his terror of the old man.

"Because there is blood upon them!" cried

Samuel Crank. "Ha, ha, did you think to deceive *me?*"

With a shrill scream of horror, the young man fell upon his knees before Mr. Crank's desk, and taking a bundle of notes from his pocket, cast them from him as if they had been scorpions.

"Mercy! mercy!" he gasped.

The old man laughed aloud.

"Mercy," repeated the wretched youth, hiding his face in his hands.

"Listen to me, young man," said Samuel Crank, in a solemn voice; "you have taken the first step upon the great high road of crime. You can no more retrace that step than you can recall the yesterday which has fallen into the grave of the past. You are a criminal, and the strong hand of the law is on the watch to strike you. You are *ours*, join us!"

"Join you?" repeated Timothy; "but who—what are you?"

"That you shall know when you have become one of us. Be satisfied now to know that we arm ourselves against the law, which is armed against us, and that we defy that law. Join us!"

"I will!" answered the terror-stricken young man.

"Good. Had you refused, I should have given information against you, and to-night you would have slept in Newgate. Now go, but return to this house at midnight, and I will then take you to the place where you will be enrolled as a member of our society."

"But——" remonstrated Mr. Hodge.

"Go," repeated Samuel Crank, in a tone of command. "My time is valuable; I can waste no more of it upon you."

The young man sneaked out of the room crestfallen and pale as ashes.

Colonel Bertrand emerged from his hiding-place.

"Samuel Crank," he said, clapping the old man upon the shoulder, "I always thought you a useful member of the society, but now I know you are a treasure."

"I do my best, renowned Captain," said Mr. Crank; "I do my best, and I like the business."

CHAPTER XII.

THE STAR OF THE BALLET

As the clocks in the neighbourhood of the Haymarket struck three on the afternoon of the day upon which Lady Edith had given her hand to Robert Merton, a stream of young girls poured out of the stage door of Her Majesty's Theatre.

A heavy rain was falling, and some of these young women, who were, many of them, humbly though neatly and respectably dressed, stopped under the colonnade in hopes that the sky would clear and the rain cease before long. Others, who were elegantly clad in rich silks and velvets, stepped into broughams which were waiting for them, and drove off after having exchanged a few words with their humbler companions.

Alas for those who wear costly dresses and glittering jewels, but who, to win these, have bartered that purest of all gems—peace of mind! Lovely and brilliant, animated and fascinating, they appear to be joyous and happy. But we know not of the lonely hours of anguish which may rack the breast of the hapless ballet-girl who has exchanged her humble lodgings for the luxuries of a palace; her shabby garments for robes of silk and satin; but who, in making this exchange, has parted for ever with the pure visions of her youth, and can only look forward to a desolate and despised old age.

Weep for them; pity; but do not too harshly blame them! Poorly paid at the best, with perhaps a drunken father or an invalid mother to support—perhaps the only provider for a band of helpless little sisters—sorely tempted by base and cruel men who hold the ballet-girl only as a toy made to minister to their amusement, and to be cast aside for some newer fancy.

Weep for them, poor erring sisters! and remember that frail though many of them may have been, yet in the ranks of the ballet are still every day to be found devoted daughters, self-sacrificing sisters, and true and affectionate wives.

Many of the fairy-like creatures who flit before us in gauze and satin are married women, and the mothers of a band of little ones, all looking to the ballet-girl for support.

The rehearsal of a new ballet has just concluded, and the troop of dancers, happy in having finished their morning's labours, were dispersing to their different homes.

Some of them had been prudent enough to provide themselves with umbrellas, and these trudged contentedly off through the crowded streets. Others hailed omnibuses into which they stepped, for many of them lived at a great distance from the theatre. One by one they dropped off, leaving at the last only one solitary young girl, who stood shivering against one of the pillars of the colonnade, as if afraid of encountering the bad weather.

She was very young, and very pretty. Her dress was shabbier than that of any of the companions who had just left her; but shabby as it was, it was neatness itself. The little thin print dress was scrupulously clean; the small black shawl was carefully arranged upon her slender figure; a snow-white linen collar encircled her thin and graceful throat; the dark brown hair was smoothly braided under her coarse straw bonnet; and the little threadbare boots which encased her slender feet had been darned and patched with careful neatness.

"I dare not go till the rain is over," she murmured to herself; "my shawl will be wet through in a few minutes, and then I shall have that nasty cough, which the ballet-master says makes me so tiresome."

Several of the passers-by turned to look at her pretty face. She was too busily engaged in watching the rain to notice their glances; but at last she was annoyed by an elderly man, with dyed moustachios and a wig, who approached her with an insolent stare that brought a vivid blush to her thin cheek.

"Are you waiting for bettaw weathaw, my chawmaw?" asked the old beau, with an affected drawl.

This padded and moustachioed old dandy was no other than Sir Frederick Beaumorris, well known to the theatrical world as a lounger behind the scenes of those metropolitan theatres which admit some favoured members of the aristocracy to the side-scenes and the green-room.

Such men as these are the tempters and destroyers of ballet-girls, who, entering a theatre young, innocent, and confiding, are exposed to the polluting addresses of heartless wretches, bent only on selfish amusement.

Such men as these have no belief in womanly virtue.

Bad sons, bad husbands, and bad fathers, they go down to the grave through a long career of vice and infamy, and die at last unregretted and despised.

The ballet-girl, whose name was Clara Melville, turned away her head as Sir Frederick Beaumorris addressed her, and affected not to hear him.

"I am shuaw you are a great deal too pwetty to be deaf," drawled the old man. "Pway allow me to see you home. My bwougham is waiting in the next stweet, if you'll accept a seat in it?"

Clara, crimson with indignant blushes, and with the tears starting to her dark blue eyes, was about to make some angry reply when a young man touched the baronet on the arm, and with one light gesture pushed him aside.

"Sir Frederick, cannot you discover when your attentions are offensive to a young lady, without being told of the fact in pretty plain terms?" asked the new comer.

He was tall and slim, elegantly dressed in the height of fashion, yet with gentlemanly simplicity. His face was handsome, his eyes bright hazel, and round his broad forehead clustered a profusion of dark brown curls.

Sir Frederick Beaumorris blushed deeply, almost as much as Clara had done a few moments before.

The old dandy's vanity was wounded at the thought of his insolent attentions having been disagreeable to any woman; and, above all, at the fact becoming known to a younger and handsomer man than himself.

"By Jove! my dear Reginald," he said, with considerable confusion, and with a marked decrease of his customary drawl, "how should I know that the little girl was so high and mighty that she wasn't to be spoken to?"

"She is not high and mighty, I'm sure," replied the young man, glancing at Clara with a look of unmistakable admiration; "and she would not have objected to being spoken to had you spoken like a gentleman. Will you allow me to call you a cab?" he asked, addressing himself to Clara. "I fear this bad weather will continue for some time."

The young girl blushed more vividly than she had done before.

"You are very kind, thank you," she said, hesitating painfully, "but I would much rather walk. I do not mind the rain. I—"

The stranger understood the cause of her embarrassment.

"You must allow me to insist," he said; and before Clara could remonstrate farther he had hailed a passing cab.

"If you will favour me with your address," he said, as he handed her into the vehicle, "I will direct the cabman where to drive."

She gave him the address of an obscure street in Blackfriars. He spoke to the driver, and then, looking in at the cab-window, said, removing his hat as he spoke—

"I have settled with the driver, and have taken his number; ladies do not understand these sort of things."

She understood his motive, and, touched by the delicacy of his conduct, was about to thank him, when the cab drove off, leaving him standing bare-headed upon the pavement.

"Upon my word, Mr. Reginald Falkner," mumbled Sir Frederick Beaumorris, as he and the young man walked away in the direction of the Athenæum club, of which the old baronet was a member, "upon my word, my young friend, I think this is one of the coolest proceedings I ever heard of. No sooner have I pitched upon a pretty little party to whom I feel inclined to say a little soft nonsense, when you walk in, shove me out of the way, and ship off the pretty little party in a cab before I can say Jack Robinson. What do you mean by it, sir? I repeat, sir, what do you mean by it?"

Though Sir Frederick endeavoured to laugh off the matter, as if he thought it a very excellent joke, it was not difficult to see that he was both enraged and mortified by the affair.

"What I mean, Sir Frederick," said the young man, "is this. There are some people so dull of comprehension, that they do not know a virtuous woman when they see one, unless she rides in her coach, with a ducal coronet painted upon the panel. When people are so dull as this, Sir Frederick, they must be taught by those who know better, and who can recognise virtue in a shabby gown, trudging on foot through the mud."

"What a sermon!" cried Sir Frederick, with an affected shudder.

"One by which I hope you will profit, my dear sir," replied the young man, laughing good-humouredly. It seemed as if he did not a little enjoy the old baronet's vexation.

"Upon my word, Reginald, you ought to have been brought up a parson."

"No, Sir Frederick," answered Reginald Falkner, "for then I could not have enjoyed the pleasure of your acquaintance. No clergyman of the Church of England could possibly be hand and glove with the celebrated Sir Frederick Beaumorris."

"Egad, you're right, Reginald," said the old roué, chuckling. "I'm not quite the sort of party for a parson's society. You're a capital fellow, Reginald, though you do sometimes take it into your head to preach. Good day to you, my dear boy, good day. I shall look that little party up at the opera-house, in spite of your sermon." And the old man hobbled off as fast as his tight varnished boots would allow him, chuckling to himself as he walked up the steps leading to his club-house.

To Clara Melville, the ballet-girl, a ride in a cab was such a novelty as to be almost a treat; that is to say, it would have been a treat had not her affectionate mind been tortured by the thought of those whom she had left at home.

"Poor little Jessie," she said to herself as the cab drove over Westminster-bridge, and turned into the New Cut, on its way to Blackfriars. "Poor dear child! I wonder whether she has cried much for sister Clara. It was half-past nine when I left home this morning; now it is nearly four. Poor children, how they will have missed me! And Papa, too, he has been waiting for me, no doubt, to get his dinner."

After driving through several small streets, the cab stopped at a dingy-looking house, in a street smaller, dirtier, and more obscure than the rest.

Half a dozen squalid, raggedly-dressed children were playing upon the pavement before the door of this house, the lower part of which was devoted to a chandler's shop.

Poverty reigned supreme in this wretched neighbourhood. It was difficult to think that the same city could contain the gorgeous mansions of the West End and the tumble-down, smoke-discoloured houses in this quarter of the town.

Clara dismissed the cab, and knocked at the shabby private door of the house. It was opened by a little boy of about seven years of age, poorly but neatly dressed. The child cried out with delight at the appearnce of Clara Melville.

"Sissy, dear sissy!" he exclaimed, "is it really you? Papa would not have dinner till you came home, and poor Jessy has been crying for you. How long you have been, sissy!"

Clara took the child in her arms and kissed him, and then followed him up the creaking, broken-down staircase, to a room in the garret.

This garret was a wretched place, with a sloping ceiling, and a narrow window looking into the gutter which ran along the tops of the houses; but wretched as it was, even here cleanliness and neatness were stamped upon every object. A sick child lay upon a little bed in one corner of the room, close to a tiny iron grate, in which burned a handful of cinders.

At a table near the one miserable window sat an elderly man, busy writing. Threadbare and shabby as was the faded chintz dressing-gown which he wore, it was not difficult to see that, in the midst of all this poverty, he was still a gentleman. His features were well formed and aristocratic; his attenuated hands, small and white; and his manner had that unmistakable grace which betrays good breeding.

He looked up with a smile of delight as Clara entered the room.

"My darling," he said, "you are back at last. Hard as I have been working, the morning has seemed very long to me without you. It is four o'clock, Clara; you have been away from me for six hours."

"My dearest Papa, I know how very long I have been away. The rehearsals of this grand ballet are so tiresome, and the ballet-master is so cross when we cannot learn the steps quickly; and sometimes, do you know, when he is teaching me, my thoughts wander to you, and Jessie, and George, and I begin to wonder how you are all getting on without me; and then I do not hear a word he says, and it puts him in a terrible passion, and he says I am the most stupid girl in the theatre."

"My Clara, my poor darling, how much you have to suffer! you, who ought to be rich."

"Ah, Papa, I never know what you mean when you say that. You so often say we ought to be rich; but you will never tell us your meaning."

"No, my dearest girl, that is my secret. It is a sad and a painful secret; but I shall never reveal it to you. Think this, Clara, in the worst sufferings that your poverty brings down upon you—the sufferings of the poor are nothing beside the sorrows of the rich. Money is a curse, Clara. It transforms the dearest friends into the deadliest enemies. It causes the mother to hate the son—the husband to betray the wife— the brother to detest the brother. It transforms men into fiends, and this world into a hell."

The old man was terribly excited. His whole frame shook with emotion, and sparks of fire seemed to flash from his large grey eyes.

"Dearest father," cried Clara, throwing her arms round his neck, "I will never wish to be rich. Am I not happy, even in this poor garret, with you and my dear brother and sister? I do not seek for wealth while I possess your love."

"My sweet one," murmured her father, returning her embrace; "but how is this, Clara? It has been raining ever since two o'clock, and you are not wet? How did you escape the rain; you had no money to pay for an omnibus?"

"Ah, Papa, that is quite a romantic story," answered Clara, with a blush and a smile; "I must tell you all about it." And she described the scene under the colonnade, and the conduct of Reginald Falkner. Of course she did not know his surname, and she could only describe him as one of the handsomest and most gentlemanly men she had ever seen, adding that she had heard the old man call him Reginald.

Jasper Melville looked very grave.

"My darling girl," he said, "how bitterly I feel this! How bitterly I suffer, when I think of your beauty and innocence exposed to such scenes as these! Remember, Clara, trust no one. Remember always that the unprotected ballet-dancer is considered the legitimate prey of every bad man about London. Do not trust to fair words, or even to actions which seem benevolent, but which may only be the smooth mask that hides a guilty motive. Do not trust to pity or remorse; towards beauty and innocence the wicked are both pitiless and remorseless. Trust no one, believe in no one."

"Dear Papa, I will not, I will not indeed," cried Clara, anxious to reassure her doting father. "I may never see this Mr. Reginald again; but indeed, his manner was so respectful,

so gentlemanly and kind, that I cannot believe he had any bad intention.'"

"Do not trust one of them, Clara," answered Jasper Melville: "they are all hypocrites."

Clara busied herself in preparing the humble meal, for which, small as it was, the family had waited until her return. She took off her bonnet and shawl, put them carefully away in the adjoining garret where she slept, and then began to boil some potatoes which she had prepared for cooking before she went out in the morning."

These, with a wretched bone of meat, made the dinner to which Mr. Melville, his daughter, and the little boy contentedly sat down.

Those who have once been rich will often endure poverty and privation with a patience and fortitude unknown to those who have been reared in penury from their cradle.

After Clara had cleared away the dinner, and washed up the two or three plates which had been used at that humble meal, she set to work to make a cup of arrowroot for her invalid sister.

The child was in a burning fever, and, in spite of Clara's persuasion, refused to take even a spoonful of the arrowroot.

"She has had nothing the whole day but part of the orange you brought her yesterday," said Mr. Melville; "I do not know what is to be done, Clara, for I am sure the child is very ill."

Clara knelt down by the bedside of her sister and looked long and anxiously into the child's flushed face.

She was a pretty little thing of about nine years of age, wasted by sickness, and with large blue eyes unnaturally bright with the glassy look which tells of fever and pain. She tossed her weary little head from side to side upon the pillow—the softest pillow which the family possessed, but still a hard one.

Clara burst out crying as she contemplated the child.

"Oh, Papa, Papa," she exclaimed, "how hard it seems, how cruel and how bitter, that this darling little one cannot have the comforts and luxuries which might perhaps restore her! Look at her lying on this wretched bed, in the stifling atmosphere of this miserable neighbourhood, and think how different her fate would be were she the child of a rich man. Dearest father, I know that the idea is a painful one to you, but let me implore you, for our darling Jessie's sake, to let her be taken to one of those hospitals which the benevolent rich have provided for the poor of London. There she would have all that she required; the highest medical aid—the most unfailing care and watchfulness. Let her go, dear Papa; it is as painful for me as for you to have to part with her, but for her sake I ask it. Let her go!"

"No, Clara, no," cried the old man, with passionate vehemence, "I will never suffer it. Never shall it be said that the child of Jasper Melville was the recipient of any man's benevolence. We can starve, my child, but we will never stoop. We may die, but we will die undegraded. My child, my youngest darling, my Jessie, a pauper! No, no, no. Think what that sweet innocent would suffer when she opened her heavy eyes to behold only strange faces! Think of her tortures when she called for her sister and her father, to be answered only by the hospital nurse! Oh, Clara, Clara, how could you ask such a thing?"

"I asked it because I thought it was right, father," replied Clara, her beautiful face assuming an expression of stony despair, "for I feel that if the child remains here she will die. She will die, my darling, my little sister;" and the ballet-dancer burst into a passion of sobs and bowed her head upon the miserable pallet upon which lay the unconscious child, for Jessie was in a high fever, and had been for some time delirious.

At this very moment the unusual sound of carriage wheels was heard in the street below, followed immediately by a tremendous double knock at the street door.

"What is the meaning of this?" said Jasper Melville, turning as white as a corpse and starting hurriedly to his feet; "have they hunted me down, the merciless wretches? Have they hunted me down at last?"

Clara lifted her head from the patchwork counterpane which covered her sister's restless limbs, and wiping away her tears, looked anxiously at her father, wondering at his unwonted agitation.

Before she could utter a word, however, the garret door was opened from without, and a lady entered the room.

A lady! She was such a creature of light and beauty that description is powerless to give the reader a just idea of her loveliness.

She was of Spanish origin, and the rich blood of the South mantled in her rounded cheek. Her eyes were large and lustrous, and of that exquisite almond-shape which is so rarely seen, except in the gazelle-like beauties of the East. Her lips were of a glowing crimson, and slightly parted, so as to reveal twin rows of teeth which glittered like pearls. Her massive black hair, in which shone those purple shadows seen in the raven's plumage, was brushed away from her face. She was tall and commanding in figure; born to be a queen, an empress, a divinity!

She looked about her for a few moments with a graceful hesitation, and then advancing to Clara, took both the young girl's hands in hers and pressed them in her slender gloved fingers.

This unexpected visitor was no other than Lolota Vizzini, the reigning star of the ballet at the Royal Italian Opera House.

"My dear Miss Melville," she said, with a slight foreign accent, but in a rich deep voice, whose every tone was music, "pray forgive this intrusion; you must think me very impertinent, I have no doubt. But you know, of course, that I am called by the world one of the most eccentric women who ever lived. You must not, therefore, wonder at anything I do. Say that you will forgive me, or I shall have to run away without telling you the reason of my visit."

Her manner had a grace and a fascination which none were ever able to resist, and in spite of Clara's embarrassment, she was won by the charm of her visitor's every word.

The poor girl blushed crimson as she glanced round the wretched apartment, and reflected what the celebrated dancer must think of it.

"This is such a poor place for you to see, Madame Vizzini," she stammered.

"My dear child, do not speak of that," cried the lovely Spaniard, "my life has been a very strange one. I have seen so many changes, that at five and twenty years of age I feel old and worn out, and find that nothing is new to me. A palace to-day, a garret to-morrow— these have been the vicissitudes of my varied life. Never blush for your poverty before me, my dear girl, for I have known the bitterest forms of destitution." She seated herself as she spoke in a little chair by the bedside of the sick child. Her superb violet velvet dress swept the floor of the room. The rich perfume which surrounded her filled the apartment with exquisite scents.

Little Jessie opened her eyes and looked wonderingly at the visitor.

"How pretty you are!" she said to Madame Vizzini; "and oh, what a beautiful dress!"

"I'll tell you what, little one," exclaimed Lolota, laughing at the child's wondering eyes: "only promise me to get well, and you shall have quite as pretty a one."

"What! a dress like that?" cried the child.

"Yes, a dress like this," answered Lolota; "and what is more, you shall go out riding in a nice carriage, and you shall come to the theatre to see your sister dance, and you shall come to my house to see me, and you shall do all sorts of pleasant things besides."

Jasper Melville's careworn brow had flushed scarlet upon the entrance of the brilliant dancer. He now spoke to her for the first time.

"Madam," he said, "we are very poor, but we

are very proud, and I do not allow my daughters to accept favours from any one."

"Favours!" cried Lolota, with a laugh of liquid music, "who spoke of favours? Do you think there would be any favour in my taking this little one home in my carriage, and nursing her as if she were my own? Mr. Melville," she said, with an entire change of manner, and with a shadow of deep melancholy upon her lovely face, "I was married at the age of sixteen, and I once had a child like this. She is dead—or at least," she added, her pensive expression darkening into a vengeful frown, "I have been made to believe that she is dead. I ask you, then, for her sake, let me nurse your little girl. Kind and good as her sister is, she cannot attend to her as I would do, for I have been a mother. Let me take her with me. Come when you like to see her—every day, every hour, if you please, I shall be always glad to receive you, and when the child is well I will restore her to your arms. Clara, plead for me."

"Papa, Papa, you hear, you will let her go?"

The haughty nature of the old man was completely overcome. He dropped his head upon the sheet of paper on which he had been writing, and burst into tears.

"You must do what you like with us, Madam," he said. "You are an angel, and we should be wretches to refuse your bounty. But tell me what all this means, and what kind Providence led you here?"

"That is very soon told," said Madame Vizzini. "My notice has for some time been attracted by your daughter Clara. I have seen her so different to the other girls with whom she mingles, that I could not help admiring—nay, loving her. I have beheld her always so patient and gentle—so kind to her companions, yet so retiring and modest: shrinking always into a corner, as if she hated to have her pretty face admired and observed. All this charmed me; and when, on making some inquiries amongst her companions, I discovered that she was the support of her little sister, and that the child was ill with a dangerous fever, and scarcely expected to recover, I determined immediately upon paying you a visit this evening, as there is no performance to-night and it is therefore a holiday with all of us. I have brought my doctor with me; he is the best and kindest of men. He is waiting in the carriage, and if I can only obtain his permission and yours, I shall take this dear child home with me at once."

"I can only repeat, my dear Madam," replied Mr. Melville, "that you must do with us as you like. There is something in your goodness which makes me powerless to oppose you. I little thought the day would come when Jasper Melville would accept the bounty of any living being, but I cannot refuse yours."

"Will you run down to the street door, my little man," said Lolota to Clara's little brother, "and tell a nice old gentleman whom you will see seated in a carriage before the house, that he is to be so kind as to step upstairs with you?"

The child obeyed, and in a few minutes returned with the doctor—a white-headed old man, with a most benevolent countenance.

"Now, my good Mr. Williams," said Lolota, "this is the little patient I have brought you to see."

After due deliberation, the old man pronounced that the child might be safely removed to Madame Vizzini's house in Arlington Street, where she would have a spacious apartment and pure air.

"Now, my dear Clara," said Lolota, when all the arrangements had been made for removing Jessie, "of course we cannot possibly separate you from your sister, for I fear that if I did all our nursing would be unsuccessful; so you must come and stay with me till Jessie is well. You can go on attending to your duties at the Opera House, and you can bring your Papa your salary every Saturday, as soon as you receive it; and I think that it will be very strange if, between us, we do not persuade the manager to double it before long."

So Clara carried her sister down to the carriage, and held her on her lap as they drove away.

Mr. Melville went downstairs with the little party, kissed his children again and again, and poured out his thanks repeatedly to the lovely Spaniard.

"You will come and see us to-morrow?" said Lolota, giving him her hand through the carriage window. "You will dine with us to-morrow, Mr. Melville, and then you will see how our little patient is getting on. Good-bye."

The carriage drove off, and Jasper Melville and his little son re-ascended to their dreary attic.

"George," said the old man, "do you know what that lady is called?"

"No, Papa."

"She is called 'the Star of the Ballet.' And if beauty and goodness united can entitle a woman to such a name, she is indeed a star."

CHAPTER XIII.

TOO LATE!

LADY EDITH MERTON sat alone by the fire in Lord Horton's splendid drawing-room on the night of her private marriage to the merchant.

THE BAFFLED MURDERESS

The vast apartment was dimly lighted by a shrouded lamp standing upon a little table by the lady's side. The corners of the room were thus left in shadow.

Lady Edith had thrown aside the book which she had been endeavouring to read, and sat with her large dark eyes fixed upon the flame in the gilded and steel grate at her feet.

She had attained the object of her life-long ambition.

She had trampled on her own heart, and the hearts of others.

She had cast truth to the winds; she had laughed purity and virtue to scorn; and she was the wife of the richest man in England.

But was she happy?

A thousand mocking demons devouring her inmost heart seemed to be for ever asking that question.

No. 4. [*Weekly, One Penny.*]

And what was the answer?

No! no!—a hundred times and again a hundred times, no! Unwomanly as she was, she could not extinguish every spark of womanly feeling.

She was the wedded wife of the millionaire, and she loved another man.

That other, Lord Lionel Montfort, seemed to her all that was perfection in mankind.

Handsome, young, generous, ardent, brilliant, accomplished, fascinating, high-born, but—poor!

Poor! Ay, there was the sting!

"I have done right," she cried; "I suffer, but I have chosen well. At least I shall be rich, and in this world to be rich is to be powerful."

The gilded clock over the chimney-piece struck twelve while Lady Edith Vandeleur was absorbed in these dark thoughts.

To her surprise she heard a cabriolet dash through the quiet square, and draw up at the door below.

Who could it be at such an hour?

Not her father, for the Earl was engaged at a debate in the House of Lords, which would last most probably till three o'clock in the morning, and, besides, he always drove to the house in his chariot, and this was a cabriolet.

Before she could reflect further, a thundering knock resounded upon the panel of the door; she heard voices in the hall below, as if in altercation, then a rapid footstep upon the stairs, and before the servant could announce him, Lord Lionel Montfort dashed into the room.

Lady Edith Merton rose to her feet with a cry of agitation and alarm.

Of all men in the world, Lionel was the last she wished to see on this night.

"Edith!" he cried, "Edith! I am here."

"What is the meaning of this intrusion at such an unwarrantable hour, Lord Lionel Montfort?" she asked, with hauteur.

"Intrusion, Edith!" exclaimed the young man; "you call my coming an intrusion? You ask the meaning of my presence here at such an hour as this? Have you forgotten the words I spoke to you in this very room only one short week ago? Have you forgotten my promise? Can you have forgotten all this?"

"Your promise! What promise?" she cried, wildly.

"The oath I swore that before the week was out I would lay wealth, rank, title, lands, all at your feet. I have kept my oath, and I have come to do so."

"Lord Lionel Montfort—you are mad!" exclaimed Edith.

The late hour, the wildness of the young man's manner, her own fevered and excited brain, all combined to bewilder her, and she fancied that he must indeed have lost his senses.

"I am no longer Lord Lionel Montfort," exclaimed the young nobleman, in strange and solemn tones; "I am Lionel, Marquis of Willoughby."

"No—no!" shrieked the agonised woman; "it cannot be; it is too horrible."

"It is true," said the Marquis, deadly pale, and handing Lady Edith an evening newspaper, still wet from the press.

"Read," he said, pointing to an account of the death of the late Marquis. "Read, incredulous woman!"

Lady Edith took the paper with a trembling hand, and with eyes that seemed well nigh starting from her head, perused the paragraph to which the Marquis pointed.

This paragraph gave a brief description of the finding of the body of the late Lord Willoughby.

"There is some hideous witchcraft here," muttered Lady Edith, "it never can be true."

"Edith," exclaimed the Marquis, "I have kept my oath. You will be mine, will you not? The barrier which parted us was the accursed stain of poverty. That is removed. Edith, you will be mine, Marchioness of Willoughby."

The wretched woman burst into a loud hysterical laugh.

"Too late! too late!" she shrieked; "I was married twelve hours ago to Robert Merton."

She fell on the floor, her whole frame shaken by violent convulsions.

"Heartless demon!" cried Lionel, "slave, sold in the market to the highest bidder! May your life be as accursed as your treachery has made mine—may your soul be racked by the agonies that now consume mine—may your days be wretched, and your nights restless—may remorse haunt you as a hideous phantom that will not be driven away—and may every coin of the filthy gold, for which you have bartered your base soul, become a separate curse and a torment to you."

Yelling these horrible words into the tortured ears of the stricken woman, the Marquis of Willoughby rushed from the room.

Lady Edith Merton's maid, alarmed by the piercing shrieks, which penetrated to the upper storey, came to her mistress's assistance.

She found the beautiful but guilty creature stretched senseless upon the ground. She was carried to her own apartment, and the family doctor was summoned to attend her. When her eyes at last opened, she gazed wildly round the room, and then closed them again with a horrified shudder.

"Why do you seek to call me back to life?" she exclaimed; "why not have pity upon my misery, and abandon me to die?"

"She is delirious!" whispered the maid.

"This is something more and something worse than delirium," said the doctor, gravely. "It is the mind which is affected here. I can be of very little use."

Robert Merton called in Hanover Square early the next day to see his bride; he was shocked at beholding the ghastly pallor of her beautiful face. But she assured him that there was no cause for alarm.

"Remember, Robert," she said, "the excitement of yesterday. You cannot wonder that it has driven the roses from my cheeks. Remember what I underwent through your jealous fancy."

"My beloved," he murmured, raising her

jewelled hand to his lips, "how can I ever forgive myself for having for one brief moment doubted your purity and truth?"

* * * * *

The Marquis of Willoughby was an altered man.

Whatever inward despair consumed his proud heart, he kept the secret of his anguish, and presented a calm face to the world.

Lady Edith and Mr. Robert Merton were married a second time by special licence at the house of the Earl of Horton.

The bride looked a queen in her voluminous robes of white satin, covered with cloud-like flounces of lace of fabulous value.

The bridegroom, trusting and happy, clasped the false woman to his heart, believing that Heaven had smiled upon his devoted love, and blest him by bestowing upon him an angel in human form.

The proudest members of the aristocracy were assembled to do honour to the union of the wealthy merchant with the lovely daughter of the peer.

Rank, fashion, and beauty all were there. The magnificent apartments sparkled with the jewels which glittered upon the brows, the necks, and the arms of the assembled guests.

Amongst others the Marquis of Willoughby was present, dressed in deep mourning for his brother. People wondered at seeing him, for it was the first time that he had appeared in public since the melancholy death of the late Marquis. Many were aware, too, that Lionel was an old admirer of Lady Edith, and they were surprised to find him among the guests at that splendid wedding.

"He has come here to show people that he's not cut up by the affair," murmured one of the visitors to his neighbour at the wedding breakfast; "he is as proud as Lucifer, and he wants to convince the world that he has not been jilted."

Whether this was, or was not, the motive of the Marquis of Willoughby, it was difficult to say. Calm and haughty, he betrayed no agitation, he revealed no emotion. He was separated by the crowd of guests from the bride, and only once had he the opportunity of speaking to her. This was as her father the Earl was about to lead her to the carriage which waited to convey the bride and bridegroom upon the first stage of their continental tour.

At this moment, when all the guests were crowding round Lady Edith to bid her adieu, Lord Willoughby advanced from amongst the rest, and addressed the bride in a clear, audible voice.

"I need scarcely say how much I wish for your happiness, Lady Edith Merton," he said; "I can only repeat the words which I said to you about three months since."

The bride turned pale as death, and shuddered violently as the Marquis spoke to her.

"This agitation is too much for you, dearest," murmured Robert Merton, as he drew Lady Edith through the crowd and assisted her into the carriage.

* * * * *

The year passed away, and another season has commenced at the Royal Italian Opera, or Her Majesty's Theatre, as it is more usually called.

Lolota Vizzini was still the reigning star of the ballet. She had not forgotten Clara Melville. The young girl's salary had been doubled, and she had removed with her father and her little sister and brother into clean and comfortable lodgings at Kensington—lodgings in a house with a large garden, in which Jessie and little George played half the day through. The family was a very happy one. Mr. Melville added to the little store by copying music, and sometimes by translating a book from the French or the German for some West End publisher, who paid liberally for his work.

Clara improved very much in her dancing, and grew prettier and prettier every day.

The ballet-master no longer scolded her or called her stupid, for he began to feel that she was one of the ornaments of the theatre, and he did not wish to disgust her with a profession which she had never much liked—for hers was one of those gentle natures made to adorn the holy circle of a happy home. Admiration had no charm for her. To find a hundred opera-glasses levelled at her as she advanced to the front rank of dancers, only distressed and annoyed her, instead of turning her head with pleasure and delight.

Her companions laughed at her for her retiring disposition.

"Upon my word," they would say good-naturedly, "you are the silliest girl in the world. But, certainly, no one could be envious of your pretty face, for you make so little use of your beauty."

Clara Melville had never seen Reginald Falkner since the day on which he had rescued her from the persecution of Sir Frederick Beaumorris. The young man, who was an officer in the army, had been absent from England with his regiment; while, happily for Clara, the old Baronet had been laid up with gout and kept a close prisoner at his country-seat, Beaumorris Castle, in Cumberland.

Clara Melville loved Lolota Vizzini as she had never before loved any living creature, except her father and her little brother and sister. The Spaniard's generous kindness had made a lasting impression upon the young girl's grateful heart, and it was with deep grief that she perceived that her friend and benefactor was not happy.

No; beautiful, rich, admired, and courted, Lolota Vizzini was still far from being a happy woman. There were dark secrets connected with her past life which the Spanish dancer revealed to none—not even to the loving and devoted Clara.

"No, Clara," she would say, "ask me no questions. My story is after all a common one. The old, old story of an idol raised up by a woman's foolish heart and found in the end to be the basest clay. I have loved, I have been betrayed, and I have suffered. That, Clara Melville, is the history of my life—seek to know no more."

The London season was at its fullest height. Lady Edith and Mr. Robert Merton had not yet returned from their continental tour, but the merchant's house in Park Lane had been redecorated, and all that art, aided by boundless wealth, could devise had been done to make the mansion a palace fit for a queen.

The Dowager Marchioness of Willoughby had retired to her country-seat, there to hide a cureless grief. She told her younger and sole surviving son that, dear as he was to her, she could not endure to see him wear the title of the noble boy for ever lost to her.

Lionel bowed to his mother's decision, and did all in his power to make her retreat agreeable; but the silver cord was loosed, the golden bowl was broken, the sunshine had for ever fled from the world it had once made so beautiful, and the desolate woman only looked forward to that merciful death which would re-unite her to her beloved son.

The Marquis of Willoughby and Colonel Oscar Bertrand were close friends. They were constantly seen together, and no party in the houses of the aristocracy was considered complete unless the wealthy young Marquis and the fashionable Colonel graced the assembly.

Amongst other places, the Austrian officer took his aristocratic friend behind the scenes of Her Majesty's Theatre, to which Colonel Bertrand's influence, and the young nobleman's rank, found them easy admittance.

It was the first night of a new ballet, entitled "The Vintage of Andalusia," and, for the first time in his life, Lord Willoughby beheld Lolota Vizzini, except upon the stage.

The lovely dancer was standing at the side scenes, ready to bound on to the stage as soon as the crash of the orchestra gave the signal for her appearance.

Her lady's-maid was standing behind her, putting the finishing touches to her mistress's costume.

Lolota was dressed in pure white gauze, with a real and valuable leopard-skin looped across one shoulder, and a luxuriant crown of grapes and vine leaves encircling her dark hair.

She was surrounded by a group of adorers as the Marquis approached; one of them holding her magnificent bouquet, and carrying a costly Indian shawl over his arm.

She looked up as Lord Willoughby drew near the group, and the eyes of the Marquis and the dancer met.

What is there in the wonderful magnetism of some glances? What is it that sends a thrill into the soul, a shiver through the heart, as we gaze upon some faces?

Who can answer such questions as these? and again, who can avoid sometimes asking them?

The southern blood burned in the Spanish dancer's cheek, a soft mist veiled her beautiful eyes.

"Who is that man?" she asked hurriedly of the gentleman who carried her shawl. "Tell me, Captain Mortimer, who is that man yonder?" she repeated, indicating the Marquis, who was talking to a group of gentlemen a few paces off, by one flash of her brilliant eyes.

"Oh, that's Lord Willoughby," said Captain Mortimer, "and a devilish lucky fellow he is, too, egad! He was as poor as Job less than a twelvemonth ago; and when his brother died, he dropped into a cool forty thousand a year."

Lolota made no reply, but remained silent with her eyes fixed upon the profile of the young Marquis, which was turned towards her as he stood.

"Surely, Madame Vizzini, you are not fascinated by that fellow Willoughby," said Captain Mortimer, who was a devoted admirer of the Spanish dancer, and never tired of following her about; "surely, after turning a deaf ear to all of us, you're not going to fall in love with the Marquis."

"Captain Mortimer," said Lolota, haughtily, "you are impertinent. Lolota Vizzini can protect herself, even though her husband may not be here to protect her."

"That's where the shoe pinches," said the Captain to a confidential friend some time afterwards. "The Vizzini has some mysterious husband hidden away somewhere or other, and it's my opinion he has treated her badly. If I only knew where to put my hand upon the ruffian, I'd thrash him within an inch of his contemptible life."

When Lolota Vizzini came off the stage, after a terrific burst of applause, which greeted the conclusion of one of her dances, she found the Marquis standing at the wing. She was laden with the bouquets which had been thrown her, and was almost hidden under the heap of exotics which she carried.

CHAPTER XIV.

THE TEMPTER

FROM the hour when Lolota Vizzini and the Marquis first met in the side-scenes of the opera-house, Lord Willoughby was counted amongst the most devoted admirers of the Star of the Ballet.

The carriage of the Marquis was seen day after day waiting at the door of Madame Vizzini's house in Arlington Street.

Through every temptation, through every trial, Lolota had preserved her fair fame, spotless and pure as the untrodden snow, and even now detraction scarcely dared assail her name. No one had ever seen her husband, Antonio Vizzini. It was only known that he was an Italian; that he was separated from his wife, and that he was not in England. No friend, however intimate with Lolota, had ever been told more than this.

*   *   *   *   *   *

Lady Edith and Mr. Robert Merton returned from their continental travels when the London season was considerably advanced.

The splendid mansion in Park Lane was thrown open for a series of parties, so brilliant that the fashionable world was taken by storm, and the beautiful Lady Edith was elected by every voice as one of the queens of the higher circles.

But was she happy?

No; she had sacrificed the only true emotion of her guilty heart for pomp and power, and she found but too soon that the sacrifice was vain to purchase peace of mind.

But the chief bitterness of the disappointment fell upon the honest heart of the millionaire.

He had hoped that love alone had won for him the hand of the woman he adored.

How cruel was the awakening from that sweet dream!

He discovered, but a few brief weeks after their public union, that he was but a cypher in the thoughts of his handsome wife.

Lost in a whirl of ceaseless gaiety, it was with difficulty he could snatch one moment in which to speak to the woman he loved, unheard by strangers.

When he remonstrated with her, she would tell him, with a scornful laugh, that he was new to fashionable life, and did not understand its usages.

The Marquis of Willoughby was a frequent guest in Park Lane. Robert Merton's unsuspicious mind beheld nothing strange in the presence of the young nobleman, and Lady Edith had ample opportunities for seeing and speaking with her former lover.

But these chance meetings only rendered her more unhappy; she remembered that, but for her marriage with Robert Merton, she might have been Marchioness of Willoughby, and she cursed her own ambition, which had brought about the luckless union.

One brilliant summer's morning, as she was lounging on a luxurious violet-velvet cushioned sofa, in her costly boudoir, she was disturbed by the entrance of the groom of the chambers, who brought her a card, on which was inscribed—

Colonel Oscar Bertrand,
THE ALBANY.

Lady Edith knew the Austrian Colonel to be a friend of Lord Willoughby's, and this was enough to give him an interest in her eyes.

"I will see him," she said to the groom of the chambers.

The Colonel entered the apartment, elegantly dressed in the most fashionable morning costume, and wearing a hot-house blossom in the buttonhole of his light overcoat.

"Lady Edith Merton," he said, "this visit will not, I trust, be deemed an intrusion. Believe me, when I tell you that it results from my strong interest in your welfare."

"You are very good," said Lady Edith, rather haughtily; "but pray may I be allowed to ask to what I owe this interest?"

"Shall I tell you, Madam?" exclaimed the Colonel earnestly; "shall I tell you?"

"Yes."

"I am interested in you because you are dear to one who is my friend and associate. One whose heart your treachery has broken, but, who, in spite of that treachery, cannot cease to love you."

A radiant flush of vivid crimson lit up the lady's handsome face; she had feared that Lord Willoughby had forgotten her.

"Sir," she said with cold disdain, "do you come to plead for your friend? Do you forget to whom you are speaking?"

"No, Madam," answered the Colonel, "I do not forget; I am speaking to the wife of a man who began life as an errand-boy; who has sat for hours bent over his writing-desk, as a poorly-paid junior clerk: I am speaking to the woman who has sold herself for gold."

"Colonel Bertrand!"

"I am speaking to her who was loved with all the fondest devotion of an ardent nature, and who repaid that devotion by the blackest treachery; I am speaking to her who should have been Marchioness of Willoughby."

Lady Edith clasped her jewelled hands before her face to conceal the emotion which she could not repress.

"Spare me," she cried, "for pity's sake, spare me!"

"No, Madam, I would not spare you, I would save you; I would dissolve this odious marriage, and restore you to the man who loves you."

"Dissolve my marriage!"

"Yes."

"But by what means?"

"Do you bid me tell you, Lady Edith?"

"I do."

"There are some natures so weak and fearful, that they would shrink from the commission of one desperate deed, though that single act might secure for them the happiness of their future lives. Is your nature one of these?"

The burning black eyes of the mysterious Austrian were fixed with a searching gaze upon the lady's face. She scarcely dared to meet those flashing eyes; a strange magnetism seemed to lurk in the Colonel's glance, and a convulsive shiver shook her whole frame as she encountered his earnest look.

"Tell me," he said, "is your nature so weak that you would shrink from a terrible ordeal, and fear to take the step which might unloose your galling fetters?"

"I think not," she murmured, in a hoarse and broken voice.

"Good," said Colonel Bertrand. "You have spoken bravely, Madam, and I may yet aid you."

"Aid me!" cried Lady Edith, looking anxiously at the Colonel's inscrutable face; "but how?"

Colonel Bertrand did not answer the question. For some moments he remained silent, as if lost in deep thought, while his fair companion, bewildered by his mysterious words, waited anxiously for him to speak.

"Your husband's fortune, Madam," he said, presently. "Do you know how that is disposed of in the event of his death?"

"He made a will a week after our marriage," answered Lady Edith, "in which, with the exception of a few trifling legacies, he left every shilling of it to me."

"And he has not altered that will since?" asked the Colonel.

"I am sure that he has not."

Again there was a pause of silence, the lady still watching the face of the visitor. After about five minutes, during which not a word had been spoken, the Colonel rose, hat in hand, to take his leave, and with his hand upon the lock of the door of the apartment, he turned, and said in a low voice—

"Lady Edith Merton, for such a marriage as yours there is but one divorce."

"And that is—?"

"Death!"

Lady Edith's handsome face changed to a death-like pallor as the Colonel pronounced this one terrible word.

"I shall be present at your ball this evening, Madam," said the Austrian, "and we can talk further of this matter."

"What!" she exclaimed, "surrounded by the crowd of dancers and loungers—in the throng of my saloons?"

"No place, Lady Edith, could be fitter for such a purpose; for who would ever suspect us there?"

*   *   *   *   *

All the beauty and fashion of the West End of London were congregated that evening in the splendid saloons of Lady Edith and Mr. Robert Merton.

Hot-house flowers lined the walls in vases of priceless china.

Valuable statues, in unsullied marble, adorned the broad staircase, with its bronze and gilded bannisters, and lamps of rose-coloured glass and silver. It was a scene of fairy splendour.

The stranger suddenly introduced into it might have fancied himself in the enchanted palace of some Arabian geni, so gorgeous was all around.

In the midst of this brilliant scene Robert Merton felt himself out of place.

"Why did I ever spend my youth in toils to win wealth, which, with all its boasted power is impotent to purchase one thrill of happiness, one throb of joy?"

Lady Edith, dressed in sweeping robes of pale blue satin, bordered by heavy fringes of silver, and wearing a coronet of priceless diamonds and sapphires around her raven hair, looked like a queen amongst even the most lovely of her guests.

Robert was proud to see her so beautiful; pleased to behold her the observed of all observers; but, for all that, he felt a pang as he remembered that her loveliness only seemed to separate him from her the more completely, and to widen the hopeless gulf which yearned between them.

"Oh, if she only loved me truly!" he murmured, as he gazed upon her perfect face, from an obscure corner of the vast ball-room; "if she would only be contented with a simple life at our country-seat, surrounded by our happy tenantry, beloved and honoured by the rich, and blessed in the daily prayers of the poor, whose lives it should be our task to make happy, what peace and cententment might be ours!"

While these thoughts filled the mind of the wealthy merchant, Lady Edith and Colonel Oscar Bertrand stood apart from the throng of dancers in a curtained alcove filled with exotic flowers.

There was something more than human in the manner and appearance of the elegant Austrian upon this particular evening.

His tall and slender figure, dressed in sombre black, his hair of that peculiar reddish auburn so rarely seen, his flashing black eyes, in which a fitful fire seemed for ever burning; all combined to give something almost of a demoniac air to his handsome person, and to inspire those who beheld him with a strange and shuddering dread.

Even Lady Edith Merton, proud and imperious as was her nature, felt herself feeble as a child in the presence of this mysterious being.

"You have been thinking of what I said to you this morning, Lady Edith," he murmured, bending his moustachioed lips to the ear of his beautiful listener.

"Thinking, Colonel Bertrand?" she hesitated.

"Nay, Madam," said the Austrian, "why endeavour to deceive *me*? *That* was never yet done by mortal man; and lovely as you are, proud and powerful as you may be in the knowledge of that superb beauty, even *you* cannot deceive Oscar Bertrand. Be candid with me, Madam, and I can and will serve you. Refuse to confide in me, and I bid you farewell. Lie to your own soul, if you will, Lady Edith Merton, but do not lie to me."

"Who and what are you?" cried the terrified woman, "that you dare to speak thus to me?"

"Dare!" he laughed, in a mocking tone of concentrated bitterness; "I am the chief of a sect so powerful, Madam, that princes acknowledge, though they fear to share, its power. Dare!" he repeated; "I have but to stretch out one of these fingers"—extending his slender and dazzlingly white hand as he spoke—"and the man you love will drop dead in the streets of London, on his way home from this house, and to-morrow morning the newspapers will be filled with the account of a terrible and mysterious murder. Lady Edith Merton, I hold the keys of life and death. One word, then, and answer me truly. Would you become Marchioness of Willoughby before this year is out?"

She looked at him with her beautiful black eyes filled with a glance of terrible meaning, but those lovely orbs sank under the piercing gaze of the Austrian.

"Answer," he said; "yes or no?"

"I would," she murmured.

"Although to accomplish that end the man who now claims you as his wife must die?"

"What is his life to me?" she exclaimed, scornfully.

"Then listen to me, Lady Edith Merton. I have been for years a traveller in the East; the harems of Constantinople are as familiar to me as the drawing-rooms of Belgravia, or the saloons of Paris and Vienna. Where it is death for the foot of other men to tread, I have entered freely; and secrets have become known to me that are undreamt of by the rest of Europe. The men of the East are jealous, Lady, and the women are not always true. It is thought by the ignorant that the favourite who betrays her lord sleeps beneath the still waters of the Bosphorus. It is not always so; the sack and the splash of a body into the dark tide give cause for scandal. There are quieter methods of dealing vengeance to the guilty; there are poisons——"

"Poisons!" she repeated with a shudder.

Still the ball went on. The gay strains of merry music floated to the gilded roof. Beauty and fashion, youth and innocence, all were assembled within those splendid walls. Who could have dreamed that even in such a scene two guilty creatures were met together whose talk was of murder?

"Yes, Lady Edith, poisons so subtle that modern science has failed to find an antidote to their deadly power, or a clue towards the discovery of their presence. The guilty favourite sups one night on milk of almonds; or she is thirsty, and drinks from a silver goblet a cool draught of sparkling sherbet. They find her the next morning stretched upon her embroidered couch; beautiful, serene, and—dead!"

"Why do you tell me this?" asked Lady Edith, her eyes fixed upon the handsome face of the Austrian, with that same look with which the fascinated bird regards the glittering orbs of the deadly snake.

"I thought the fact might interest you, Madam," he said, indifferently. "See," he added, taking from his waistcoat pocket a tiny phial of emerald crystal and filagree gold; "I have here twenty drops of that mysterious essence of which only the science of the East holds the fatal secret. Take it, Madam, it is a pretty trinket for a lady's toilette. Take it, but beware how you use it. One drop is certain death—death as peaceable as an infant's. A death which is mistaken by doctors for disease of the heart."

She extended her hand half mechanically, and her slender fingers closed convulsively upon the phial.

"And now, my dear Lady Edith," said the Colonel, gaily, "I must, with the deepest regret, bid you adieu. Unhappily I have one or two important engagements to-night, which will deprive me of the pleasure of soliciting your hand for the next quadrille."

CHAPTER XV.

THE SPANIARD'S LOVE

A LITTLE before midnight upon that evening on which Lady Edith Merton and Colonel Bertrand had held the secret conversation above described, Lolota Vizzini returned from the opera to her house in Arlington Street.

She looked pale and jaded, and as she entered the exquisite little drawing-room, followed by her maid (who was loaded with the bouquets that had been thrown to her mistress at the close of the ballet), she glanced eagerly at the vase of Parian marble and gold, in which lay a heap of cards and notes of invitation.

"Are there no other letters than these, Joseph?" she asked of her footman, who was busy lighting the wax candles upon the mantel-piece and piano.

"No, Madam, none but those."

She sighed impatiently, and throwing herself into an easy chair, took off her sable-lined mantle, and gave it to her maid.

"You may go, Joseph," she said, "and you too, Jeanette."

The man obeyed immediately, but the girl lingered for a few moments, looking anxiously at her mistress.

"Will not Madam take any refreshment?" she asked.

"None, Jeanette; leave me."

The girl quitted the room slowly and reluctantly, and the lovely Spaniard took a gorgeously-bound volume from the table near her, and tried to read.

But it was in vain; the book dropped from her hand, and she sank into gloomy thought.

"How cruel he is," she murmured; "he was not at the opera to-night! How sadly I missed him from his accustomed seat! What were, to me, the plaudits of the heartless crowd, their smiles, their bouquets, their cries of admiration? *He* was not there; and the vast theatre was empty to me. And then, on my return, to find no letter, no message! Oh, it is too bitter!"

Her head sank on the damask cushions, and she sobbed aloud. In her simple robes of pure white, with her heavy plaits of raven hair, twisted about her head so as to form a regal diadem worthy of that queen-like brow, she looked even more beautiful than when bounding on to the brilliantly-lighted stage in her most dazzling and fairy-like costume.

Presently, she raised her head from the cushions, and dashing the tears from her almond-shaped eyes, cried impatiently, "Oh, where, where is my pride—where is the spirit of that haughty Spanish race, whose purple blood flows swiftly in these veins? Is this *love?* Does Lolota Vizzini bow down at last to that cruel passion which crushes the proud and the haughty into the very dust? Is it *I* who suffer thus? And it may be for one who does not give me love for love, truth for truth, heart-throb for heart-throb!"

Then, after a long pause, she murmured—

"A week ago I felt as sure of his love as of the light in the skies, the sun at noontide; but for this last few days a change has come over him; he has been cold, reserved. When I have spoken, his thoughts have wandered, and he has replied with ill-concealed embarrassment. Can it be that he loves another? No! no! that cannot be! Heaven grant that may never be. It would make me a murderess."

A shudder convulsed her superbly-moulded frame as she uttered these last words, with her teeth clenched, and a sombre flame burning in her great black eyes.

At this moment a cabriolet dashed into the quiet street, and an instant after a double knock resounded upon the door below.

"It is he—it is he!" cried Lolota. "I thought—I thought he would come at last!"

She looked anxiously in the glass at her disordered hair, and smoothing it, hastily snatched a wax-like scarlet camelia from a vase of hot-house flowers, and placed it amidst the massive and velvet-like plaits that encircled her head.

"I would not have him see that I have been weeping," she murmured.

The door opened, and the Marquis of Willoughby entered the room. He wore the evening costume which he had assumed for the ball at Lady Edith's. He looked pale and care-worn, and dark circles surrounded his hollow eyes.

"Forgive the lateness of the hour, dearest Lolota," he said, as the impetuous Spanish girl bounded forward to meet him. "I should have been here long ere this; I should have been in my box at the Opera, but I was forced to attend a ball in Park Lane. Will you forgive me?"

"Forgive you?" she exclaimed. "Do I not see you, clasp you by the hand, hear the low tones of that dear voice; and is not that enough for me? Come," she added, leading him to a chair, "tell me all that has passed since we met. Ah, Lionel, it is only three days, yet what an age it seems to me! and to you, does it seem long to you, truant?"

"Yes, Lolota, yes," he said, with considerable embarrassment.

"But tell me, whose was this tiresome ball which kept you away from your Lolota?"

"It was given by Mr. Robert Merton, the millionaire," said the young man, a crimson flush overspreading his face.

"Mr. Merton? Ah, I remember; I have seen him at the Opera with his handsome wife, the daughter of the Earl of Horton."

Lord Willoughby did not answer, but resting his head upon his hand, averted his face from the Spanish girl.

For some moments she watched him intently, in profound silence; then entwining one of her rounded arms about his neck, she said, with tender gentleness, "Lionel, Lionel, what is this? I see that you are unhappy."

He dropped his hands from his face, and turning round, looked full at the loving girl.

"Lolota," he cried! "Lolota, I am indeed the most miserable of men!"

"Lionel, dearest Lionel!"

"Yes," he repeated, in accents of unmingled despair, "the most miserable, Lolota. Heaven knows how I have tried to love you truly."

"Tried to love me!" she exclaimed, lifting her proud head from its drooping attitude.

"Yes, Lolota. Forgive me—forgive me, if you ever can! When first I saw you I was suffering from a terrible blow which had been struck at my peace by the treachery of a woman I adored—a woman who, in my presence, publicly gave the hand which should have been mine to another man; a man whom she despised. On that day of anguish and madness I swore to forget her, and heaven knows that I have endeavoured to do so. I saw you, Lolota, and dazzled by your beauty, your grace, your genius, the witchery of your manner, the sweet magnetism of your melodious voice, I said to myself, 'Surely, blest by the love of such a being, the woman who betrayed me may be forgotten.'

"We became acquaintances—friends; and though by the tie that binds you, we could not be more than friends, friendship melted into love, and I did love you, Lolota."

"I thought you did. Alas, alas! how truly I believed you did!" she murmured, in a voice broken by her passionate sobs.

"Lolota Vizzini! three days ago I met the woman who has been, and who is yet, the evil genius of my life. In a breath all the old madness returned—once more I was her abject slave, scarcely holding my own soul, save at her behest. Lolota, you alone can save me from this fiend in angel form."

"Save you," she said, with passionate vehemence, "how, Lionel, how?"

"Fly with me to some far distant land; amidst the fountains of Granada, by the waters of the Guadalquiver, amid the orange-groves of Seville, the dark shades of Valambrosa. Fly with me, Lolota; forget the tie which binds you to a villain, and be mine for ever. In your presence I can forget my evil genius. I am wealthy beyond calculation. I will anticipate every wish of your true heart, every dream, every fancy. We will form for ourselves a paradise on earth, and you, Lolota, shall be its queen. Say that you will come," he cried, sinking on his knees at her feet.

"Lionel, Lionel," she murmured, "for pity's sake do not tempt me."

"Lolota, Lolota, will you refuse to save me?"

She did not answer, but the tears fell from her lovely eyes upon the uplifted face of the young man.

"Lolota, will you refuse?"

"I *cannot*, Lionel," she cried, passionately; "beloved, I would save you at the cost of my life."

"My own Lolota!"

He rose from his knees, and was about to clasp her to his breast, when the door was softly opened, and Colonel Oscar Bertrand walked into the room.

"So," he exclaimed, with a laugh, which had the mocking bitterness of some triumphant fiend in its very note, "so, my Lord, you were summoned this evening to attend a meeting at the central office of the company to which you belong, but you were better engaged. I guessed where you would be found, and came myself to seek you."

"Sir," cried the Spaniard, haughtily, "this is my house, and I do not know by what right you entered it, or why my servants were so imprudent as to admit you."

"Your servants, Madam!" exclaimed the Colonel; "Oscar Bertrand does not wait to ask admission from servants. When I am interested in the inhabitants of a house, I take care to provide myself with the means of access to its innermost chambers."

He held up a tiny key of glittering steel as he spoke, and Lolota saw that it was attached to a bunch of other keys of the same kind.

"Who are you?" demanded Lolota, angrily.

"Ask that question of the Marquis, Madame," answered Colonel Bertrand.

"Oscar Bertrand," said Lord Willoughby, "by what right do you intrude upon this lady?"

"By the right which I hold over you," replied the Colonel. "In every place, and at every time. You would fly to a foreign clime, would you? Do you forget that you are mine, body and soul, and that so long as I please to command, you must do my bidding?"

"Demon!" exclaimed the young nobleman, ghastly pale, and trembling with passion.

"I cannot spare you yet, my dear Lionel," said the Colonel, laying his hand lightly upon the shoulder of the Marquis.

"Lionel!" cried Lolota, "what does this mean?"

"Ask me not, my beloved," he answered; "I have told you that I am the most miserable of men."

"Come, my Lord," said Colonel Bertrand, pointing to the door.

Lionel clasped Lolota in his arms, pressed his lips once to her pale forehead, and then, snatching up his hat, rushed out of the house, followed by the Austrian, who turned on the threshold of the door to say to Madame Vizzini, with his mocking smile, "I am sorry, Madam, to rob you of your midnight visitor."

CHAPTER XVI.

THE POISONER IS DEFEATED

THE following day Lady Edith Merton and her husband dined alone. It was to the millionare an unexpected pleasure to find himself in the society of his beautiful wife without being surrounded by a crowd of guests, for whose frivolity and heartlessness he had no feeling but contempt.

"How delightful, my dearest Edith, to feel, even for one brief hour, that we are something more to each other than mere strangers! I assure you I look forward to the simple dinner of this evening as the most delightful festival of the season."

Had Robert Merton s been a suspicious nature he might have observed on this day a strangeness in the manner of his wife; a death-like pallor on her handsome face; dark rings about her eyes, that told of a sleepless night; and a nervous restlessness in every action, bespeaking a mind ill at ease.

"As you think so much of our quiet little dinner, Robert," said Lady Edith, in her sweetest tones, "suppose we dine in my boudoir. We can dismiss the servants, whose presence is always such a hindrance to conversation, and I will wait upon you with my own hands."

"My dearest Edith," cried the merchant, "nothing could be more delightful to me."

That day Lady Edith Merton was gayest of the gay as she drove round Hyde Park, her carriage surrounded by horsemen, only too proud to get a bow from one of the reigning queens of fashion. Only a very close observer would have perceived the hollowness of that silver laugh, the false ring of that musical voice, the fever in those lustrous eyes; only a close observer would have known that the woman of fashion was acting a part.

As the clock struck eight, Lady Edith and Robert Merton seated themselves at the elegantly-appointed dinner-table in the boudoir of the millionaire's wife.

Though it was scarcely sunset the light of day was shut out by curtains of rose-coloured silk, and the apartment was illuminated by alabaster lamps, which shed a subdued radiance over all around.

Exactly opposite to Lady Edith, and behind the chair of the merchant, an immense mirror stretched from the ceiling to the floor. Robert Merton had at first seated himself opposite to this mirror, but on some pretext or other the lady changed places with him.

The butler had placed a small dinner-waggon loaded with bottles of wine in silver coolers, exactly before this very mirror. The servants removed the covers and retired. Robert had told them that he would open the champagne himself. The merchant was in the highest spirits and ate with more appetite than usual Lady Edith, on the contrary, scarcely took a mouthful.

"You do not eat, Edith," said her husband, most anxiously.

"I am fatigued with my drive," she answered carelessly. "I will take a glass of champagne presently, and I have no doubt that will give me an appetite."

"You shall not wait long for it, then, dearest," cried Robert gaily, and rising from his seat he took one of the bottles from the silver cooler and began to unfasten the wire that secured the cork. As he did so, Lady Edith drew from her bosom the tiny crystal phial given to her by Colonel Bertrand on the night before, and stretching her jewelled arm across the small dinner-table, poured one drop of the poison into her husband's champagne glass.

She had forgotten the mirror.

Robert Merton turned round with the bottle of wine in his hand, and after filling his wife's glass replaced the bottle upon the dinner-waggon, whence he had taken it.

"You have not filled your own glass, Robert," said Lady Edith, anxiously.

"I shall not take any champagne."

"Not even to please me?"

"No; not even to please you."

Lady Edith bit her lip until the blood flowed from the wound inflicted by her small ivory teeth.

The murderess was foiled.

When the servants were clearing the table, Robert Merton stopped the man who was removing the glasses, saying carelessly—

"You may leave that champagne glass, Jarvis, I may fancy a glass of wine in the course of the evening; place it upon that ivory cabinet."

The man obeyed; and the glass containing the one drop of the deadly fluid was placed upon a cabinet near the merchant.

"What an absurd idea!" exclaimed Lady Edith, angrily. "Jarvis, remove the glass. I cannot have my boudoir littered by the remains of the dinner-table."

The man hesitated, puzzled whom to obey.

"Remove the glass, immediately," said Lady Edith.

"Jarvis," said the merchant, quietly, "you are my servant, and you will do as I bid you. Leave the room."

"He *cannot* suspect," thought Lady Edith, pale as a corpse, and with an undefined dread at her heart; "he would never be so calm if he had suspicion of the truth."

She forgot that in these quiet natures there is an element of power unknown to the more vehement and impulsive. She did not know that the vengeance of the man who says little is always the most terrible and unfailing. The shrouded lamps left the face of the merchant in shadow, or she might have seen that he was very pale .

Presently he threw aside his newspaper, and walking to an elegant little desk at the end of the room, he seated himself and began to write.

The wretched and guilty creature followed him with watchful eyes.

"How dull you are to-night, Robert!" she said, preserving her calmness by a fearful effort. "It is not very polite of you to write letters when we are alone together."

"Excuse me," he said, " this letter is of importance. It will not detain me long."

He wrote a few lines, addressed an envelope, and then rang a bell at his right hand.

"See that this is taken immediately to the Earl of Horton," he said, handing the letter to the servant who answered his summons.

"You were writing to my father, then, Robert?" said Lady Edith, whose agitation every moment increased.

"Yes, to your father," answered the merchant gravely.

"But what reason could you possibly have for writing to my father?" she asked.

"You will see presently."

"How so?"

"Because if that letter finds your father at home, he will most likely come here immediately in accordance with my request."

"But what can you want with him to-night?"

"I decline saying anything further till your father himself is present."

"Robert, Robert," cried the guilty creature, in an agony of apprehension, "what does this mean?"

He did not answer her.

For upwards of half an hour she remained a prey to the most acute terror and anxiety. Grave, calm, and self-possessed, the merchant sat awaiting the arrival of the visitor he had summoned. Once or twice he looked at his watch, and rising from his chair took one or two turns up and down the room. To Lady Edith Merton that half-hour seemed by its length of agony an eternity of suspense and torture. At last footsteps were heard in the richly-carpeted gallery without, and the groom of the chambers announced Lord Horton. The old man looked pale and uneasy.

"My dear Robert," he said, "what in goodness' name induced you to send for a poor old fellow like me, at ten o'clock at night?"

"Pray be seated, my Lord," said the merchant gravely.

"My Lord! Why, Robert, what are you thinking of?" cried the old man.

The merchant seated himself opposite his father-in-law, and in solemn tones, which vibrated through the lofty apartment, he addressed the Earl thus—

"Lord Horton, nothing but the solemn and dreadful nature of the subject on which I have to address you would have induced me to send for you at such an hour and in so abrupt a manner. I have something to tell you, my dear Lord, which I fear will break your heart."

"Robert, Robert!" cried the terrified old man; "Edith, tell me what your husband means."

But the baffled murderess sat rigid and unmoved as stone.

"I would willingly spare you the bitterness of this pang, my Lord, but it cannot be. This night, in this room, that woman, who is, unhappily for both of us, your daughter and my wife, attempted to poison me."

"Great heaven!" cried the Earl, "you are mad!"

"I would I were, my Lord, rather than have lived to see what I have seen this night. Look at this glass," said the merchant, taking the champagne glass from the cabinet; "into this I distinctly saw Lady Edith pour the poison which was to have been drunk by me."

The merchant then described how he had seen in the looking-glass the outstretched hand which contained the crystal phial.

"But," gasped the Earl, eager to catch at the frailest straw that could afford a hope, "are you certain that the fluid contained in that phial was indeed a poison?"

"We will soon set that doubt at rest," said Robert Merton, ringing a bell.

"Jarvis," he said to the servant who came in answer to his summons, "fetch Lady Edith's Italian greyhound; and bring, also, a small piece of raw meat."

The man was too well-bred a servant even to look astonished at this order. He left the room, and returned in a few minutes, carrying a valuable lap-dog and a small square of raw steak upon a dinner-plate.

The collar of the dog was of the finest gold set with large turquoise, so lavishly had the millionaire scattered his wealth to please the extravagant tastes of his wife. Robert took the dog in his arms, and after rubbing the meat in the bowl of the champagne glass offered it to the animal. Well fed as the dog was he ate the morsel greedily. Five minutes afterwards, without one throe or struggle, the greyhound fell dead at the merchant's feet.

"Great powers of mercy!" exclaimed the wretched father; "I must be mad, or dreaming."

"Calm yourself, I implore you, my Lord," said Robert; "it is no time for lamentation: serious measures must be taken. Under the present circumstances I have only one alternative with regard to my unhappy wife, your daughter; either she is a murderess or she is mad."

"Mad!" cried the old man—that thought had never before struck him, and he clung to it as a spar of hope.

"For the credit of an ancient name, for the honour of human nature, I would rather think her mad."

"Look at her!" said Robert, snatching a lamp from the table, and holding it before the face of his wife; "look at her, and become convinced of either her guilt or her madness."

"Alas! it is indeed too true," said the Earl, gazing at his daughter's stony face.

"For your sake, Lord Horton," said Robert, "as well as for the sake of her whom I once called my wife, the events of this night shall never be revealed to mortal ears. Amongst my other property purchased of late years, I have an estate in the north of Scotland—a castle

hidden among the craggy peaks of the Highlands, far from all human habitation. Thither shall this wretched woman be conveyed, and there, watched by careful attendants, shall she spend the remainder of her life."

The lips of the guilty creature were unloosed, she sprang from her chair, and rushing to her husband, clung convulsively about him.

"No, Robert, no, no, no," she shrieked, "anything but that, anything, anything! A prison, a court of justice, even the scaffold. I am not mad; I am a vile and wicked wretch— but I am not mad."

"In mercy to your unhappy family you will be treated as a mad woman," said the merchant, pushing her from him; and then walking to the door, he turned, with his hand upon the lock, and said solemnly—

"Lady Edith Merton, I have loved you with all the intensity of an honest and truthful nature; you will now find that I can also hate."

She uttered one long and piercing scream, and fell fainting into her father's arms.

CHAPTER XVII.

ON THE WATCH

THE lamps were being lighted in the dusk of the July evening, in the neighbourhood of St. James's Park, when a woman, dressed in dark garments, and with her face concealed by a thick black veil, might have been seen by the passers-by, walking slowly up and down, under the avenue of trees at the back of Carlton Terrace. Some of the passers-by did turn to look at her, for there is something in the aspect of a person who has no particular business, but who for some unknown reason hangs about a spot, that generally attracts the attention of curious passengers. Eight, half-past eight, a quarter to nine, struck from the clock of the Horse Guards, but still the woman paced slowly up and down; sometimes pausing at the foot of the steps leading to the Duke of York's column to watch the people ascending and descending, and then resuming her solitary ramble. It was almost impossible to guess whether the woman was young or old, ugly or handsome. She was tall and slender, and had something of the carriage of a person of superior station. This, and this alone, was revealed in the dim lamplight. The clock struck nine; the passers-by became fewer; but still the woman watched and waited. At last, as the strokes that tolled the hour died away upon the night air, she was suddenly joined by a man, muffled in a thick coat, and with his face concealed by the broad brim

DEATH-STRUGGLE IN THE USURER'S CHAMBER

of the hat which he wore slouched over his eyes.

As this man approached, a tall, raw-boned, awkward-looking country lad, who had passed backwards and forwards several times unobserved by the woman, while she had been waiting, descended the steps by the column and followed the two, keeping at a respectful distance.

"You are late, Mr. Lucas," said the woman.

"I was busy," answered the man, in a strange metallic voice—a voice which sounded as if its owner so seldom held communion with his fellow-men, that the very voice within him had grown stiff and rusty, and creaked like some piece of disused iron machinery which creaked with every word he uttered.

"You were busy; that is always your answer. Did you forget that you had appointed to meet me here at a quarter to eight this evening?"

"I scarcely forgot—" said the man, in the same harsh grating tones. "I did not exactly forget; but the hours crept on one by one, the darkness gathered, and yet I could not leave my work—it was such interesting work, so very interesting."

"Well, you have come at last, at any rate—that is something. Have you brought the money?"

"No, Mrs. Montmorenci! No: we are not quite so reckless as that. We don't bring money into the streets, to be robbed of it as we walk along, or to be knocked down in a solitary place, like this for instance," he muttered, looking about him, "and have the precious stuff taken from our pockets while we lie stunned by some treacherous blow. Why, how do I know that you may not have a bottle of chloroform about you, and a handkerchief steeped in it, ready to fling in my face, that you may rob me? Yes; that you may rob me. But it would be wasted labour," he added, with a chuckle, "for I haven't a farthing about me, not a farthing."

"You must have lived amongst strange people, to have grown up so suspicious," said the woman whom he had called Mrs. Montmorenci.

"I *have* lived amongst strange people—stranger people than you ever met with in your life, though you may have seen a great deal of the world. People so strange, that if I were to tell you of them, you'd think I was dreaming, or mad, or a liar. Unless—unless you were—— but no, no; that can't be."

"What can't be?" asked Mrs. Montmorenci. If her veil had been raised at that moment, the man might have perceived, in the light of the lamp near to them, a strange sardonic smile upon her careworn face.

"Never mind what; never mind what, Mrs. Montmorenci. No business of yours, you know, my dear good soul; nothing whatever to do with you. All you want of me is the money, and you shall have it. You shall have it, if you're prepared to pay well for it. Fifty per cent., remember; not a penny less!"

"I'll pay what you like," answered the woman, with the same sardonic smile, "only let me have the money."

"You shall have it, my dear Mrs. Montmorenci, you shall have it."

"Can I come to your chambers for it?"

"Yes, yes, you shall come there; that will be the safest."

"To-night?"

"Yes, to-night; directly, if you please."

At this very moment, the tall, raw-boned country lad, of whom we have spoken before, walked slowly past them, whistling as he went along. He carried a small basket on his arm, and if the old money-lender noticed him at all, it was only to take him for some tradesman's boy, going an errand after the shops were closed.

As this young man approached, Mrs. Montmorenci happened to drop her handkerchief, and the country lad, with more politeness than might have been expected from his rough exterior, stooped to pick it up and restore it to her.

"Thank you, young man," she said; "I did not expect to be treated with such gallantry."

She uttered the words in a clear and distinct voice, the young man staring at her intently all the time, as if he feared losing one syllable of what she said to him; then, with an awkward bow, he walked on, still whistling.

The usurer would have perhaps felt considerable surprise had he beheld this young man, entirely altering his manner the moment he was out of sight, run rapidly up the steps by the Duke of York's column, then into Pall Mall, where he hailed a passing hansom cab.

"To the Albany!" he said to the driver, as he sprang into the vehicle.

Still the man and woman walked slowly up and down behind Carlton Terrace. It seemed almost as if Mrs. Montmorenci, in spite of her eagerness to secure the money, was, for some reason or other, anxious to detain the usurer in the deserted thoroughfare of St. James's Park. Once or twice he had proposed returning to his chambers, and each time she had made some frivolous objection. At last he said, with the peevish irritability of an old man unused to consult the wishes of others—

"If you want that money, Mrs. Montmorenci, you'd better come for it at once. I don't feel inclined to waste much more of my time out here in the damp night air. I'm an old man, and I'm not so strong as you, ma'am, I dare say."

"When you please, Mr. Lucas," she answered; "I am quite ready to accompany you."

"Then we'll take a cab at Charing Cross," said the old man; "you'll pay for it, of course. My clients always pay cab-hire under such circumstances, and you ought to pay my fare here too. I can't waste my time in dancing attendance upon you."

"I can pay for no cabs to-night," said Mrs Montmorenci; "I told you I wanted the money desperately, and of course if I'd a full purse, I shouldn't have said so. I am about as rich as yourself. I have not a halfpenny."

"Let's be off, then," said Mr. Lucas; "you can walk pretty fast, I suppose, at any rate?"

They went straight from the park through Whitehall, Parliament Street, Bridge Street, and across Westminster Bridge, not turning until they came to the York Road. From the York Road they passed into Stamford Street; and here the old man, who had walked so rapidly that his companion was almost exhausted by her efforts to keep pace with him, stopped to draw breath.

"I lead a hard life, Mrs. Montmorenci, he said, as he clung to the railing, before a house against which they stopped: "a cruel hard life, and a life that has neither hope nor joy, end or aim, except the grave—except the lonely, dismal, forgotten grave, in which I shall lie and rot before many years are over. I've had a bitter disappointment, woman, which has changed me into a demon: a disappointment that has turned my blood to gall, and transformed all the love that there once was in this withered heart into hatred and fury: one of those disappointments that make a man loathe his fellow-creatures, and love to visit upon the innocent the tortures inflicted upon them by the guilty."

"What was this disappointment?" asked the woman, gently, for the wildness of the usurer's manner almost alarmed her.

"It was the disappointment of finding black ingratitude where I looked for tender love," cried the old usurer. "It was the disappointment of finding a viper in the nest, where I thought that I had reared a dove. It was the disappointment of having an only child, for whose happiness I would have sold my soul, turn from me and leave me in my desolate old age, without a word, without a tear; leave me to starve, for aught she knew, or to kill myself in the despair of losing her."

"It was very cruel," murmured Mrs. Montmorenci.

"Cruel!" cried the old man, walking slowly on, and speaking in a hoarse suppressed voice, that told of the powerful emotion which convulsed him. "Cruel! it was the work of a demon; and in all outward seeming my child was an angel. For her sake I, the last male descendant of one of the proudest families in England, lived like a pauper in the lodge at the gates of the house of which I had been master years before. For her sake I became the companion of bad men; for her sake I soiled my hands with foul deeds which have made me the wretch I now am. Pshaw! woman," he said, testily, as Mrs. Montmorenci was about to interrupt him; "don't attempt to flatter me. I know what I am, and am used to myself as I now am. All this I did for the child I loved, that she at least might be rich, powerful, honoured, happy; that she might restore those old halls in which the bat now roosts, and the fearless spider weaves her web; that she might know all the joys which for years had been denied to me."

"And she —— ?" said Mrs. Montmorenci.

"She deserted me," cried the usurer. "She stole away from me, without leaving so much as one line in her handwriting to break the bitterness of the blow. She fled from me with a villain, and from that hour to this I have never heard of her."

By this time they had nearly reached the end of Stamford Street, opening into the Blackfriars Road. Mr. Lucas stopped before a house which, from its ruined and dilapidated appearance, the blackness of the window-panes, the broken iron railings slowly rusting away, the dirt and straws accumulated about the door, and the general aspect of desolation and decay which overshadowed the whole building looked as if it

must have been in Chancery. It was not so, however, for the usurer, taking a latchkey from his pocket, unlocked the door and walked into the hall, followed closely by Mrs. Montmorenci.

There was no lamp in the hall, and the lamps in the street were situated at some distance from the house occupied by Mr. Lucas. The summer night was dark and starless, and as the usurer entered his hall and walked quickly towards an inner baize door, he did not perceive that he was followed by another person besides Mrs. Montmorenci.

This third person was a man, tall and slender, and muffled in a loose overcoat. As Mr. Lucas was about to open the baize door, Mrs. Montmorenci started, with a cry of surprise.

The usurer turned quickly to see what was the matter.

"I thought I heard a knock," she said.

"A knock! where?"

"At the street door."

"Pshaw! woman; mere fancy. There was no knock; my ears are sharp enough, and I heard nothing."

During this brief dialogue the stranger had contrived to open the baize door, and had crept lightly up the staircase.

"Stay!" said Mr. Lucas; "there is a lamp somewhere about here, and as you are a stranger to the place, I'd better light it."

He took a lamp from a niche in the wall, and lighted it with a match that was lying near.

The lamp gave a bright and vivid light, and for the first time Mrs. Mortmorenci beheld the interior of the usurer's house. A strange sight met the eyes of the astonished woman.

Marble statues were ranged on each side of the panelled hall, the woodwork of which was crumbling to pieces from sheer neglect. Upon these decaying panels hung pictures whose value was something fabulous—pictures by the greatest of the Italian masters—pictures which had only to be offered in the auction-room to bring the richest noblemen of the land together, eager to possess them. Several lamps hung from the arched ceiling, one of bronze, another gilt, one of solid silver; but silver, bronze, and gilt were alike black with dust and dirt; the broken glass of the globes had fallen on the ground to be trodden into the rich carpet, the once splendid colours of which were scarcely perceptible for the dust which shrouded them.

The staircase presented the same appearance as the entrance-hall. Here, again, valuable paintings adorned the walls, marble statues stood in niches on the landing-places. Everywhere the same wealth mingled with the same decay. The apartment into which the moneylender ushered his visitor was furnished with a splendour and luxury which bewildered the senses of those who beheld it for the first time.

Magnificent cabinets, inlaid with gold and gems, velvet-covered sofas with heavy fringes and tassels of bullion, gaudy curtains of rich satin hanging from the blackened windows; Dresden and Sevres china upon the cracked marble mantelpiece—all that the mind could imagine of wealth and luxury, yet all alike bearing the traces of long years of neglect.

"Mine," muttered the money-lender, as he held up the lamp and watched his client's astonished gaze, "mine, all mine—the property of fools who could not keep what they once held—the property of women who coined their smiles into gold, till old age and wrinkles overtook them and they were glad to come to the money-lender for help—the property of idiots who believed in love and friendship, and who squandered their money upon knaves and false women—all, all, all glad to come to the usurer at last."

He laughed aloud, rubbing his shrivelled hands together as he looked about him. "I have had this place for fifteen years," he said; "ever since the daughter, who has now deserted me, was a little toddling child. Fifteen years, and all that time I have been supposed to live at the lodge gates of the mansion over which I was once lord. Fifteen long, laborious years, during which I have been backwards and forwards—backwards and forwards—calculating, and plotting, and working, to get the fortune which was to make my child rich and powerful. Well, well, it was a bitter disappointment, a hard and cruel disappointment—but now to business."

His whole manner changed as he spoke, he hurried across the room, and on going to a cabinet of ivory and gilt work, unlocked a drawer and began to search through a packet of papers.

* * * * * *

While Mr. Lucas, the usurer, is thus employed, we must retrace our steps a little and follow the awkward country lad to the entrance of the Albany.

Here he was about to dismiss the hansom cab, but appearing suddenly to recollect himself, he told the driver that if he cared about getting another fare, he might wait for ten minutes.

Having said which, the young man walked at once to the chambers occupied by Colonel Oscar Bertrand.

These chambers, as the reader will easily imagine, were furnished with more than aristocratic elegance and splendour. A drawing-room, a library, a tiny smoking-divan, all opened one out of the other, and a winding bronze staircase led from the divan to the Colonel's bed and dressing room.

The Austrian was not at home, the servant who opened the door told the young man, but if his name was Timson he was to wait.

He said his name was Timson, and the man led him into the hall, where he told him to take a chair.

"The Colonel came in at half-past eight," the footman said, "and asked if you had been; he said he should return at half-past nine."

"It's a quarter to ten by this time," answered Mr. Timson, and as he spoke a loud double knock resounded upon the outer door.

"That is the Colonel's knock," said the servant, hastening to admit his master.

"Ah, Timson," exclaimed the Colonel, as the young man rose from his chair; "I thought you had quite forgotten my little mission. Come this way!"

He led the young man into the library as he spoke. The country lad stared about him at the carved oak book-shelves loaded with volumes bound in crimson morocco and gold. The glittering lamp, the green cloth curtains and rich Turkey carpet, all were so strange to him that he stood open-mouthed with admiration.

"I thought you had forgotten me, Timothy," said the Colonel; "for though it is wiser to call you Mr. Timson before other people, Timothy will do very well between ourselves. I thought you had forgotten me, or that you had failed in the commission I had entrusted you with; and yet though you are but a country lad, I give you credit for being able to succeed."

"I haven't forgotten you, Sir," said Timothy, whom our readers will already recognise as Timothy Hodge, "I haven't forgotten, and I haven't failed in what you gave me to do, but I had to wait, for him as you set me to watch didn't come till it struck nine, and then I had to wait till she give me the signal, and that was nigh upon half an hour first, and I wasn't above ten minutes coming up here."

"Good," said the Austrian; "we shall be there before them."

"I told the cabman as brought me here to wait," said Timothy; "I thought you might want a fast cab where you couldn't trust your own carriage."

"Good again!" cried Colonel Bertrand; "why, Timothy, you are by no means the fool your personal appearance would lead one to mistake you for. You are by no means an unworthy member of the Black Band. A brain that can think, an arm that can strike, and a tongue that can be silent, these are the three qualities, remember, Timothy, that make a good member; and now, good-night; you will call at Mr. Samuel Crank's to-morrow for your wages."

The young man made an awkward bow, and left the room. The servant was waiting in the little hall to show out the humble visitor, wondering what his master could want with such a rough lad; for it was not the Colonel's ordinary practice to transact business at his private residence. The affairs of the mysterious company, of which he was the Grand Master, were too well organised for this.

As soon as the Colonel was alone, he opened the door leading into the divan. This tiny circular apartment was illuminated by a globe of ground glass, that shed a subdued and chastened light over the maroon-coloured velvet cushions round the side of the room. Upon one of these cushions lay the Marquis of Willoughby, fast asleep.

"Lionel!" exclaimed the Colonel, endeavouring to arouse the young man from his heavy slumber.

Lord Willoughby awoke with a start. "You have been so long away, Bertrand, that I smoked a couple of cigars, and then fell asleep. What has detained you?"

"Policy!" said the Anstrian; "policy! I have been seen this evening by all the fashionable world. I have been at Lord Vandesert's dinner-party, which I only left, as I said, to go to the ball at Chornington House. Whatever happens to-night, I have provided proof of my *alibi*. Come! a cab is waiting to convey us to Stamford Street, where we are to meet, face to face, with a renegade from our company."

"A renegade!"

"Yes, a man who joined us fifteen years ago; who, though being associated with us, has scraped together wealth which I cannot calculate, but which I know to be immense, and who six months ago deserted us; to-night he will render an account for that desertion. You are young amongst us, Lord Willoughby; it will be well for you to see the manner in which we act towards an old associate who breaks his oath. In this case, I do not trust to the executioners of the order, I go myself, and I would have you accompany me; I may want your aid, and in any case the business of to-night will be a warning to you, should you ever feel tempted to be false to the oath you took upon the 20th of last December."

The flashing eyes of the Colonel were fixed upon the young nobleman's face as he spoke these last words. Lord Willoughby quailed beneath that searching glance: how often had he not thought of breaking the terrible oath which made him until the hour of his death, one of the Companions of Midnight!

CHAPTER XVIII.

THE MIDNIGHT ENCOUNTER

THE usurer handed a packet of notes to Mrs. Montmorenci. She had removed her veil on entering his apartment, and displayed a face that had once been handsome, but which already showed the traces of premature old age: a face which told of late hours and midnight orgies; a face which was sad to look upon, from the thought that it might have been illumined by the smile of purity, now faded and gone for ever.

The Black Band did not reject the aid of women. There were women who took, in fear and trembling, those terrible oaths which gave their lives into the keeping of the Companions of Midnight.

In many capacities women were useful to this marvellous band—as spies, to decoy, to ensnare, to blind, to creep into places where men could never penetrate, to obtain confidences accorded to them on account of their sex. For such purposes as these a select number of women were necessary, and Mrs. Montmorenci was one.

She took the money, signed some papers, and bidding good-night to the usurer, left the room. But she did not leave the house. A strange feeling of mingled curiosity and fear possessed her, and instead of descending to the hall-door, she crept into a corner of the first landing-place, and concealed herself behind one of the statues.

When she was gone, the money-lender seated himself at his desk, with the lamp close behind him, and busied himself with his papers.

His interview with Mrs. Montmorenci and the settlement of the loan had occupied a considerable time—it was now half-past eleven.

Mr. Lucas had worked for about five minutes, pen in hand, and with a row of figures upon the paper before him, when he was suddenly aroused by a hand being laid upon his shoulder.

He turned with a start of surprise and terror, and beheld a man standing by the side of his chair.

This man was tall and slender, dressed entirely in black, wearing a velvet mask that completely covered his face, and having on his wrist a band of black crape, fastened with a slip-knot.

"Lucas Clavering," said the stranger, in a solemn voice, which reverberated through the large apartment.

"Who calls me by that name?" asked the terrified old man.

"Look and see!"

"An executioner of the order," cried the usurer, with a shudder.

"What!" exclaimed the other; "you looked for us, then! You knew that we did but wait a fitting time for our revenge. You remember that the turncoat and the renegade is never either forgotten or forgiven by the Companions of Midnight."

"Do your duty," said the old man calmly. "The Clavering blood has never yet flowed in the veins of a coward. Whatever my fate may be, I am prepared to meet it. I left you because there was a villain in your ranks, at whose hands I had received the deadliest of injuries; but I have never betrayed you. The Claverings do not lie. Do your duty, executioner."

"I am no executioner," answered the other, casting aside his mask; "look at me. I am the Grand Master."

"Then you are a scoundrel!" shrieked Lucas Clavering, in an outburst of rage, "a base and treacherous scoundrel, who crept beneath an old man's roof to steal from him his only and beloved child. Revenge on me!" he cried, with a laugh that had something of insanity in its mocking fierceness. "Who shall refuse me *my* revenge? Fool, thrice blind and reckless fool, to trust yourself within the gripe of an outraged and desperate man!" With a movement so rapid that Colonel Oscar Bertrand had not time to intercept it, the old man snatched a loaded pistol from his desk, and fired it full at the breast of the other. In his passion, Lucas Clavering missed his aim, and instead of the bullet entering the Austrian's breast, it glanced aside, and only grazed his ribs.

Like a baffled tiger the usurper leaped upon his foe, and, feeble as was his wasted form compared to that of the Austrian officer, he contrived in his mad rage to fling the Colonel to the ground, and grapple with him there like some savage beast.

Alarmed at the sound of the pistol, the woman who called herself Mrs. Montmorenci rushed into the room, shrieking aloud for help. At the same moment, too, Lord Willoughby, who had been hiding throughout the interview in a room at the back of the house, rushed towards the apartment. He was too late to interfere. Releasing himself from the old man's relaxing grasp, and, rising to his feet, with one terrific blow Oscar Bertrand hurled Lucas Clavering to the ground, senseless and bleeding.

For some moments the Austrian knelt beside his unconscious foe, watching the stream of blood which flowed from the wound in his head; then laying his small hand upon the old man's heart, he listened intently.

"Each pulsation is more feeble than the last," he murmured. "Life is ebbing fast."

He rose from his knees, holding a cambric handkerchief to the wound in his side, from which the blood slowly oozed. He was pale and exhausted, but perfectly self-possessed. He seated himself in the expiring usurer's luxurious chair, and looked about as if trying to collect his thoughts.

As he did so his eye rested on the woman, who stood pale and trembling near the open door of the apartment.

"What has detained you here after your business was finished?" he said, angrily. "It is against the laws of the order. You may be a spy upon others, but not upon the members of the society. Retire."

The woman caught up her bonnet and shawl, which she had flung aside in her terror, and left the room without a word.

"Now to business."

"What more business have you here?" exclaimed Lord Willoughby. "I thought all was finished."

He glanced as he spoke to the prostrate form of the dying usurer.

"You do not know all, Lord Willoughby," replied the Colonel; "you do not know that the man who now lies senseless there is the father of my lawful wife. The woman whom I wedded as a penniless girl, knowing when I did so that she was heiress to thousands. Help me to search these cabinets: I must find the old man's will."

After a search that lasted till the clocks in the neighbourhood had struck the quarter after two, the Austrian found the document of which he had been in search. It was a will bequeathing the whole of Lucas Clavering's fortune to his only and beloved child, Ellen Clavering. But this will was tied up with a bundle of old deeds and documents, labelled, "*To be burned.*" There was a will of a much later date in one of the other cabinets, in which the old man left his fortune to an hospital. The Colonel made a note of the names of the witnesses to this latter will, and of the lawyer who drew it up, after which he deliberately destroyed the parchment, placing the older will in its stead.

"The witnesses are to be bribed, and the lawyer is to be bribed," muttered the Colonel, with a sardonic smile. "Neither of them are mentioned in the body of the will, and men who leave their money to hospitals get very little sympathy from their parasites."

It was nearly daylight when, tired out and exhausted, the Marquis re-entered his splendid mansion.

His valet, who assisted him to undress, told him a piece of gossip which was exciting all the attention of the fashionable world. The lovely Lady Edith Merton had become a raving madwoman, and had been conveyed by her husband to his castle in the Highlands of Scotland.

Our readers can imagine the feelings of the young nobleman on hearing this intelligence from the lips of his servant.

The real truth of the story he had yet to learn, and that could only be revealed by Colonel Oscar Bertrand.

THE BLACK BAND; OR, THE MYSTERIES OF MIDNIGHT

59

CHAPTER XIX.

A MERITED REWARD

CLARA MELVILLE, the ballet-girl, was very happy in her strangely altered circumstances. She saw her father surrounded by every comfort —no longer toiling by day and night in a cold and cheerless garret, and she hoped to see him as happy as herself. But it was not so. At times a brooding melancholy would take possession of the old man, and he would sit for hours in his easy chair, by the open window, his face buried in his hands, and so lost in thought that it was almost impossible to arouse him.

Clara was a great favourite in the theatre. Her modesty and gentle retiring disposition endeared her to her bolder and more daring companions; while her pretty face made her old enemy, the ballet-master, feel that she was a valuable acquisition to his band of lovely dancers. The season was drawing to a close; the last days of July were passing away, and still life flowed on smoothly for the simple-hearted ballet-girl.

It had grieved her to observe, for some time, that her kind friend and benefactress, Lolota Vizzini, was sadly altered. As brilliant as ever upon the stage, she still dazzled and charmed the admiring audience; but Clara saw her, after her triumphs, retire to her dressing-room with a dark and gloomy face that told of hidden sorrows.

"Ah, Clara!" she would say, when the young girl ventured to express anxiety about her sadness, "the world little knows how often a weary heart beats beneath a spangled bodice—how often the glittering diadem of gems presses upon a fevered brow—how often the gayest smile is but a mask to hide the deep despair that broods within the silent heart! They envy me my successes, do they? Envy me! Heaven help me! if they but knew all."

In vain Clara sought to know the nature of these secret griefs which weighed upon the noble heart of her friend: Lolota Vizzini's proud spirit shrank from revealing its sorrows.

But for Clara the season had not been altogether an uneventful one. Her innocent heart had learned to throb with an emotion she would have blushed to tell. Clara was in love!

She stood, one evening, apart from her noisy comrades, waiting for her turn to appear upon the stage. She had a little piece of needle-work in her hand—for the more industrious of the ballet-girls often work until the moment of their entrance upon the dazzling scene. She was busy with a tiny strip of embroidery, which was to trim a frock for her little sister; and, with her head bent over her work, she took no notice of the passers-by. She had become accustomed to the loungers, whose wealth, position, or title, procured for them the privilege of going behind the scenes; and though she always shrank from their notice or admiration, she had learned to look upon their presence with indifference.

This evening, however, as she stood with her fair head bent over her task, one gentleman passed before her once or twice, each time regarding her earnestly. Presently he stopped, and, taking off his hat, said in a tone of respectful politeness entirely different to the cool insolence with which some of the so-called gentlemen were in the habit of addressing the dancers, "Miss Clara Melville, I hope you have not forgotten me?"

Clara started, and, looking up, recognised the young man who had rescued her from Sir Frederick Beaumorris's disagreeable attentions.

"Forgotten you!" she exclaimed, blushing; "no, indeed; I should be very ungrateful, could I have forgotten your kindness. You are Mr. Reginald—"

"Falkner," he said; "Reginald Falkner."

"I knew that your name was Reginald," she said, with innocent candour, "for I heard that horrible old man call you so."

"That horrible old man is Sir Frederick Beaumorris; and I am very glad you dislike him so much, for I know that his character is a very bad one. I am sorry to say that I saw him in his box in the theatre, to-night; so he has returned to town."

"I hope he will not come behind the scenes," said Clara.

"But I very much fear he will," replied the young man; "but remember, Miss Melville, that if he ever presumes to annoy you, you have only to appeal to me, and I will read him a lesson he shall not forget in a hurry."

At this moment Clara was summoned to join the throng of dancers hurrying on to the stage, and when she returned to the wing, Mr. Falkner had gone.

The next evening, when she came to the theatre, she was surprised by the doorkeeper, who put a bouquet of hothouse flowers into her hand.

"Am I to carry them to Madame Vizzini?" she asked; for the man had sometimes entrusted her with bouquets and messages for the Star of the Ballet.

"Lor', no, Miss!" said the old man, good-naturedly—for Clara's gentle amiability had won her friends throughout the establishment—"don't you see that that there pretty nosegay is directed to you? I ain't much of a scholar, but I can read that much."

He pointed as he spoke to a slip of paper

attached to the stem of the bouquet, on which was written, in a bold and flowing hand, " Miss Clara Melville, with Mr. Falkner's compliments."

" Now, Miss," said the old man chuckling, " you're satisfied now, I suppose, as to who the nosegay is meant for. Heart alive, how you blush! you're as red as one of those roses."

The young girl had, indeed, blushed crimson with delight at receiving this pretty and delicate present. A diamond bracelet, such as was often presented to her companions, she would have rejected with anger and disdain; but her heart told her that this simple bunch of flowers had been offered by one who would not have wounded the feelings of the unprotected ballet-girl by so much as a word. Clara dropped a shilling into the hand of the door-keeper, but the old man rejected it with unflinching obstinacy.

" Lor', Miss Clara!" he said, " do you think I'd take a sixpence of yours? Lord bless your pretty face! a smile from you is better than other people's money. Keep it to buy your little sister a doll, Miss, and tell her that old Davis, the door-keeper, sent it to her, with his love—excuse the liberty."

Clara tripped away, carrying the bouquet into the crowded dressing-room, and prouder of it than many of her richer comrades were of their gold and gems.

" From *him*," she murmured. " How kind and thoughtful! how good he is!"

The rules of the theatre did not permit of her carrying the bouquet on the stage; she therefore selected two or three of the handsomest of the flowers, and fastened them to the bosom of her dress.

But when she ventured to cast a timid glance round the crowded house, she was disappointed at not seeing Reginald Falkner in the box he had occupied the night before.

Later in the evening, to add to her disappointment and vexation, she was annoyed by the attentions of the old dandy, Sir Frederick Beaumorris, who made his appearance behind the scenes, and who persisted in persecuting Clara with his odious attentions.

In vain she endeavoured to repel him by glances and tones of cold disdain. Too vile himself to believe in virtue, he only saw in her scorn the calculating policy of a coquette, anxious to enhance her attractions.

" Sly little fox," he whispered, " we shall understand each other by-and-by."

She turned and looked at him with flashing eyes, her lips quivering with indignation.

" I beg, Sir Frederick Beaumorris," she said, with a degree of spirit unusual to her gentle nature, " that I may be no longer annoyed by your society. I think I have given you sufficient reason to see that it is most disagreeable to me."

She walked away from him as she spoke, and hurried towards a staircase that led to her dressing-room, which apartment was situated below the level of the stage, so that, instead of the dancers having to ascend to the room in which they made their toilettes, they descended as if into a cellar.

It is necessary for the reader to understand this in order to comprehend the scene which we are about to describe.

Clara hurried towards the swing door at the top of the staircase, hoping to escape from her persecutor, but the Baronet, in spite of the attack of gout to which he had so lately been a martyr, contrived to hobble after and to overtake her just as she reached the door.

Here again he endeavoured to engage her in conversation, and this time her courage failed her, and instead of replying to him with indignation, she burst into tears.

Thinking by this that she was about to relent in her anger, the old roué attempted to put his arm round the dancer's slender waist.

But at the moment that he did so he felt himself suddenly grasped by the collar by a firm and powerful hand, and before he could utter one exclamation he was hurled against the swing-door at the head of the staircase leading to the dressing-room.

" You shall not be insulted with impunity, Miss Melville," said Reginald Falkner, for he it was who had so fortunately appeared upon the scene.

But the young man, who knew nothing of the arrangements of the theatre, was not aware that it was a swing-door against which he flung the old Baronet. He beheld, therefore, with horror that the door gave way as the old man fell against it, and precipitated Sir Frederick to the bottom of the stairs.

A stage carpenter and one of the scene-shifters picked up the prostrate old dandy, and brought him to the top of the stairs. He was happily not seriously hurt, but he was bruised and shaken by the fall; his wig had tumbled from his head, and rage, mortification, and pain combined to make him a hideous spectacle.

The door of the dressing-room happened to be wide open, so that his rapid descent had been seen by about twenty merry girls, who all laughed aloud at his misfortune.

" You shall pay for this, Mr. Reginald Falkner," he said, rubbing his shins and looking with a glance of ferocity at the young man. " And as for you, Miss," he added, turning with scarcely a less savage countenance to Clara Melville, "there's a reckoning that shall be had between you and me before you are many weeks older."

___

CHAPTER XX.

MACLOMOND CASTLE

LADY EDITH MERTON was a prisoner in her own apartments in the merchant's palace-like mansion. What now, to her, was the gold for which she had bartered her wretched soul in the first flower of her youth, in the earliest blush of her glorious beauty, in the very day of her triumph? She found herself watched over by a hired servant, and confined as a dangerous mad-woman.

In the first tempest of her rage she flew like a tigress at the female attendant who had been engaged to wait upon her.

This very fury convinced the woman that Lady Edith was indeed a maniac. The wretched creature's wild protestations of her sanity were uttered to ears accustomed to such assertions; for it is of course well known that the wildest inmates of a lunatic asylum will always declare, with piteous entreaties, and with, to a stranger, apparent truth, that they have been falsely called insane, and that it is their keepers, not they, who are mad.

In vain, therefore, did Lady Edith Merton vow, with loud and angry vehemence, that those who attempted to deprive her of her liberty knew that she was as sane as themselves. The attendant was a masculine-looking woman, of about forty years of age, with a sallow complexion, and thick black eyebrows meeting over a prominent nose. Her life had been spent within the dismal walls of a private mad-house. She was without pity for afflictions which she had been familiar with from her earliest youth —stern, gloomy, and severe, she was a creature calculated to fill the breast with terror, and subdue the proudest spirit.

This woman's name was Martha Crookman. Lady Edith Merton had found her seated by her bedside on awaking from a fitful slumber upon the morning after her vile attempt upon Robert Merton's life.

For three days Lady Edith remained in Park Lane, watched night and day by this Martha Crookman, and never seeing any other human creature. The outer doors of her apartments were locked, the keys being kept by Martha, who received food for herself and her charge from the hands of one of the servants.

Sometimes the Earl of Horton's wretched daughter would sit for hours, her face buried in her hands, as if almost stupefied by the horror of her situation; but there were periods when she would lose all power over herself, and when, possessed by a wild fury, she would endeavour to escape from the apartment.

"Let me pass, woman!" she cried to Martha Crookman, who was always ready to take her place before the door if her charge made any attempt to escape.

"Not till you are better, my Lady," said the nurse.

"Better!" cried Lady Edith, with an hysterical laugh; "who says that I am ill?"

"I beg your pardon, my Lady, but I know that you are ill. As soon as ever you recover, you will be allowed to go where you please."

"Look you, woman!" exclaimed Lady Edith, fixing her lustrous black eyes upon the inflexible face of Martha Crookman, "they tell you that I am mad, do they not?"

Martha made her no answer.

"I tell you, woman, that they lie! They lie! Lie wilfully and knowingly. Knowing in their cowardly hearts that I am as sane as they! Look at these!" She rushed as she spoke to the dressing-table, and, unlocking a jewel-casket, threw a glittering heap of exquisitely-mounted gems at the feet of the nurse.

"Look!" she shrieked, "these are worth thousands. Take them, and give me in exchange the key of that apartment. Let me but once escape into yonder corridor, and though the staircase were in flames of fire, I would rush through the blaze into the street below. Once out of this accursed house, I have friends, good and noble friends, who will shelter and save me. Take these jewels then, they are worth a fortune such as you could never have dreamed of possessing. Take them, and let me go."

The dull green eyes of Martha Crookman, which were as lustreless as those of a fish, looked thoughtfully at the splendid gems lying in disorder, where Lady Edith Merton had thrown them.

A bitter struggle was going forward in the woman's covetous heart; she would gladly have taken the jewels, but she knew that in doing so she might be ruined, and her caution got the better of her avarice.

"Pick up those ornaments, my Lady," she said, pointing to the gems, and speaking to the haughty Edith in the same tones she would have used to a naughty child, "pick them up directly! If I were to take them it would be my ruin, and I should not be allowed to keep them half an hour. I've got a good place here, your Ladyship, and I don't want to lose it."

Lady Edith Merton looked at the woman in

blank despair. How hopeless to attempt to bribe such a creature as this! How more than hopeless to try to move her to one spark of pity or compassion!

"Tell me," cried the millionaire's wife, "tell me, woman, one word. Do *you* believe me to be mad?"

"I don't know, my Lady; I've been with many mad people in my time, and them as are the maddest always pretend they're the most sensible. It's hard to tell, sometimes. But that's nothing to me; I'm here to wait upon you, and to watch you, and my orders are not to let you out of my sight—that's my business. I'm paid good wages for doing it, and I'm not going to quarrel with my bread-and-butter."

Lady Edith turned away from Martha Crookman with a gesture of profound disgust, and began restlessly to pace backwards and forwards through the superb apartment. She could hear the roll of carriages, the rapid hoofs of horses, the sound of many voices and joyous laughter in the street beneath. Her friends were, perhaps, close at hand. Some, it might be, who had seen her, only a few evenings before, in the glorious pride of her beauty and power. Lord Willoughby himself, even, might be near her; near, but unable to approach or to help her.

The thought filled her with wild despair; she pushed her long and heavy raven tresses away from her fevered brow and rushed to one of the windows.

In her anguish and frenzy she might have precipitated herself into the street below, had not due precaution been taken to prevent such a catastrophe. Heavy pieces of furniture had been placed against each of the windows, and it was impossible for her to approach near enough even to look in the park beneath.

Maddened by this, she flung herself upon the ground, and lay for hours, racked with convulsive agonies, and refusing to accept any aid from the hands of Martha Crookman, the nurse.

Exhausted by this passion of despair, for the first time since Robert Merton had made the fearful discovery which gave him so dreadful a power over his guilty wife, the wretched woman slept heavily during the early part of the night.

She was awoke from a dull dreamless slumber, that was more like a stupor than a natural sleep, by the harsh voice of Martha Crookman, and on opening her eyes beheld the dark figure of the nurse, standing by the bed-side.

Martha held a lamp in her hand, the light of which was painful to Lady Edith's dazzled eyes.

"What do you want?" she cried, impatiently. "Cannot I even be allowed to forget my miseries in sleep? Even in slumber, do you still follow and persecute me?"

"You must get up, my Lady, and prepare for starting on your journey to Scotland."

"What! in the middle of the night?"

"In the middle of the night, my Lady. Those are Mr. Merton's orders. He said it would be less painful to your feelings, to leave London at a time when you might be sure of being unobserved."

"He is very kind," cried Lady Edith, in tones of bitter mockery; "he is really too kind and considerate. Tell him that I do not choose to go to Scotland to-night. That perhaps I may never go there at all."

Martha Crookman smiled. It was the first time that her wretched charge had seen her smile, and in that one moment Lady Edith Merton perceived the nature of the being to whose mercy she had been committed. It was the smile of a hard and pitiless creature, conscious of her power, and utterly heedless of the sufferings of others.

"Tell Mr. Robert Merton," repeated Edith, "that I do not choose to go to Scotland."

"The carriage will be at the door in half an hour, to convey you to the Great Northern Railway Station, where Mr. Merton has engaged a special train that will take you, without more than half an hour's delay upon the road, into the heart of the Highlands. To-morrow night you will sleep within the walls of Castle Maclomond."

"But I refuse to go."

"Then we shall be obliged to use force," said Martha Crookman, in cold and measured accents.

"Force!"

"Yes, my Lady, force!"

"What force?" cried Lady Edith.

"A strait waistcoat, my Lady," answered the nurse, touching a bell upon the table near the bed.

Before the sound of this bell had died away, it was answered by two women closely resembling Martha Crookman in dress and appearance.

These women were assistant nurses, whose duty it was to obey the orders of Mrs. Crookman, should the patient become troublesome.

From their rapidity in answering the bell, it was evident that they had been waiting close outside the door, ready to rush in the room should their help be wanted.

One of them carried a hideous-looking garment, composed of whalebone and some thick material. This garment was a strait waistcoat. The other woman had several leather straps hanging across her arm.

These straps were to be used in fastening the arms of the patient to her sides, or even in strapping her down to her bed, should she become troublesome.

The horror of her situation, and the sight of these women, amongst whom she felt as powerless as an infant, filled Lady Edith's heart with the madness of despair, and screaming aloud, she struggled with them for a few brief moments before they subdued and bound her.

These piercing shrieks penetrated through the midnight stillness of the house, and every servant in the vast establishment believed its mistress to be indeed what her husband had represented her—a raving maniac.

Her struggles, and the violence of her conduct, had the same effect upon the narrow mind of Martha Crookman.

"Do you know, Jane," she whispered to one of the assistants, "I give you my word that, not above three hours ago, she talked to me so sensible and went on so pitiful, that I really began to think that perhaps there was some foul play at the bottom of it, and that she was no more mad than you nor me. But now look at her; who can doubt after this that she is a raging lunatic?"

Thoroughly exhausted by her struggle with the three powerful women, Lady Edith Merton cried like a child, and promised that if they would consent to remove the straps with which they had bound her to the bed, she would suffer them to dress her for the journey. The women therefore released her, and assisted her to attire herself in a dress of the richest silk, a mantle of costly Genoa velvet and priceless sable, and a bonnet provided by the most celebrated milliner in Paris.

Of what use now were these gewgaws? She would gladly have exchanged them all for one brief half-hour's liberty.

As soon as the women had hurried on their own garments, after dressing their patient, Martha Crookman unlocked the door of the outer apartment, and taking Lady Edith by the arm, in such a manner as to keep her a prisoner, without appearing to use violence, led the way down the broad staircase, followed by the two assistant nurses, Jane and Susan.

In the dimly-lighted hall Lady Edith perceived her husband, standing near the door of the library with two gentlemen, both elderly, gravelooking, and dressed in black.

The wretched woman knew these two men to be distinguished physicians—men who were known to the world for their skill in all cases of madness. She remembered that two days before they had each waited upon her, engaging her in conversation for some little time, and then quietly retiring.

At sight of Robert Merton, the man whom she looked upon as her bitterest foe, Lady Edith uttered a wild shriek of grief, and would have rushed towards him but for the strong hand of Martha Crookman, which grasped her delicate arm with the force of an iron vice. The two assistant nurses were close behind, ready to secure her at a moment's notice.

"Fiend!" she cried, in hissing accents. "Vengeful and malignant demon!"

Before she could utter another word, one of the assistant nurses had drawn a silk handkerchief tightly over her mouth, so as to render utterance impossible.

Robert Merton shuddered as he beheld this.

"Let her speak," he said; "her most cruel words cannot injure me. And remember," he added sternly, addressing himself to the three nurses, "remember my orders are that she shall be treated with the utmost gentleness."

The two doctors shrugged their shoulders. Custom had blunted their feelings as it had those of the nurses, and they could look upon this painful scene without one pang.

"A little determination is sometimes necessary," said one of the physicians; "for, remember, whatever soonest ends the struggle is always best for the patient. The women are experienced nurses, and know their business. You may safely trust Lady Edith in their care."

Robert Merton turned away from the physician with a groan, and re-entered the library. Cruelly as he had been treated, though his heart had been broken, his peace destroyed, and even his life attempted by the woman he had so passionately loved, still he could not look upon her sufferings without anguish, more intense even than her own.

"Oh, Edith, Edith!" he cried, when he had closed the door behind him, and stood in the solitude of his own chamber, "why were you so guilty, so treacherous and pitiless? Why have you forced me into measures which fill me with horror, and which I only pursue in the hope of bringing you to repentance, and sparing you by your sufferings in this world from eternal suffering in another?"

The millionaire's carriage dashed quickly through the deserted streets to the King's Cross Station. Robert Merton had entrusted his house steward with the management of the journey. The man had gone on before in a cab, and was waiting at the station to receive the party. By this arrangement the delay even of a moment was avoided, and Lady Edith Merton was conducted straight from her own carriage into the luxurious compartment provided for her special use.

Martha Crookman seated herself by the right side of her patient, one of the assistant nurses took the seat on the left, and the other placed herself opposite to Lady Edith.

Look where she would the unhappy lady met the watchful eyes of one or other of these three nurses.

If Lady Edith's mind had not been occupied solely by her own miseries, and had not the nurses been employed in keeping a close watch upon their charge, either she or they would most likely have noticed a cab which drove after their carriage, from the corner of Park Lane to the gates of the Railway Station.

The mere fact of a cab driving behind the carriage would, perhaps, have appeared nothing singular; but the unusual lateness of the hour, and the deserted state of the streets, made the fact appear strange; especially when it is remembered that this cab stood waiting at the Oxford Street end of Park Lane as the carriage conveying Lady Edith turned the corner, and that the driver immediately dashed off after the vehicle, and never once relaxed his pace until he reached King's Cross.

The express train which conveyed Lady Edith Merton into the Highlands of Scotland flew onward with fearful rapidity. The shriek of the engine, as it rushed screaming through a tunnel, alone broke the stillness of the night. A lamp illuminated the carriage, and, by the dim light, Lady Edith beheld the hard and pitiless faces of her three nurses; faces as cold and relentless as if they had been hewn out of stone. Hours passed without a word being uttered during that terrible journey. On flew the engine through the starless night, until the dim grey of the dawn began to peep in faintly at the window with a wan and ghostly light.

It was broad daylight, but a dull, wet morning when they stopped at Carlisle.

Martha Crookman conducted Lady Edith into the waiting-room, where she brought her a cup of coffee and a few biscuits. But the unhappy woman refused to eat.

"They may deprive me of every weapon," she murmured; "they may bind my hands, and shut me in on every side with bars of iron, but they cannot compel me to sustain life."

She did not know that the women under whose care she had been placed would not have scrupled to force nourishment down her throat had they found it necessary. As she was crossing the platform to return to the railway-carriage, a person who looked like a clerk belonging to the station advanced towards the little group. This young man was a clerk from the telegraph office.

"Madam," he said, addressing Lady Edith, whom he knew, by her rich dress, to be the chief person in the party, "have I the honour of speaking to Lady Edith Merton?"

A thrill of delight ran through her veins at this unexpected mention of her name. What if friends were at hand, prepared to rescue her?

"That is my name," she cried eagerly, before either of the nurses could interfere; "I am Lady Edith Merton."

"We have a telegraphic message for your ladyship. We knew by what train to expect you, as the message informed us. Will you be good enough to step into the office?"

Still followed by the nurses, Lady Edith hurried after the clerk, and having, at his direction, signed her name in a book, she received from him the dispatch.

She did not open it till she had returned to the carriage; then, with a trembling hand, she tore asunder the envelope, and looked at the contents.

The telegraphic message consisted only of one word.

That word was "*Hope.*"

She crumpled the paper in her hand before either of the nurses seated beside her could have time to read the message over her shoulder, and thrusting it into the bosom of her dress, closed her eyes as if in slumber.

But, as the reader may easily imagine, this slumber was only pretended, in order that she might conceal the violent agitation which shook her whole frame.

HOPE! Was there indeed, then, *hope?*

A moment before, in the bitterness of her despair, the guilty woman had prayed for death; now her proud soul thrilled with a hope that, in spite of all, she might escape from the just punishment of her attempted crime, and triumph over her injured husband.

"Hope," she murmured within herself. "Yes, yes, I will hope."

There was only one person whom she could imagine as the sender of this message.

That person was Lord Willoughby.

"Lionel," she thought, "my noble, generous Lionel! He has heard of my sufferings, and he will yet rescue me."

It was late in the afternoon when the train stopped at an obscure little station in the Highlands of Scotland.

Dark mountains, the lofty peaks of which were still wrapped in snow, met the eye in every direction. Bleak moors stretched around, and craggy precipices frowned upon the lonely traveller, while the eye sought in vain over the dreary prospect for one trace of any human habitation.

In spite of the hope which was hidden in the innermost depths of her soul, Lady Edith Merton shivered as she looked around her, while the special engine which had conveyed her to Scotland flew shrieking back to town.

SECRETS OF THE PAST

A carriage and pair stood waiting for her at the gate of the little station, to which she was conducted by her three watchful attendants.

A drive of about an hour and a half along a winding mountain-road, scarcely wide enough to admit of the carriage-wheels, brought the dreary party to the gates of Maclomond Castle. The castle was shaped as a square. Thick and massive walls, fourteen feet in height, shut in a solid pile of stone buildings, with turrets at the four corners, and a moat surrounding it on every side. It had stood many a siege in the days of feuds and war, but it had fallen out of the possession of the noble family to which it had once belonged; and the halls in which Scottish knights and lovely ladies had once held their revels were now the neglected property of the merchant prince, Robert Merton.

No. 6. [*Weekly, One Penny.*]

An old Scotch woman, and a couple of shepherds who reared their sheep on the sides of the craggy mountains around the castle, were the only occupants of this dismal mansion.

The heavy, iron-bound oak door shut with a loud and hollow clang upon the wretched prisoner, and Lady Edith Merton, once the favourite of fortune, the courted, admired, and beloved, found herself standing in a vast stone hall, the flooring of which felt cold and damp beneath her slender feet.

One of the turrets had been prepared for her use. A wood fire burned in the wide chimney of a circular stone-flagged apartment, over which had been thrown a square of old and faded tapestry, which served as a carpet. The same mouldering tapestry hung upon the walls, and in one corner of the apartment stood a heavy oaken four-post bed, hung with curtains of dark green cloth, and ornamented with plumes of a funereal aspect.

The spoiled child of fortune would have bitterly complained of such accommodation at any other time, but her mind was full of the strange telegraphic message which she had received, and the discomfort of her abode scarcely made any impression upon her.

Two of the nurses slept in an apartment above the one occupied by Lady Edith, but Martha Crookman had a small bed made up for her by the side of that in which her patient lay.

The unhappy woman's mind was too much distracted by her many miseries, and the one ray of hope which shone like a star through the darkness, to allow of her sleeping.

She did not close her eyes throughout the night.

Lying awake thus, out of mere weariness, Lady Edith took to watching the nurse who slept by her side.

She saw that Martha Crookman's slumber was a very light one; at the least sound—a groan, a murmur from her patient, she awoke suddenly, and looked towards Lady Edith's bed.

"Good heavens!" thought the merchant's wife; "even in her sleep this woman watches and listens. How hopeless is the thought of escape from such a creature!"

The long experience of the mad-house nurse had given her a second nature—a nature of watchfulness and suspicion, of fear and doubt. She had awoke sometimes to find a lunatic standing by her bedside, razor in hand, with eyes glaring with murderous rage. She knew that, however quiet, however in outward seeming subdued, the maniac is never really and truly *safe*.

The next day passed in dull monotony to the unhappy Lady Edith.

Hour after hour she sat at the narrow window of her turret-chamber, gazing out upon the dreary mountain-tops and the scattered sheep cropping the short grass. In her secret heart she hoped to see a carriage winding up the solitary mountain-pass, or a horseman approaching the high walls of her prison.

She looked in vain, and late at night she retired to rest, thoroughly exhausted in mind and body.

To rest, but not to sleep. She lay awake, staring vacantly at her slumbering attendant, and at the worm-eaten furniture of her turret-chamber. This night she saw to her surprise that Martha Crookman slept with a dull and heavy slumber, from which it seemed almost impossible to wake her.

It was a stormy night, and the wind howled violently about the old castle, and rattled the narrow casement of Lady Edith's apartment; but still the nurse never stirred. Three times her patient ventured to rise from her couch, and walked up and down the room wrapped in thought, but still the nurse never stirred.

But at last, in the course of her walk, Lady Edith knocked over a heavy oak chair, which fell with a loud crash to the ground.

She turned towards the little bed expecting to see the nurse start up in alarm; to her surprise she saw that Martha Crookman slept as soundly as before.

"I should not wonder if the woman has been drinking," she thought; "there is something unnatural in this heavy sleep."

She threw herself down upon the bed, and this time, as she lay awake, her attention was attracted by a picture on the wall opposite to her.

It was a full-length portrait of one of the former owners of the house. A knight clad from top to toe in chain-armour, and with a dark vengeful face that promised little mercy for the foe that fell into his iron grip.

The flickering flame of the expiring embers shone ever and anon upon the warrior's face, now lighting up the bearded mouth, and now glowing in the dark eyes. Once Lady Edith started from her pillow with a scream, for those vengeful eyes had appeared to her to move.

"Fancy," she murmured, "the wild fancy of a disordered mind. If I stay long in this terrible place I shall indeed be mad."

She fell back upon her pillow, and closing her eyes, endeavoured to sleep. But at this moment the wind outside the castle sank into stillness with a low sobbing moan, and in the silence Lady Edith heard the creaking of a hinge. Opening her eyes she looked wildly around her.

The picture of the iron-clad knight had disappeared, and in the frame stood the tall and commanding figure of Colonel Oscar Bertrand.

With one bound Lady Edith Merton sprang from her bed, and flung herself on her knees at the feet of the Austrian.

"Saved! saved!" she cried hysterically, "Lionel has not forgotten me."

"I have not forgotten you," answered the Colonel; "the Grand Master does not forget the humblest member of the company which he rules. You must be one of us, Lady Edith. You obeyed me and you failed. Be it my care to save you from the consequences of that obedience and that failure. You received my message?"

"What? It came from you?"

"It did," replied the Austrian, quietly seating

himself before the expiring embers, and motioning to Lady Edith to take a chair upon the other side of the hearth. "Listen, Lady Edith, patiently and quietly, for I have much to say to you."

"But my attendant—" said Lady Edith, pointing to Martha Crookman.

"Will sleep for twelve hours more as soundly as she sleeps now," replied the Colonel. "She took a powerful opiate in her glass of whisky toddy."

"Administered by you?"

"Administered by those who serve me."

"But tell me how you entered this place?"

"That is one of our secrets, lady. Stone walls cannot keep us out; we laugh at double-locked doors and granite walls; the moat, the draw-bridge, the mountain-precipice are all alike to us. There are secret ways in Maclomond Castle which its present owner little dreams of, but which are as familiar as the high road to the Master of the Black Band."

CHAPTER XXI.

THE ABDUCTION OF CLARA MELVILLE

SEVERAL nights elapsed after the quarrel between Sir Frederick Beaumorris and Reginald Falkner, and to Clara's delight the old Baronet did not make his appearance behind the scenes. Reginald came every evening, and every evening the doorkeeper had a beautiful bouquet for Clara when she came to the theatre.

The ballet-girl was perfectly happy. Reginald Falkner seemed to her so unlike the other gentlemen who came behind the scenes of the Italian Opera. He paid her no idle compliments, but he talked to her of her father, her little sister and brother, her home employments, and her home amusements, till by this means he became fully acquainted with her simple and artless nature. Then he would talk to her of his own family; describing his sisters one by one, telling her how much she would love them, and that some day, perhaps, she would come to know them as well as she knew him. Sometimes he talked to her of books, of his favourite poets, and his best-loved authors, and he seemed pleased to discover that the hard-working ballet-girl could talk to him on these subjects with a taste and knowledge that he had not expected to find.

Once she found a parcel of books waiting for her with the nightly bouquet, and on opening them was overjoyed to see the works of the authors whom she best liked, beautifully bound in dark green morocco, while on the first page of each her name was written in the flowing hand she knew so well.

This period seemed to Clara almost too blissful to last. In the innocence of her heart she little knew how deep an impression the handsome and gentlemanly Reginald Falkner had made upon her young mind; she only knew that she was very happy; that even her toil seemed sweet to her, and that life was all sunshine during these few bright days and nights.

Reginald Falkner had begged her very often to allow him to see her home to her lodgings at Kennington, but she had always firmly refused. He asked her once what her motive was for denying him this pleasure. She hesitated for a few moments, and then said, with that rosy blush which the young man so much admired, "My father has forbidden me to allow any one, however kind, to see me home. He has made me give him my promise. I therefore cannot consent."

"You cannot, Miss Melville," he answered, looking at her with a glance of admiration; "I would be the last in the world to ask you to disobey your father."

Clara was generally in time after the conclusion of the ballet, to catch an omnibus which started from Charing Cross at about a quarter-past eleven, and which dropped her close to her own door.

The conductor of this omnibus knew her well, so regularly had she ridden in the vehicle. He was a good-natured, rough-spoken man, with daughters of his own, and he would have protected Clara from insult by the aid of a pair of good British fists, had there been occasion.

The evening she had received Reginald Falkner's present of books, she left the theatre rather later than usual, carrying the precious brown-paper parcel under her arm.

It was a windy night, with a sharp driving rain that beat in the ballet-girl's face, and almost blinded her. Her comfortable cloak blew about her, and made it difficult for her to make her way along the slippery pavement.

For the first time in her life Clara Melville envied the ladies driving past in their luxurious carriages.

She heard the clocks chime the quarter after eleven and was afraid of being late for the omnibus by which she always travelled. She hurried on, neither looking to the right nor the left, till just as she was passing Spring Gardens her foot slipped upon the wet pavement, and she fell to the ground.

Her head struck upon the curb-stone; for a moment she was stunned by the blow, and her senses forsook her. But before she could recover herself she was raised from the ground in the strong arms of a man, and in another moment she was lifted into a carriage, which drove rapidly through the lamp-lit streets. The terrified girl would have screamed aloud, but a powerful hand was placed over her mouth; and as she looked wildly about her, she saw that two men were seated in the carriage, one of whom had his arm about her waist, and his hand held tightly over her mouth.

On flew the carriage—across a bridge, through several narrow, dark, and lonely streets, then out on to a high road.

In the darkness it was impossible for Clara to distinguish the features of the two men, and before she could remonstrate with either of them, she felt that she was far away from any friend who could help or save her.

"There must be some error," she cried, wildly; "you have brought me here in mistake for another person."

"Not a bit of it," answered one of the men; "there's no mistake at all, Miss; you're Miss Clara Melville, of Her Majesty's Theayter, and our orders is to take you to a party wots uncommon fond of you."

"Who, in heaven's name, can you mean?" asked Clara.

"Why, it's a old maiden aunt of yours, Miss, wot lives ever so far away from here. It's in France she lives, to cut it short, and she's sent us over here to fetch you."

If there had been light enough, Clara might have seen the ruffian's villainous grin as he uttered these words.

"My aunt," she said; "what aunt?"

"Why, a very rich old lady, Miss, wot means to leave you a uncommon large fortune one of these days, if you do what she asks you, and go over to France to see her, now she's sent for you."

"A rich maiden aunt!" murmured Clara; "what is her name?"

"Lor, Miss, what should it be but Melville, the same name as yours? She's your father's own sister, ain't she? You must have heerd him speak of her scores of times, haven't you?"

"Never once," said Clara. "He has never mentioned her name."

"Why, he is a close-mouthed old gentleman," said the man; "but I've heerd as how his sister and him had a very desperate quarrel nigh upon twenty years ago, and they've never been friends since; so perhaps it's rather a sore subject with the old chap."

"My father is always very reserved," answered Clara; "but, tell me, why has my aunt sent for me in this mysterious manner?"

"Why, because of this very quarrel, as I've been a telling you of, Miss. She thinks to herself, does the old lady—I've heerd as how my niece, Clara, is a very deserving young woman. Now, what I must do is to get her over here, unbeknown to her father, and if I find she is, I shall leave her the whole of my fortune, and she can spend it on her poor old father, or on her brother and sister, or how she likes; so, all you've got to do, Miss, is to play your cards well, and mind your p's and q's, and before you know where you are you'll be riding in your own carriage."

Clara was an infant in the ways of the world. Truth itself in every thought and word, she never suspected falsehood in others. Her father's history had always been a secret to her. What, then, was there more likely than that he had a maiden sister whose name he had never mentioned?

"I would not mind going to my aunt," she said, innocently, "but I cannot bear to leave my father without a word to tell him where I am going. Pray, drive back to our lodgings, and let me see him a moment before we start."

"Well, Miss, I'm uncommon sorry," replied the man, "but that can't be done, for time's precious, and we're fifteen miles on our road already; but I'll tell you what: when we get to Dover you shall write your pa a nice little note, and me or my fellow-servant shall put it into the post. My name's Thomas, you know, Miss, and I'm your aunt's gardener. My mate's name is John, and he's head footman."

Consoled by the man's promise Clara waited patiently until, after changing horses once upon the road, they stopped, by broad daylight, at an hotel at Dover.

Here she wrote a letter to her father, which the man who called himself Thomas put into his pocket, saying that he would go out and post it immediately.

Towards noon they left Dover in a steamer, and in a couple of hours reached Calais, where a post-chaise was waiting to convey them into Normandy, where, as the man told Clara, her aunt resided.

Late the next afternoon the little party reached a splendid chateau, surrounded by a park, but far from either town or village.

Here Clara was received by an old housekeeper, who could not speak a word of English, but as the ballet-girl was very well acquainted with French, she was able to ask to be immediately taken to her aunt.

To her great disappointment the old woman told her that her aunt's health was in so dangerous a state that the doctor had forbidden her seeing any one, not even her niece, until the next day.

The housekeeper then led her to a gloomy

but splendid apartment, looking into the court-yard of the chateau, and having begged her to rest herself after her journey, departed to order refreshments for the fair traveller.

Tired and worn out, Clara had no inclination even to examine the strange apartment in which she found herself. She sank into a luxurious sofa near the fire-place, and closing her eyes, fell into a gentle doze.

She was suddenly awoke by the jingling of bells, the rattle of harness, the roll of wheels, and the trampling of horses over the stones in the courtyard.

Wondering who could have arrived at the chateau—wondering, too, at so much noise and riot being allowed under the window of her invalid aunt, she rushed to the balcony to look at the new-comers.

A foreign post-chaise was standing in the court-yard, the postillions occupied in removing a pile of portmanteaus from the roof. Two men had just alighted from this carriage—one a Frenchman, the other an Englishman—and stood close together in earnest conversation.

With a cry of horror Clara Melville recog-nised the face of the Englishman. She had seen him behind the scenes of her Majesty's Theatre. He was the confidential servant of Sir Frederick Beaumorris.

"Lost!" she cried, "lost! The story these wretches told me was a cruel falsehood. Heaven help me, for I am in the power of my direst foe!"

Overcome by fatigue and agitation, she sank fainting to the ground.

CHAPTER XXII.

HELP AT HAND IN THE HOUR OF PERIL

WHEN Clara Melville recovered her senses, the dusky shadows of the summer's evening were gathering in the large apartment.

Dizzied by her fall, bewildered by the strangeness of the place, and scarcely able to recall to recollection the events of the past day and night, the wretched girl tottered to her feet and crawled once more to the window, from which she had beheld the servant of her perse-cutor, Sir Frederick Beaumorris. The wide stone court-yard of the chateau was still and deserted; there was not a human being to be seen at either of the windows in the opposite wing of the building, and nothing but the faint rustling of the leaves of the trees in the park broke the evening silence. Clara clasped her hand to her forehead, and endeavoured to consider her situation with some degree of calm-ness.

There was little doubt that the same carriage which had brought Sir Frederick's valet had also conveyed the Baronet himself. Her perse-cutor was near at hand therefore; how near, she trembled to think; at any moment he might intrude his detested presence upon her—here, where there was none to help or save her. Alone in that solitary chateau, and surrounded only by the dependants of her persecutor, far from friends or country—what was to be her fate?

In their hours of greatest trouble, Clara Mel-ville's father had never forgotten or neglected the religious instruction of his children. The lonely and unhappy girl felt this in the midst of her danger, and, falling on her knees, uttered a prayer to that Heaven from which alone in her peril and suffering she could hope for aid.

Strengthened by this brief prayer, she rose with a lighter heart, and set to work to examine the apartment.

Her first action was to seek for a key to the door.

There was none; the heavy oak door was fastened from the outside, and she felt herself indeed a prisoner.

But her courage did not utterly desert her; glancing hastily round the apartment, she selected one of the heaviest pieces of furniture, and dragging it from its place, with an effort pushed it against the door. By this means she was secured, for a time at least, from intrusion.

But the night waned, it grew quite dark, and her persecutor did not approach. The old woman whom she had seen on her arrival knocked at the door, but Clara refused to admit her, telling her in French that she wanted nothing. The refreshments which had been brought to her upon her first entering the apartment stood untouched upon the massive oak centre table; and on the high chimney-piece she found a pair of wax candles, one of which she lighted by means of a great log of wood which was slowly smouldering on the hearth.

A temporary bed had been prepared for her upon a massive carved oak sofa, covered with rich green velvet. The whole of the furniture of the apartment was heavy and old-fashioned; and had a look of gloomy splendour.

The old chateau had been unaltered since the days of Lewis the Thirteenth; it had escaped the ravages of the Revolution, or escaped with only a few cannon-balls in its massive turrets; but it had passed from the hands of the noble French family to whom it had belonged into those of Sir Frederick Beaumorris. Dark deeds

THE PERSECUTOR'S PLOT IS REVEALED

had been enacted in this solitary chateau in the long ages now wrapped in obscurity, but none perhaps darker than those which had been done within its gloomy walls since it had become the mysterious retreat of the old Baronet.

In this lonely spot, surrounded by servants who were paid to keep silence, with unlimited wealth at his command, the old roué defied the laws of his own country, as well as of that in which the chateau stood.

Seated in a low chair by the hearth, Clara Melville waited hour after hour, listening with a beating heart for the dreaded sound of footsteps in the corridor outside her chamber. But no sound broke the oppressive silence of that wing of the chateau. Sometimes she crept to the balcony, and watched the lights flashing from the narrow casements opposite to her, but she was too far from those windows to be able to distinguish the forms within.

Let us enter one of these apartments in the more frequented wing of the chateau.

It is an immense chamber, the walls, floor, and ceiling being of oak, blackened by the hand of time; along each side of the room there stretches a line of full-length portraits of former inhabitants of the chateau. The heavy furniture is exquisitely carved, and covered with rich crimson damask. Brazen chandeliers hang from the oaken ceiling, and a pile of logs blaze in the deep square recess in which the hearthstone stands, surmounted by great iron dogs.

In order to understand the scene which is now taking place in this chamber, we must retrace our steps for a few hours, and describe the events which have occurred since the arrival of Sir Frederick Beaumorris. The old Baronet crossed the Channel in the very boat that conveyed Clara Melville and the wretches who had been employed to carry her off; but he had contrived to remain in the cabin during the brief voyage, and to land after Clara and her conductors had left the boat.

For the rest of the journey he had followed on the heels of the post-chaise carrying the unhappy girl, and had arrived, as the reader knows, ten minutes after Clara reached the chateau.

He was in an excellent temper at the success of his scheme, which had been concocted by his valet and himself.

"It was an admirable idea, Danvers," he said, "and has succeeded gloriously. I shall bring the proud young lady to her senses now we've got her over here; and it will be a splendid revenge upon Mr. Reginald Falkner, for I know he's smitten with her. As for the girl herself, I care very little for *her*; but I'm determined to make that gentleman know what it is to insult Sir Frederick Beaumorris."

Full of such reflections as these the old beau retired to his dressing-room, still attended by his valet, Danvers, who had some difficulty in making his master satisfied with his personal appearance after the ravages made by seasickness. At last, however, Sir Frederick smoothed his dyed moustache, unfolded his perfumed cambric handkerchief, and surveyed himself in a cheval glass with perfect satisfaction.

"I shall do, I think, Danvers," he said. "I feel faint after my journey, so I shall dine before I pay a visit to our pretty little prize. Tell them they may serve the soup."

Sir Frederick Beaumorris was one of those men whose whole lives are devoted to self, and whose sole study is self-gratification. He never travelled without his French cook, and by this means never ran the terrible risk of eating a bad dinner.

At the very moment when he was hurrying to the dining-room, armed with a most excellent appetite, he was disturbed by hearing the sound of wheels in the court-yard without, followed by a loud ringing at the principal entrance.

The wicked old man's cheeks grew white with fear even beneath the rouge he wore to conceal his wrinkles.

"Who can it be, Danvers?" he said, in tones of unmistakable agitation. "Surely no one can have traced us here with the girl! And yet who can possibly have arrived? I associate with none of my French neighbours, and none of my English friends know where I am. Run and tell them not to admit a soul, Danvers."

The valet hastened to obey his master's orders, but he was too late. Before the Baronet could pass into the dining-room, the doors of the inner hall were thrown open, and the servants announced—

"Colonel Oscar Bertrand!"

A thunder-clap bursting over his head could have scarcely more astonished Sir Frederick Beaumorris than the sound of this man's name. The Baronet and the Colonel had met in the fashionable world of London, but they had never been more than casual acquaintances. Picture then the surprise of Sir Frederick at finding this man on the threshold of the door of his solitary chateau in the very heart of Normandy.

Three nights before the Captain of the Black Band had penetrated into the inmost recesses of a castle in the Highlands of Scotland. To-day, cool and self-possessed, he entered the hall of Sir Frederick's chateau in the very moment of the Baronet's triumph in a base and cowardly plot against an innocent girl.

"My dear Sir Frederick," said the Austrian with a smile that revealed two rows of glittering white teeth, "this is indeed a delightful surprise to me. I have been travelling through Normandy for the last few days, availing myself of the hospitality of some of my noble friends, who have residences in this part of the country. I heard this morning, by the merest chance, that you had bought this chateau of my dear old friend, the Marquis de Carillac, and I made up my mind at once that however hurried I might be, I would not leave Normandy without paying you a flying visit. I have sent my carriage and servants round to your stables, and mean to throw myself upon your hospitality for the night."

Sir Frederick bit his lip; the Colonel's easy and self-possessed manner completely threw him off his guard. Oscar Bertrand's position in the higher circles of English society was a very powerful one; his rank in the Austrian army was high; he was the chief descendant of a great Viennese family, and his wealth was supposed to be enormous. It was impossible, therefore, to affront such a man, and the Baronet tried hard to put a good face upon the matter, and to conceal his mortification.

"You are just in time, my dear Colonel," he said; "they have taken the soup into the dining-room, and as I always carry my cook with me wherever I go, I can venture to promise you a good dinner. The chateau is dull, and damp, and reported to be haunted; but if you can put up with these things, we will do our best to make you comfortable in one of the spare rooms, none of which have been occupied for a long time."

The Baronet was in hopes that, by such a speech as this, he should alarm Colonel Bertrand and prevent his wishing to sleep at the chateau.

The elegant Austrian only shrugged his shoulders, with a gay laugh.

"I will run the risk of a damp bed for the sake of your delightful society, Sir Frederick," he said cheerfully; "pray do not allow the soup to get cold. I have no doubt that we shall contrive to pass a very pleasant evening."

The dinner was excellent; Colonel Bertrand ate with the discretion of a finished epicure. He praised the cook, and admired the wine, told his host amusing anecdotes, and laughed and talked in his most brilliant style; but a close observer might have remarked that he never once took his eye from the crest-fallen countenance of the old Baronet; while once or twice a malicious smile curved his thin lips as he watched the preoccupied and uneasy manner of the roué.

After dinner the Colonel proposed a hand at *écarté*, and the two gentlemen retired to the oaken chamber with its pictured walls, which we have before described.

Sir Frederick was far too much disturbed in mind to be able to attend to his cards; the Colonel, therefore, who was, as we know, a most accomplished player, won every game, much to the aggravation of his host.

It was midnight before the Austrian consented to be conducted to his apartment. The chamber which had been assigned him by Sir Frederick's orders was at the very opposite extremity of the house to that in which poor Clara was imprisoned. Even when twelve o'clock had struck, the wretched girl was afraid to throw herself upon her couch, to seek the rest that she felt would never come to her in that house. The last spark of her wood fire had died out, and she sat shivering by the cold hearth, with a prayer every now and then trembling upon her parched lips, and with despair and anguish at work in her half-broken heart.

As the clock chimed the quarter after twelve she started from her low seat, and trembling violently, strained her ears in the endeavour to distinguish a sound which she heard slowly approaching the apartment.

This sound was that of a man's footstep; but it did not approach in the direction of the door. She heard it at the other side of the room, where there was no visible means of entrance.

But to her horror the doors of a carved ebony cabinet, which stretched from the ceiling to the floor, flew suddenly open, and her dreaded persecutor entered the apartment.

Of what use was the barricade she had placed, at the cost of such labour, against her door? There were secret ways and mysterious corridors in this ancient chateau, whose every chamber had been stained with some dark and hideous crime, undreamt of by the innocent girl.

Pale as death she stood, with her two slender hands clasped over her beating heart, awaiting the first words of her tormentor.

"Well, my sweetest of Claras," the old Baronet said, with a malicious chuckle; "I told you there was an account to be settled between you and me, and I think I've kept my word. But never mind, my pretty one, it was only a lover's stratagem to get the sweet little bird into a cage better fitted for so much beauty. All's fair in love, you know, as well as in war. You're not angry, my angel, are you?"

As he spoke he advanced towards the trembling girl, and attempted to take her hand. Clara Melville drew back with a shudder.

"Angry?" she cried, her tender blue eyes flashing with a light that was strange and new to them—"angry? There is no word that can speak my contempt and loathing for conduct such as yours. Yes, Sir Frederick," she said, in reply to his angry gesture, "contempt! So deep is my contempt that I do not even fear you; you are too mean a thing to be successful even in the attempt to injure and destroy an unprotected girl. I might dissimulate—I might endeavour to gain time and palter with my own conscience, by pretending to listen to your hateful words; but I scorn to do this. Even in this foreign country—at this dead hour of the night—in this solitary chateau, surrounded only by the base wretches who serve you—I still can dare to defy you, and tell you, in the very hour of your fancied triumph, that Heaven will not permit you to succeed."

The Baronet, pale and convulsed with passion, stood gazing upon the daring girl with an aspect of utter consternation.

"Hear me, Clara!" he gasped, the words coming in short and hurried sentences; "hear me! Your defiance is as useless as would have been the tears of another woman. Every word you utter only makes me more determined on mastering the haughty spirit which I admire, but must conquer. Vengeance and love alike have urged me on to this course; consent to remain in this chateau, as its mistress—its queen—the idol of its master, and your life shall be one long sunny day of luxury and delight; refuse, and—"

"What if I refuse?" asked Clara, calmly.

"What if you refuse? Are you mad, girl? Do you forget where you are? The purple stains of blood spilt by the murderer's hand have darkened the very spot on which you are now standing. There are lonely vaults in the walls of this chateau, in which wretched creatures have rotted piecemeal, for having dared to thwart the masters of the soil. There are secret traps which open beneath the foot of the man marked for destruction, and hurl him to the black abyss below. On every side there is death and danger; and the man who now stands before you, though he wears the fashionable costume, and assumes the polished manners of the nineteenth century, is as unscrupulous as the knights who were once masters of this place—if his hatred is aroused. Remember this, Clara Melville, and do not try to provoke that hatred."

He paused, exhausted by the suppressed violence of his passion, and evidently awaiting an answer from his victim; but the young girl stood calm, silent, and motionless, her large clear blue eyes fixed upon his wrinkled face.

"Have you no answer to this?"

"None," she said, quietly.

"You defy me, then?"

"By the help of Heaven, I defy you."

"Be it so, then; the consequences of your folly be upon your own head," said the Baronet, in hissing tones; "you are mine, mine by the power which places you like an infant in my hands. You might have been a queen, you now shall be a slave; and for your lover—the young coxcomb who dared to come between me and my caprice, he shall die in ignorance of your real state—die, thinking you a willing party to the elopement."

At these words Clara uttered a cry of anguish.

"Oh, for pity's sake," she said, "do not let him think that."

Sir Frederick laughed at her distress.

"*That* grieves you," he answered; "I've discovered a tender point, have I, my proud young lady? Come, this dreary chamber is no place for you: there are richer apartments prepared for our pretty prisoner— come!"

He caught her by her slender wrist, and, in spite of her wild shriek of despair, dragged her towards the doors of the ebony cabinet, which had closed behind him with a spring when he entered the apartment.

But as he approached this mysterious cabinet, dragging his wretched victim with him, the ebony doors flew asunder for a second time, and Colonel Oscar Bertrand advanced through the opening.

The Baronet was beside himself with rage at this interruption.

"What brings you here?" he cried, furiously.

"My instinct," answered the other in cold and measured accents; "my instinct, which told me that a woman was in danger. Release that girl!"

"Not for you, nor for any man living."

"Once more, Sir Frederick Beaumorris, I say to you, release that girl!"

"And once more I tell you that you waste your breath. What is the girl to you, and what brought you through a passage, the secret of which is only known to the owners of the house? What brought you here?"

"I came to save you."

"To save me?"

"Yes. You asked me just now what the girl was to me. Shall I tell you what she is to you?"

"Fool, let me pass!" cried Sir Frederick.

"Not till you have consented to allow that young lady to return to her friends; not till you have atoned for the insults you have offered to your brother Arthur's eldest daughter, your niece, Clara Beaumorris."

The cold perspiration broke out in great beads upon the forehead of the old Baronet, as with a cry of horror he released Clara's wrist.

"What do you mean?" he gasped; "you are mad!"

"Fool!" cried the Colonel, with a scornful smile; "did you see no likeness in those pale and delicate features to the face of one whose bitterest foe you have been? did you perceive no expression that reminded you of that only brother, whose prospects you destroyed, but who may yet arise to claim his own, and to make the astonished world ring with the tale of your black villany? Fool, thrice besotted fool! a child might have seen your brother in that face."

He pointed as he spoke to the pale and agitated girl, who had sunk into a chair, half unconscious, and utterly exhausted by the violence of the varying emotions she had endured.

"Summon your women-servants, and let them attend to this poor child, and come with me to the oak chamber below; I have much to say to you."

The Baronet, stricken down and helpless as a child, obeyed Oscar Bertrand without a murmur; he rang a bell, which brought a good-natured peasant girl to the door, and, having admitted her, he told her to attend to the young lady, with whom she could remain all night. Then, taking a candlestick in his trembling hand, he followed the Austrian to the oak chamber.

———

CHAPTER XXIII.

A DARK STORY

THE Colonel calmly seated himself in the luxurious couch before the hearth, on which the logs still blazed with a red glare, which was reflected across the oaken floor. Sir Frederick Beaumorris paced up and down the long apartment, absorbed in dark and confused thoughts. The calmness of the other chafed and irritated him. Who was this man who could thus reveal a secret unknown even to himself, whom it so nearly concerned?

Oscar Bertrand sat gazing lazily at the fire in perfect silence, while his agitated host walked hurriedly up and down the room.

At last Sir Frederick stopped suddenly, and walking close up to the Colonel, exclaimed in a broken voice—

"Colonel Bertrand, what was the meaning of the scene of five minutes past?"

"The meaning was simply this, Sir Frederick —I happened to recognise the niece of whose existence you were almost ignorant."

"But how should you recognise her?"

"There are secrets, Sir Frederick Beaumorris, which it may not please me to reveal. What if I tell you that I have watched your scheme from first to last? What if I tell you that I have followed you step by step, from the time when you left London with your intended victim, and that my visit of to-day was made for a deep and settled purpose? What if I tell you this, Sir Frederick Beaumorris?"

"Then I deny your right to play the spy upon me, Colonel Bertrand," cried the Baronet, pale with passion; "whoever and whatever you are, I call you to account for having dared to cross my path and dog my actions."

"You deny the right!" said Colonel Bertrand, with a ringing laugh of scornful meaning. "You would call me to account! I have fought nearly twenty duels, Sir Frederick Beaumorris; but I never yet crossed swords with a forger and a cheat!"

"Forger! Cheat!"

"What is that man, Sir Frederick Beaumorris, who robs those of his own blood, and reduces his kindred to poverty, that he may waste his stolen wealth in heartless vices? Sir Frederick, shall I tell you a story?"

"Mocking devil!" cried the Baronet, fiercely. "What are you, that you should thus torture me? How have you acquired the knowledge that——"

"The knowledge that gives me power to crush you, eh, Sir Frederick?"

"By what infernal means have you become possessed of this information?"

"Sir Frederick Beaumorris, the secrets of other men are the wealth of the wise. In Paris, in London, in Vienna, in St. Petersburg, in Rome, in Florence, in every city of civilised Europe, there are men who tremble at the faintest echo of the name of Oscar Bertrand—men whom I could crush with a word; men who ride in carriages to-day, but who, if I pleased, would crawl on foot and beg from door to door to-morrow. I hold the destinies of hundreds in my hands. Amongst others, I hold yours. Pshaw, Sir Frederick!" he added, as the Baronet clasped his hands wildly above his head, with a gesture of despair, "I thought you were more a man of the world. Remember this, and take it for a rule through the rest of your life—there never was a crime committed, since the world began, that did not, sooner or later, become known to some one. The secret may never be revealed to the world; but it is known."

"Do not juggle with me," said the Baronet, sinking into a chair. "What is this knowledge by which you could injure me?"

"Listen to my story," replied Colonel Bertrand, calmly; "it is not a long one. Hear it patiently."

"I am listening."

"Five-and-thirty years ago there were two brothers, both young, both handsome; one younger and handsomer than the other, and far more beloved. The tender mother clung to this bright and noble-hearted younger son; the proud father admired and loved him; a cousin, a fair and beautiful girl, who was loved by both the brothers, chose the younger. A wealthy uncle selected the younger for his heir, and proudly acknowledged his choice to the world. The elder beheld all this, and a cruel and deadly hate took possession of his cold heart—a hate which was fostered night and day, and which, night and day, grew stronger."

"It did, it did!" muttered the Baronet. "It became the ruling passion of a life. It poisoned the well-springs of existence; it grew into a curse."

"It was a self-created curse!" replied Colonel Bertrand. "Time passed; the younger brother married, and the elder stood by him at the altar, and swore, even in that sacred place, to be the destroyer of bride and bridegroom. The father and mother died, and the elder son succeeded to his inheritance—a barren title and a mortgaged estate. Meanwhile, the wealthy uncle willed his princely fortune to his younger and favourite nephew."

"That was the injustice," murmured Sir Frederick.

"He had a reason for his choice. Young as the elder brother was, his name was already stained; his honour already tarnished with black and cowardly actions. The old man knew this, and determined to leave his wealth to him who would employ it nobly. He had a steward—a faithful servant, as he thought—called Anthony Verner."

"He had."

"That man was a scoundrel. The elder nephew discovered this, for there is a free-masonry in villany which has no need of words to communicate bad thoughts. This Anthony Verner admitted the elder nephew to the house at the time that the old man lay upon his death-bed. Between the two men a second will was concocted, to which the nephew forged his uncle's signature. The old will was, as he thought, destroyed in his own presence by the steward, Verner; but he was mistaken."

"Mistaken!" cried Sir Frederick Beaumorris.

"Yes: the other villain tricked him at the last. It was a blank sheet of parchment which was destroyed. Verner wished to retain a hold over his accomplice; the real will still exists."

"Still exists! It is false!"

"Is it? I tell you that it is true; and to me alone is known the secret of its hiding-place. Anthony Verner is dead; in his last moments he would have confessed, but the hand of death was on him, and he expired in the struggle to reveal the secret upon which he had traded for thirty years; for he was well paid for his fidelity to the villain who had employed him."

"Is that all you have to tell?" asked the Baronet, in a hoarse and broken voice.

"The fate of the younger brother remains to be told. The blow which fell upon him at the reading of his uncle's will was as terrible as it was unexpected. He had been taught from his boyhood to consider himself the sole heir to an enormous fortune. His young wife had been reared in luxury, and had looked forward to the inheritance of the old man's vast estates. In one hour they beheld every hope shattered, and found themselves penniless, for they had hitherto lived upon an income allowed them by the uncle. The young man disputed the will, but clever lawyers laughed in his face, telling him that it was but natural his disappointment should have made him bitter. From that hour he became an altered man; broken-hearted and despairing, he left the luxurious mansion that now belonged to the brother who hated him; left the home of his boyhood to seek for a living, in a world of which he was as ignorant as a child. Need I say that he failed; the fair young wife drooped day by day, and hour by hour, and at the end of a few brief years, died in a wretched garret, leaving behind her three children. The man grew old before his time, and dragged on a wretched existence, earning his scanty bread by copying music, or translating from the French and German. From the hour of his disappointment he had changed his name, and fled from all those who could possibly recognise him. His children were brought up in utter ignorance of their real birth, and when the eldest appeared on the boards of the Italian opera-house, she never dreamed that the man who persecuted her with his odious admiration was her father's elder brother—her uncle, Frederick Beaumorris."

"My curses on the whole brood of them!", cried the Baronet, in an outburst of fury; "other men would have died under the effects of such a disappointment; Arthur Beaumorris has lived to torment me."

"And perhaps to be avenged upon you, Sir Frederick. You know now the power I hold over you. A word from me and the genuine will of Martin Beaumorris will be given to the world; your princely fortune, your whole estates, will pass into the hands of the brother you abhor, and you will be branded by society and by the law of the land as a forger and a scoundrel."

"What is it that you want of me?" exclaimed Sir Frederick.

"*Yourself.* I am the GRAND MASTER of a society, which numbers a hundred such men as you amongst its associates; men of high rank and lofty position, whom suspicion cannot touch, and whose crimes are never discovered. Join that society, and your secret shall be kept; refuse to join us, and in four-and-twenty hours every newspaper in London shall be full of the story I have told to-night; every club-house at the West End shall ring with your infamy; every door in the fashionable world shall be closed against you. Join us!"

"But if I join you, what would you have me do?"

"That will be revealed to you when you have taken the oaths of the society, and not till then. Do you consent?"

"I have no other course," said the Baronet, gloomily; "I *must* consent."

"You do not put it in the most gracious manner," replied Colonel Bertrand, laughing; "but no matter; you will return to London as early as possible, and once arrived there you will meet me at a place appointed between us. As for your poor little niece, Clara Beaumorris, or Clara Melville, as she has been taught to call herself, I will undertake to conduct her back towards England, and will myself place her in her father's arms—taking care to ensure her silence as to your share in the transaction. Her poor father must have suffered tortures in her absence."

"Let him suffer," said the Baronet savagely; "he can never know the pangs I endured when I beheld him the beloved by all, and my heart was hourly tortured by the throbs of jealousy."

The clocks in the court-yard and in the interior of the chateau struck three as the two men separated after this long and painful interview. They did not rise till late on the following day, when the Colonel, before even stopping to breakfast, went to the solitary wing of the chateau to seek for Clara Beaumorris.

He found the apartment empty; the prisoner had escaped. He questioned the servants; but they could tell nothing. The girl who had waited on Clara had left her, at her own request, half an hour after the departure of Sir Frederick and the Colonel.

The window leading on to the balcony was open, and the cloak worn by Clara was fastened to the iron railing. The apartment was only one storey above the ground, and the terrified girl had, no doubt, lowered herself from the balcony by this means.

Sir Frederick sent his servants to search for her in the adjoining villages. "She cannot have gone far," he said; "and if the worst should happen, and they do not find her, I care little.

She comes of a stock I hate, and she showed an instinctive dislike to me, which bespeaks the blood of her father, Arthur Beaumorris!"

* * * * * *

Clara had indeed escaped from her persecutor. In the darkness of the night she lowered herself with a desperate courage from the iron balcony. Her experience as a dancer enabled her to descend as lightly as an infant. Once having reached the ground, the rest was easy. She softly opened one of the great mouldering gates of the chateau, which always stood half ajar, and crept into the park without.

Beneath the dark shade of the neglected avenue she felt herself safe once more. She hurried along the grassy path, and in less than half an hour gained the high road. Here she paused for a moment to think which way she should go.

"When they discover my escape," she thought, "they are sure to seek for me upon the road between this and Calais, as they will imagine that I am trying to return to England. My best chance of safety, therefore, is to take the other road, and trust to Providence for the place to which it will lead me."

There was no moon, but the stars faintly illumined the darkness of the night. She saw before her a long white high road, which glittered in the dusky light, edged in by a wide expanse of flat open country, fringed here and there with rows of scanty poplars that swayed to and fro in the night breeze.

It was a dreary road for the young and defenceless girl, who found herself penniless and alone in a foreign country; but her horror of Sir Frederick Beaumorris was so great that had the way been peopled by wild beasts, she would have dared its dangers to avoid him. She had not even heard Colonel Bertrand's assertion that her persecutor was her own uncle. The shock of the Austrian's appearance, and her sudden rescue from her tormentor, had been too much for her over-excited mind, and she could remember nothing of what afterwards happened till she found herself lying upon the couch attended by the honest peasant girl. Escape was now her only thought. She hurried on, neither looking to the right nor the left, only turning now and then to take one hurried glance at the lights of the chateau behind her. These flickering lights were soon hidden by the trees, and after another half an hour's rapid walking, she found herself far from any human habitation. Still on she hurried, brave and fearless, strong in her trust in that Providence which had already interposed, as if by a miracle, to save and shield her.

REGINALD FALKNER BIDS CLARA FAREWELL

CHAPTER XXIV.

THE LADY IN THE SCARLET JACKET

LADY EDITH MERTON waited, day by day, for tidings of the Austrian, Colonel Bertrand, but the long and dreary hours passed one by one, and the promised help did not come.

He had told her on the night of their secret interview to wait—and to wait patiently, for that all would be well in the end.

"Long or late," he said, as he bade her farewell, "long or late, fear not, for I will save you. The Grand Master never forsakes the meanest member of the Black Band."

He departed through the frame of the mailed knight's portrait, and left the Castle by the secret passage only known to himself and the former owners of the estate.

After that night he departed, as the reader knows, for Normandy, on the track of Sir Frederick Beaumorris.

No. 7. [*Weekly, One Penny.*]

It was by activity such as this, which made the movements of Oscar Bertrand appear almost supernatural, that the wonderful organisation of the Black Band was carried out in all its branches. There were others to work, to watch, and to carry out the designs of the Chief, but Oscar Bertrand's was the master mind which held all together.

"Dissimulate," he had said to Lady Edith. "Throw your enemies off their guard. Appear to grow reconciled to your captivity; they are ignorant and stupid; they will be easily deceived by a superior intellect; and they will soon relax their watchfulness."

The haughty woman followed Colonel Bertrand's advice. She no longer complained of her prison, or avoided her keepers. She sat hour after hour at the narrow window of her turret-chamber, looking out at the bare hills before the Castle.

Martha Crookman found her place a very

easy one. Desolate as was Maclomond Castle, it was well furnished with hung beef, dried venison, kippered salmon, and Scotch whiskey. Martha and her two assistants, the nurses Jane and Susan, did ample justice to the national beverage, and strong tumblers of toddy were brewed every night in the great stone kitchen, where the three nurses supped with the old woman who had charge of the Castle, and the two shepherds who slept in one of the deserted chambers of the building. Nothing could have presented a greater contrast than the appearance of these two men. The younger, whose name was Donald, was a stalwart, good-looking young fellow of six feet high, with blue eyes, rosy cheeks, and a fine open countenance. The elder, who was called Sandy, was a man of about fifty; a broad-shouldered hideous ruffian, with a mouth that stretched from ear to ear; a row of tusks such as those of a wild beast; and a great head, covered with stiff bristling hair that almost stood on end. The old woman and the young shepherd Donald both feared this man, who rarely addressed either of them, but sat silently drinking his allowance of whiskey, or eating great bowls of oatmeal porridge.

He was always accompanied by his dog, which was not an ordinary sheep-dog, but an immense hound, savage to every one but his master, who could subdue him by a look.

The shepherd Donald did his best to make himself agreeable to the three grim and stony-faced nurses, though, as he did so, he remembered with a sigh the pretty rosy-cheeked lasses he had known about his own home, from which he was now far away; for Maclomond Castle was far removed from the more populated part of the Highlands.

About three days after her midnight interview with Colonel Oscar Bertrand, Lady Edith expressed a wish to see the interior of the Castle.

"I am kept such a prisoner in this turret-corner," she said, "that I know nothing whatever of the building in which I live; there can surely be no objection to my seeing the other apartments."

Even Martha Crookman could scarcely refuse so simple a request, from the lovely woman who had once been one of the queens of the fashionable world.

"As to that, my lady," she said, "I suppose there's no particular objection to your seeing the Castle, but I can tell you before you begin that there's very little to look at in the old tumble-down place."

"It will at least amuse me for an hour," replied Lady Edith, "and I have little enough to amuse me here."

She wrapped herself in a heavy Indian shawl, as the corridors of the Castle were cold and draughty, and prepared to follow Martha Crookman, who had summoned the two assistant nurses to attend herself and her patient.

"She seems quiet enough," she whispered to the women; "but there is never any knowing when she may break out. She might try to throw herself out of one of the windows. We'd better be on the safe side."

Martha Crookman was not far wrong in saying that there was very little to see in the old Castle. The furniture in the great oak-panelled rooms belonged to an age long gone by, and was fast falling to decay. The tapestry hung in mouldering shreds from the walls of some of the apartments, while the portraits of the race that had given the Castle its name were discoloured and blackened by the defacing hand of time.

Lady Edith shivered as she gazed around the dreary rooms.

"The place seems a grave of the past," she said; "it is a fit place for the broken-hearted to die in."

She shuddered as she thought that if Colonel Bertrand did not keep his promise, the Castle would be her living tomb.

At the top of the staircase belonging to the turret opposite to that in which her own chamber was situated, Martha Crookman passed a door without opening it, as she had all the others.

This circumstance immediately attracted Lady Edith's attention.

"Why did you not open that door as well as the rest?" she asked.

"Because," said Martha, sinking her voice to almost a whisper, "it is the door of the haunted room."

"The haunted room?"

"Yes, my lady; it is haunted by the ghost of the lady in the scarlet jacket."

"The lady in the scarlet jacket! What a singular idea!"

"But old Mother Macpherson, who has the care of the Castle, and who has lived here since she was a child, says that it is perfectly true, and that she herself has often seen the lady in the scarlet jacket, after midnight, gliding through the corridors of the Castle. Once, when she was quite a girl, and had a bolder spirit than she has now, she ventured to follow the ghost, and traced her to the very door of this room, which closed behind her with a noise that shook the Castle to its foundation. Ever since then this room has been called the chamber of the scarlet lady."

"I must see the room," said Lady Edith, eagerly; "but first tell me all you have heard about the ghost."

"It's rather a long story, my Lady," replied Martha Crookman, "so you'd better sit down while I do my best to tell it."

Lady Edith seated herself in a deep window-sill on the turret-staircase, and, wrapping her shawl closely round her, prepared to hear the story, while the other women placed themselves at a respectful distance upon a worm-eaten old oaken bench.

The story related by Martha Crookman was to the following effect. Early in the reign of George the Second, Sir Hector Maclomond, the then master of the Maclomond estate, married a beautiful Frenchwoman, whom he met when upon a brief visit to Paris. He was so fascinated and enraptured by her beauty, that, proud as he was as the head of an ancient Scottish house, he asked no questions as to her pedigree and connections, but married her, only knowing she was a penniless widow. But penniless as she was when Sir Hector made her his wife, Lady Maclomond soon showed a proud and impatient spirit, which was scarcely likely to ensure the Baronet happiness. She was never contented in the quiet retirement of their lonely Highland home, but was always restless and uneasy when away from the court, where she shone as one of its proudest and loveliest ornaments.

Her beauty was of the most dazzling order. She had a pale olive complexion, large flashing black eyes, and a marvellous wealth of lustrous raven hair, which, contrary to the fashion of the time, she wore unpowdered, and which, when released from the combs which confined it, fell in heavy tresses below her knees. It was only to be expected that in the profligate court of the second George this lovely creature would have many temptations. Insidious tongues whispered their poisonous flatteries into her ear; unscrupulous courtiers sighed at her feet, and sent her amorous verses, signed by their own aristocratic names, and purchased for a crown of some needy poet. Royalty itself descended from its throne to breathe proposals, which, at that time, the loftiest lady of the land would have scarcely blushed to hear, into the unwilling ear of the lovely Frenchwoman. But, through every temptation she preserved her husband's honour, and the proud name of Maclomond remained untarnished. Happy in this security, in a circle where so few husbands had any certainty of the truth of their wives, Sir Hector loved his beautiful Leonie with a passion that knew no bounds. He forgave her her pride, her caprices, her violent temper, her extravagance; he forgave all, for—was she not true to him! For three brief years all went happily with the young couple; but at the end of that time a dark cloud overspread the fair horizon, and the threatening sound of the coming storm rolled in the distance.

There appeared at the court of King George a Frenchman, of noble extraction, as it was said, but of whom very little was known, beyond his name and title.

He called himself Count Gaston de Lancy, and spoke frequently of his estates in the south of France.

His elegant appearance, and his numerous accomplishments, soon secured for him friends at the English court. He was a perfect musician, and a clever painter. Fascinating in his manners, brilliant in his conversation, and gifted with one of those faces which all women admire, and which many cannot help loving, the accomplished Caroline, the queen of George the Second, took especial notice of the young Frenchman, and, blest by the smiles of royalty itself, he very rapidly became the rage amidst the capricious and frivolous votaries of fashion.

This was how matters stood when Sir Hector and Lady Maclomond arrived in town after a brief sojourn at their Highland mansion.

The Count de Lancy and his fair country-woman, Leonie Maclomond, met constantly in the houses of the great, and during their attendance at the court. It was not long before scandalous tongues began to whisper that Lady Maclomond and the Count were more than chance acquaintances. There were some who hinted at secret meetings in the gardens of Kensington Palace, or in St. James's Park; others told of whispered conversations in the deep recesses of windows, where Gaston and Leonie felt themselves secure from the watchful eyes of the crowd; but not one of these dark reports reached the ear of Sir Hector. Blinded by his passionate love, and by the security of the past, he placed implicit confidence in his wife's honour. But the day came at last when the danger and the falsehood of the woman he loved was suddenly revealed to him.

Returning by accident to his house in St. James's Square, at a time when he was not expected, he entered the drawing-room, which was empty, and throwing himself upon a sofa, exhausted by the heat of the day, fell into a doze. He was awoke by the sound of voices in a conservatory opening out of this drawing-room, and before he recovered his surprise at the first words which met his ear, he overheard a conversation between Leonie Maclomond and Gaston de Lancy, which poisoned the happiness of his life.

From what he heard, however, he had reason to imagine that his wife was not actually guilty, in that sense in which the world looks upon a woman's guilt, but he knew that she was tottering on the very verge of the terrible abyss which separates virtue from vice, and that nothing but the strongest measures could save her.

In less than an hour Count de Lancy received a challenge from Sir Hector Maclomond. Before dusk that evening the two men had met upon the marshy ground of the Lambeth shore of the Thames, and by daybreak the next morning Sir Hector and his wife were seated in a post-chaise drawn by four horses, on the road to Scotland.

Count de Lancy had been only slightly wounded by his opponent, but the duel made a considerable sensation in court circles, though the matter was hushed up, and the real history of the encounter was never known.

Lady Maclomond did not utter a word to Sir Hector upon the subject of their sudden return to the Highlands. She seemed perfectly satisfied at the change, and once or twice remarked that she was not sorry to leave the fatiguing gaieties of London for the quiet of Maclomond Castle.

Overjoyed at this, Sir Hector imagined that her flirtation with the French Count might have merely proceeded from the frivolous coquetry of a beautiful woman, and once more he trusted her as he loved her, looking forward to a serene and happy future.

He little knew Leonie Maclomond, and the depth of deception that lay beneath that smooth and lovely surface. Sir Hector was a great sportsman, and one of the chief reasons of his love for the Castle was the delight which he took in deer-stalking upon his native hills. Lady Maclomond was a superb horsewoman, and often accompanied him upon these expeditions, galloping across the mountains, while her husband and his attendants chased the deer upon foot.

On these occasions she always wore a scarlet-cloth riding-jacket, braided with gold, in which costume her spirit still appears in the corridors of Maclomond Castle.

The autumn passed slowly by; Leonie rode her spirited horse amongst the barren hills, and Sir Hector fondly imagined that his rival was quite forgotten.

One day the Baronet went out alone on a deer-stalking expedition, attended only by his dogs—three powerful and faithful hounds, who had been reared by him from puppies when he was a boy. The attachment of these faithful animals was something more than common, even in the noble nature of a Scottish deer-hound. The Laird of Maclomond and his dogs had become almost a proverb through the Highlands, and many a shepherd pointed out to the traveller the noble figure of the Baronet, attended by his three hounds, upon the bleak hill-tops.

A few hours after the departure of Sir Hector and these faithful animals, Lady Maclomond ordered her horse, and galloped away from the Castle.

In the dusk of the evening the servants were alarmed by a strange and terrible sound approaching the court-yard of the Castle. It was the clattering of a horse's hoofs, at a violent gallop upon the mountain-road, and the furious baying of hounds.

They flew to the hall door, and reached it in time to behold Lady Maclomond ride into the court-yard, her horse bathed in foam and flecked with blood, staggering beneath its burden, while close at the animal's heels came the three hounds which had left the Castle with Sir Hector. A strange and hellish fury seemed to possess the dogs; before the terrified servants could rush to the rescue, they had dragged the shrieking and agonised Leonie from her horse, and springing on her with one savage bound, tore her limb from limb as they would have torn their mountain prey.

When, with terrible difficulty, the men belonging to the Castle succeeded in driving the three hounds from their wretched victim, a mangled and blood-stained corpse was all that remained of the once lovely Leonie.

The mystery was explained the next day, when the body of Sir Hector was found shot through the heart, lying in a lonely mountain-pass, while close beside the corpse lay a tiny jewelled pistol, which was known to have belonged to Lady Maclomond.

The wretched woman had murdered her noble and generous husband in a lonely spot, where no human eye could behold the hideous deed.

She had forgotten the hounds, those faithful animals, who, to a sagacity little inferior to human wisdom, joined a strength of affection rarely beheld in man.

She had forgotten also that there is a Providence, ever ready to confound the guilty, and that the murderer's utmost cunning is powerless to shield him from the wrath of Heaven.

Such was the story which Martha Crookman related in other words to Lady Edith Merton. A dark and terrible history of crime, which must have borne to the lady's mind a strange parallel with the events of her own life.

"And now, my Lady, if you'd like to see the haunted room, we can have a peep at it. It's broad daylight, and there are four of us, so I shouldn't think we're likely to see the ghost, which, as Mrs. Macpherson says, never appears till after midnight."

Lady Edith bent her head. The story of Leonie Maclomond had made a powerful impression upon her guilty mind.

The haunted chamber was a room very much resembling that occupied by Lady Edith in the opposite tower, except that it was in a far worse state of neglect. Shadowy cobwebs obscured the ceiling, and hung about the damp stone walls; on every object the dust lay thick and white, and the carved oak furniture was dropping to pieces. There were only two pictures in this apartment. One was the portrait of Sir Hector, in Highland costume, attended by the three hounds who avenged his murder, the other was that of Lady Maclomond, in her scarlet riding-dress. Lady Edith saw that she was a dark, imperious beauty, in style not at all unlike herself, and that she wore her raven hair combed off the forehead and falling in heavy curls upon her sloping shoulders.

In one corner of the apartment stood an immense chest, exquisitely carved, though worm-eaten and rotten, and with the massive brass hinges dropping away from the wood.

"What does that chest contain?" asked Lady Edith, after she had examined the other furniture.

"It belonged to Lady Maclomond," answered Martha Crookman. "It contains some remnants of her wardrobe; amongst other things, the very scarlet jacket in which they say her ghost walks the Castle."

"I should very much like to see it," said Lady Edith. The women lifted the heavy lid of the chest, and took out one by one the old-fashioned articles of dress which it contained. Old brocades of the richest silk and most exquisite embroidery, laces of priceless value, now yellow and rotten with age, were contained in this roomy chest, but that which Lady Edith regarded with the most interest was the scarlet jacket spoken of by Martha Crookman.

The gold lace which adorned it was tarnished and discoloured, but the cloth was of so superior a quality as to have retained its bright scarlet hue for upwards of a hundred and thirty years; and except for the dulness of the gold, the garment looked almost as if it had been made but yesterday.

"Leonie Maclomond must have been a tall woman," said Lady Edith, thoughtfully; "this jacket looks as if it would fit me."

The women replaced the garments in the oak chest, and Lady Edith having declared herself tired with her morning's ramble, Martha Crookman led the way back to her patient's turret-chamber.

That night Lady Edith Merton lay awake long after the eyes of her watchful attendant were closed in slumber. She was brooding over the story of the ghost of Maclomond Castle, and meditating a scheme which, should Colonel Bertrand fail to keep his promise, might render her independent even of the accomplished Austrian.

CHAPTER XXV.

THE GHOST APPEARS TO DONALD, THE SHEPHERD

A WEEK had passed since the Colonel's secret visit to Maclomond Castle, and still no tidings reached the lonely and wretched captive in her dreary turret-chamber. A week to her impatience seemed an age, and by the seventh day after her interview with the Austrian, her patience was almost entirely exhausted, and she began to think that Colonel Bertrand had deceived her, and that he meant to leave her to perish in her Scottish prison-house.

But through all this weary time of watching and waiting she had never once forgotten the Austrian's advice, and she had every day appeared to grow more contented with her lot and resigned to her dismal northern abode.

The effect of this was exactly that which Oscar Bertrand had predicted. Martha Crookman, who was selfish and lazy, and who had been all her life subject to the strict discipline of a public mad-house, where the conduct of the nurses is always exposed to the vigilant eye of the physicians, was glad enough to enjoy herself in the Castle kitchen, gossiping with Mrs. Macpherson, the housekeeper, and drinking whiskey toddy with the two shepherds, Donald and Sandy.

Lady Edith began to observe that when Martha made her appearance in the turret-room, after taking her supper below-stairs, there was an unsteadiness in her gait and a leaden dulness about her cold greyish-green eyes that told of the potent effects of good Scottish whiskey. The nurse no longer started from her sleep every time her patient stirred, but she would lie half the night in a heavy slumber, snoring continually.

On the seventh evening from the Colonel's visit the little party in the kitchen sat round the blazing fire rather later than usual, after a very hearty supper.

It was a stormy night; the thunder rolled amid the distant hills, and ever and anon a vivid flash of lightning illuminated the narrow windows of the great stone kitchen in which the old Scotchwoman, the two shepherds, and the nurses were congregated.

Mrs. Macpherson was frightened by the storm;

HUNTED DOWN

she sat crouching in a corner of the wide fire-place, her elbows resting on her knees, and her teeth chattering with terror.

"Hech, Sandy," she said to the ugly shepherd, " it's on such uncanny nights as this that ' the lady ' is seen about Maclomond Castle."

(Lady Maclomond's ghost was always spoken of by the servants of the Castle, as " *The Lady*.")

Sandy only nodded his hideous head in reply to this remark. He sat in the opposite corner of the fireplace, with his hound by his side and his great rough hand on the animal's head.

"Puir body," said the old woman; "she has walked a hundred and thirty years, through hail and thunder, through lightning and tempest. It's weary thinkin' o' her puir lost soul."

Donald looked at the old woman with an awe-stricken expression in his bright blue eyes. The young shepherd was as brave as a lion, but his simple Scottish nature made him credulous, and he fully believed in the story of " the lady," and crept about the Castle after dark in constant fear of meeting her.

"Is it true that all dogs attack the ghost of ' the lady ' if she comes in their way ? " asked Martha Crookman.

"Not all dogs," answered the old Scotch woman, " only the Scottish deerhound—only the faithful Scottish deerhound."

This was perhaps the most romantic part of the legend of Maclomond Castle. It was said that the faithful deerhound always knew when the ghost of the wretched Leonie was wandering the earth, and that it would hunt her spirit down as Sir Hector's dogs had hunted her a hundred and thirty years before.

A great deal more was said about the ghost, for the three nurses were full of curiosity upon the subject, but the old shepherd never spoke. Once, when Mrs. Macpherson said, " I ha' seen her, puir leddy, and Sandy ha' seen her himsel'," the shepherd nodded, and patted his dog's head significantly.

Still the storm did not abate—the thunder shook the massive walls of the old Castle, and the hail came drifting down the wide open chimney. The little party sat a long time in silence, listening to the tempest without. At last Martha Crookman looked at a great silver turnip-shaped watch, which she wore at the waist of her black stuff gown.

"Why, I declare," she said, " it's past eleven ! My Lady will be wanting to go to bed. Good night, Mrs. Macpherson. Good night, Sandy and Donald. Come, Susan and Jane, here's an hour ! "

Martha Crookman found, on reaching the turret-chamber, that Lady Edith Merton had already retired to rest. She lay in apparently profound slumber, with the faint light of the night-lamp flickering on her handsome face.

The nurse threw herself down upon her little bed by the side of her patient, and in five minutes had fallen fast asleep.

In the meantime the other two nurses had ascended to their room in the storey above. Mrs. Macpherson had retired to some obscure chamber in the vast edifice, and the two shepherds had stretched themselves upon a couple of oaken settles, before the blazing kitchen fire, in which comfortable quarters they meant to remain for the night.

For upwards of an hour both the men slept soundly ; but as the Castle clock struck twelve, Donald, who was a light sleeper, was awoke from a dream of the ghostly lady, by a sound in the corridors above his head.

It was the faint sound of a footstep, and of a woman's robes trailing upon the stone floor.

Donald sprang from the settle, snatched a lighted brand from the hearth, and, without awakening his companion, crept softly out into the hall of the Castle. His hair almost stood on end, for, straight before him, upon the broad staircase, was the form of the dreaded apparition of Lady Maclomond. Yes, she stood indeed before him !—the pale olive complexion, the flashing dark eyes, the raven hair brushed off the forehead and falling in ringlets on her shoulders ; and, above all, the scarlet riding-habit so celebrated in the legend.

The terrified shepherd shrank back to the furthest extremity of the hall, whilst the ghostly figure of " the lady " slowly advanced towards him.

The red and fitful light from the burning brand he held flashed upon the pale face of the ghost, while the rest of the hall was wrapt in darkness.

The shadowy form descended the stairs, and slowly crossed the hall; but at the heavy iron-bound door of the Castle the apparition paused.

"She'll just go through yon door without unfastening a bolt," muttered the affrighted Donald.

But he was mistaken ; the ghost did not glide through the oaken panels of the door, as he had expected, but, after pausing for a moment, the apparition turned, and looked full in the direction of the corner into which he had squeezed himself. Fixing its large black eyes upon him, with an imperious motion of its white and slender hand, the ghost of Lady Maclomond pointed to the lock of the door.

"Lord save us !" cried the shepherd, " the leddy wants me to unlock the door ! "

In his agitation he uttered this aloud. The spirit slowly bent its head.

This was enough for the trembling Donald. The *leddy* wanted the door unlocked, and he must unlock it, for to provoke the wrath of the apparition was no doubt certain destruction. With tottering steps and chattering teeth, he advanced to the door, his eyes opened to their widest extent, and fixed in a terrified stare upon the face of the ghost.

Again the spirit pointed to the lock, and, this time, with an impatient gesture.

Trembling in every limb, Donald took a bunch of keys from a little recess against the door, and inserting one of them in the lock, turned it, drew back some bolts, and flung open the massive portal of Maclomond Castle.

Before he could recover from his terror the apparition had glided through the open door, and disappeared in the darkness of the court-yard. Pale as death, the shepherd returned to the kitchen, where he found his companion still asleep with the dog beside him.

Donald shook the old shepherd by the collar of his tartan jacket.

"Sandy!" he cried, "Sandy!—Wake, now, wake!—The leddy!"

The shepherd sprang to his feet; and the dog, awaking at the same moment as his master, growled, and showed his great teeth.

"The leddy?"

"Yes, the ghost!"

The taciturn old shepherd made no reply to his comrade, but, looking at the dog, cried—

"D'ye hear him, Wallace?—D'ye hear?—The leddy!—The leddy!"

As if prompted by some supernatural instinct, the animal began to bark violently.

"Come, Wallace, come!" cried the shepherd, his eyes flashing with a savage fury, and an unwonted animation in his manner. "Come! come," he shouted; "come, lad!"

He rushed towards the hall followed by the dog.

"Sandy! Sandy! Where are ye ganging?" cried Donald.

"After *her*, mon!" shouted the old shepherd; "after *her!* to hunt her down as she was hunted down before, and as she shall be hunted for a thousand years to come. It isna the first time I've been through storm and tempest on the track o' the leddy of Maclomond.

Before Donald could remonstrate further, the old shepherd had dashed into the court-yard, followed by the hound.

While this scene was enacting below, the greatest confusion reigned in the turret-chamber occupied by Lady Edith and the nurse. The barking of the dog, and the voices of the men

in the hall, had aroused Martha Crookman, who awoke suddenly and looked about her.

The night-lamp was extinguished, and the chamber was in utter darkness.

"My Lady," said Martha, addressing her patient, "my Lady, did you hear that noise?"

There was no answer.

"How soundly she sleeps!" muttered the nurse.

Rising from her narrow mattress, Martha Crookman crept to Lady Edith's bed. She laid her hand upon the pillow and the tapestried counterpane, meaning to arouse her patient.

The bed was empty.

She flew to a little table upon which matches were always kept, and striking a light, kindled the lamp.

The door of the turret-chamber stood wide open. Martha had always slept with the key under her pillow, but a cautious hand had abstracted it.

"She's gone," cried the nurse, "she's gone! What will become of me? I'm ruined for life, unless I find her."

She rushed down the turret-stairs, and through a long passage leading to the kitchen, where she found Donald crouching over the fire.

"Donald," she cried, "Donald, help me to find my Lady. She's gone!"

*   *   *   *   *   *

On sped the phantom through the beating hail, across the thunder-shaken hills; the lightning ever and anon illuminating for an instant the dreary landscape with the bright scarlet raiments of the hurrying figure. On sped the spirit; never pausing, never looking to the right or the left till, about a mile from Maclomond Castle, it stopped before the broken door of a hut, standing alone upon the mountain-road.

The white hands knocked feebly at the door through the cracks of which, in spite of the lateness of the hour, there shone the feeble glimmer of a light.

The door was opened by a girl, who started back with a cry of horror at beholding the form without.

"The leddy, the leddy!" she shrieked, rushing away from the door; "the ghost of Leddy Maclomond."

"No, no!" cried she whom Donald had taken for the ghost of the wretched Leonie. "No, no! I am no phantom, girl; only a wretched woman, without friend or shelter. Save me! If there is any pity in your heart, save me!"

"What!" said the girl; "then you're no the spirit—you're just flesh and blood? Come in, puir body, come in, and welcome; but yer braw scarlet jacket mad' me tak' ye for the spirit. Come in!"

Lady Edith Merton waited for no second invitation, but rushing into the hut, implored the girl to shut the door.

"I am pursued," she said; "they are on my track. Hide me! hide me, girl, for the love of Heaven."

But she was too late; the loud baying of the furious hound approached the hut, and in another moment the hideous face of the old shepherd peered into the little window, with the dog at his side.

"See her, Wallace; see, boy!" cried Sandy. "She's there, she's there, the uncanny creature. After her, Wallace, hunt her down—the wicked Leddy of Maclomond! Hunt her down! hunt her down!"

The old man was beside himself. He could not hear the agonised shrieks of Lady Edith; he only saw in her the spirit of the murderess of Maclomond.

"Upon her, Wallace!" he shouted.

The fatal moment had come. With a savage howl the animal sprang through the narrow casement; but at the same instant a bullet whistled sharply through the air, and with one long and piercing death-cry, the hound rolled bleeding upon the floor of the hut.

An unknown hand had saved Lady Edith from the most horrible of deaths.

CHAPTER XXVI.

POOR CLARA

WE left Clara Melville (for we shall continue to call her by that name by which she was first known to the reader) alone, under a midnight sky, upon a dreary road in the wildest part of Normandy.

The densest forests of Southern Africa could not have been more strange to the ballet-dancer than this dismal Norman road; but under her gentle and amiable disposition there lay hidden a brave and enduring spirit, often found in such sweet natures; and once escaped from the chateau of her hated persecutor, Clara scarcely cared what dangers she had to encounter.

The bright autumn morning dawned and found her still travelling upon the broad high road, foot-sore, and sinking with fatigue, but steadily pressing on towards the unknown regions that lay before her.

The cottagers began to open their rustic casements; thin threads of blue smoke rose from the tiny charcoal fires; sturdy peasants in blue blouses and great wooden shoes went merrily by to their work; farmer's men led the cattle into the barns and yards to be milked. All was astir with the cheerful bustle of country life, and the drooping girl revived as she felt that she was no longer alone. Her knowledge of the French language enabled her to address the honest peasantry, but their provincial manner of speaking, which is as strange to a Parisian as the broader Yorkshire or Lancashire dialect is to a Londoner, puzzled the English girl, and she was often terribly at a loss to understand them, while they had considerable difficulty in comprehending her.

But the hearts of these simple peasants were good and noble, and charity has but one language throughout the world. The savage will understand the cry of distress, though uttered in a foreign tongue, and will fly to succour the wretched, of whatever country he may be.

The compassionate Normandy peasants saw at once that Clara was a stranger in a foreign land; that she was weary and broken down by fatigue, and that the first thing she required was rest.

A stout rosy farmer's wife led the fainting girl into her great kitchen, and placing her in a warm corner of the stove, removed her dusty shoes, and brought her a pair of comfortable slippers.

She then placed before her a basin of new milk, and a long roll of coarse, but sweet bread; and having insisted upon her partaking of this refreshment, began to question her upon her story, while she bustled about the kitchen, polishing her copper stewpans, and removing every speck of dust from the gaily-coloured crockery upon her broad white dressers.

With some difficulty Clara contrived to make this kind-hearted creature understand the story of her troubles; how she had been carried off by force by her vile persecutor, and how she had escaped from his house in the dead of the previous night.

The farmer's wife grew scarlet with indignation as she listened to Clara's story. She told her that if she chose to remain there till she could obtain tidings from her friends in England, she was welcome to do so.

Clara thanked her generous friend with tears in her eyes for this offer.

"I will freely accept your kindness," she said; "I have good friends in England, who will repay you for your generous goodness to an oppressed and penniless girl. Only tell me how I can write to England, so as to ensure my letter reaching its destination quickly."

Her benefactress told her that the best plan

she could adopt was to take her letter to Caen, which was the nearest town of any importance.

"But before you write a line," she said, "you shall take six or eight hours' good sleep. I can see by those cruel dark circles round your pretty blue eyes that you have not slept soundly for many nights."

It was vain that Clara endeavoured to remonstrate. She felt a feverish anxiety to write to England, that her poor father's agonised mind might be relieved; but her hospitable friend told her that she must first sleep, and she could not oppose one whose kindness had touched her to the heart.

The farmer's wife conducted her to an apartment above the kitchen. The boards were white as the driven snow; the walls hung with gaudy-coloured prints and Catholic images, before which were arranged bunches of sweet-smelling flowers. The curtains to the casement, as well as those to the little bed, were of white dimity, with scarlet borders, and the coarse linen sheets smelt of the lavender gathered in the fragrant garden attached to the farm.

Clara laid her head upon the humble pillow with a feeling of security, which was new to her after the sufferings through which she had passed; and breathing a heartfelt thanksgiving to that Providence whose mercy had rescued her from perils far worse than death, and secured for her a noble friend in the generous-hearted farmer's wife.

It was late in the evening when she awoke from a peaceful and refreshing slumber; but late as it was, she implored her hostess to allow her to write her letter immediately, that she might take it to Caen that very night.

Luckily for Clara, a cousin of the farmer's, who lived in Caen, had been spending a day in the corn-fields, assisting his kinsman in getting in his little harvest. He had come in an old-fashioned, rumbling vehicle, half-gig, half-cart, drawn by a stout Norman donkey, harnessed with ropes, and with bells jingling about his sleek head.

In this rough equipage he was to return to Caen that evening, the distance being about fourteen miles. He freely volunteered to take Clara, that she might post her letter with her own hands.

"The poor little ma'amselle can sleep at our house," he said: "my wife will be glad to see her pretty face, and will take good care of her. I, or a neighbour, will drive her back some time to-morrow, unless, indeed, she has a mind to stay with us till she gets an answer to her letter. If she does, she is welcome to the best we have."

Clara thanked the warm-hearted fellow for his generous offer.

"You are all so good to me," she said, "that you bring the tears into my eyes. But," she added, twining her slender arms affectionately round the neck of her hostess, "I will come back to my first friend, and when I forget her kindness, may I be once more a weary wanderer in a strange country, and without a friend to help me!"

With some little difficulty the farmer's wife, whose name was Margot Lorin, succeeded in finding a sheet of paper and ink-horn and pen, with which her husband, the worthy farmer Lorin, kept his accounts.

Clara seated herself close to the window, to catch the last light of the declining day, and began her letter.

It was not to her father, but to Lolota Vizzini that she wrote; begging the generous Spanish woman to drive over to Mr. Melville's lodging immediately that she received Clara's letter, to inform him that his child was safe, and that she would soon be restored to him.

"Tell him nothing of what I have suffered, dearest friend," she wrote, "for his life has been a troubled one, and I would gladly spare him every pang. Tell him only that I was carried away from England in mistake for another person."

Clara only added a request that Madame Vizzini would advance her the money to enable her to return to England without delay.

Jean Gougon's vehicle was standing at the door by the time Clara had sealed and directed her letter, the donkey jingling his bells with impatience to be off.

Jean handed the English girl into his rough gig, sprang in himself, fastened the broidered apron, and, with one shake of the reins, and a merry good-night to his cousins, drove off towards Caen.

It was a lovely evening; the new moon rose above the woods, on one side of the road by which they went, while on the other side the sun sank amidst rosy shadows, that faded slowly away in the meadows, in which the cattle reposed after the heat of the September day.

It was late when they drove over the rough pavement of Caen, and saw the lights gleaming in every narrow window.

"Now, Ma'amselle," said Jean Gougon, "I shall set you down close to the post-office. The post-master is a very civil fellow, and if you tell him that you are a friend of Jean Gougon's, I know, for old acquaintance sake, he will give you all the information you require. So I'll just leave you to post your letter, while I drive on to Madame Gougon and the children, who will be all of them wondering what can have become of me. You'll find it easy enough to get to our house, Ma'amselle, everybody in Caen knows Jean Gougon, wine and brandy merchant."

Before Clara could reply, the worthy fellow had driven off, with the bells about his donkey's head jingling through the narrow street.

She had no difficulty in finding the post-office; and though the hour for business was long past, the post-master, who was gossiping with a neighbour before the door of his house, took charge of her letter, and answered all her inquiries.

Three or four days must pass before she could receive an answer from England; but she felt that though with strangers, she was not the less with kind and generous friends, and her only anxiety was that her father might be informed of her safety. She inquired the way to John Gougon's house, and, having left the post-office, passed through a short alley, into a large open square.

By this time the moon had risen, broad and full, and every roof and gable-end, every stack of chimneys and diamond-paned casement, was distinctly visible in the clear blue light.

Though Clara had been fully directed to the honest wineseller's house, the strangeness of the scene bewildered her, and for a moment she forgot which way she was to take. While she stood looking about her, in this brief instant of hesitation, her attention was attracted by a group of gentlemen on one side of the square.

They were smoking cigars, and talking to each other gaily, with the exception of one, taller and more elegant-looking than the rest, who stood a little apart, and seemed absorbed in anxious thought.

Something in the appearance of this stranger attracted Clara Melville's attention. In spite of herself she stopped and regarded him earnestly.

At the very moment that the ballet-dancer's eyes were riveted upon this young man, he was addressed by one of the other gentlemen, and, in turning round to answer his friend, the moonlight fell full and bright upon his face.

Clara well knew those aristocratic features, and that calm, thoughtful expression. The stranger was dressed in a slightly foreign style. He wore a loose coat, richly braided, and bordered with fur, but it was easy to see, notwithstanding this, that he was an Englishman.

Before the ballet-dancer had time for reflection, the surprise and the impulse of the moment had betrayed her.

"Mr. Falkner," she said, advancing eagerly to the young Englishman; "Mr. Falkner, is it indeed really you? What a surprise to see you here!"

"What a surprise to see you here, Miss Melville," he replied gravely. "I thought you were an inhabitant of Sir Frederick Beaumorris's chateau, thirty miles from this place."

The coldness of Reginald Falkner's reply sent a chill through Clara's heart. She had expected to find a friend and protector, and he addressed her in a manner which seemed rather akin to contempt than to friendship.

"What!" she exclaimed; "you knew then that I was in Normandy; you knew of the cruel plot put into execution by my persecutor, Sir Frederick!"

"Pray spare yourself this unnecessary falsehood, Miss Melville," he answered sadly; "I would not willingly see one whom I once believed to be all that was good and pure so uselessly degraded. I knew of no plot of Sir Frederick's; but I knew of your willing flight with an old roué, whom you had pretended to despise."

"My willing flight!" exclaimed Clara, almost too bewildered for utterance.

"Your willing flight, Miss Melville," replied Reginald, with mournful gravity; "I had evidence of it in your own hand. Your own letter written to Sir Frederick Beaumorris. Nothing but that could have convinced me that she whom I would have made my idol was fashioned like her fellows, of the vilest clay."

He turned away as he spoke, as if he would have left her. They were standing at some distance, and quite out of hearing of the other men, who were still quietly smoking their cigars in the moonlight.

But Clara thought of nothing but of justifying herself in the eyes of one whose opinion was so dear to her.

"Mr. Falkner!" she cried; "Reginald! for pity's sake, hear me! What can this mean? What hideous error can there be which has led you to believe me so base a wretch? My own hand! My letters! As there is light in yonder heaven, I never addressed a line to Sir Frederick Beaumorris in my life!"

"Miss Melville," said Reginald Falkner, earnestly, "once more I must implore you; do not stoop to falsehood; it cannot remove your guilt, it only can add to its baseness. Let the past be for ever past." He bent his head upon his breast sadly, and seemed as if about to leave her; then turning back, he fixed his eyes upon her with a mournful lustre in their earnest gaze, and, in a voice broken by emotion, said—

"Clara Melville, it was but a little time ago that I thought you the most innocent, as well as the loveliest, of women—incapable of deception as you were incapable of wrong. You know how roughly that dream has been broken. I saw you amongst a giddy crowd, and I fancied you as superior to that crowd as though you had been a creature descended from some higher and purer sphere. Others might stoop to guilt, but not you; others might deceive, but not you. There are many men, calling themselves gentlemen, who would have despised you because you trod the boards of a theatre to earn bread for your father and his helpless children. It was not thus with Reginald Falkner. I revered the motive which ennobled the profession you were pursuing, and which would have still ennobled you, had you been but a sweeper in the streets of London; and in the face of the whole world I would have made you my wife."

"Reginald, Reginald!"

"That was my solemn intention, when, at the very moment that I loved you most dearly, and trusted you with the deepest confidence, I was told of your elopement with Sir Frederick Beaumorris."

"But, Reginald, for pity's sake, if indeed you once loved me, hear me now!" cried the wretched girl, in a voice broken by her sobs.

"Not one word, Clara," he said; "I should but be deceived once more. Farewell—farewell for ever."

She was standing at the foot of a flight of steps leading to the principal house in the square. As he uttered these words a cry of anguish escaped her lips, and her head sank on the stone balustrade by which she stood.

He watched her for a few moments in mournful silence, and then withdrew.

Her sobs redoubled as she heard his footsteps die away in the distance, and felt that he was indeed gone.

"Oh, Heaven!" she murmured; "unhappy wretch that I am! What a heart have I lost!"

CHAPTER XXVII.

THE GRAND MASTER AT WORK

THE hand which had saved Lady Edith Merton from the fangs of the infuriated hound was no other than that of the Grand Master of the Black Band, Colonel Oscar Bertrand. As the old shepherd rushed into the cottage and sank on his knees by the side of the expiring animal, with a howl of rage and grief (for to his rugged nature the dog had become dearer than child or wife, than friend or kindred), the Austrian officer strode into the rude dwelling, and, removing his hat with the careless grace peculiar to him, saluted Lady Edith, exactly as he would have done had he met her in Rotten Row, or in her own elegant saloon in Park Lane.

"A narrow escape, my dear Lady Edith," he said, laughing. "It was very lucky that I happened to be passing."

"My preserver!" cried the rescued woman, clasping her hands.

"Why could you not trust and wait?" said Colonel Bertrand, sinking his voice into a whisper; "foolish woman, did you forget what I told you? The Grand Master never deserts the meanest member of the Black Band."

"I was to blame; I was very, very foolish," replied the once haughty Lady Edith, with the humility of a child. "But every day and hour seemed so long. My sufferings almost turned my brain."

"I have but just arrived in time to save you," answered Oscar Bertrand; then raising his voice, he added, "my groom is waiting without, with the horses, Lady Edith. If you would suffer me to convey you before me on my saddle, we can easily regain Castle Maclomond."

"Return to the Castle!" cried Lady Edith, with a shudder, "return to that living grave!"

"And why not?" said the Colonel gravely; "where else would you go?"

"Where else——?" exclaimed Lady Edith; then checking herself abruptly, she dropped her eyes beneath the impressive glance of the Colonel: a glance that seemed to say, "Wait, and leave all to me!"

"Your husband's Scottish retreat is, strange to say, my own destination," said Colonel Bertrand. "I am the bearer of a letter from Mr. Robert Merton authorising me to use Castle Maclomond as if it were my own house during my stay in Scotland, which will not be a long one, as I only visit the Highlands for a fortnight's deer-stalking."

At the word "deer-stalking," the old shepherd Sandy for the first time raised his head, which had fallen in an agony of grief upon the side of the dead hound.

"Deer-stalking!" he cried; "the deer may roam free upon the mountains noo; ye've killed the bonniest dog in the Hielands. Ho, Wallace, Wallace!" he added, lifting the animal's bleeding head in his great hands, "there's many a fayther wouldna greet for his dead bairn, as I could greet for thee."

There was something touching in the Highlander's anguish. It was the grief of an almost savage nature mourning for the loss of the one thing it had learned to love.

"I am sorry I killed your dog, my worthy fellow," said Colonel Bertrand, "but it was a toss up between the life of the hound and the destruction of the lady, and gallantry forbade that I should sacrifice so lovely a lady as the wife of Robert Merton."

"Why did she wear a scarlet jacket, then?"

THE ROBBERY AT THE SHAM HOTEL

cried the shepherd; "why did she dress herself in the accursed garments of the Leddy o' Maclomond? There is nae a dog o' the true stock in a' the Hielands that would nae ha' hunted her to the death in yon uncanny claes."

"I know the old legend," said the Colonel; "I knew the last of the Maclomonds, a fated and ruined race; glad to sell the home of their ancestors to the merchant prince. Come, Lady Edith."

Colonel Bertrand led her from the cottage, and springing into his saddle, held out his arms to receive her, and placed her carefully before him upon the horse. The groom then mounted, and the party galloped off, the shepherd slowly following him, carrying the dead hound upon his shoulder, and the cottage-girl looking after them through the darkness of the stormy night.

They were not long in reaching Maclomond

No. 8. [*Weekly, One Penny.*]

Castle, where they found the small household in a state of terror and confusion, the young shepherd repeating every moment his story of the ghost of the Leddy, the nurses searching in every direction for their missing charge, and the old Scotch housekeeper too deaf to fully understand what had happened.

The doors were opened by the terrified Donald, whose hair still stood on end from his meeting with the ghost. He gazed with redoubled terror upon the two horsemen, the lady in the scarlet jacket, and the old shepherd carrying the dead hound. It was some time before the Colonel could convince him that the midnight visitors to the Castle were, at any rate, flesh and blood.

"Foolish lad," he said, laughing; "cannot a lady wear a scarlet riding-jacket without your mistaking her for a ghost? Open the doors, and let us get out of this pelting storm. Your comrade has lost his faithful dog by this night's folly. Let us in, my lad, and get us a good tumbler of toddy, and you'll soon see we're honest flesh and blood."

The manner of the Colonel completely re-assured the superstitious young Highlander; he flung the heavy doors of the Castle open to their widest extent, and bade welcome, in his honest Scottish fashion, to the visitors.

"Let me see Mr. Robert Merton's house-keeper," said Colonel Bertrand, shaking the rain from his dripping garments.

The old Scotchwoman, Mrs. Macpherson, appeared at this summons, and the Colonel handed her a letter, which, after polishing her spectacles upon her stuff petticoat, she, with considerable difficulty, managed to read.

The letter was a brief one, and ran thus—

"Mrs. Macpherson,—My esteemed friend, Colonel Oscar Bertrand, is travelling through the Highlands of Scotland. Bid him your heartiest welcome to Castle Maclomond, and see that he uses my house as if it were his own.   ROBERT MERTON."

The old woman saluted the Colonel with half a dozen curtsies, after reading this letter.

"We'll just do our best to make you welcome, sir," she said; "but it's a poor place, and little better than bare walls and empty chambers; I mind the time when there was mirth and revelry, and when the old rafters rang with merry voices."

During this brief interview the three nurses had surrounded Lady Edith, and were busied in removing the scarlet jacket, which had so be-wildered the two shepherds, and which was now soaked through and through with the rain.

Martha Crookman was violently enraged against her patient, though she knew how to conceal her fury beneath the cold and impassible manner of an automaton; but Lady Edith had aroused the hatred of the nurse's selfish nature; she had endangered Martha's situation by her attempted escape, and the woman was deter-mined on being revenged upon her.

"I'm thinking that a strait-waistcoat's about the next thing you'll be wearing, my Lady," she said, as she flung the scarlet jacket upon the floor of the hall.

At this moment the Colonel beckoned the nurse aside.

"I have brought you back your patient," he said, in a whisper; "but if you wish to keep your place you must look to her a little better for the future. You've had a very narrow escape of losing her and your situation at the same time. This stormy weather has a strange effect upon the insane."

Martha Crookman curtsied humbly as she re-ceived this sharp reproof from the Austrian officer. She little knew that it was only in-tended to throw her off her guard. She might, perhaps, otherwise have suspected the motive of Oscar Bertrand's visit to the Castle; after this, she only saw in him a friend of Robert Merton's, commissioned, perhaps, to see to the safety of the merchant's mad wife.

Before Lady Edith was conducted to her usual apartment, the Colonel contrived to speak to her, unperceived by the vigilant eyes of Martha Crookman or the assistant nurses.

"In Heaven's name," she said, "how did you obtain that letter from my husband?"

The Colonel smiled at Lady Edith's question.

"Do you suppose," he said, "that the Grand Master of the Black Band would wait for a genuine letter when a forgery would answer his purpose as well?"

"What? The letter you showed the house-keeper was a forgery, then?"

"It was."

"But she has been in my husband's service ever since he bought his estate. She must know his handwriting."

"I have no doubt she knows it well, but the same penman who can deceive the most expe-rienced banker's clerk in the City of London or Paris could surely impose upon a purblind old Scotchwoman."

"Colonel Bertrand!" cried Lady Edith, looking with a bewildered gaze of mingled admiration and terror upon the handsome and tranquil face of the Austrian, "you are surely something more than human."

The Colonel smiled at this speech.

"You utter the very words which I once heard spoken by your lover, Lionel Montfort, now Marquis of Willoughby. My reply, then, was—"

"What, Colonel?" cried Lady Edith.

"I am neither more nor less than human. I am only the Grand Master of the Companions of Midnight—the Captain of the Black Band!"

CHAPTER XXVIII.

THE SECRETS OF THE ASSOCIATION

THE lamps were being lighted in the streets of London, and darkness was slowly closing in upon the shadow-shrouded river, when a man of foreign appearance might have been seen leav-ing the Waterloo Railway Station, and wending his way slowly across the bridge towards the Strand.

His dark olive complexion and closely-cut hair, of a bluish black, proclaimed his southern origin. His eyes were small and piercing : but, by a strange peculiarity, the left eye seemed to be immovable in his head, while the right rolled restlessly in every direction. This peculiarity gave a sinister expression to his face, which was further increased by the bird-like sharpness of his small hooked nose, and the compression of his thin and colourless lips.

He was a man whose face, once seen, would haunt you afterwards in the dead hours of the silent night; a man whose aspect told of mystery; of dark and terrible secrets, and fathomless abysses of undiscovered guilt. But in the busy streets of London, the passers-by rarely pause to observe those whom they meet; the changing faces shift as rapidly as the shadows in a magic-lantern; the mysteries of life lie deeply hidden under the noise and bustle of the hurrying crowd.

The foreigner strolled across the bridge, looking furtively with his one active eye to the right and left, and no one in the crowd stopped to observe him.

He paused at the toll-bar, and going close up to the lamp above the gate, took out a small slip of paper, which he examined carefully.

There was very little written on this fragment of paper, and what there was must have been unintelligible except to one who possessed a secret key to its meaning. It ran thus :—

" C. O.,—For direction wait at the corner of Castle Street, 10 p.m. Badge, per order of   G. M. B. B."

The clocks were chiming the half-hour after seven as the foreigner stopped to read these words. He shrugged his shoulders as he listened to the chimes.

"Half-past seven," he muttered, with a slightly foreign accent, but in very good English. "Two hours and a half to wait, and only a few pence in my pocket."

He paid his halfpenny, passed through the toll-bar, and walked slowly towards the Strand.

That busy thoroughfare is perhaps more crowded at this hour than at any other period of the day or night; men hurrying home from business; others on their way to the haunts of pleasure; crowded omnibuses rolling by; cabs taking merry parties of smartly-dressed people to the different theatres; humbler pedestrians waiting in dense crowds about the pit and gallery doors of the Lyceum and the Adelphi; brilliantly lighted shops, replete with every necessary or luxury of life : all the many signs which bespeak a city's prosperity, greet the eye on every side.

The stranger loitered along the pavement, staring now at one shop, now at another, with the vacant, listless air of a man who seeks to kill time. His shabby overcoat was worn threadbare about the sleeves and collar; the felt hat slouched over his swarthy face had seen long service ; his hands were ungloved, and the long, sharply-pointed nails gave his bony fingers something the look of the claws of a bird of prey. He seemed, altogether, one of those shabby, penniless adventurers, who, rejected from their own country by reason of some evil deed, are thrown upon the wide sea of London for a refuge.

He turned in the direction of Temple Bar, and passing under the archway, walked the entire length of Fleet Street and back again into the Strand.

The clock of St. Clement Danes was striking nine as he repassed Temple Bar.

"An hour to wait yet," he said, shrugging his shoulders. " An hour in these cheerless, cold streets, under this dull, smoky sky, and with empty pockets. I dare say *she* is riding in her carriage, lolling on the satin cushions, and displaying her diamonds to the crowd. Curse her ! "

He uttered these last words with an expression of deep and concentrated hate. Suddenly a thought seemed to strike him. He quickened his pace from his former listless lounge into almost a run, and hurried off in the direction of Charing Cross.

From Charing Cross he made his way to the Haymarket, not once slackening his pace till he reached Her Majesty's Theatre.

The colonnade was dark and deserted; there was no long rank of carriages, no glitter of diamonds, or rustle of silks and velvets; no waving of plumes, or bright flash of sparkling glances from the orbs of beauty and fashion. The massive doors of the opera house were closed—the season was over.

The foreigner turned away from the box entrance with an oath; then pausing for a few minutes he read the bill of the last performance which had taken place.

" Shall I go to her ? " he muttered, thinking aloud. " Shall I go to my fine lady, in her splendid house, and ask her for the money which is mine by right ? No, there might be danger in that; secrecy is the condition of my presence in London. I must first do my work for *them*. *They* are doubtless on the watch."

He left the colonnade, and looking at a clock in a tobacconist's shop, saw that it wanted only ten minutes to ten.

Foreigner as he was, he seemed familiar with all the byeways of London; for he passed through several intricate courts and turnings, and emerged, as St. Martin's clock struck ten, into the lower end of Castle Street, Leicester Square.

A man of respectable appearance was looking into the window of a small shop; and as the foreigner entered the street, he glanced round, and the eyes of the two met.

The foreigner put his hand in the pocket of his coat and drew out a small strip of black crape, which he fastened in a peculiar manner round his left wrist, the other man watching him attentively all the time.

As he drew the slip-knot tightly, with a jerk of the finger and thumb, the man addressed him—

"You have hurt your wrist," he said, carelessly.

"I wear the badge of my craft," answered the foreigner.

"The arm—" said the Englishman.

"That can strike!" replied the foreigner.

"The head—"

"That can think!"

"The tongue—"

"That can be silent!"

"Good," said the Englishman. "Come with me."

The two men walked into St. Martin's Lane, where the Englishman hailed a cab, and gave some directions in an undertone to the driver, who wore around his wrist a shabby strip of crape, like that assumed by the foreigner.

It is needless to conceal from the reader that these three men were alike members of that mysterious society of which Oscar Bertrand was the powerful and unknown chief. The Black Band had its own vehicles as well as its own places of meeting; vehicles which, apparently at the service of the public, were in reality driven by humble members of this mighty association.

The ceremonies which Colonel Bertrand had used in the case of Lord Lionel Montfort were employed on this occasion. The eyes of the foreigner were bandaged, and he was handed out of the cab at the entrance to that very building in which Lord Lionel Montfort had taken the vows of the society, and the real situation of which was known only to a privileged few.

When the bandage was removed from his eyes, the foreigner found himself in the office which contained the books of the society, and that marvellous and terrible cabinet, armed with its triple rows of loaded pistols, and furnished with the wonderful machinery of death, the secret of which Colonel Bertrand had revealed to Lord Lionel.

A man dressed in black, and wearing a velvet mask, was seated at a desk covered with papers, under the brilliant light of two lamps, so contrived that their light could be turned at will in any direction, and thrown with a concentrated glare upon the face of any person in the room.

The foreigner found himself alone with this man, who wore a small jet star on his breast, which bespoke his high rank in the society. He lifted his delicate hand, which sparkled with diamonds, and threw the light of the two lamps upon the face of the foreigner.

"You are an Italian?" he said.

"A Neapolitan."

"Passing under the name of Antonio Vecchi?"

"Yes."

"A member of three political societies, and traitor to each?"

Antonio Vecchi shrugged his shoulders.

"Enough," answered his interrogator. "We do not need your acknowledgment of facts we know. The important questions are these:— Has your treachery ever been discovered?"

"Never."

"Neither discovered nor suspected?"

"Neither discovered nor suspected," answered Vecchi.

"Is there any fear of suspicion arising?"

"No."

"Good. If this is so, you can serve us. Now, then, for your letters."

He referred to a pile of documents on the desk before him, and selecting three narrow slips of thin paper, closely written in a cramped foreign hand, he addressed Antonio Vecchi in the following words—

"In number one you tell us that the Prince de Z., one of the most powerful members of the Society of the Good Cousins, has been entrusted with a mission of importance. You have not yet discovered the purport of this mission?"

"I was but a humble member of the society," answered Vecchi. "I had to watch and wait."

"Good. In your second letter you inform us you have discovered London is the city to which the Prince de Z. is to be sent. In number three you tell us more. His mission is to the members of the Society of Good Cousins scattered throughout England; and he is charged with an immense sum of money, with which he is to organise the secret return of the exiles to the Two Sicilies, in order to renew the struggle of '48, and this time with more prudence and better success. This is the information you send us. Are you prepared to swear that it is correct?"

"I am," replied Vecchi.

"By the oaths of the society, which are severe and terrible."

"By any oaths you may please to administer."

"Good. You are a villain, Signor Vecchi, but I do not think you are a coward."

"You shall never find me one."

"Now, then, to business. When does the Prince arrive in London?"

"To-morrow night."

"And what is the sum of money he carries?"

"I do not know the exact amount," answered the Italian; "but it consists of several thousand pounds."

"You know the terms of the society?"

"I do."

"A third of the booty to the informer and originator of the robbery; a third to defray all expenses; and the remaining third to the society."

"The conditions are just."

"They are. Justice, even in crime, is the first condition of the society. Now for the means of action."

"I am all attention."

"Is the Prince de Z. familiar with London?"

"He is not."

"Has he many friends in London?"

"No. He is a very young man, and his youth has been passed in the mountain strongholds of Calabria, where he possesses a vast estate. He has only lately joined the Good Cousins, but he is trusted on account of his character for truth and chivalry."

"Good; he is a young man, and he is therefore inexperienced; he is truthful, and he is therefore unsuspicious; he is a stranger to London, and he can therefore be easily deceived. The society has houses of resort in every quarter of the town. The Prince must be taken to one of these houses at the West-end, under the impression that he is being conducted to a fashionable hotel."

"But who will do this?" asked the Italian.

"The working members of the society. They will watch at the station for the arrival of the train conveying the Prince from Dover; it will be easy for them to contrive the rest. You will furnish us with a minute description of his appearance."

"I will."

"Good. Tired with his journey, the Prince will sleep well on the night of his arrival, and when the grey dawn breaks over the housetops of London, the money he carries will have passed into the hands of the association."

There was something terrible in the consummate coolness with which the man in the velvet mask arranged the details of this treacherous and diabolical robbery; and even the Italian, villain as he was, shuddered at the business-like tone of the unknown being before whom he stood.

"You will receive your orders for action below," said the mask; "our interview is ended."

He then took a black cloth mask from a drawer near him and handed it to Antonio. "You will assume this," he said; "secrecy is the policy of the association; you will be known only to the higher members of the band by your name; for all ordinary purposes you will, like all other associates, be distinguished by a number; your number will be 161."

He touched a bell, which gave forth one single stroke, and the small square flooring upon which the Italian stood sunk slowly, until Antonio Vecchi found himself in a large apartment, which very much resembled the office of an ordinary house of business.

There were some striking peculiarities, however, in this apartment. At one end there was a desk at which a clerk was seated, and on the right hand of which an iron pipe communicated with the ceiling above. Benches were arranged across the room, upon which men of all ages, and apparently of all grades, were seated. They were all silent, and they all wore masks similar to that of Antonio Vecchi. Along one side of the apartment was a row of doors; on the centre panel of each, a peculiar cypher was painted in black characters.

While the Italian was looking about him, a sharp whistle vibrated through the iron pipe by the desk of the clerk, followed by a rustling noise of papers falling through the tube.

The clerk busied himself in selecting and sorting these papers, all of which were folded in long narrow slips, and sealed at each end with black wax.

"No. 43," he said, in a loud, clear voice; "No. 79, 104, 18, 62, 37, 91, 161."

Antonio Vecchi stepped forward at the same moment with seven other members of the masked assembly, who crowded eagerly round the desk.

Each of the eight men received a sealed slip of paper from the clerk. Antonio Vecchi observed that no one stopped to open his paper, but placed it at once in his pocket; the Italian therefore did the same.

"The assembly is dismissed," said the clerk; "the members will leave the office by the seventh door from the right."

The assembly crowded round the door indicated, which opened outwards with a spring, revealing a dimly-lighted passage.

Into this passage the crowd flocked, the Italian following the stream. They had not gone half a dozen paces before the passage took an abrupt turn to the right; it then gradually curved to the left; after that it appeared to describe three parts of a circle, and then branched off suddenly in a new direction. In fact, it was so constructed as to defy all topography; the curves were so peculiar and so varied, that it was impossible to guess whether they led east, west, north, or south.

In about ten minutes the Italian felt a stream of cold air blowing upon his face, and a few moments afterwards the crowd emerged in a dismal, narrow street in the heart of the city.

"Curse this place!" said one of the men; "I've been fifteen years a member of the Band, and all that time I've tried to discover the real position of the central office without being a jot nearer success to-night than I was when first I took the oaths."

One of the other men laughed at this remark.

"Nor would you be any nearer," he answered, "fifteen years hence. The secrets of the association are like the secrets of the grave—they were never yet discovered by mortal man."

CHAPTER XXIX.

THE ROBBERY AT THE SHAM HOTEL

THE young Prince de Z. was brave, generous, high-minded, and enthusiastic. The tyranny of that Bourbon ruler, who had been christened by his unhappy subjects "King Bomba," in commemoration of having, besides perpetrating other cruelties and massacres, bombarded his own capital; and whose tyrannies did much to lay the foundation of that spirit of revolt which smouldered in the heart of Italy through long years of oppression, which burst forth in the brief revolution of '48, and which finally triumphed, so far as Naples and Sicily were concerned, under the leadership of Garibaldi in 1860.

The spirit of freedom has never been extinct in the breasts of the noble children of Italy. It may have slumbered, but it has not died. The Prince de Z., at the age of twenty-five, was foremost in the ranks of the patriots, of whom Mazzini was then the chief. Eager to serve his party, he had prayed earnestly to be employed for the interests of the society, and, overruled by his enthusiasm, the heads of the association had consented to overlook his inexperience, and to entrust him with a mission which, though critical, was not difficult.

He had simply to distribute a sum of money amongst a number of exiles, whose names and addresses had been entrusted to him.

He was accomplished, handsome, elegant; the scion of an ancient house; the owner of a princely estate. He was used to all the sweet intoxications common to his position; the flattery of women, the servility of men. Credulous and unsuspicious, almost to a fault, he knew not what it was to doubt the truth of another.

The Prince arrived at the London Bridge station at the hour indicated by the traitor, Antonio Vecchi. He was attended only by his valet, who was as ignorant of English customs as the Prince himself.

As he alighted from the railway carriage he was approached by a man, dressed in a suit of black, resembling that of a gentleman's servant, who asked him, in French, if he was provided with an hotel.

The Prince knew that abroad it was customary for men called commissionaires to seize upon newly-arrived foreigners, and carry them off to the hotels by which they were employed; but he did not know that the custom is unknown amongst our more independent English citizens.

"No," replied the Prince, also in French; "if you belong to a desirable hotel, in the fashionable quarter of London, you may make arrangements with my servant."

The man bowed respectfully to the Prince de Z., and addressed himself to the valet, who selected his master's luggage and placed it on one cab, while the Prince seated himself in another.

The whole transaction had occupied little more than five minutes. The strange man gave directions to the Prince's cabman, and then seated himself in the vehicle with the valet, with whom he contrived to get into conversation as they drove towards the West-end. They stopped at a small house in a quiet street in the neighbourhood of St. James's Square, and the sham servant of the hotel ushered the Prince into a small but handsomely-appointed suite of apartments upon the first floor.

He led the valet to a chamber situated two floors above the rooms occupied by the Prince.

It was the plan of the robbers to separate the master from the man.

The Prince ordered dinner, and three waiters entered the room and busied themselves in preparing the table.

These waiters were three of the most accomplished members of the Black Band—men who had been engaged in some of those mysterious robberies that have bewildered the cleverest police in the chief cities of Europe—men to whom crime was an art, and who studied the details of a robbery as a great painter studies the details of his picture.

They understood half-a-dozen languages, and though the Prince and his valet conversed in

Italian, the attendants remembered and noted every word that was uttered.

The Prince de Z., young and inconsiderate, spoke at random before these men—never for a moment imagining that the ordinary servants of a London hotel were likely to understand Italian.

"You carried the portmanteau containing the money in your own hands the whole time, Nicolas?" asked the Prince.

"I did, your excellence."

"That is well, Nicolas. I've heard that these English are terrible thieves. The portmanteau might have been tampered with if you had let it out of your sight. Where is it now?"

"I have placed it in my own sleeping-apartment, your excellence. I have locked the door, and have the key in my pocket," answered the valet, tapping his waistcoat triumphantly.

One of the men, whose back was turned to the Prince and his servant, smiled involuntarily at this remark.

The reader need scarcely be told that there were duplicate keys to every door in this house.

"Cautious Nicolas!" said the Prince, laughingly, "you had better have left your door open; people will think your conduct strange in locking it. Remember you are now in a respectable hotel, the master of which is answerable for the honesty of its inmates, and you need no longer be alarmed for the safety of the specie."

The three men exchanged stolen glances.

The money, then, was in specie!

They had now learned all they required to know.

Their directions were to leave all for night—to drug the man they had to rob, and to make away with the property while he slept.

A sumptuous dinner, procured from a neighbouring confectioner's shop (for it is needless to say that there were no cooks in this sham hotel), was served; and the Prince, who was very well satisfied with his accommodation, retired to rest at about eleven o'clock, exhausted by the fatigue of his journey.

The valet went to his room at the same time. He had not been five minutes in the apartment before he was disturbed by one of the waiters, who brought him a tumbler of hot wine, spiced and sweetened, and smelling most delicious.

Nicolas grinned his thanks for the steaming liquid, and nodded and smiled to the waiter, by way of good night.

"An English custom, no doubt," he thought; "unluckily the wine will be cold before I can drink it, as I must first write to Pepita."

Pepita was the valet's sweetheart—a pretty little Calabrian damsel, who was, no doubt, anxiously awaiting a letter to tell of her lover's arrival in London.

But writing this letter was by no means an easy task to Nicolas. He had some difficulty in thinking what he was to write, and still more difficulty in writing it. He squared his elbows on the little table, dipped the pen in the ink, and began to write—"My darling Pepita—"

In the very first stroke of his pen he made an awkward sweep with his right elbow, and knocked over the tumbler of wine.

The poor fellow was in despair at his loss, but it was not to be remedied; so he shrugged his shoulders, laughed good-humouredly at his ill-luck, and went on with his letter.

He was nearly an hour finishing it, and by the time it was done he was so sleepy that he threw himself dressed upon the bed, having first taken care to lock his chamber-door, and to examine the fastenings of the precious portmanteau, which stood on a chair close to his pillow.

He was asleep in less than five minutes, after having murmured a brief prayer to his patron saint.

A little after two o'clock he was suddenly awoke by a noise at the casement of his room.

He opened his eyes, and beheld a young man enter his room by means of a ladder placed against the open window.

Nicolas sprang from the bed, and flung himself on the intruder with the bound of one of the animals native to his own mountains. But the robber was more powerful than the valet; and after a brief but desperate struggle, he contrived to disengage himself from Nicolas's grasp, and drawing a clasp-knife from his sleeve, stabbed the Italian in the breast.

The valet fell with a cry of anguish.

"The gold! the gold!" he cried. "I would have died sooner than have been robbed of that. I have betrayed my trust."

The room swam round before his dizzied eyes, and darkness shadowed his senses, as he fainted from loss of blood.

As Nicolas sank senseless to the ground, the robber took the portmanteau in his hand, and lowered himself from the window with his precious load.

CHAPTER XXX.

CAST OFF

CLARA MELVILLE did not appeal in vain to the generous heart of Lolota Vizzini; the return of post brought her a letter from the Spanish dancer containing ample funds for her journey, and the warmest expressions of sympathy and regard. "Come to me, poor little Clara," she wrote, "come to me, who can pity, and believe your story; for I, too, have suffered from the baseness of men, calling themselves gentlemen, but wearing the false and tinselly polish of the world as the mask for every vice and cruelty. Come to me, Clara, and I will never again part with my protégée."

Lolota wrote very little of her interview with Clara's father; she merely said that she had seen Mr. Melville, and that his mind was now relieved from all anxiety. She instructed Clara as to how she was to return to London, and promised to meet her at the railway station.

But the heart of the ballet-dancer was almost broken. Reginald, that good and noble Reginald, whose friendship had been so bright an oasis in the weary desert of her life, was lost to her for ever. And worse than lost, for he thought her base and unworthy, and he would henceforth remember her name with scornful loathing.

He thought her the mistress of the man whom she abhorred.

Her heart sank with a deadly sickness at the hateful thought. The good farmer's wife soon discovered that some deep and bitter grief was preying on the mind of her English visitor. By a thousand little tender attentions she showed a sympathy so unobtrusive and sincere, that, in spite of herself, Clara took comfort from the Frenchwoman's goodness.

"She, at least, does not mistake me for the guilty wretch that Reginald believes me to be. Her woman's instinct would revolt from me, were I indeed so base a creature. Heaven will not long suffer me to be so wronged. Sooner or later Reginald will learn the truth."

That firm faith and those fixed religious principles which had sustained the unhappy girl through her past trials supported her in this new affliction. When the first bitterness of her grief was over, she learned once more to place her trust in Providence and patiently await the issue.

But a new and even harder trial was yet in store for her.

She bade adieu to her kind Norman friends, the farmer's wife weeping to lose the stranger on whom her hospitality had been so freely bestowed. Lolota's generosity enabled Clara to offer her friends presents which compensated them for all they had bestowed on her, though it was with great difficulty that the ballet-dancer could prevail upon them to accept anything but her affection in return for their goodness.

Fifteen hours' travelling brought Clara to her destination. Lolota was waiting on the platform as the train entered the station, and Clara was once more in the arms of her truest friend.

"Dearest Madame Vizzini!" she exclaimed, as soon as she and Lolota were seated in the Spanish dancer's luxurious brougham, "how kind you have been!"

"No kinder than I will always be, Clara," answered Lolota, laying the girl's fair head upon her shoulder, and fondly smoothing the soft clusters of pale auburn hair—"not kinder than I will be while life is left to me," she added, sadly. "My poor little girl! how much you must have suffered through these weary trials! What a pale face you have brought back to England! But we will soon restore you."

"Dear madame, you are too good to me," replied the young girl, embracing her protectress.

The brougham crossed London Bridge, and drove slowly through the crowded City. Clara had been too absorbed by her friend's welcome to notice the direction in which Lolota's coachman was driving; but by-and-by, glancing through the front windows of the vehicle, she observed with surprise that they were going westward.

"Your coachman is driving to Arlington Street, dear Madame Vizzini," she said; "will you add one more kindness to all that I owe you, and drive me home? Or if you are anxious to return to Piccadilly, will you let me take a cab? My first duty is to fly to my poor father."

There was a sorrowful accent in Lolota's voice as she replied to this request—

"I know, dear Clara," she said, "how anxious you must be to see your father; but remember that I love you as dearly as ever he can. Grant me the happiness of having you with me to-day, and to-morrow——"

"No, no, my best friend," interrupted Clara; "you would not ask this if you knew my father. His life has been one of suffering. Sorrows, which to me have been dark and mysterious secrets, have embittered his days, and the only poor consolation he can have is in the affection of his children. Pray, pray, let us drive there at once."

Her hand was on the check-string as she spoke, but Lolota arrested her by a rapid gesture, and encircling the ballet-girl's slender form with her arms, drew her to her bosom.

"My Clara, my poor, poor girl!" she said, tenderly, "you must not go to your father to-day."

"Oh, Heaven!" cried Clara; "something has happened to him!"

"No. I left him an hour ago in perfect health."

"And yet I must not go to him?"

"No, Clara," answered Lolota, firmly; "you must not go to those who disbelieve and misjudge you, while you have friends who can trust in you, even against all conflicting evidence."

"What!" cried Clara, in accents of despair; "can my father misjudge me?"

"He does, Clara."

"He thinks me guilty?"

"Unhappily, my poor child, he does."

Clara buried her face in her clasped hands, and abandoned herself to a tempest of grief.

"I could have endured all but this," she sobbed; "the contempt of the world—the scorn even of one who had loved me, but not this. Oh, Heaven! why am I afflicted past my powers of endurance?"

"Patience, Clara, patience. All this is but for a little time. The truth must triumph in the end."

"But let me go to my father," cried the ballet-girl; "let me go to him and fall on my knees at his feet. He cannot disbelieve me then. He cannot look on me and think me guilty."

"You shall see him to-morrow, Clara," answered her friend. "You are too much broken down by fatigue and agitation to endure the interview to-day. To-morrow you will be calmer, and will be able to plead your cause more coherently."

It was only by this last inducement that Madame Vizzini prevailed upon Clara to accompany her to Arlington Street, and to defer the interview with her father till the following day.

All that the tenderest sympathy could effect —all that a sister's love could imagine, was done by the Spanish dancer to soothe the wounded spirit of the weary traveller. Lying on a sofa in the shady drawing-room, surrounded with luxury and comfort, Clara told her story to her friend and benefactress.

Lolóta listened in perfect silence till the mention of Colonel Bertrand's name, and the mysterious intervention which had saved Clara from a fate far worse than death.

"Strange and superhuman being!" exclaimed Madame Vizzini. "That man exercises an influence that no living creature can either fathom or resist. Whence comes this sinister and invincible power?"

"I only know that he appeared at a moment when I thought myself far removed from all human aid," answered Clara, "and that but for him I should not now be in safety."

"But can you remember nothing of what he said after his appearance?" asked Lolota.

"Nothing. The surprise, the shock of my rescue, was more powerful even than the anguish that had gone before; I must have fainted immediately. I remember nothing until I awoke and found myself alone with a peasant girl who was one of the domestics belonging to the chateau."

Clara did not hesitate even to confide to the Spanish dancer the history of her meeting with Reginald Falkner. Lolota was deeply grieved to hear of the young man's cruel suspicions.

"There has been some fatal treachery at work in all this, Clara," said Madame Vizzini; "there have been letters written in your name —vile forgeries, in which you are made to appear the falsest and most heartless of women. One of the counterfeit letters was shown to me by your father, and it is on evidence such as this that even a parent has condemned you."

"Oh, Heaven," cried Clara, "this is too cruel."

"Do not fear, my poor child. The day will come when this base treachery shall be exposed to the contempt and loathing of the world. I, too, have suffered from the plots of the base and designing; yet I do not fear. I had long perceived Mr. Falkner's attachment to you, and I had hoped to see you elevated to a superior position, and far removed from all the dangers that surround the ballet-dancer.'

"It was too bright a hope!" murmured Clara, sadly.

Early the next morning Lolota Vizzini ordered the carriage to be in attendance for Clara Melville.'

"You shall go alone, Clara," she said; "my presence can do no good, and you will best plead your own cause. A father's grief, a father's love, and a father's anger, are alike sacred. The presence of a stranger would but be an intrusion. Go alone; tell your story as simply as you have told it to me, and the most incredulous could scarcely fail to believe you. Trust only to the eloquence of truth and sorrow."

Clara embraced her friend, and hurried down to the carriage. The ballet-dancer was looking careworn and haggard. Purple circles surrounded her soft blue eyes, and not a tinge of colour illumined her pale cheeks, but still there was a light of hope in her face.

"My father cannot refuse to believe me," she murmured.

The way seemed to her long and tiresome in her anxiety to be at her father's feet. Every obstacle annoyed her, and she thought that Madame Vizzini's coachman had never before driven so slowly.

At last, however, they reached the Kennington Road; the carriage drew up at the well-known house, and Madame Vizzini's page ran up the garden-walk and sounded a long and resounding peal upon the knocker.

Clara looked eagerly up at the windows of her old apartments. She fully expected to see her little brother and sister looking at the carriage which had stopped before their door; but she was disappointed. No fair and curly heads appeared at the open casements; no merry voices sounded in the familiar rooms.

"Little George and Jessie must have gone for their morning's walk," she said. "Perhaps it is better so, I shall see my father alone."

She sprang from the carriage and hurried to the door, which had just been opened by the mistress of the house.

"Oh, Miss Clara," she said, "you are too late to catch your Papa before his journey."

"His journey!" cried Clara. "What journey?"

"Why," said the woman, "didn't you know, Miss, that your Papa and your little brother and sister were to start this morning for the country?"

"No, no!"

"Well, it was rather sudden certainly, Miss. Your Pa only made up his mind last night, after that handsome Spanish lady had been here. He calls me up stairs, and I thinks what was up directly I sees my rent for a fortnight laid out upon the table. 'Mrs. Morris,' says your Pa, 'my little ones want change of air, and so I've made up my mind to take them for a trip in the country; so when my eldest daughter comes here you must tell her that we have gone away, and give her a letter I will leave with you. In the meantime, as my movements are very uncertain, it will be best for you to dispose of your lodgings to the best advantage.' You know your Pa's quite the gentleman, Miss, and I was that sorry to lose him and the dear children, that as soon as the cab drove off to the railway station this morning, I laid my head on the kitchen table and had a good cry; but, Lor' a mercy, how pale you have turned, Miss!"

Clara had, indeed, grown as white as death. This intelligence seemed a death-blow to all hope.

"The letter!" she exclaimed. "For pity's sake, Mrs. Morris, the letter!"

"Your Pa's letter. Lor', yes, to be sure, Miss. I left it on the kitchen dresser; but pray don't take on so! You look so flustered and frightened like. Your Pa's only gone away for change of hair. The front parlour's gone to Greenwich for the day, so just step in, Miss

Clara, and sit on the sofa while I fetch your Pa's letter."

The unhappy girl complied. She tottered to a seat, the room swimming before her eyes, and her brain bewildered by the mental shock she had received.

She had but one thought—her father's letter and the tidings which it might contain.

She took it from Mrs. Morris with an eager but a trembling hand.

It ran thus :—

"I have been throughout a troubled life the victim of treachery and falsehood: falsehood from those of my kindred, to whom I should have looked for truth; I ought not, therefore, to have been surprised at the treachery of my child. Yet, so weak are we at the best, that I will freely confess to you that your conduct has been a bitter blow to me. I go far away, in order that I may learn to forget that I ever had a daughter. Enclosed you will find the evidence of your guilt, against which even a father's trust in his child's truth could not survive."

The enclosure was an open letter, written in a hand so closely resembling her own that the bewildered girl gazed at it in amazement.

"I must be dreaming," she said, "for surely this is my own writing."

The forged letter was worded thus :—

"Dearest: I will grant your request, and fly with you to that luxurious bower in the solitudes of Normandy, which you so eloquently describe. You are right; I am weary of this dull, monotonous life; I am weary of working for my father, and brother, and sister. I sigh for splendour, for carriages, and diamonds—gorgeous dresses and a princely home, and to obtain these I will become all that you desire. Yours till death, Clara."

"Merciful Heaven!" cried Clara; "can such treachery exist, and yet go unpunished?"

Scarcely knowing what she did, she placed the two letters in a little pocket-book which she always carried, and which contained the few brief but treasured notes addressed to her by Reginald Falkner. Her old landlady, Mrs. Morris, was alarmed by her lodger's pale face and agitated looks.

"Come, bear up, Miss Clara," she said, soothingly; "no bad news from your Pa, I hope?"

"No, no," murmured Clara. "Tell me, Mrs. Morris, where have they gone?"

"Your Pa did not say, Miss."

"What! he gave you no address—no direction where to send his letters?"

"No, Miss; he only said he was going somewhere in the North."

Somewhere in the North! Clara's heart sank within her. She felt herself, indeed, abandoned. Had it not been for Lolota Vizzini she would have been without a friend on earth.

She had left the house, and returning to the

carriage, flung herself back upon the cushions, and abandoned herself to gloomy thoughts, as the vehicle returned to Arlington Street. Lolota received her with open arms.

"Cheer up, Clara," she said, "the storm is but a brief one; the sunshine will burst forth in redoubled splendour. Remember, I, too, have passed through the tempest. Give me that vile forgery, Clara; it shall be my task to bring the shame he deserves upon its base author."

Lolota opened a cabinet, and placed the letter in a secret drawer.

In an early issue of the *Times* newspaper appeared the following advertisement:—

"C. M. implores her beloved father to communicate with her. The evidence produced against her is false, and she has been the victim of the treachery of others."

In vain Clara watched and waited for a reply to this advertisement. Days, weeks, months passed, and none came. Lolota Vizzini was compelled to leave England to fulfil her Parisian engagements; for in the brilliant capital of France the lovely Spanish dancer was as much admired as in England; and Clara Melville felt that she would be indeed alone.

———

CHAPTER XXXI.

THE WINDING WAYS OF LIFE

LOLOTA VIZZINI did not forget her protégée. Before leaving England, she wrote to the Manager of a minor theatre on the Surrey side of the Thames, requesting him to wait upon her in Arlington Street.

The worthy Manager, who had begun life as a jockey, and who had picked up a small fortune, among such crooked in-and-outs of London life that few were able to trace the winding ways of his career, was only too happy to respond to the summons of the fashionable dancer. To have secured Lolota's services for one night only at the Royal Paragon Theatre would have been to ensure a house crowded to the ceiling, and to put three or four hundred pounds into the pocket of Mr. Rupert de Lancy.

The Manager's cab dashed up to the door in Arlington Street at the hour appointed, and Mr. de Lancy, flinging the reins to his tiger, sprang from the vehicle, and hurried into the drawing-room where Lolota and her protégée awaited him.

Rupert de Lancy was rather a handsome man of about five and forty years of age. Tall and slender, with good teeth and dark hair, he retained the appearance of youth after a life of dissipation. He was dressed in the height of the fashion, and decorated with jewellery, which said more for his wealth than his good taste.

Lolota was reclining in an easy chair by the fire, with her tiny slippered feet resting on the low bronze and ormolu fender. She wore a loose morning robe of rose-coloured silk, and a black lace veil floated round her superb coils of glistening raven hair.

Clara was seated in the window, simply dressed in black, with her soft auburn hair clustered round her delicate face.

Mr. Rupert de Lancy opened his eyes to their widest extent as he glanced at the two ladies. So much beauty had never yet adorned the Royal Paragon Theatre.

"My dear Madame Vizzini," he said, as Lolota motioned him to a seat opposite her own, "your letter has filled me with delight. Dare I hope that you have at last relented, and that, if but for one night only, you have determined on allowing the audience on the other side of the Thames to behold and admire the Star of the Ballet?"

"You are very good, Mr. de Lancy," said Lolota, smiling; "but I have no intention of changing my mind just at present as to the Royal Paragon Theatre; anxious as I should be to oblige its manager. I start for Paris next week. My object in asking you to be so kind as to call on me had reference to a friend."

"A friend. Oh, indeed!"

Mr. Rupert de Lancy's face fell at this intelligence. He had been summoned from an important rehearsal to gratify some absurd whim of the Spanish dancer's. She was, however, far too distinguished a person to offend, so the Manager smoothed his face, and said, with his sweetest smile—

"Pray, may I ask you who this friend is?"

Lolota laughed.

"Come here, my dear Clara," she said. "Let me introduce you to Mr. Rupert de Lancy, the most courteous and liberal of managers. I want him to engage you as columbine for the pantomime he is about to produce at Christmas."

Mr. de Lancy looked admiringly at Clara's blushing and downcast face.

"Columbine!" he said, gravely—"that's a serious matter. Had it been for the ballet the young lady's appearance would have been enough to secure her an immediate engagement."

"The ballet!" exclaimed Lolota, looking the Manager full in the face. "I believe at the Paragon Theatre you give your ballet-dancers twelve shillings a week? You hear, Clara— with a pretty face and a good figure—with a considerable knowledge of dancing—you may earn twelve shillings a week. Ah, Mr. Rupert de Lancy!" continued the lovely Spaniard, her face flushing with generous indignation, "it is these small and pitiful salaries that drive the ballet-girl to become that which on first entering the profession she little dreamed of ever being. Bad men offer their jewels and wealth to girls who perhaps are almost starving; and the virtuous world, riding by in their carriages, wonders that the ballet-girl falls."

Mr. Rupert de Lancy grew very red in the face. He knew that this was true. He knew that while he was making a superb fortune out of the Paragon Theatre, his salaries were cut down to the furthest limit; and this, in the face of the bright example of other managers, whose liberality made them beloved by the lowest servant in their theatre.

"But do not let us talk of these things," said Lolota; "let us rather hope to see them some day reformed. Miss Melville is an excellent dancer. I believe you would as soon take my word for that as the word of any one—but the ballet-master at Her Majesty's will tell you the same. She only asks five guineas a week, as her name is not yet known to the public. Tell me, then, Mr. de Lancy, is it a bargain?"

"Five pounds a week!" murmured the Manager.

"You would have to give anybody else seven or eight," answered Lolota.

"But the young lady is a novice."

"But I assure you she is a better dancer than many of the most experienced."

"I can refuse you nothing, Madame Vizzini," said the Manager, in his most insinuating tone; "Miss Melville may consider herself engaged. If she will call on me to-morrow at the Paragon, I will draw up our agreement." ·

"I shall leave you some of my handsomest stage-dresses," said Lolota, when she and Clara were alone, "and you can occupy this house while I am away. Benson, my housekeeper, will remain in England, and will take good care of my little protégée."

Clara felt herself at first strangely alone in the crowded Green Room of the Paragon Theatre. It was early in December, and the pantomime was not to be produced until the twenty-sixth of the month; but Clara went every day to the long and fatiguing rehearsals necessary to ensure the perfection of the forth-coming performance.

She found the members of the company kind and friendly towards her, and in a little time she grew to prefer the minor theatre to the opera house, in which the great Italian singers held themselves aloof from the humbler ballet-girls.

The leading tragedian of the Paragon Theatre was a Mr. Antony Verner, that very Antony Verner whom we met by the death-bed of his uncle. The young man, cut off by poverty from entering any other profession, had chosen to devote himself to the stage, for which an unfailing instinct told him that he had talent. Gifted with an excellent appearance, a rich, deep voice, and an intellect capable of appreciating the varied phases of every character he attempted to perform, Antony Verner could scarcely fail to succeed. He did succeed; but the theatrical profession is a jealous one; he had yet much to achieve, and he was glad to hold a leading position in the Paragon Theatre, awaiting that lucky hour when the flood-tide of fortune should drift him to West-end celebrity.

Clara met him several times in the Green Room. She had not been introduced to him, but she could not help observing that, every time they met, his attention seemed attracted to her as if against his own will. There was nothing impertinent in his gaze, but there was an anxiety, a curiosity, which the young girl could not understand.

One morning, however, Mr. Antony Verner entered the Green Room with Mr. de Lancy, and the Manager, walking straight up to Clara, said to her with a facetious smile—

"Here is a gentleman who is very anxious to be introduced to you, Miss Melville. Pray take pity on him, for I assure you the impression you have made upon his susceptible heart is something terrible."

Clara bowed, Mr. de Lancy strolled out of the Green Room humming a popular air, and the dancer was left alone with Antony Verner. They talked for some little time on general topics, then, after a brief pause, the tragedian said—

"You would never guess, Miss Melville, my strongest reason for wishing to be introduced to you."

"No, indeed," replied Clara.

"It is on account of a likeness———"

"A likeness?"

"Yes, a marvellous likeness which you bear to a picture in my possession."

"Indeed," answered Clara, carelessly, "that is singular; but these accidental likenesses are so common. You often see strangers who more closely resemble each other than the nearest relatives."

"True. Yet something tells me that this likeness is not accidental. I fear you must have often thought me impertinent, but, from the first moment of seeing you, I have never been able to withdraw my eyes from your face. I will bring the picture to-morrow morning and you shall judge for yourself."

NICOLAS FINDS THE GOLD CONCEALED BY ANTONIO VECCHI

"Pray do so," said Clara, smiling, "and perhaps when you see me and the picture side by side, this marvellous likeness will disappear."

"I do not think so," answered Mr. Verner.

Clara attached very little importance to this alleged likeness; indeed, she had nearly forgotten all about it the next day when the tragedian met her in the Green Room.

"By Heaven!" he said, as she advanced to shake hands with him, "it is positively wonderful!"

He took a small case from his pocket—a dark red morocco case, ornamented with massive silver clasps, and with a coat of arms engraved upon a shield of the same metal.

This case contained a miniature set round with large pearls—the miniature of a young man in the dress of thirty years ago.

It was the likeness of Jasper Melville.

No. 9. [*Weekly, One Penny.*]

The colour faded from Clara's check as she looked at the picture.

"You are agitated," said Antony Verner; "the face is known to you."

"It is indeed," answered Clara; "this is a portrait of my father."

"What!" exclaimed the young man; "is it possible that you are the daughter of Arthur Beaumorris?"

"Arthur Beaumorris?"

"Yes," answered Mr. Verner. "This is the portrait of one of the two nephews of my late uncle's old master—the youngest of the two Beaumorrises."

"And the brother of Sir Frederick?"

"Yes, the younger brother of Sir Frederick."

"Good heavens!" cried Clara, "what can this mean? There is not a line in this face, which—allowing for the lapse of time—does not reproduce the same line in the face of my father; and yet he is poor and obscure, and his name is Jasper Melville."

"And you never heard that that was an assumed name?"

"Never."

"Miss Melville," said Antony Verner, solemnly, "there is some mystery in all this. I know that my uncle, who died only a year and a half ago, was involved in dark secrets—secrets, perhaps, which closely concern Sir Frederick Beaumorris. On his death-bed he would fain have revealed some guilty mystery, but the icy hand of the King of Terrors arrested the words of penitence even as they hung trembling on his lips. But, never fear, Miss Melville, if these secrets should indeed concern you, as I am half inclined to believe they do, my happiness, too, is involved in seeing the wrong made right, and the task of my life shall be to accomplish that end."

"My poor father!" murmured Clara; "I know that his life has been an unhappy one. Some unknown sorrows have darkened and embittered his days. Oh, Mr. Verner, if it should indeed be your lot to restore him to happiness, the gratitude of a life shall be yours."

The young man shook his head sadly.

"I might ask too much," he said, fixing his dark grey eyes upon Clara's blushing face.

"Alas!" she thought, "noble and generous as this young man may be, earth holds for me but one, and he despises and abhors me."

*   *   *   *   *

The last rehearsal of the pantomime took place on Christmas-eve. A few friends of Mr. de Lancy's were admitted to the private boxes of the theatre to see the gorgeous scenery and well-arranged dances—both arrived at perfection. Clara, dressed in a graceful dishabille, looked almost as lovely as in the more brilliant dress which she was to assume on the first night of the pantomime being performed. A little lace handkerchief, knotted loosely under her chin, shrouded her braided auburn hair; she wore floating skirts of purple-white muslin, and her little feet glistened in their snowy satin shoes. Even Mr. de Lancy could not help admiring her.

"I might have done worse," he whispered to his stage manager, the confidant of all his schemes. "She's very pretty, a first-class dancer, and I get her cheap into the bargain."

Every now and then, when Clara executed some difficult and brilliant step, the few spectators assembled in the boxes rewarded her by a burst of applause.

"The Vizzini has taught her," murmured Mr. de Lancy. "I could swear to the Spanish woman's style."

The important night of the twenty-sixth of December came at last—a night which in the London theatres is one of confusion and agitation. Scene-shifters hurrying hither and thither; managers, stage managers, prompters, carpenters, and property-men, running over each other, and tumbling against each other in every direction. Ballet-girls nervous and anxious; crying and lamenting over shoes that will not fit, petticoats that have not come from the hands of the laundress, and wreaths that are not becoming. Everybody flurried and ill-tempered, and all absorbed in one thought—the success of the evening's performance.

The Columbine, as the reader is of course fully aware, does not appear until the first part of the pantomime is over, and the enchanted wand of the Fairy Queen transforms the heroine of the opening scenes into a radiant and sparkling dancer.

The wand was waved; the merry strain of music commenced, and Clara Melville bounded on to the stage. Her dress was one floating cloud of azure and silver—like the moon in the blue depths of a cloudless summer sky. From her wreath of forget-me-nots dropped a rain of the same silvery fringes, as if the flowers had been gathered wet from under a hedgerow, and were still glistening with diamond spray.

Thunders of applause hailed her brief opening dance. She advanced to the front of the stage, and for the first time ventured to cast a glance round the crowded house.

Merry children with bright and joyous faces were assembled in the boxes; happy tradespeople, dressed in their best, filled the crowded benches in the pit; stalwart mechanics, in tier after tier, looked down from the immense and noisy gallery. All was noise, bustle, and confusion; but all, too, was good-temper, and hearty, simple-minded enjoyment. It was altogether a pleasant sight to see; and the austere teachers, who cavil at the harmless amusements afforded by a well-conducted theatre, might have learned a lesson that night. Husbands were there, surrounded by their wives and children; brothers with their sisters. Surely, this was better than the gin-palace!

But Clara had no time to think of these things; at the first glance the crowded house swam before her eyes, and the lights blinded and dazzled her. In a box close to the stage were assembled a party of elegantly-dressed people; a young man and a young girl were seated opposite to each other in the front of the box.

The young man was Reginald Falkner. A deathly sickness overcame the ballet-dancer; she felt the lights grow dim before her eyes; she felt her limbs powerless to sustain her, and in another moment she had fainted in the harlequin's arms. They had carrried her off the stage, and the prompter hastened to fetch vinegar and cold water.

A murmur of sympathy ran through the house, and the clown, a good-natured fellow, contrived to amuse the audience, and keep them in good temper. But the polished Mr. de Lancy dropped the mask. He had been hidden in a corner of his box, and had witnessed the whole scene. He rushed through a side door communicating with the prompt entrance, and at once attacked poor Clara.

"Upon my word, Miss Melville," he said, "this is pretty conduct; fainting on the very first night of my pantomime! Pray, do you know, Miss, what this pantomime has cost me to produce? and do you think I am going to have my business spoiled by such airs and graces as these? I suppose you thought the audience would be fascinated by this sort of thing, but I can tell you we don't like such affectation on this side of the water."

Clara, who had by this time, thanks to the friendly help of those around her, entirely recovered, looked at Mr. de Lancy with a glance of chilling contempt.

"Any loss you may sustain in my absence from your stage for the last five minutes can be deducted from my salary, Mr. de Lancy," she said; then, as the music for her next dance struck up, she once more bounded on to the stage.

She was received by an outburst of applause. The sympathies of the rough but honest natures composing the gallery audience had been enlisted by the fainting girl, and the horny hands of labour were raised to welcome her back to the stage which her beauty and her grace adorned.

"Curse them!" murmured Mr. de Lancy as he returned to his box; "there's no knowing where to have them. The artful minx will be wanting her salary raised after this."

Once more Clara beheld Reginald Falkner—he whom she had last seen in the lonely moonlit square of Caen. But her womanly pride, and the remembrance of his cruel words, armed her to sustain the agitation of the meeting. She whirled round in the rapid and sparkling waltz, and smiled gaily on her delighted audience, even though the dance took her close to the box in which Reginald Falkner was seated.

How much will a woman endure when sustained by love!

How much more when armed with pride!

CHAPTER XXXII.

THE TWO DETECTIVES

LET us retrace our steps once more in order to relate the incidents which followed the robbery at the sham hotel.

The Prince slept soundly after his long and fatiguing journey. The luxurious bed-chamber which had been prepared for him was situated at the back of the house. No sound broke the stillness of the room; the windows were shrouded by thick velvet curtains; the heavy four-post bedstead was surrounded by the same hangings, which had been drawn closely round the Prince's couch after he had retired to rest by the careful hands of the faithful Nicolas. Thoroughly wearied, the Prince lay in a profound and dreamless slumber, from which he awoke to find the morning sunlight peeping in through a narrow crevice in the heavy window-shutters. Care had been taken to keep every gleam of light out of the Prince's chamber, but this one crevice had escaped even the vigilant glances of the members of the Black Band.

The Prince pushed aside the heavy curtains at the head of the bed, and lay for some time lazily watching this one gleam of light illuminating the darkness of the apartment.

He listened for the footfall of a passing servant on the staircase without, but all was silent.

"I must have awoke very early," he thought, "and yet I feel as if I had overslept myself."

The Prince had that dull, heavy sensation which one always experiences after having slept longer than usual.

After lying for half an hour, still listening for some sound to bespeak the household being astir, the Prince buried his head in the pillows and endeavoured to fall asleep once more.

But the effort was vain; he was restless and wakeful, and at last growing impatient, he rang the bell at the head of his bed.

"They must be a lazy set of people in this house," he said to himself; "I am convinced that it is getting late. However, be it as it may, Nicolas is sure to answer my summons."

But for once the Prince was mistaken. The valet did not respond to the bell. The Prince rang again, but still no answer. Again, and with the same result.

"All the bells in the house must be broken," he muttered; "or perhaps, after all, I have awoke at early morning. I will open the shutter myself and see how late it is."

The Prince rose, and going to one of the windows, endeavoured to open the shutter, but he found the task more difficult than he had imagined. The bolts were heavy, and the fastening of the shutters peculiar and complicated; but the Italian nobleman was renowned for his energy and determination, and he was not to be foiled by a few iron bars. With a powerful effort he drew back the last and heaviest of the bolts, and flinging open the shutter, admitted a broad glare of sunlight into the apartment.

His first action was to look for his watch; he had placed it under his pillow on retiring to rest. The reader need scarcely be told that he looked in vain. His purse, some valuable rings, and a set of studs composed of single diamonds, worth some dukedoms, had disappeared from the dressing-table upon which he had left them.

"Merciful Virgin!" exclaimed the Prince; "I must be in a den of thieves."

For a moment he paused, gazing around him, utterly bewildered. Then the thought of the specie with which he had been charged flashed suddenly upon him.

"The money!" he cried. "Not mine, but a sacred charge, entrusted to me by my countrymen. What if that, too, is lost?"

The very thought rendered the passionate and high-souled Italian almost frantic. He flung open the door of his apartment, and rushed to the floor above, upon which he knew his valet slept.

But he knew not in which chamber to seek for Nicolas. He threw open the doors of several apartments, only to find them empty, the furniture undisturbed, and everything appearing as if no creature had ever occupied the chambers.

At last the Prince entered the room in which Nicolas had slept. This room, like the others, was empty.

The chamber, we repeat, was empty; but a pool of blood upon the floor revealed the desperate nature of the struggle which had taken place. The overcoat and hat worn by Nicolas, and the luggage belonging to the valet, convinced the young Italian that he was indeed in his servant's apartment, but the portmanteau was gone.

"Good heavens!" exclaimed the Prince, "this is too horrible. Nicolas has been murdered, and the money stolen. Are these English, then, nothing but thieves and assassins —these English, whom I have been taught to think so honourable?"

There was, however, no time for reflection. The Italian possessed the courage of a lion. He rushed from room to room, seeking for the occupants of this den of iniquity—but he sought in vain. Every apartment in the house was empty. No trace of occupation was to be seen in any corner of the mansion.

"What is to be done?" exclaimed the Prince. "A robbery and an assault, perhaps a murder, has been committed. My faithful Nicolas has been carried away, I know not where, and I, a stranger in a foreign land, feel myself utterly powerless."

The suddenness of the calamity had bewildered and stunned the Prince; but he was not one to succumb beneath even such a blow as this. He seated himself in the deserted dining-room, and endeavoured to collect his thoughts.

"The Neapolitan Consul!" he exclaimed; "I have letters for him, and he will of course assist me in this mysterious affair."

But on examining his packets the Prince found that his papers also had been stolen. He had no means of even establishing his identity. A stranger in London, unable to speak the language, penniless, and without credentials; was he not most likely to be mistaken for one of those disreputable adventurers whose names every day figure in the English newspapers, linked to some act of audacious swindling?

Fortunately for the Prince, he happened to remember the address of the Consul.

"He is a distinguished member of the Society of Good Cousins," he thought; "and there are signs by which the initiated recognise each other, and which no impostor can use. He will know by those that I really am what I represent myself."

The young Italian further reflected that the return of the post would bring him fresh supplies and new credentials from Naples; but this post would take long to go and return.

He left the house; but before he descended the steps before the door, he took care to closely observe the exterior of the sham hotel.

It was not numbered, and it resembled all the other houses in the street. With one or two exceptions, every window was furnished with green Venetian blinds, and a peculiarly-shaped lamp ornamented the fanlight over the door.

"I shall remember the house by that lamp and by the green blinds," he thought; and then, hurrying down the steps, he walked onwards in the direction of a cab-stand, which he perceived at the corner of an adjoining street.

As the Prince left the street in which the sham hotel was situated, two men emerged from a small public-house at a corner—a public-house used by the servants of gentlemen resident in the neighbourhood. The two men crossed the street, and, ascending the steps leading to the door of the house the Prince had just left, admitted themselves by means of a latch-key. These two men were members of that infamous association of which Colonel Oscar Bertrand was the guilty chief.

The merciless robbers had overlooked a little loose silver in the waistcoat-pocket of their victim. This happy accident enabled the Italian to hire a cab.

He directed the driver to proceed at his fullest speed to 14, Portland Place, the house of Signor Marelli, the Neapolitan Consul. In half an hour he found himself seated in the Consul's library, relating to his countryman the misfortunes that had befallen him the previous night.

Fortunately for the Prince, Signor Marelli remembered his father, and perceived at once the strong likeness which the young man bore to the last scion of his noble line.

"My heart warms to your Excellency," said the Consul; "your father was one of my best friends; and even had we not been united by the sacred bonds of the Society of Good Cousins, we should have been drawn together, perhaps, by a still stronger link—the memory of the past."

"You are too good, Signor Marelli," murmured the Prince.

"Your noble father was good to me when I was an obscure clerk in the house of a Neapolitan banker," replied the Consul; "but let us think of more important matters; your money must be recovered."

"Alas!" exclaimed the Prince; "I fear that it is hopeless to think of such a thing."

"Nothing is hopeless to the detective police of London," replied Signor Marelli. "I have already despatched my servant for Inspector Martin and his colleague, Sergeant Boulder. I know these men to be two of the cleverest detectives in London. They scent crime as the thorough-bred hound scents a fox. What is as dark as midnight to us may be as clear as dawn to them. Without them we cannot stir a step; with them we may do anything."

As the Consul uttered these words, the two men were announced.

"Show them in immediately," said Signor Marelli; "I may keep a Duke waiting, but the time of Inspector Martin is too valuable to be trifled with."

The two men entered the room, and, bowing respectfully to the Consul, dropped into the chairs offered to them without taking the least notice of the Prince. They were unlike in every particular, except in the one respect of a certain grave and reflective look in the face of each, utterly different to any expression ever seen in the countenances of other men.

To the eye of the initiated, "Detective" was written in unmistakable characters in the thoughtful lines about their mouths, and in the wrinkles clustered round their eyes.

Inspector Martin was a short wizen little man, whose insignificant appearance was of the greatest use to him in his professional capacity. He was a man who might pass unnoticed anywhere, by reason of that very insignificance of appearance.

Sergeant Boulder, on the contrary, was tall and stalwart, broad-shouldered and strong-limbed. He had come off victorious in many a personal encounter with some of the most powerful ruffians that had ever picked oakum in Coldbath Fields or ornamented the hulks by their presence. Heaven help the delinquent who fell into the grasp of Joseph Boulder! He was known to his colleagues as the Lion of the Detective Force.

Signor Marelli slowly and deliberately related the whole circumstances of the robbery, and the disappearance of the valet.

The two detectives listened in perfect silence, Inspector Martin rubbing his chin, and looking at the ground, as if only interested in the pattern of the Consul's carpet, while Sergeant Boulder sat with his hands on his knees, staring vacantly at the geraniums in the balcony outside the open window.

The Prince looked at the two men with a feeling of disappointment.

"If these are Signor Marelli's boasted English police," he thought, "I don't think much of them."

When the Consul had finished the relation of the robbery, there was a considerable pause, during which neither of the detectives uttered a word. The Prince fidgeted in his chair, scarcely able to conceal his impatience, but Signor Marelli quietly waited the pleasure of the two colleagues. Presently, without lifting his eyes from the carpet, Inspector Martin said, slowly—

"This has been done by a gang."

"A gang of twenty or more," added Sergeant Boulder.

"And a rich gang—a gang that has plenty of money to carry out its schemes," continued the Inspector.

"It's been done by an organised company—as well organised as even our Force is," said the Sergeant.

THE MEETING AT THE PARAGON THEATRE

"And do you think there is any chance of discovering the guilty parties?" asked Signor Marelli.

"I don't know," muttered the Inspector, thoughtfully; "if it is to be done, me and my comrade will do it. But we've been baffled many times already in some of the greatest robberies that have ever been perpetrated in London, and it's my belief there's a company so organised as to defy detection."

"But if ever we do come across any of the lot," said the Sergeant, involuntarily clenching his fists, "it'll be worse for 'em, that's all."

"Anyhow, we'd better lose no time," added the Inspector; "call a cab, Sergeant, and the Prince will take us to the house in which he was robbed."

"As my friend cannot speak English, I had better accompany you," said Signor Marelli. "We shall easily recognise the house by the green blinds and the peculiar shape of the lamp."

The two detectives looked at each other and laughed.

"I wouldn't count too much upon that, Sir, if I were you," said the Inspector; "I shouldn't wonder if we find the blinds yellow, and a turnip hanging up instead of this here peculiar lamp."

A cab was called, and the Consul, the Prince, and the two detectives drove off to the street in which the sham hotel was situated.

The Prince, the detectives, and the Consul examined every house in the street; but they could find neither the green blinds nor the lamp. The Prince was in despair.

"This was the house, I am convinced," he said, pointing out a door to the Consul; "it had no number, but it was between numbers sixteen and eighteen."

There was no lamp behind the fanlight, nor were there any green blinds in the windows of this house.

Upon a bright brass plate in the centre panel of the door was engraved MR. T. HOBSON.

"You must be mistaken, your Excellency," said Signor Marelli.

"No," exclaimed the Prince; "changed as the house is in outward appearance, I am convinced that it is here I slept last night."

Signor Marelli told the two detectives the Italian's conviction.

"I thought as much, Sir," said Inspector Martin, with a sardonic grin, "though the foreign gent was so precious knowing, with his green lamps and peculiar blinds. It ain't any lamps of that sort as will throw a light on this robbery, and if any one's blind and green, blest if I don't think it's the Mossoo."

"I'll tell you what, Sir," said Mr. Joseph Boulder, "me and my mate are pretty well knowed among these sort of customers; suppose you knock at the door, and ask for Mr. T. Hobson; though it strikes me very forcible you won't find the gent at home."

Signor Marelli declared his willingness to make himself useful, and the Prince and the two detectives having walked to the other end of the street, the Consul knocked at the door of the mysterious mansion.

His summons was answered by an elderly servant, dressed in a suit of respectable and faultless black. His grey hair and prim and orderly manner proclaimed him at once to be one of those faithful dependants, remnants of the old school, now so rarely to be met with.

He told Signor Marelli that Mr. Hobson had gone to the City that morning at ten o'clock.

"As he does every day of the year, Sir, except Sundays and holidays, as you must know, being a friend of his. But if you'd like to see my mistress, I'll take your name up."

"Mrs. Hobson is at home, then?" said the Consul.

"She is, Sir. Her health is not so good as it used to be, and she rarely stirs out now."

The Consul was thoroughly convinced by this time that the Prince had been mistaken.

"I will not trouble Mrs. Hobson," he said; "my visit is of no importance. I will call on Mr. Hobson to-morrow, and explain my reason for waiting on him."

The old butler bowed, and closed the door upon Signor Marelli—the Italian rejoined the Prince and the two detectives.

"Well, Sir?" said the Inspector, interrogatively.

The Consul described his interview with Mr. Hobson's butler.

"It's the biggest and best organised gang in London that's in this," said Sergeant Boulder, slapping his colleague's shoulder; "but if they succeed in throwing dust in our eyes we ought to be ashamed of ourselves. I feel that my honour as a detective officer is concerned in unearthing them, and by the Heaven above me I'll do it!"

"*We'll* do it, Joseph Boulder," said the little Inspector, with an air of wounded dignity; "we've worked together for years, and we aren't going to work single-handed in this. I'll tell you what you can tell your friend, Sir," added Mr. Martin, addressing himself to Signor Marelli; "you can tell him that before to-night we'll find his valet alive or dead, if his valet wasn't in this business. That's number one. For number two, you can tell him that if the valet isn't in it, the thieves got their information from Naples, and were ready to receive the Prince. Let him try and think of any one as is likely to have given that information; for that'll be a clue as will help us along; and now, gents both, good-day; me and my mate will lose no more time, but go at once to work."

The two detectives nodded with rather a patronising air to the Prince and the Consul, and walked off in different directions, without having exchanged a word. These men knew, by an unfailing instinct, the part each had to play.

"As to Nicolas," said the Prince, when Signor Marelli told him the detective's suspicions, "I would pledge my life upon his honour. There is little doubt that I have been betrayed by some one who knows the secrets of the Good Cousins; but who the traitor may have been I cannot imagine. Heaven help him if he be a member of the society."

Signor Marelli insisted on the Prince's taking up his abode in Portland Place during his stay in London.

"My old friend's son shall not be exposed to the chance attentions of an hotel in a country whose language he does not speak. Stay with me, your Excellency, and we shall hear from day to day of the proceedings of Martin and Boulder. I trust yet to their sagacity for tracking the robbers."

CHAPTER XXXIII.

THE MISSING GOLD

WHILE the two Italians were seated at dessert, the servant announced Mr. Joseph Boulder.

The worthy Sergeant was of course immediately admitted. He strode into the dining-room, and on being requested by Signor Marelli to help himself to wine, seated himself at the table and poured out a bumper of claret.

"None of your ports and sherries for me, Sir," he said, as he sipped his wine; "somethin' light and cool, that'll allow a man to keep his head clear for business. Very tidy St. Julien this!" he added, smacking his lips.

"You've brought us some news, I know, Mr. Boulder," said Signor Marelli.

"Well, not over much, Sir, I'm sorry to say, but something, anyhow. The Prince's valet is found!"

"Indeed!"

"Yes; he had been took in at St. George's Hospital. A respectable, benevolent-looking old gent, with white hair, had taken him in a cab, telling a long, pitiful story as how the Italian had stabbed himself owin' to jealousy, and he being a clergyman of the parish where the soicide lived, had brought him off immedi-

ate to the hospital. I know their dodges and their benevolent games. There was a chap as I got seven pennorth for only last week, Bill Simmons by name, as was celebrated among the swell mob for doin' the venerable old coves with white hair. He was as big a ruffian as ever walked, was Bill; but he looked the bishop or elderly nobleman what belongs to a missionary society and speaks at Exeter 'All to the very life; yes, and acted it too, did Bill."

The Prince was delighted at finding Nicolas. The valet had been brought up upon the young nobleman's estate, and the two men were bound by a link which rarely unites master and servant; they were foster brothers. The same black-eyed peasant woman had nursed them amidst the green hills of sunny Calabria; they had played beneath the same clustering vines, and seen their childish faces reflected in the clear waters of the same crystal fountain. The pure memories of innocent infancy united them by ties that the harsh experience of the world could not loosen.

Nicolas lay for upwards of a week at the hospital before it was considered safe to remove him; for, although his wound was not a serious one, he was considerably weakened by loss of blood.

He had been carried to the hospital in an insensible state, and remembered nothing from the moment of the robbery until he regained his consciousness under the treatment of the surgeon.

The warm-hearted fellow wept at the sight of his beloved master.

"The money!" he exclaimed, "the money you trusted me with, Eccelenza!—gone!—gone!"

"Think no more of that, my poor Nicolas," replied the Prince; "only get strong and well, and we may yet recover the money. Remember, I want your aid in the matter."

The valet clasped his master's hand, and kissed it passionately. The poor fellow was too much affected to utter a word.

In nine or ten days he was able to walk out of the hospital almost entirely restored to health and strength. His temperate life had rendered the wound a mere trifle. To a drunkard it might have been fatal. Would that the intemperate could only remember this one fact!

Signor Marelli accommodated the servant as he had done the master.

"I am an old bachelor," he said, laughing; "my house is a great deal too large for me. Bring your faithful Nicolas; he shall be well taken care of."

For the last ten days nothing had transpired

to reward the exertions of the two detectives. Inspector Martin had called two or three times in Portland Place, but only to confess the failure of all their endeavours. The stalwart Sergeant was too low-spirited to come at all.

Nicolas was a wretched man. He could not be made to think that he had been blameless in the affair of the robbery. He was firmly impressed with the idea that he was responsible for the money that had been entrusted to him.

"My honour!" he exclaimed, when his master endeavoured to console him; "I am but of humble parents, ignorant and poor, but my honour—it has never been tarnished until now."

The services which the Prince required of his valet were very trifling. After Nicolas had assisted his master to dress for dinner his duties were over until the Prince retired to rest. He might spend his evening as he pleased.

It was noticed by the servants of the Consul that Nicolas took good care to avail himself of this liberty. Every evening, as soon as ever the Prince's toilet was completed, the valet left the house, rarely returning until eleven o'clock.

"I am afraid he is very dissipated," said the housekeeper.

"It's a pity!" murmured the housemaid, "for he's very handsome. At any rate, he never comes home tipsy; so he doesn't go to public-houses."

One night, however, about a week after Nicolas had left the hospital, the housemaid had reason to change her opinion; for when she opened the area-gate to the valet, as the clocks were striking eleven, she noticed a great peculiarity in his manner.

The Italian's garments were strangely disordered; his hair fell in tumbled masses about his face, and his whole manner bespoke the bewilderment of a drunken man.

Although, on ordinary occasions, distinguished by the urbanity of his manners, on this particular evening Nicolas ran down the area-steps without taking any notice of the pretty housemaid, and hurrying through the kitchen, rushed upstairs to the room in which the Consul and the Prince were seated.

"Can I see you alone, Eccellenza?"

"Yes, Nicolas," replied the Prince; "but tell me what has happened?—you are as pale as death."

"Do not ask me anything till we are alone together, Eccellenza," rejoined Nicolas; "the good Signor shall know all in due time; but I must first speak to you alone."

"Then I shall wish you good-night, Signor Marelli," said the Prince, shaking hands with his friend; "to-morrow you shall know all. Come, Nicolas."

The Prince led the valet to his apartment, and seating himself in an easy chair by the fire, for the autumn evening was cold, prepared to hear what his valet had to say.

"Eccellenza," said Nicolas, "there are men who remember faces. I am one of those men. I was walking the streets of London this night, hoping against hope, I think, to find in this big crowded city some clue to the mystery which is driving me mad, when I saw amongst the faces of the passers-by one that I knew—the face of a scoundrel—one Antonio Volni, whom I knew in Naples. I knew, too, that this man, scoundrel as he is, is one of the Good Cousins. How he ever got himself admitted into the Society I cannot tell, but he is a specious hypocrite, and has doubtless deceived the chiefs of the association. You follow me, my Prince?"

"I do. You believe this man——"

"I believe this man to be the villain who has betrayed us. He is as poor as Job. Then what brings him to London? He is one of the Good Cousins. He, therefore, had a means of knowing our secret. Eccellenza, he is the traitor."

"But how are we to proceed against him?"

"Fortunately, though I recognised him, he did not remember me. He is a man whose face, once seen, is never to be forgotten. I was but a boy when he knew me, and my face has most likely utterly escaped his memory. I followed him for upwards of an hour, and traced him to a small house in one of the shabbiest parts of the City. Luckily for me, the landlord of this house happens to be a Frenchman, and from him I ascertained all about his lodger. He calls himself Vecchi; describes himself as a Genevese, and pretends to employ himself by watchmaking. All falsehood, Eccellenza, and all so much proof that he is engaged in evil deeds."

"You have done nobly, Nicolas," said the Prince; "to-morrow we will consult these English police-officers of whom the Consul thinks so much, and perhaps we may yet find a clue to the scoundrels who robbed us."

The Inspector and his colleague listened very attentively to the Italian's story as related to them by Signor Marelli.

"That young man ought to be educated for the detective force," said Mr. Martin; "he's got a very pretty talent. He's as right as ninepence, and before the week's out we'll have Mounseer Vecchi, or Volni, or whatever he calls himself, safe under lock and key."

The house in which Antonio Vecchi lodged was situated in a back street in Clerkenwell. At dusk the next evening the two officers started with another man who understood French, and could therefore serve as interpreter between the detectives and Nicolas. They easily found the house, only one window of which was lighted.

"As he lodges upstairs, and there's only a light in the parlour, he's most likely out about some of his pretty business," said the Inspector. "Our luck's going to take a turn, perhaps. You just tell the Seenor, in your French lingo, that he'd better knock at the door, and ask after this Vecchi, will you, Green?"

Mr. Green, the interpreter, did as requested, and the three men then retired, leaving Nicolas to execute the detective's orders. They did not, however, go far, for it was arranged between them that if Nicolas found the coast clear, he was to go in, and they were to follow him.

It was exactly as the Inspector had anticipated. Signor Vecchi was not at home.

The Frenchman very politely asked him to step into the parlour, a clean but shabby apartment.

"You will, perhaps, like to wait till your friend returns," he said. "He is very uncertain; but he may be home earlier than usual."

"He is generally very late, then?"

"Yes; he is often late."

There was nothing in the man's manner to indicate that he was an accomplice in any evil deeds of his lodger. The whole aspect of the house spoke for the honesty of its master.

While Nicolas was making these reflections the Inspector knocked, and on the Frenchman opening the door entered the house with his two colleagues.

The interpreter made some excuse for this intrusion; they were looking for apartments, he said, and understood that they could be accommodated.

The Frenchman told them politely that his house was full.

During this brief colloquy the two detectives had examined the Frenchman's face with that peculiarly searching glance known only to themselves—a glance in which the clever detective can read the inmost secrets of a man's soul.

"I'll tell you what it is," said Inspector Martin, aside to his companion; "this yer cove's an honest cove, I'll stake my affidavy. Let's tell him all about it."

The Frenchman understood English well, though he only spoke it imperfectly. Sergeant Boulder and Inspector Martin had, therefore, the satisfaction of telling the story their own way.

"Now, what we want," said the Inspector, when he had finished, "is just this here. If this Vecchi has been the traitor, as seems only likely, why he has had a share of the booty, and he may have it yet. The first thing is to search his room."

"You are at liberty to do so immediately," said the Frenchman, eagerly.

"Very nice and fair spoken," replied Inspector Martin.

"Very well, then; you just tell Mounseer Nicolas to walk upstairs with you, and you and he can search Mounseer Vecchi's room, while me and my comrade stops down here to lay hands on Mounseer Vecchi when Mounseer Vecchi comes home."

Nicolas and the Frenchman were about to obey, when the Inspector called them back.

"You just catch hold of these," he said, taking two or three bunches of keys from his pocket. "I dare say Mounseer has locked up his property; but he's quite welcome to be careful, for it's a queer lock that one of these won't fit."

The valet and the landlord ascended to the top of the house. It was only a garret that Antonio Vecchi occupied, but it was clean and comfortably furnished.

The two men began their search. For a long time they sought in vain for any clue to the object of their inspection. The bed, the chest of drawers, the cupboards, every possible hiding-place was examined, without any result. The roof of the garret was supported by heavy wooden beams. In one corner of the room these beams made a resting-place, into which had been hoisted a trunk that stood on end between the two beams and the ceiling. An old coat of Vecchi's hanging on a nail entirely concealed this hiding-place, and it was only on removing this coat that the Frenchman and Nicolas perceived the sharp corner of the box jutting out from behind the beam.

"The money is here," cried the Italian; "my life upon it, the money is here!"

With considerable difficulty the two men dislodged the trunk, and placing it on the ground, Nicolas knelt before the lock, and tried the keys given to him by Inspector Martin.

He had nearly tried every key in the three bunches, when at last, to his delight, he succeeded in opening the box.

It was filled with old garments, which the valet tore out of it one after another in his mad impetuosity. He had not been deceived. At the very bottom he found a bag filled with gold. This bag was afterwards found to contain exactly the third part of the very sum of which Nicolas had been robbed in the sham hotel.

THE DEMON WORK SUCCEEDS

"Perhaps."

One morning, however, Jessie found Mrs. Atkinson busy at work at a little black frock.

"Is that for me?" asked the child.

"Yes, my dear," answered the warm-hearted Tilly, looking mournfully at the eager little questioner.

"It's very pretty," exclaimed Jessie; "I shall like it very much. But I thought people wore black frocks when their friends died. Nobody that I know is dead."

By-and-by, as the two children were playing in the garden, their father called them aside—

"George, Jessie," he said, "I have something to tell you that has made me unhappy, and which I know will also make you so. But, young as you are, you are not too young to learn that life is not all sunshine. You will never see your sister again."

No. 10. [*Weekly, One Penny.*]

"Papa, Papa!"

"Never, my darlings. She is dead."

This was the determination at which the broken-hearted father had arrived. Clara, his dearest child, was indeed dead to him. He little knew the sin of this falsehood; still less could he dream of the dire effects which it would some day bring upon him.

The children's grief was something terrible. In vain their little playfellow, Charley, endeavoured to console them. In vain the warm-hearted farmer and his wife tried to make them forget their troubles. Their little hearts were well nigh broken.

Time passed, and the November weather set in—long foggy days in which the children could no longer wander in the meadows.

Every morning John Atkinson went about his farm wrapped in a heavy greatcoat, and with high jack-boots that enabled him to stride through muddy lanes and fields half under water.

He was always armed with a good stout cudgel, which swung loosely in his strong hand.

One misty morning when the yellow fog filled the meadows, Mr. Atkinson's attention was attracted by two men, who were creeping along under the shelter of one of the leafless hedges in the direction of the farmhouse.

The field in which these men were walking was a public thoroughfare leading across the farm, and John Atkinson would have taken no notice whatever of the two pedestrians had it not been for something peculiar, and almost suspicious, in their appearance, and from their evident wish to avoid observation.

They were dressed in the garments of gentlemen upon a shooting expedition. One of the two wore a beard and moustache cut in the last fashion, and walked with a dandified swagger which ill assorted with the character of a country gentleman.

As they perceived John Atkinson crossing the field, they suddenly stopped and shouted to him to come to them.

But honest John was not the sort of man to be ordered about in this unceremonious fashion; he stood stock still, and the sportsmen were obliged to pick their way across the field in order to reach him.

"Why didn't you come when we called you?" asked one of the men.

"Haw, to be sure!" echoed the wearer of the moustachios, "why didn't you come?"

"Because I've got something else to do than to run after every fool that can't follow his own nose," answered John, sturdily.

"The low person!" muttered the moustachioed dandy, who wore a large-patterned suit of Stuart plaid, and patent leather boots, adorned with mother-of-pearl buttons, "I must chastise the low person."

"Hold your tongue, Colonel FitzMortimer," said his companion: "pray can you tell me the way to a farm called Beresford Meadows?" he added, addressing himself to John.

"There's little need to do that," answered the Farmer, "for you're on the farm now. If you want the house, I'm going there, and I can show you the way."

"Oh, but I can't possibly walk with the low person," muttered Colonel FitzMortimer, in an audible aside to his companion.

"Hold your tongue, Fitz."

"Your friend don't seem much used to carrying a gun, Sir," said John, pointing to the gallant Colonel's fowling-piece, which he carried with the butt end over his shoulder, and the muzzle pointed downwards, very much as if he wanted to fire into his own boots. "I should think, for a military man, he was rather awkward with fire-arms."

"We never use fire-arms in my regiment," answered the Colonel; "we think them low."

"Pray," said the other man, as if anxious to change the conversation; "pray, my good friend, do you know this Atkinson?"

"Well," answered John, with a quiet smile, "me and him have passed a good bit of time together, one way and another; but for all that I mayn't know much of him."

"He's a countrified fool, I suppose. A sort of easy, simple-hearted booby, that you could do anything you like with?"

"Why," replied the Farmer, "as for that, I don't suppose he's over and above clever. He ain't much of a Greek scholar, very like, and he don't *parley vous*; but, for all that, I wouldn't try on too much with him, if I was you."

"Indeed," answered the man, scornfully, "I should have thought he was the sort of fellow that you could twist round your finger."

"Oh, I dare say you might," said John, "as long as you twisted him the right way; but I'm afraid if you was to give him just one awkward twist the wrong way you might find him rather a toughish article."

"Ged gracious, haw, by Jove!" exclaimed the elegant FitzMortimer, "how extraordinary."

"If you've got corns, and want to cure 'em, you can't do better than shoot your toes, Sir," said John, pointing once more to the Colonel's fowling-piece; "but if you haven't, and your gun's loaded, I'd advise you to let me carry it for you."

"Oh, it isn't loaded," answered FitzMortimer; "I don't mean to load it till I see the bird I want to fire at, because I find the shot better when it's fresh; haw, by Jove! Ged gracious!"

"Well, you're a rum sportsman!" said John, laughing aloud, as he contemplated the dandified Colonel. "I'll back myself to eat all the game you shoot this season, and a good dinner after it."

"Haw! By Jove! Ged gracious! The low person's laughing at me. I shall have to chastise him."

By this time they had reached the house. John Atkinson led the way into the noble stone-floored kitchen, and seating himself in an arm-chair before the blazing fire, said quietly—

"Now, gentlemen, if you want to talk to this simple-hearted booby, this countrified fool that you can twist round your finger, here he is, at your service."

The Colonel's companion was visibly disconcerted by this discovery. The gallant Colonel, himself, dropped into a chair, letting his gun fall clattering upon the flag-stones.

"Haw! By Jove! Ged gracious!" he exclaimed, "the low person is the very man we want."

But his companion soon recovered from his discomfiture.

"This," he said, drawing a slip of pasteboard from his card-case, "is my card. You will perceive, Mr. Atkinson, that you have to deal with gentlemen."

The card was inscribed:

Dr. Marmaduke Dorington,
DORINGTON PARK,
HANTS.

"The business on which I have to address you," said Dr. Dorington, "is of a very serious —I may indeed say, of a very painful character. You have a gentleman lodging with you?"

"I've had a many gentlemen lodging with me one time and another," answered John.

"Pray do not prevaricate; my errand is a solemn one. My profession entitles me to respect."

"Very likely," said John; "but I'm rather a queer chap, and I never respect folks till I know 'em. I shouldn't respect the Queen of England if I didn't know her to be as good a woman as ever stepped on British ground."

"Haw! By Jove! Ged gracious!" exclaimed the Colonel, "the low person's quite a character!"

"You have a gentleman now residing under this roof," continued the Doctor, "whose name is Arthur Beaumorris."

John Atkinson stared as vacantly at the Doctor as if he had never heard the name of Beaumorris in his life.

"Some of those folks as is over fond of meddling with other folks' affairs has been leading you a fine dance, Mr. Doctor," he said; "there's no Beaumorris here."

"Come, come," said the Physician, sharply, "this prevarication will not avail you; call him Jasper Melville, if you please, but the man now beneath your roof is no other than the younger brother of Sir Frederick Beaumorris."

"Don't know the gentleman," muttered John, shaking his head.

"Oh, I shall soon be able to improve your memory. You have, no doubt, been bribed by Arthur Beaumorris to keep his secret. I will bribe you higher to reveal it. I think I know human nature."

"You seem to uncommon well," answered John; "I should think you'd studied it by looking at yourself with a double-barrelled microscope."

"Listen to me," cried the Physician; "I see you pride yourself upon being a sharp fellow, so I'll no longer treat you as a fool. It is necessary that Arthur Beaumorris should be removed to some place of security. A lunatic asylum is the most secure. Whether he is a madman or not is a question for the doctors to decide. I am a physician, and it is to my house he will be taken. I need not tell you that he will be treated with the same tender indulgence which I should bestow upon a beloved child of my own."

"No you needn't," said John, quietly; "I wouldn't waste my breath, if I was you— because I'm a queer chap, and might happen not to believe you."

"Now, if you will assist us in quietly removing Arthur Beaumorris, we will give you a hundred pounds down for your trouble."

"Will you?" said the farmer, slowly rising from his chair, and twisting his cudgel round and round in his powerful hand. "Now, that's what I call a liberal offer, and as I don't like not to be equally generous, I'll give you and your friend, the Colonel, as sound a thrashing as ever you got in your lives, if you don't make yourselves scarce before I catch you."

At this speech, which burst upon them as unexpectedly as a thunderbolt, the Physician and the Colonel both forgot their dignity, and with one accord made, as fast as their legs would carry them, for the door of the farmhouse.

The worthy Doctor did succeed in escaping, but the unfortunate Colonel got his gun between his legs in such a manner as to throw him upon his nose on the very threshold.

Before he could pick himself up, John Atkinson caught him by the velvet collar of his coat, and, lifting him in his arms as if he had been a baby, flung him into the middle of a duck-pond before the farmhouse, from which the ducks and geese flew shrieking away, alarmed by the apparition of the gallant Colonel, who, with his legs and arms stretched wildly in every direction, and his coat-tails flying in the wind, looked by no means unlike some extraordinary species of foreign fowl.

For full five minutes the gallant officer stood up to his waist in the pond, fearing to emerge, as he must encounter John, who, with his cudgel in his hand, waited for him upon the brink of the water.

At last, however, he screwed his courage to the sticking-point, and, scrambling up the bank, covered with duck-weed and mud, took to his heels in the direction of the high road.

The honest farmer pursued him for some little way, intending only to frighten him, as he saw that no more punishment was needed to prevent the wretched coward ever re-entering the farmhouse of Beresford Meadows.

"I wonder whether I ought to tell the poor gentleman of this," said Atkinson, as he returned to the kitchen. "Better, I think, to keep it to myself. He has unhappiness enough, I fancy, without any new troubles; and as for those two fine gentlemen, I'll take precious good care to keep them off the premises."

But the simple-hearted Yorkshireman, himself true as the light of heaven, knew little of the dark and winding ways of those whose whole life has been passed in the plotting of villanous schemes.

He was like an honest prize-fighter, who only wards the blows that are struck in the open. He was not prepared for the secret thrust of the knife given behind a man's back.

Three days after the scene between John and his two visitors, Jasper Melville, accompanied by the two children, walked into the town of Beresford to post a letter.

It was broad daylight—a sunshiny winter's afternoon, or John would never have allowed his lodger to venture out unattended.

The farm was situated little more than a mile and a half from the town; but Jasper was delayed at the post-office, through the stupidity of a clerk, and was also hindered for some time by George and Jessie, who were delighted with the old town, its noble Minster, and quaint houses.

It was striking the half-hour after four as they left the town behind them, and it was rapidly growing dark.

The road between the town of Beresford and John Atkinson's farm was very lonely.

The country people who were accustomed to it thought little of this, but Jasper Melville, whose life had been spent in noisy cities, looked about him with a shudder.

On one side there was a thick and dense fir wood; on the other a deep ditch ran darkly under the shelter of the leafless hedge.

"Surely," thought Jasper, as he glanced about him, "this is the very place which a murderer would select for his deed of guilt."

He clasped his children's little hands more tightly in his own as this dark fancy passed through his mind.

"Luckily," he thought, "we are safe, for we have nothing to be robbed of."

Did he forget that most inestimable gift of Heaven—more precious than all earthly treasure—dearer even than life? Did he forget LIBERTY, that jewel beyond all price, whose value the prisoner alone can appreciate—whose blessings the slave can only dream of?

Half way between the town and the farmhouse Jasper Melville's attention was attracted by a carriage and pair which was drawn up close under the shelter of the pine wood.

Three men were standing in the road close to this carriage.

Another man was seated on the box holding the reins.

"See, Papa," said Jessie, as they approached the group, "there's a beautiful carriage. How I should like to ride in it!"

"And so you shall, my little dear," answered one of the men, seizing her in his arms, and wrapping her head and face in a thick shawl, while the second caught hold of her brother.

"My child!" cried Jasper. "Wretch! what would you do with my child?"

He was about to throw himself upon the man, but before he could do so a handkerchief, soaked in chloroform, was thrust into his face, and he sank senseless into the arms of one of his assailants.

They lifted him into the carriage with the two children, and at one smack of the whip the spirited horses dashed off into the high road leading from Beresford to Hull.

At Hull they changed horses. Travelling further north, they stopped at midnight in a lonely moorland district, and dashing through the open gateway of a walled-in courtyard, drew up before a dismal stone-built house, of about seven storeys, each storey being lighted by twenty narrow windows, closely studded with iron bars.

Of all the prisons, those terrible, but, alas! necessary buildings which disfigure the fair face of beautiful and merry England, there is not one of aspect half so appalling as this hideous stone-built house.

Horror and death seemed to brood about the lofty roof. Despair had set her seal upon the stony walls.

One of the men had stopped at Hull with the two children, whose rosy little mouths had been gagged with cambric handkerchiefs tied closely round the jaws.

Jasper Melville lay in a dull stupor upon the seat of the carriage, utterly unconscious of whither he was being taken.

It was only the next morning that he awoke to some dim consciousness of his condition.

He found himself in a square stone room, little better than a dungeon in appearance, lighted by one gloomy barred window, so deep in the massive wall that the wretched inmates of the apartment could see nothing from the casement but a square patch of the blue sky.

He was not alone in this wretched prison.

His companions were three men of dark and forbidding appearance.

One smoked a dirty clay pipe. The second sat upon a stone ledge jutting out from the wall. The third lay on the ground, gazing stupidly at the stones in his prison floor.

Jasper Melville asked no questions of these men. He felt no curiosity. He sat close against the wall, with his eyes fixed upon blank space.

The demoniac hate of his vile enemies had done its work.

Arthur Beaumorris, the once proud heir to a princely fortune, the beloved favourite of a wealthy uncle, the once happy husband of a beautiful wife, was now a melancholy madman.

It was no common lunatic asylum to which he had been taken.

It was a house supported by the Society of the BLACK BAND.

This terrible association had its own methods of revenging itself on the members who betrayed or endeavoured to desert the Society.

Bloodshed was not always convenient. It was not the hand of mercy that stayed the stiletto of the assassin; it was prudence. The traitor or deserter whose life was spared languished for the remainder of his days in this terrible stone dungeon.

He entered it, possessed of all his faculties; often to die a raging maniac, or a gibbering idiot.

How, then, the reader may ask, was Arthur Beaumorris brought here, since he had no connection with the Black Band?

Time will solve that question.

CHAPTER XXXV.

STILL WATERS RUN DEEP

AFTER a brief examination before a magistrate, Antonio Vecchi was removed to Coldbath Fields Prison to await his trial. It was desirable that his trial should be delayed as long as possible, in order that the detectives, Martin and Boulder, might discover the accomplices of the Italian.

"Let the scoundrel rot in prison, so as it gives me a chance of tracing this here gang that he's concerned with, Sir," said Sergeant Boulder, in a private interview between himself and the magistrate at the Clerkenwell Police Court. "I'd give a year of my life to find 'em, and now we've got one of 'em, it's hard if we're not too many guns for the lot."

But for once that wonderful science which tracks the dark pathway of crime with such marvellous success, that we come at last to look upon the detective police officer as the magician of civilised life—for once, the most skilful men in London were utterly at fault.

Night and day the quiet little Inspector and his colleague toiled with brain and body, now following up one clue, now another; and then unravelling some tangled skein, only to find hopeless confusion and disappointment.

What was the horror and despair of the two men when, after six weeks of devoted labour, they received the intelligence that the prisoner had escaped from Coldbath Fields!

An extraordinary amount of skill had been employed in this escape, and more hands than one had assisted the Italian.

He was missed a quarter of an hour after his departure, and in less than an hour the two detectives were seeking for him through all the most disreputable haunts of London criminals. They sought in vain.

The Prince de Z. returned to Italy, carrying with him the third portion of the specie which the authorities had restored to him on his identification of it—returned heartbroken at the failure of his mission.

Meanwhile Sir Frederick Beaumorris returned to fashionable society; and it was at his estate, Beaumorris Castle, in Cumberland, that Oscar Bertrand publicly married the lovely Ellen Clavering, declared by her father's last will to be heiress to all his hoarded wealth. None amongst the brilliant assembly who assisted at this wedding knew of the secret midnight marriage in the ruins of Clavering Park, nor of the death-struggle in Stamford Street, Blackfriars.

Thus the tragedies of life are ever acted behind a dark and sheltering curtain, while each actor presents a gay and smiling face to his neighbour.

Who that sat at the costly banquet at which Sir Frederick Beaumorris presided, with Colonel Bertrand as his most honoured guest, could have believed that the first of these men was a trickster and a forger, the second a murderer and the instructor of thieves?

Surely they would have shuddered had they known that the white and jewelled hand which raised the wine-cup to those smiling lips was stained by the life-blood of a helpless old man.

No one amongst them all was more ignorant of the truth than Ellen herself.

Her husband had told her of her father's death; of his entire forgiveness of her, and of the will, which, in testimony of that forgiveness, left her all his wealth.

She asked no further questions; and her first grief for the loss of this beloved father once past, she felt that life was now brilliant and joyous.

Her beloved husband no longer hid his marriage from the world in which he lived. He no longer appeared to her as a mysterious being with whose life some strange secret must be connected. No; she now beheld him, courted and admired, clasping noble hands in his, leading her amidst the highest of the land.

The guests at Beaumorris Castle were delighted with Ellen's beauty and simplicity. Her frank and girlish manner made for her friends wherever she went.

"And you are happy now, Ellen?" said her husband, as they walked up and down the terrace before the Castle, upon a frosty winter's afternoon.

"Happy! yes, indeed," she exclaimed, clasping her two little hands upon the Colonel's arm; "more happy than I can find words to say. So it was not a poor penniless little girl, but a rich heiress, whom you ran away with, after all."

"Yes, my darling," said the Colonel, "but, remember, I knew nothing of this hoarded wealth."

"I know, dearest Philip—ah, forgive me, I mean Oscar," she added, correcting herself— "but I love the old name best, for it was that by which I thought of you in my first love-dreams. I know, my beloved, that no mercenary feeling, no calculation of my paltry thousands, ever led you to your poor Ellen's side. You loved me, did you not, Oscar?"

"Yes, dearest; and I love you still. I am preparing a surprise for you, Ellen, against next summer."

"A surprise! Oh, pray tell me what."

"Why, if I tell you it will be no longer a surprise."

"But, indeed, you must tell me! Now you have excited my curiosity, do you think I could possibly wait till the next summer for its gratification? Why, Oscar, how little you can have studied the fair sex!"

"The fairest of them all has little interest for me when you are not by, Nelly," answered her husband, in those deep and thrilling tones which, as much even as his handsome face, had won her heart in the shady avenues of Clavering Park. "You are all the world to me, Nelly!"

"But the surprise, the surprise!" she cried, looking archly up at him from under her furred hood. "The surprise, Colonel Bertrand; all this is only prevarication, Sir."

"Well, then, my darling, the secret is, that I

have sent an architect and a troop of bricklayers down to Clavering, with orders for the restoration of the Abbey. The work will last six months, and at the end of that time you will see the stately pile towering once more over wood and meadow, village and common land, as it did in its proudest day when the Claverings were lords of the land."

"Oscar, Oscar, this is indeed a surprise!"

"Yes, Ellen, it was your father's highest ambition, when, for your sake, he assumed the character of a miser, that the wealth hoarded by him would enable you to be queen again in the once deserted chambers of Clavering. That wish will now be fulfilled. I am making arrangements for myself assuming your ancient name, as successor, in some measure, to your father's property. The name of Bertrand is an aristocratic one, but I am so much an Englishman in habit that I would fain be one in name. I shall ere long be known as Bertrand-Clavering."

"Dearest," exclaimed Ellen, glancing with a look of profound affection at her husband's handsome face, "it is for my sake and in my honour that you do all these things!"

"Perhaps it is, Nelly," he answered quietly, while a scarcely perceptible smile curled his finely-chiseled lips.

The Marquis of Willoughby was amongst the guests who arrived at Beaumorris Castle to share in the Christmas festivities.

He looked pale and careworn. In vain he tried to stifle the love which he felt was hopeless; in vain he endeavoured to chase from his heart the image of the woman who had reigned there from his very boyhood. Go where he would, do what he would, he could not forget Lady Edith Merton.

Strange chances of this tangled web, which we call Life! The wealthy cotton-spinner, the merchant-prince, was once more amongst Sir Frederick's many Christmas visitors.

He, too, had changed since the blow which had rendered his life desolate. He, too, had loved only to be deceived; and a bitter spirit had taken possession of his once generous nature, which seemed to transform him into a different man.

A tale of distress no longer melted his heart as it once had done. Might it not be false, however seeming true? For had not *she* been false? She, whose every accent seemed truth itself. He despised the lovely woman whose flashing eyes beamed on him like rays of summer sunlight. "Beauty," as the outraged husband exclaimed, "is but a mask." Might not they hide beneath that dazzling mask hearts as black as that of her who had deceived him?

THE BLACK BAND; OR, THE MYSTERIES OF MIDNIGHT

Robert Merton looked on everything with a jaundiced eye. What was wealth? He hated his wealth, since with all its boasted power it could not purchase for him the one heart which, had it been true, might have transformed a garret into a palace.

Lord Willoughby had shunned as much as possible the society both of the merchant and of Colonel Oscar Bertrand. But the Austrian never relaxed the hold which he had once obtained over his victim. He did not loosen that fatal grasp once.

"My dear Lionel," he said one morning, when he found himself alone with the Marquis, "what in mercy's name have you been doing with yourself? What is the meaning of the pale cheeks and hollow eyes? When will you acquire the true philosophy of life, and learn to take things easily?"

"I have no secrets from you," answered the Marquis, moodily.

"Of course not, my dear boy. There are very few people who have any secrets from me. I have a talent for finding the clue to the darkest mysteries of life."

"You ask when shall I learn to take things easily," continued the Marquis, fiercely. "I tell you in reply, that I shall never learn to root this fatal passion from my breast. I shall never forget Edith Vandeleur."

"You mean Edith Merton. What a good thing her husband is not anywhere about to hear this passionate avowal!"

"I care not," cried the young nobleman; "I care not if all the world hears it."

"Lionel, Marquis of Willoughby," said Oscar Bertrand, sinking his voice to its deepest and most solemn tones, "have I ever failed you yet in any crisis?"

"Never."

"Two years ago, amidst the midnight revels of a masked ball, I promised you your brother's wealth and title."

"You did, you did," cried the Marquis, sinking into a chair, and covering his face with his hands.

"Within six months from my making you that promise you were called by that title, and you possessed that wealth. Was it not so?"

"It was."

"Then you will not doubt me now, when I tell you that before many moons have waned below the blue mountains of yonder Scottish land, Edith, the widow of Robert Merton, will be yours."

The young man started to his feet, and falling on his knees before the Austrian Colonel, with his clasped hands elevated above his head, cried wildly—

"No, no! Let there be no more crime, no more bloodshed. Enough has already been done to stain my soul with the blackness of death. Let my sufferings be what they may, but do not lift your hand again to strike for me. Demon, I renounce my allegiance—I call upon you to release me from my bonds!"

"Fool!" exclaimed Oscar Bertrand, scornfully; "before the coming year is out Robert Merton, the merchant prince, will have died a natural death, and the fortune made in cotton-spinning will have passed into the coffers of the Marquis of Willoughby."

The room in which this conversation had taken place was an immense tapestried chamber, which had been devoted to billiards.

As the Colonel finished speaking, a square of the tapestry was drawn aside, and Robert Merton stepped into the room.

He was perfectly calm and self-possessed, and looked about him with a quiet smile.

"I was never aware until this moment," he said, politely, "that the next room was only divided from this by a tapestried curtain. Pray, gentlemen, have you seen the *Times* newspaper? I have been looking for it in the library, but cannot find it anywhere about."

CHAPTER XXXVI.

MR. RUPERT DE LANCY RECEIVES A VISITOR

ANTONY VERNER seemed never happier than when standing at the side scenes watching Clara's light figure gliding through the graceful mazes of the dance.

The applause of her enthusiastic audience; the consciousness that she excelled in her captivating art; the inspiriting influence of the music; the dazzling lights, and the friendly smiles of the crowd, all combined to inspire her with a wild sense of gaiety, which possessed her while she was dancing, and which left her sad and thoughtful when the last chord of the music had been struck, and she returned to her quiet corner in the crowded Green Room.

It was in vain that the young tragedian endeavoured to become more intimately acquainted with the lovely *danseuse*. She was always polite, even friendly, in her manner; she acknowledged his respectful compliments with a modest, deprecatory smile, but she seemed to be utterly unconscious of the warm interest which she had inspired in the breast of the clever young actor.

"My mother was in the boxes last night, Miss Melville," he said, one evening when Clara entered the Green Room, "and I need scarcely tell you how charmed she was with your exquisite dancing; she begged me to prevail on you if possible to spend a day with her this week. Our house is a queer old place, but I fancy you would find much to amuse you in the rambling and tumble-down building. Pray say that you will come."

"Indeed, Mr. Verner, your invitation is so kind that I cannot well refuse it," said Clara; "but a very great shock which I experienced last September has left my spirits so low and variable that I scarcely dare trust myself in society."

"Do not say that, Miss Melville," replied Antony Verner, earnestly; "you might indeed shun crowded assemblies in which smiling faces are only masks assumed to deceive; in which joy is a livery worn alike by all, and where men grasp the hands of those at whose funeral they would gladly attend. But with us you would be with friends. If you forgot your sorrows, and were gay, we would gladly join in your gaiety; if you were sad we should be too wise to intrude upon your mournful thoughts. I hope you will come."

"I will, Mr. Verner," answered Clara, holding out her hand to the young tragedian. "Pray give my best thanks to your mother for the kind invitation, and tell her that I cannot refuse it."

"A thousand thanks," cried Antony, eagerly; "remember, Miss Melville, it is no common interest which I take in your welfare. The mystery of the portrait of Arthur Beaumorris is yet to be solved. I only wish your father were here to assist us."

Clara's bright blue eyes filled with tears as the young man said this.

"Alas!" she murmured, "the most unhappy misunderstanding has arisen between my father and myself, and I do not even know where he is."

Antony Verner was silent. He had far too much good feeling to attempt to fathom the mystery which had separated father and daughter.

*　　*　　*　　*　　*　　*

Let us introduce our readers into the Manager's dressing-room early on the evening after that on which the above conversation took place.

To those who have never entered this *sanctum sanctorum*, the aspect of the apartment will be something almost bewildering.

A rather large room, the walls covered with a gay flowered paper, a pair of gas burners at the opposite corners of the mantelpiece, and on either side of a large glass placed against the wall. An immense dressing-table before this glass is crowded with all the mysterious and miscellaneous articles used in the toilette of an actor—vermilion, black paint, Indian red, burnt cork, false eyebrows, whiskers, beards, moustachios of every shape and shade, chalk with which to imitate the pallor of hunger, disease, or death, vermilion for the rubicund hues of health, scowling black eyebrows which convert the pleasantest face into the sinister-looking visage of a villain.

Above this dressing-table, and on either side of the glass, hangs almost every variety of wig, suspended on nails; fiery red, curly flaxen, black and flowing ringlet wigs, such as were worn when rollicking Charles the Second held the helm of power, and drove the good ship Old England through such perilous ways; powdered wigs, such as those in fashion at the courts of the Georges; in short, every variety of hair that ever adorned the human head.

The would-be actor should remember this. The materials of his art are numerous and expensive, and, what is more, they have to be purchased out of his own slender salary; and he must often, perhaps, deprive himself of many comforts in order to procure them.

There are few arts so difficult as that of the actor, and perhaps none that, in a general way, are so badly paid.

Let the sturdy mechanic, the thriving young tradesman, the smart apprentice, and the rising lawyer's clerk bear this in mind; and whatever talent they may have for either tragedy or comedy, let them think twice before they abandon a certainty for an uncertainty.

About six o'clock on this bleak January evening, Mr. Rupert de Lancy sat before the dressing-table we have just described. His valet, a very meek young man, who was so accustomed to be sworn at by his master that he scarcely heard, and still less heeded, the Manager's energetic language, was standing at Mr. de Lancy's elbow, holding a long raven black curling wig, which the actor was to assume as soon as he had finished what is technically termed "making up the face."

This "making up the face," in Mr. de Lancy's case, comprised putting a thin coating of vermilion over the cheeks and forehead, to represent the bronze of a Southern sun, and gumming an intensely black beard and moustachios about his lips and chin, to say nothing of a pair of marked black eyebrows, also gummed upon the forehead.

The piece in which Mr. Rupert de Lancy was about to appear was a powerful melodrama, such as are most popular on the Surrey side of the water. It was called, *The Massacre of the Mountain; or, Mandini's Revenge*; and Mr. de

Lancy, in common with managers in general, who do not often (as our readers may imagine) play the worst parts, enacted the hero, a dashing brigand, who, though living at war with society and its laws, was beloved by every lowly mountaineer, as the protector of the innocent, and the avenger of the wronged.

The Manager's toilet was nearly finished. He wore tight breeches of emerald green silk velvet, embroidered with gold; a snowy shirt, the lace trimmings of which were worth a considerable sum; a scarlet silk sash with heavy bullion fringe, and embroidered gaiters adorned with rich bunches of satin ribbon. A high-crowned black velvet hat, also ornamented with gold cord, bunches of ribbons and a superb diamond brooch stood on the table at his right hand.

"I think the dress is rather the thing, eh, Thomas?" he said to his valet, as he examined the effect of his costume in a cheval glass.

"It's regular 'ansome, Sir," answered the man; "and it ought to be, for it cost enough."

"So it did, Thomas; but I never wear anything cheap," answered the Manager, contemptuously.

At this moment one of the carpenters came with a message from the stage-door.

"A gentleman sent this card for Mr. de Lancy," said the man.

The Manager took the card from his valet's hand.

Upon it was engraved the name of

Sir Frederick Beaumorris, Bart.,
ST. JAMES'S SQUARE.

"Sir Frederick Beaumorris!" exclaimed Mr. de Lancy; "I don't know the gentleman, but I suppose he wants a box, or a season ticket, or something of that kind. Go and ask him to walk upstairs, Thomas."

"Here, Sir?"

"Yes, here, of course. Look sharp, will you, booby?"

We will spare our readers the oath with which Mr. de Lancy accompanied these words. The next moment he had settled his face into an agreeable smile, and, throwing himself into a luxurious velvet-covered easy-chair, took up an evening paper, and arranged himself in an elegant attitude for the reception of his visitor.

Mr. Rupert de Lancy was a handsome man, but, like many others possessed of a moderate share of good looks, he was painfully conscious of the fact.

He rose when his valet ushered the Baronet into the dressing-room, and, wheeling forward a chair, requested his visitor to be seated.

"Leave us, Thomas," he said, with a dignified wave of his hand, which was covered with valuable rings. It was with this jewelled hand that he doled out the pitiful twelve shillings which was the weekly stipend of those ballet-girls whose pretty faces were often the chief ornament of the stage.

How different from another Manager, whose distinguished name we refrain from mentioning; a star whose light is about too soon to be withdrawn from the dramatic world!

"I have called on you, Mr. de Lancy," said Sir Frederick, "to wequest a favour, which it is in your power to gwant."

The Manager bowed obsequiously.

"Anything," he murmured, "that I can do for Sir Frederick Beaumorris will be only too great a pleasure."

"You're vewy good," said the Baronet, with his favourite drawl—that artificial drawl which, in moments of passion, was exchanged for the sharp accents of vexation or rage, "you're vewy good. Of course, any twouble I put you to will be amply wecompensed by a cheque on my bankers, Messrs. Wansom."

Mr. Rupert de Lancy merely bowed. He was not above accepting a cheque, provided it was a sufficiently heavy one.

"Thwee figures, of course," said the Baronet. The Manager bowed again.

"I believe you have a dansaw heaw," said Sir Frederick, "wather a pwetty girl, who calls herself Clawa Melville."

"Miss Melville is my Columbine," replied Mr. de Lancy; "I have engaged her at great expense for the run of my Pantomime."

"Deaw me!" murmured the Baronet, "a Columbine! Pway, what's a Columbine? I nevaw saw any Columbines at the Opewa."

"A Columbine is the principal dancer in a Pantomime," answered Mr. Rupert de Lancy.

"A Pantomime! Ah, I think I wemember once seeing a Pantomime. An extwaordinawy piece of amusement that vulgawians delight in; a howid man who steals babies, and swallows sausages, and jumps through shop windows. I wemember."

Mr. Rupert de Lancy looked rather spitefully at his aristocratic visitor. His Pantomime, which had cost him upwards of a thousand pounds, and eight weeks' trouble and anxiety, to be spoken of in this contemptuous manner. It was too much!

"Now," continued Sir Frederick Beaumorris, "this Miss Clawa Melville has been wemarkably insolent to me, and I want to punish her for her airs and gwaces. I have hit upon wather a clevaw little plot, and I want you to assist me in cawying it out. I shan't fawget the cheque. Thwee figures, you know."

Mr. de Lancy bowed once more, and the Baronet resumed.

But as our readers will presently become acquainted with the infamous scheme which was working against an unprotected girl's peace of mind, we will leave these two unscrupulous gentlemen to arrange their honourable plot between them.

It was seven o'clock when the Baronet left Mr. de Lancy's dressing-room. The two men shook hands very cordially as they parted.

"You're a vewy clevaw fellaw, de Lancy," murmured Sir Frederick, "and you wichly deserve to make a fortune. *Au wevoir.* Thwee figures, you know."

In making his way from the Manager's dressing-room to the stage-door it was necessary for Sir Frederick to pass the side scenes. In doing so he met Clara Melville, who had just entered the theatre, dressed in her simple dark shawl and straw bonnet. The young girl's cheeks blanched to a marble whiteness as she beheld her persecutor; but, save by the involuntary curl of her scornful lip, she gave no sign of her consciousness of his presence.

The Baronet bowed with mock respect.

"Good evening, Miss Melville," he said; "I am charmed to meet you once more, if it is only to remind you of the gratitude I feel for your polite manner of leaving my house in Normandy. I rarely forget these obligations, and shall not do so in this case, believe me."

Clara glanced at him with one brief flash of contempt sparkling in her deep blue eyes, and then sweeping past him, moved towards the Green Room.

But before she could reach the door a strong hand was laid upon her wrist, and Antony Verner arrested her steps.

"That man has been insulting you, Miss Melville," he said, eagerly.

"No, no, indeed, Mr. Verner."

"Remember, Clara, remember, Miss Melville, that your foes are mine; those who insult you insult me, and mine be the task of chastising them! Nay, Clara," said Antony Verner, with a mournful smile, as he perceived the young girl's embarrassment, "I ask no better right to do this than that of one—who respects you as a friend—who loves you—yet only dares to love you as a brother."

*   *   *   *   *   *

Upon the third evening after that on which Sir Frederick Beaumorris had visited the Paragon Theatre, Clara Melville was summoned to the stage door by a message from a poor woman who wished to speak to her.

The appeals made to actors and actresses, dancers and vocalists, by decayed members of their own profession are numerous and distressing; but they are never addressed to deaf ears.

In scarcely any other profession is such universal sympathy between the rich and the poor. The popular tragedian who plays *Hamlet* to-day to an admiring audience is ever ready to open his purse-strings to the broken-down old actor who was once as popular as himself.

Clara Melville was no exception to the general rule. She remembered the unfailing generosity of Lolota Vizzini, to whom she owed so much, and she would have gladly shared her last sixpence with her poorer sisterhood.

She found a very miserable-looking creature waiting for her at the stage door. An old woman, whose shrunken face was disfigured by a hundred wrinkles, and whose withered form was bent by a painful stoop. A bonnet adorned with artificial flowers, that had once been fine, but which were now tumbled and dirty, covered her grey hair, while a tattered Indian shawl, which, when new, must have been of considerable value, hung about her attenuated limbs.

Clara wished to feel nothing but pity for this wretched object, but, in spite of herself, she felt an instinctive shudder as she looked at her wrinkled face. Two great fangs protruded from her thick and wide lips, while her chin was garnished by a grey and bristling beard which would have done credit to an elderly grenadier.

"I told this here old crittur that you couldn't see her, Miss Melville," said the door-keeper; "and I told her that it warn't to be expected you could come down here into this windy place, catchin' cold in your thin dress, but she stood there and worritted till I let one of the men bring you her message."

"I am sure that Miss Melville will not refuse to listen to a poor old woman who was once a popular dancer."

"That old crittur a popular dancer," muttered the door-keeper; "she's a pretty figure for a dancer she is! I should like to see her in the *cowchoker* or a *pas de ducks!*"

"Yes, young lady," continued the old woman, "I was once a dancer as popular as yourself."

"That must have been a precious long while ago," said the door-keeper, in the same undertone; "I should think it must have been when Noah was gettin' his ark ready."

In vain Clara endeavoured to repress the feeling of disgust and aversion with which she looked upon the old woman. In spite of herself she drew a few paces away from her, as if afraid that her dress should touch against the garments of the other.

"Any assistance I can give you," she said, gently, "is quite at your service. My purse is upstairs in my dressing-room; but as soon as I have been on for my next dance I will fetch it. Meantime, pray be good enough to sit down. I dare say John can find you a seat."

"To be sure I can, Miss Melville," answered the door-keeper politely, and then added, under his breath, "I'd find her a precious warm one if I had my way; a comfortable shelf in a nice hot oven, or an heasy-chair on a hob, bless her ugly old mug!"

Clara was about to leave the hall, but the applicant for charity was not quite so easily satisfied.

"No, no," she said, "I will accept no alms till you have investigated and proved the truth of my story. Hearts as generous as yours are often made the prey of clever adventurers. In this case, at least, you shall be convinced before you open your purse that the want you are called on to relieve is genuine. I will not accept a farthing until you know more of me."

"But I do not ask to know more than that you are in want," said Clara; "it is a happiness to relieve the deserving, but it is a crime to leave even the undeserving to starve, when it is in our power to save them, perhaps, from further sin."

"You are an angel, Miss," exclaimed the old woman; "but you shall know at least that in this case you are only asked to assist the helpless and innocent. It is not for myself that I have to solicit your aid, but for two dear little children, left orphans by the early death of my only daughter."

"Indeed! How old are your grandchildren?" asked Clara.

The old woman named their ages. They were almost exactly those of little George and Jessie, the loved brother and sister whom Clara might, perhaps, never see again. In a moment the dancer forgot every feeling of aversion, and was all eagerness to know more of her applicant's distress.

"Poor dear children!" she exclaimed; "and orphans, you say? You shall have every farthing there is in my purse."

"Not until you have seen them, young lady," answered the old woman, resolutely.

"Seen them! Are they near here?"

"Only a few streets off. We have a wretched garret in Morley Street, Blackfriars."

Strange to say, it was the very street in which Clara had once lodged; the street in which her little sister Jessie had lain for weeks in a fever; the street into which Lolota Vizzini had entered as a ministering angel.

Clara felt that it was now her turn to be the comforter and preserver of the wretched.

"I will come and see the poor little darlings this very night," she said; "it will only take me a few streets out of my way."

"Will you really come, Miss Melville?" asked the old woman, anxiously.

"Oh yes! you may depend upon me. I never break a promise. John, try and send some one round to the refreshment saloon to get me a great bag of oranges. My little Jessie was always so fond of an orange."

With a friendly nod to the old woman, Clara tripped away, for she knew that it was nearly time for her entrance upon the stage.

The old woman curtsied, and hurried out of the stage-door with an activity of step remarkable in one so advanced in years.

"How mistaken we may be in the expression of a countenance!" thought Clara, as she pondered over the interview above narrated. "Strange to say, that old woman's face made me actually shiver, and yet she has noble and refined feelings, which would well become the proudest lady in the land. Her love for her grandchildren, too, that alone would secure my respect. It is a warning to me never to judge hastily."

Clara forgot that these natural instincts, which inspire us sometimes with a dread of a particular person, are the inaudible whispers of Providence, ever on the watch to warn us of the dangers which on every side assail us.

The animals, too, have these instincts, and know their friends from their foes. We are too proud, in our wisdom, to heed these warnings.

Half an hour after this the pantomime was finished, and Clara threw off her brilliant costume to assume the simple dark woollen gown and heavy shawl in which she shrouded her graceful figure.

Lolota had left her carriage behind for Clara's use, and the brougham always waited every evening for the tired dancer.

She gave the man the address given her by the old woman.

"You will not object to driving round there, will you, Peters?" she said; "it is only two or three streets off, and I will not detain you ten minutes."

The coachman was only too glad to oblige Clara, whose simple and unaffected nature made her a favourite with all who knew her.

In less than a quarter of an hour he had threaded his way through a maze of wretched streets, and stopped at the door of the house to which Clara had directed him.

It was now nearly midnight, and not a creature was astir in this poverty-stricken neighbourhood. Poor souls! the winter weather sadly tried their powers of endurance. Often unable to purchase either fuel or candle, they were glad to creep at an early hour to their wretched beds.

Clara knocked gently at the street door, which was opened by the old woman in person.

"My dear young lady," she exclaimed, "this is indeed noble of you. Pray step upstairs; the boards are loose in many places, and you'll have to tread cautiously. "I'd better go first with the light."

The old woman had spoken the truth. The woodwork of the staircase was crumbling to decay, and the banisters were broken every here and there. The house was one of the oldest in Blackfriars, and a great quantity of wood had been used in its construction.

They had to ascend to the very top of the house, but Clara's heart yearned to the helpless children she had come to relieve, and she scarcely thought of whither she was going.

"This is the room," said the old woman, opening the door of the front attic, and standing aside for Clara to enter the room. "Walk in, Miss."

Clara hurried across the threshold, but suddenly drew back upon beholding a man, in the dress of a gentleman, standing against the fire-place, with his back turned towards her.

"This must be the wrong place," she exclaimed.

"Oh no, it's quite right, Miss," answered the old woman, and before Clara could remonstrate she had suddenly shut the door upon her and locked it on the outside.

Clara Melville heard the key taken from the lock, and the receding footsteps of the woman upon the staircase without, and felt that she was alone, at midnight, in a strange house, in a disreputable neighbourhood, and with a man who was a stranger to her.

As this horrible thought flashed across her brain, she heard the clocks of the City churches strike the hour of twelve, every stroke vibrating in the clear atmosphere of the winter's night.

A light wind from the river was blowing towards the Kentish hills, and the sonorous booming of the bell of St. Paul's seemed to shake the garret in which the young girl stood.

The chamber in which Clara found herself was a miserable-looking apartment, furnished with only a couple of pitiful broken wooden chairs and an old deal table, upon which stood one candlestick, with a guttering tallow candle.

The sloping roof was supported by wooden rafters, and the narrow window was obscured by great beams which had been placed against the outside of the house to preserve the attic storey from falling.

A door leading into an inner apartment was ajar, and Clara could see that the chamber contained no other furniture than a wretched truckle-bed, upon which lay what she took for a heap of old garments.

For some moments Clara stood perfectly still, lost in the terrible stupor of horror and bewilderment; then, with a wild outburst of despair, she exclaimed, "Whither have I been brought? —and what new plot has been devised to destroy me?"

The gentleman standing against the fireplace turned round, and to her surprise and relief she beheld the smiling face of the Manager of the Paragon Theatre.

For a moment Clara fancied that her fears had been groundless. She had connected all thoughts of danger with the presence of Sir Frederick Beaumorris, and he was not there. Alas! she little knew the villany that often exists under the smoothest exterior.

"Good Heavens! Mr. de Lancy here," she exclaimed; "what is the meaning of all this? But you are here, and I am at least safe."

Rupert de Lancy smiled.

"Perfectly safe, my dear Miss Melville, believe me," he answered, laying his hand upon his heart, or upon that portion of his fashionable waistcoat beneath which a kindly and generous heart *should* have beaten.

"But why do I find you here? Have you, too, come upon an errand of charity?" asked Clara.

"Not precisely, perhaps," replied Rupert de Lancy, still smiling.

"Have I been deceived, then? Was the tale which brought me here a false one?"

"It was not, Miss Melville. You have indeed been brought here on an errand of charity. But that which you are called upon to relieve is not the wants of the poor, but the agonies endured by a heart which your beauty and grace have subdued."

The Manager, who was by no means too good a husband to one of the most excellent of wives, was well versed in the arts of gallantry, but he had some difficulty in meeting the scornful glances of Clara Melville.

"Forgive me, Clara," continued Mr. de Lancy, "if I have decoyed you thus to this lonely spot; there are ears ever on the alert in my theatre, and there I dared not address you. You will hear me out, will you not, Clara?"

"I will hear you to the end, Mr. de Lancy," she answered quietly, looking the Manager full in the face.

THE BRAVE DELIVERER RUSHES TO THE RESCUE

Her calm reply almost disconcerted him, but he recovered himself, and continued—

"Clara, I love you! Ties from which I cannot extricate myself bind me to another, but what of that? Be mine, and you shall be a queen, an empress, blest with all that wealth can bestow. You are listening, Clara?"

"To every word."

"And your reply—your reply!" he asked, with well-acted impetuosity.

"My reply!" said Clara, in distinct and measured tones, and with her eyes fixed on Rupert de Lancy's changing countenance, "my reply is this : You have learned your lesson well, Mr. de Lancy, and those who selected you to execute their hateful work chose their instrument wisely ; but, clever actor as you may be *on* the stage, and accustomed as you are to act *off* it, you are scarcely natural to-night. As a

No. 11. [*Weekly, One Penny.*]

profligate and unfaithful husband I should **have** good reason to despise you ; but as the base **tool** of a more aristocratic profligate than **yourself,** you are too degraded even for contempt."

"Fine words, Miss Clara Melville!" cried the infuriate Rupert de Lancy, with an oath ; "but you shall pay dearly for every syllable of them. Do you know where you are, my fine lady?"

"I am beneath Heaven's own blue sky," answered Clara, resolutely, "and I know that He who watches over the innocent will not suffer me to be wronged by a wretch such as you."

"Oh, indeed, my pretty church-going miss! Now I'll tell you where you are. You are in one of the worst houses in the worst neighbourhood of Blackfriars. You are with a man who can repay you tenfold for every hard word you have said to him, and you are far away from every friend you have in the world."

Clara rushed to the door, and beat violently against the lock.

"That won't do you much good," said Mr. de Lancy, with a sneer: "we're locked in safe enough: old Mother Bonner has the key, and as I gave her the money for a bottle of gin when I came in, she's not much in a state to unlock the door, even if she felt inclined."

"I will call the neighbours," cried Clara; "they at least may save me."

"Call away," said Mr. de Lancy: "they're used to screaming about here. I think they rather like it. It's a pleasing excitement upon a cold winter's night."

"Fiend!" exclaimed Clara, with a wild and feverish energy, her blue eyes sesming to emit sparks of fire, as she looked at Rupert de Lancy; "mocking and pitiless fiend!"

"Go on, Miss Melville," said the Manager: "pray don't stand upon ceremony."

"You say that yonder door is locked?"

"It is."

"And the key is in the possession of another?"

"Precisely so."

"She is, as you surmise, tipsy?"

"I have not the least doubt of it."

"And were I to scream till I rent the sky above us, she would scarcely hear me?"

"She would not heed you if by any chance she did hear you. I tell you she's used to screams; she rather enjoys the fun of them. She has her orders to unlock this door at a certain hour, and come what may, she won't open it five minutes before."

"Is there no other outlet from this chamber?"

"None, unless you'd like to try a jump from the window. It's four storeys high, without counting the ground floor."

"Then escape is impossible?"

"Quite impossible."

"Hopeless?"

"Utterly hopeless."

"Yet, stay one moment," cried Clara: "degraded as you have shown yourself to-night, you may not be utterly pitiless. Rupert de Lancy, hear me! By the memory of your mother, in the name of your wife, whose dishonour would be your degradation, spare me!"

She fell on her knees at his feet, her long fair hair, which she had only gathered together loosely on leaving the theatre, streaming wildly about her shoulders, and her large blue eyes lifted to the Manager's face.

Rupert de Lancy shrugged his shoulders.

"I might have spared you, Miss Melville,"

he said, "if you had been a little more civil; but you have said a few hard words, for which I am determined to make you suffer. You are quite right; I am a tool in this business, but you forgot to mention one thing, and that is, that I'm extremely well paid for it."

"Monster!" cried Clara; "then your doom is sealed. Since my destruction is certain, you shall perish with me."

She snatched the flaming candle from the table in the centre of the room, and rushing to the window set light to the thin calico curtains hanging before it.

The wintry breeze, blowing from the river, rushed in through the broken panes of glass, and spread with fearful rapidity.

"Madwoman!" shrieked Rupert de Lancy, "you know not what you have done. The children, your own brother and sister, are sleeping in the next room."

It was but too true. Little Jessie and George, whom Clara had last seen in a comfortable home, lay fast asleep upon a miserable bed in the adjoining apartment.

Heedless of herself, Clara rushed to the two children, and snatching Jessie in her arms, called to George to awake.

"Awake, awake," she cried; "the house is on fire!"

Children as they both were, there was a horrible meaning in these words which they could not fail to comprehend.

They knew that this cry meant terror, destruction, anguish, perhaps death.

They cluug wildly about their sister, crying again and again—

"Save us, Clara, save us!"

"Save you, my precious treasures," shrieked the tortured girl; "save you, alas! it is I who have destroyed you!"

Rupert de Lancy displayed some presence of mind in this horrible emergency. He rushed to the window, and showing himself amidst the raging flames, shouted to the people below.

"Save us," he shouted, "save us! A thousand pounds to the man who saves us."

Late as the hour was, and lonely as the neighbourhood had appeared only five minutes before, the street was already crowded with people, and a number of men and boys rushed off to fetch the nearest engine and fire-escape.

The cry circulated as if by magic amongst the crowd—"a thousand pounds to the man who saves them."

The flames curled about the crazy woodwork of the old house; the terrible fire-serpent licked the crumbling rafters with his red-hot tongue. The red and hissing blaze mounted to the wintry sky, while huge volumes of smoke burst forth in blinding masses of black vapour from every new chasm in the burning roof.

The screams of the agonised neighbours, the shrieks of half-naked children awakened from the heavy slumbers of poverty and hunger, the terrified groans of old men and women too feeble to fly from the danger, and the wild panic amongst the horrified spectators in the dense crowd below, all mingled into one great yell of terror and despair.

Rupert de Lancy rushed to the locked door communicating with the staircase, but the fire-fiend had been there before him; already the flames enveloped the doorway, and crept about the rotten woodwork of the staircase.

For one brief moment he gazed into the burning gulf below, but the heat of the fiery vapours rose to his face and blinded him—the noxious smoke stifled and stupefied him.

The bad man felt that his hour had come.

Of what avail now was his wealth? Powerless to save him from one of the pangs that accompany a horrible death.

With rage and despair at his heart, and blasphemy upon his lips, he groped his way to the window, whence alone he could hope for human aid or rescue.

At this moment a loud huzza resounded through the street. Every voice in the vast crowd was lifted in one hoarse cry of rapture.

The deliverers had come!

They came, those brave and valiant men, for whom danger has no fear—for whom death has no terror; whose noble lives are one long self-sacrifice, ever ready to be laid down for the rescue of others.

What death upon the battle-field can boast of greater glory than that of him who rushes into the burning ruins to save the helpless?

The trampling hoofs of the horses resounded through the streets— the crowd parting, as by a common instinct, made a pathway for the engine, and in another moment a ladder had been lifted against the crumbling frontage of the house, while volumes of water hissed against the red-hot brickwork.

Another loud huzza from the excited crowd.

The fireman had mounted the ladder.

Another and another! He reached the summit; one of the children was in his arms; in a moment he had clasped the other with one strong hand, and descending the ladder about half way, dropped them into the open arms of the crowd.

They were saved!

The moment of suspense was terrible. Clara, with her long hair streaming in the night breeze, and her beautiful but terror-stricken face illluminated by the flames, stood trembling upon the brink of destruction, awaiting her fate at the hands of Providence and her deliverers.

Sublime fortitude of self-sacrificing woman! Even in that moment of peril she could look on Death with calmness. The children, her darling brother and sister, were saved.

A moment more, and she was clasped in a pair of strong arms, and carried, half unconscious, down the ladder.

But it was not the fireman who had rescued her.

The brave man had not saved the children without undergoing frightful danger. His face had been scorched by the flames, and he had fainted in the arms of those about him.

In this crisis, a stranger, who had but that moment joined the eager throng below the burning house, leapt upon the ladder and mounted, amongst the cheers of the populace, to the summit.

When Clara recovered her senses, she found herself in the arms of the stranger, who was no other than the young tragedian, Antony Verner.

The flames were arrested by the brave efforts of the firemen, and though the house was left with only the shell-like walls remaining, the neighbouring buildings were spared.

Rupert de Lancy paid the price of his infamy. His charred and blackened corpse was found amongst the ruins.

A cab took Clara and the two children to Arlington Street, where she found the servants sitting up awaiting her return.

The coachman had waited for about ten minutes in Morley Street, when the old woman had come down to him to tell him that Miss Melville did not wish him to wait for her, as she meant to return in a cab.

The young man was fresh from a country village, where he had lived in the service of a clergyman. He knew nothing of London life, or he would never have left a young girl alone at such an hour and in such a neighbourhood.

George and Jessie told Clara the history of all that had occurred to them since their separation. The Yorkshire farmhouse, the abduction by the three men, and their meeting with their father at Hull. From Hull they had been brought to London, where they were given over into the custody of the old hag, Mother Bonner, who had taken them out every day to beg with her in the streets round the Borough, but who had never suffered them to escape from her sight.

"My darlings," exclaimed Clara, clasping them in her arms, "never again will I abandon you even for an hour. Poor children, we have powerful enemies, who are allied against us. My father, what may not be his fate? But if a daughter's devotion can restore him to happiness, he shall not long languish in despair."

In the papers next morning this paragraph appeared—

"TERRIBLE FIRE AND LOSS OF LIFE IN MORLEY STREET, BLACKFRIARS.—At two o'clock this morning one of the houses in Morley Street was burned to the ground. Mr. Rupert de Lancy, the Manager of the Paragon Theatre, fell a sacrifice to the burning element, and the favourite *danseuse*, Miss Clara Melville, who only last night appeared as Columbine at the same theatre, also fell a victim to the most terrible of deaths.

"Some dark mystery is supposed to be connected with this unhappy event. Our reporter is on the scent, and we shall ere long be able to furnish the fullest particulars."

Antony Verner read this paragraph to Clara.

"This mistake must be set right, Miss Melville," he said.

"What does it matter?" answered Clara; "better that my enemies should think me dead."

"Not so; the day may come when this may be of the utmost importance; nay, more than that, I am convinced that this very paragraph is the work of your enemies."

CHAPTER XXXVII.

CLARA'S PROMISE

ANTONY VERNER hurried to the office of the paper which had published the statement of Clara's untimely death. He was received by the Editor with the utmost politeness and attention.

"A foolish mistake of our reporter," said this gentleman; "it is to the interest of those people to make the worst, and not the best, of these kind of things. I will see that it is rectified in our next edition."

But the next edition appeared without a word in its columns to contradict the false statement, and when Antony Verner wrote an indignant letter to the Editor, complaining of this breach of faith, the letter was not inserted.

"Why do you give yourself so much trouble about all this?" Clara said, wonderingly. "Surely it can matter little."

"I have told you before, Miss Melville," answered Antony, gravely; "the day may come when this false statement may be a difficulty in our path. I should not be thus annoyed about

it did I attribute it to the mere stupidity of a newspaper reporter; but I suspect the hand of your enemies, and, above all, of your uncle, Sir Frederick Beaumorris, in this matter."

"What, you really believe me to be the niece of Sir Frederick!" said Clara, with an incredulous smile.

"As surely as I believe you to be the most amiable and beautiful of women," answered Antony Verner; "you are the daughter of Arthur Beaumorris, and the niece of that bad and designing man who has laid this wicked plot for your destruction. He must have some very powerful motive for his persecution of you. Some motive far more powerful than his anger at your rejection of his infamous addresses."

"And you imagine that motive to be——"

"Fear! He is anxious to destroy you. Why? Surely not simply because you are his niece, since you do not even attempt to obtrude upon him the claims of that relationship. No, Clara, he sees in you something more than a mere relation. He dreads in you the rightful owner of the fortune which he now possesses."

"You cannot mean this!" exclaimed Clara.

"What other clue can you find to his conduct? My uncle's dying words spoke of a dark and wicked secret. Of thirty long years of fraud and injustice. He was the steward and confidential business adviser of Sir Frederick, and your father's uncle. What more likely than that he may have betrayed his master, at the instigation of the base and unprincipled young Baronet? How else account for the abduction of your father and the two helpless children? How else explain the motive of this treachery? The keystone to the whole mystery is fear. Men of rank and fortune do not plot to assail the weak and helpless, whom they may spurn into the mud beneath their feet. They only fear those who possess some power, hidden though it may be. You, Clara, must have this power, and your foes know and tremble before it, though you yourself know it not. May the task be mine of unravelling this tangled skein."

"And to release my father! Oh, Mr. Verner, do that, and my eternal gratitude will be yours."

A crimson flush mounted to the young man's usually pale face; his dark grey eyes were illumined by one rapid flash of joy.

"Ah, Clara," he murmured, his deep voice trembling with emotion, "gratitude is a sweet word; but there is one sweeter still, which I fear I shall never hear from those lovely lips."

"And that word——?" faltered Clara, blushing.

"That word, Clara, is LOVE!"

A sudden ray of enthusiasm lighted up the young girl's truthful countenance—a bright and transient radiance, which gave something of inspiration to her lovely face.

"Antony Verner," she said, in calm and deliberate accents, "painful and humiliating as may be the avowal, I will candidly own to you that I have loved another—dearly, deeply!— far too deeply for my peace. That other believed my traducers rather than myself; he believed the witness of a forged letter rather than that of my own lips; and at the very moment in which he revealed his love, he flung me off for ever. Womanly pride forbade that I should do more than I had done in the endeavour to justify myself. I bowed to my fate, and banished the dear and fatal dream from my heart. But the dream for ever fled, a dreary chasm alone remained. No other image could ever fill that void left in my soul when his was banished from my heart. You know now, why it is that, good and noble, gifted and generous, as you are —I respect—I admire—but I can never love you!"

"I do, I do, Clara."

"But life is too sacred a gift to be wasted upon one broken dream. Restore me to my father; let me be once more clasped in those dear arms; let me be once more the comfort of his declining years; and if this poor hand, and the gratitude and duty of a lifetime can indeed repay you for your noble work, they shall be yours—yours on the day that my father's liberty is restored to him. Antony, will you accept them?"

No ray of a lover's passionate enthusiasm shone in the pale and thoughtful face of the young tragedian. It was with grave, nay, almost mournful accents that he replied—

"I will remember your promise, Clara, and if your father be yet alive, I will restore him to you." Then drawing the trembling girl towards him, he pressed his lips to her cold forehead.

"My poor, poor girl," he murmured, tenderly, "this is my first kiss, it shall be my last until the hour when I place you in a father's arms. Not in the arms of Jasper Melville, the outcast and the pauper, but Arthur Beaumorris, restored to wealth and station, friends and fortune."

* * * * * *

Two bodies were found amongst the ruins of the house in Morley Street; but so little was known of the wretched inmates of that haunt of iniquity, that neither of them were identified, and they were described in the coroner's verdict as two persons, names unknown. None knew what had become of the many inhabitants of the house, nor whether the infamous hag, Mother Bonner, had perished among the other victims of the catastrophe.

The hand which Clara had had in bringing about this punishment upon the guilty was known to none but herself and Antony Verner, to whom she had told the whole truth.

The Paragon Theatre passed into other hands, but Mr. Verner's engagement still continued, and he became every night more and more popular upon the Surrey side of the water, while West-end managers began to "have an eye upon" the successful young tragedian.

Clara was too much shaken by the terrible scenes through which she had passed, and was also suffering too much from her anxiety about her father, to be able to face the gay crowd and dazzling lamps of a theatre.

She had saved money during her winter's engagement, and she now devoted herself to her brother and sister, only leaving them for a few hours in the morning, during which she went out as morning governess, thus contriving to support herself and those dependent upon her, without becoming a burden to Lolota Vizzini.

The children soon recovered their good looks, and even their spirits, under Clara's tender care. They were too young to suffer as their elder sister did from the painful mystery of their father's disappearance; too young to understand much that was involved in the old man's abduction.

The winter wore away. The Houses of Parliament were reopened. London again began to fill with the gay crowds of rank and fashion; but Sir Frederick Beaumorris still remained at his country seat, and still did the honours of a house full of company.

Her Majesty's Theatre opened to its brilliant audience, and the lovely Spanish girl returned from her Parisian triumphs to win fresh laurels in the English metropolis.

Clara told her all that had taken place during her absence.

"My poor child," exclaimed the warm-hearted Lolota; "what new miseries have been your lot! So young and so friendless, but for this good Mr. Verner, who seems to have been your guardian angel. Ah! Clara! Clara! I fancy that the handsome tragedian would brave the dangers of a hundred burning houses for the bright glances of those sweet blue eyes. Is it not so?"

Clara blushed, but did not reply to the Spanish dancer's laughing interrogatory.

"Speak! speak! Miss Clara Melville. Is it not so?"

"Dearest, best of friends," exclaimed Clara,

THE OPENING OF THE STONE COFFIN

"why should I have one secret from you?" And in a few words she told the story of her fatal love for Reginald Falkner, and of her promise to Antony Verner.

"I am glad of this, Clara," answered Lolota, earnestly. "Better, better a thousand times as it is. I too have wasted the long hoarded treasures of my heart upon a phantom—upon a dream that can never, no, never be realised. I know, then, what these terrible delusions are—the slow agonies of a love that meets no return—the wasted tortures of a passion which we know to be hopeless, against the bondage of which our womanly pride revolts, but whose chains once worn must bind us until death. And for this poor and mocking shadow we would reject true love—true love, the beautiful flower which blooms but once in a lifetime; the sacred offering which the loveliest woman sometimes goes through life without beholding laid upon her altar. Oh, Clara, if this man does indeed love you—if he loves you with that pure and deep affection which is a stranger to the alloy of mere animal passion, and has no thought of self—if this be so, beware how you reject him; beware how you cast aside a gift which may never again be yours to refuse."

CHAPTER XXXVIII.

THE VAULTS BELOW CLAVERING ABBEY

EARLY in the month of April Oscar Bertrand accompanied his young wife in a journey from Beaumorris Castle to Clavering Abbey.

The state of Ellen's health forbade them travelling otherwise than by easy stages. She could not bear a long and fatiguing railway journey. An heir was expected for the hoarded thousands of her dead father. One child had been born during the period of Ellen's solitary retirement, but the helpless infant had only opened its soft blue eyes upon the light of day to close them again, as if in terror of the strange aspect of this troubled world. Ellen Bertrand had bitterly grieved at the ill-concealed indifference of her husband to the loss of this child.

A few cold words of consolation to the tearful mother, a few hackneyed expressions of regret, and the subject seemed to be for ever dismissed from the mind of the brilliant Colonel. Deeply as Ellen had felt this, she was too much a woman, and too tenderly attached to her husband, not to make excuses for him, even to herself.

"He is ambitious," she pleaded; "and the goodness of his noble heart is only alloyed by the distractions of the world. He has no time to think of these things as I do. Life is for him one long career of triumph. I cannot blame, however I may regret, this seeming coldness."

But this time Ellen Bertrand had no reason for these sad reflections. Her husband's devotion knew no bounds. He was untiring in his attentions, indefatigable in his care of the lovely invalid. Every guest at the Castle observed his affectionate anxiety; some even laughed at his tenderness.

They travelled from Beaumorris Castle to Carlisle, where they stopped for a couple of days to recruit Ellen's strength. From Carlisle they went to Lincoln, where they again paused in their journey, and from Lincoln they proceeded to London, where they spent a week at Mivart's Hotel. Happy in her husband's love, proud of his devotion, Ellen had but one sorrow in this journey. The Colonel had been attended by his valet, but he had dismissed an honest north-country girl, who had officiated as temporary lady's maid during Ellen's stay at Beaumorris Castle. In vain had Mrs. Bertrand pleaded for this girl who had grown wonderfully attached to her kind young mistress, and had served her with a devotion often met with amongst these simple rustic natures.

The Austrian Colonel had laughed at his wife's entreaties, affecting to treat her wish as a childish fancy, which it would be folly to indulge.

"My darling Ellen," he said, playfully, "surely you would not wish to keep this rough and hoydenish country girl in your service. Of course, as the wife of Oscar Bertrand—whom you have discovered, by this time, to be by no means an unfashionable man—you must be able to hold your place in the fashionable world; and how in mercy's name will you be able to do so, if you entrust the cares of your toilette to this village rustic?"

"But she has served me very well so far," remonstrated Ellen. "I am so accustomed to wait upon myself that I needed little attendance. But whatever help I did require, Maggie was quite clever enough to afford."

"Yes, my dear girl, that was very well in the wilds of the North, where a white muslin dress, with a simple hothouse flower twisted amongst your curls, was sufficient for the evening's costume. But in town it will be quite a different matter—there, and at Clavering Abbey too, you must shine as a star of fashion and elegance. An accomplished French maid will be indispensable to you, and I will myself find a suitable person."

"Poor Maggie, she was so fond of me," murmured Ellen.

"I dare say, my dear; but it is utterly impossible that you can keep her as your maid. Then, again, her name! Maggie! the very sound is abominable!" said Oscar Bertrand, laughing.

"But if I may not keep her as lady's maid, at least you will let me take her with me to Clavering Abbey? There she could be useful in a hundred ways, and I shall be happy if I know she is in the establishment."

"My dear Ellen," replied the Colonel, resolutely, "I cannot encourage such a silly caprice."

"Not even when it is the caprice of an invalid?" whispered Ellen, pleadingly.

"No, dearest; for I would see you above such childish fancies. I would see you a sensible woman; and, dearly as I love you, I must still refuse what I cannot help considering a foolish request."

The tears rose to Ellen's eyes at these measured words, but she pleaded no further, and on her arrival in London she was without any attendant whatever.

One morning during their stay at Mivart's, Oscar looked up from his paper as they sat at breakfast, and said, carelessly:

"Oh, by-the-bye, my dear Ellen, I think that I have succeeded in securing you an accomplished maid to attend to the all-important cares of your toilette. I saw the Countess of C—— at the opera last night, when I left your box for a turn in the corridors. She is going to reduce her establishment upon the marriage of her daughter, Lady Adela, and Lady Adela's maid is at your disposal. I belief she is a paragon of cleverness and a model of honesty."

"But if she is such a desirable person, why does not Lady Adela retain her?"

"Oh, on account of the merest whim. She is going through Germany for the bridal tour, and will not take any servants with her who do not understand German. I am sure, from the account I heard last night, that you will be delighted with the maid."

"As you please, dear Oscar, since I cannot have my poor Maggie; and since you say I must have some one, I care little who it is. I will call upon the Countess and make inquiries respecting this person."

"That will be impossible, my dear Ellen," replied the Colonel, hastily; "you must be satisfied with the information I obtained last night from Lady C——. We must leave for Hampshire by the twelve o'clock train, and I have made an appointment for you this morning with your new maid."

"As you please, Oscar," murmured Ellen.

"My dear, dutiful little wife!" exclaimed the Colonel, laughing. "It is now ten," he added, looking at his watch; "we have only two hours for all our preparations. You will have to avail yourself at once of the services of your new maid, and set her to work to pack your trunks."

A few minutes after this one of the liveried servants of the hotel brought Ellen a letter upon a silver salver. This letter was written on the thickest glazed paper, sealed with a coronet imprinted upon cream-coloured wax, and highly perfumed with attar of roses.

Ellen broke the seal, and read aloud as follows :—

"The Countess of C—— presents her compliments to Mrs. Bertrand, and begs to assure her that the bearer of this note is worthy of her every confidence."

"The young person is waiting below, ma'am," said the servant.

"Show her up," replied Colonel Bertrand.

In less than five minutes the footman returned, ushering in a woman of about five-and-forty years of age.

The young naturally cling to each other with an involuntary and instinctive sympathy, and Ellen could not repress a feeling of disappointment on finding that her new maid was not a girl, but a staid, matured woman. She was dark and tall, with a hard face, whose handsome features were unadorned by any charm of expression. It was almost a stony face—a face which took no light whatever from the soul within, and which, for any power it had of betraying emotion, might, indeed, have been hewn from granite.

The eyes were of a pale lustreless grey; the eyebrows black, and with a tendency to meet in the centre of the forehead; the mouth had a look of determination which degenerated almost into cruelty, and the chin was bony and prominent, the teeth white and regular, and the complexion sallow.

The lady's-maid was attired in a black silk dress, which fitted tightly to the throat, where it was adorned by a small linen collar. Her plain shepherd's plaid shawl had fallen a little off her shoulders, but was worn with the grace peculiar to a Frenchwoman. Her bonnet was of white straw trimmed with black ribbon.

It was impossible to point out anything objectionable in her appearance; and yet Ellen would have been delighted to find some objection to her.

Our likings and dislikings are not our own, and Mrs. Bertrand felt an involuntary distrust of this new maid.

Little as she in reality cared for any attendance at her toilette, she questioned the Frenchwoman very searchingly as to her acquirements; but it was in vain that she tried to find her at fault. Rosine Rousel was evidently well acquainted with all her duties.

At last Colonel Bertrand interfered.

"Really, my dear Ellen," he said, "you are unnecessarily particular; you have the Countess's assurance that this person is in every way suited to you, and yet you seem to hesitate; pray remember we have very little time to lose."

Ellen looked at her husband as if she would gladly have delayed her decision, but his brow was set in an almost severe expression, and she dared not hesitate longer.

"You may consider yourself engaged, then, Rosine," she said, coldly; "and, as I require you to commence your duties immediately, you had better send a cab to where you have been staying for your luggage."

That evening Ellen Bertrand entered the gates of Clavering Park for the first time since that wintry midnight on which she had fled from the old Abbey after her secret and hasty marriage within its ruined walls.

The two years which had elapsed since that time seemed to her an age, when looking back to her tranquil and eventless childhood and youth passed amid the stately avenues of the park.

The little lodge in which Ellen and her father had lived had been rebuilt, and was now a smart Gothic edifice, occupied by a comely couple and their rosy-cheeked children.

Everywhere the hand of improvement had been busy, and everywhere the good taste of the accomplished Austrian had left a trace. But the restoration of the old Abbey was as yet only half complete. A suite of apartments had been hastily prepared for the reception of the Colonel and his wife: these apartments consisted of a superb chamber, with an arched roof of black oak, which in old times had served as a refectory for the monks of Clavering. Adjoining this apartment (which had been richly decorated with a Turkey carpet, massive oak furniture, and crimson velvet hangings, and which was now the dining-room) was an octagon library, also of black oak, hung with crimson velvet, and from which a carved oak winding staircase led to an upper chamber, which was fitted as a luxurious sleeping-room, and which communicated with two dressing-rooms, a bath-room, and a boudoir.

A well-trained groom of the chambers carried a pair of wax lights before the Colonel and Ellen as he ushered them through these apartments.

After the two travellers had made their toilettes they met in the white boudoir, where an elegant little dinner awaited them.

The hangings of this peerless chamber were of the purest cream-coloured watered silk, with glittering fringes of silver. The carpet was of velvet pile; the ground white, scattered with peach-blossoms. The chimney-piece was of Parian marble, supported by water-nymphs, whose heads were crowned by wreaths of the most valuable pink coral. The lamp which hung from the exquisitely painted domed ceiling was of ground glass, shaped like a large water lily, and surrounded by frosted silver leaves.

The cabinets were of carved ivory; the chairs of a polished white wood, with peach-coloured velvet cushions.

Ellen was almost bewildered with admiration and delight.

"Tell me, dearest," said her husband, as they seated themselves at the dinner-table, after dismissing the servants, whose presence was irksome to the refined Colonel; "tell me what you think of all this?"

"Think, Oscar!" exclaimed the delighted girl; "why I can but think that you must be possessed of the lamp of Aladdin. How else could you raise such a palace as this out of the ruins I remember playing amongst in my careless childhood?"

"Wealth, Ellen, can do anything," replied the Colonel. "You know that I am rich, so rich that your father' thousands are less to me than a few pounds would be to a poor man!"

Ellen opened her large hazel eyes with a wondering glance.

"Yes, dearest; I am so rich that you may rest assured there was no mercenary feeling in my love for you."

*   *   *   *   *   *

The weather was cold and dull, but the hunting season was not quite over, and Colonel Bertrand found plenty of amusement in following the Clavering foxhounds with the gentlemen of the hunt.

Accomplished in all things, and at home in all places and amongst all people, the Austrian officer was a bold and daring rider. Dressed in a dark green coat, buckskin breeches, and polished hunting-boots reaching nearly to the knee, his tall and elegant figure appeared to the greatest advantage. It was with a feeling of pride that Ellen watched her husband from her boudoir windows as he mounted his covert hack and galloped off to the meet in the fresh wintry morning.

But in spite of the splendour of her abode, the young wife's days seemed long and lonely. In vain she tried to become reconciled to the society of her maid, Rosine Rousel. The French woman inspired her with a feeling which was almost akin to antipathy. Rosine had been ten years in England, and spoke the language with a precision and fluency rarely met with even after so long a residence. She seemed, however, silent and reserved by nature, and she rarely answered her kind young mistress except by measured monosyllables.

The Colonel's household was not yet complete, but there was one of the servants who particularly attracted Ellen's attention. This man was the butler, a person of the name of Griffiths, who powdered his hair, and always wore knee-breeches and black silk stockings.

He was also a foreigner, a German, notwithstanding his English (or rather Welsh) name. Oscar Bertrand appeared particularly attached to this man, who had, as he said, lived from his childhood upwards in the service of the Colonel's late father.

Griffiths certainly bore the stamp of the old servant of a noble family. His advanced age, his powdered hair, and old-fashioned costume, all combined to give him a venerable and respectable appearance; and the smart London servants who had been engaged to assist him in his duties, although they ridiculed his ceremonious manners and old-fashioned ways, did not dare to treat him otherwise than with the utmost respect.

Ellen and her husband had been three days at Clavering Abbey. The cold spring twilight was closing in on the third evening after their arrival, and the young wife sat in a low chair by the glittering steel fireplace in her luxurious boudoir.

She had hoped for her husband's return before dusk, but the leafless woods grew dull without her windows, and still he did not come. Rosine Rousel entered the room, and, after drawing the rustling silk curtains, lighted the lamp, which emitted a delicious perfume as it burned.

"The Colonel has not yet returned, Rosine?" asked Ellen, with a faint, lingering hope that Oscar might have re-entered the house unheard by her.

"No, Madame."

"Is it late, Rosine?"

"Half-past six, Madame."

"Tell them that I shall not dine unless Colonel Bertrand returns. You may bring me a cup of tea here in an hour. I have a terrible headache, and shall not sit up late."

The Frenchwoman curtsied and left the room.

Ellen sighed heavily as she glanced round the luxurious apartment.

"Oscar is all goodness and generosity," she murmured, "and I must be indeed a sceptic could I doubt that he loves me. And yet—and yet—I wish that he cared more for my society. These long weary days and lonely evenings are very hard to bear."

A little after ten o'clock she summoned her maid and retired to rest. Rosine did not utter a word as she brushed the long chestnut-coloured tresses of her young mistress, who had flung herself into an easy-chair before the cheval-glass.

This evening Ellen was peculiarly sensitive and out of spirits. The silence of the large bed-chamber seemed almost oppressive to her. She could not withdraw her gaze from the dark face of the Frenchwoman reflected in the glass before her. At last, scarcely knowing what she said, and as if anxious to break the spell, she spoke.

"You must find Clavering Abbey a dull place after the West-end of London?" she said, carelessly.

"No, Madame. I do not care for gaiety," answered Rosine.

"And you are happy in the country?"

"As happy in the country as in London."

"You say that almost as if you felt little happiness in either," said Ellen. The woman's manner puzzled her, and she felt her curiosity strangely aroused by the answers of Rosine.

"Perhaps, Madame, you are right. But why should you wish to know my sentiments, my opinions, my likes and dislikes? You have wealth, youth, beauty; a husband who, if appearances are not delusions, loves you dearly. What interest can you have in a lonely wretch like me?"

There was a tone of suppressed bitterness, of stifled passion, in the voice of the Frenchwoman which made Ellen shiver. The dark brow in the cheval-glass was contracted by a convulsive frown; the dull grey eyes flashed with an unwonted fire.

"There are some," continued Rosine, in the same harsh and grating voice, "to whom life is all sunshine. Others who know nothing but the storm-cloud and the tempest. Men wonder that these last grow bitter—but the evil spirits who watch life's battle rejoice in the darkness of these vengeful hearts. They can but come to fate, which is stronger than themselves. But sooner or later the hand of vengeance must come. They are patient; they submit; they are silent: nay, more, they are almost content; they have a purpose. They wait until that hour strikes."

Ellen Bertrand's cheeks whitened as she listened to these strange words.

"The woman is certainly insane," she thought. "I will tell Oscar of her strange manner, and she shall not stay at the Abbey another night."

She hurried over the rest of her toilette, and dismissing Rosine before she retired to rest double locked the door of her apartment.

"I will open it to no one except my husband," she thought.

A strange terror had taken possession of her mind. She feared that this woman might murder her.

* * * * * *

It was long past eleven when Oscar Bertrand rode into the court-yard of Clavering Abbey. He was admitted into the hall by Griffiths, who had dismissed all the other servants, and waited up alone for the return of his master.

He held a massive silver candlestick with an immense wax candle in his hand as he opened the door, and led the way across the hall into the ancient refectory.

At one end of the long dining-table a cloth had been spread, and a cold chicken and a bottle of claret were laid out for the Colonel's supper. Griffiths placed the candle at this end of the table, and, lighting another, wheeled forward an easy-chair, into which the Colonel flung himself with an air of fatigue.

"I have had a hard day's work, Herman," he said. "I rode over to Basingstoke, caught the ten-o'clock express; and was in the City by twelve o'clock, and while my poor little wife fancied that I was riding after the Clavering foxhounds, I was up to my eyes in business at the Central Office. Have you too been at work, Herman?"

"I have, Captain. The mason you sent from London was a member?"

"He was."

"I thought you would entrust none other with our secrets. The man worked well and quietly, and he has constructed a passage leading into the vaults below the Abbey."

"Good! But where is the entrance to this passage?" asked the Colonel.

The old German smiled significantly.

"Not a dozen yards from the chair in which you are seated, Captain," he replied. "You see that ponderous black oak sideboard yonder?"

"I do."

"It has two cupboards. The one on the right is filled with valuable plate; that on the left——"

"Ah, I can guess the rest!" exclaimed Oscar Bertrand. "You have done well, Herman."

"I thought you would approve, Captain. No one would suspect yonder sideboard. It is too massive a piece of furniture to be removed, and I have taken a still further precaution by having it fastened to the flooring with heavy iron screws. The door on the left opens with a spring, which works with a double action, and is too complicated to be discovered by any accident. Inside the cupboard is a trap-door communicating with the passage."

"Good, Herman! It could not have been better had I myself superintended the business."

"And now, Captain, that all has been done to your satisfaction, may I ask your motive for having this passage constructed?"

"You may, Herman; but in order to tell you this, I must go back to some three hundred years ago, when Clavering Abbey still belonged to a body of monks, the wealthiest order in the South of England."

"I am all attention, Captain."

"In the remotest depths of the New Forest was a princely estate called Pierswood. It belonged to Godwin de Piers, the eldest scion of a noble family, whose escutcheon was as ancient as any in England, but whose annals had been stained by so many deeds of crime, bloodshed, rapine, and cruelty, that the surrounding peasantry shrank from Piers of Pierswood, and all his hated race, almost as they would have shrunk from the Evil One himself. But crime had enriched this haughty house. Oppression had swelled the coffers of this dreaded family; and when Godwin de Piers succeeded to the estate, he was one of the wealthiest men in England.

"He was twenty-four years of age at the death of his father, handsome and athletic, with a commanding figure, a face of statuesque-like beauty, curling flaxen hair, and large bright blue eyes.

"This was at the close of the reign of Richard the Third.

"But handsome as Godwin de Piers was, he rarely showed his manly form beyond the battlements of his own castle. He never joined the chase; he had never been seen at a tournament or festival. Young as he was, he led the life of a recluse within the dark walls of Pierswood.

"Strange rumours began to circulate in the surrounding districts. Men whispered that Piers of Pierswood was an idiot.

"The crimes of generations long passed away had been visited on this young man.

"He had a younger brother, a dark-faced, active youth, whose burning black eyes had a feverish and an evil lustre, and wherever the idiot lord was seen, Gaveston, the younger, was at his elbow—always on the watch, ever ready to conceal Godwin's deficiencies, to gloss over his sad infirmity.

"Men, short-sighted and shallow-pated as they ever are, lauded the affectionate devotion of the younger brother.

"Every morning at early sunrise, and every evening at sunset, the two brothers walked together upon a stone gallery which ran round the topmost roof of the castle.

"From this gallery to the moat below was a distance of three hundred feet.

"One evening the brothers walked later than usual; the sun sunk below the changing woods, the trembling moon-rays were reflected in the dark waters of the moat, the castle clock was on the stroke of nine, when a terrible shriek rang through the vaulted staircases of the turret, and Gaveston de Piers rushed into the hall where the inmates of the castle were assembled at their evening meal.

"'My brother!' he cried, 'my unhappy brother! He has thrown himself from the roof of the castle. He is killed!'

"It was true. They found the mangled form of Godwin de Piers lying on the brink of the moat, the castle walls spattered with his blood.

"But none suspected the entire truth. Few cared to inquire into the matter, and none knew until years afterwards that the unhappy idiot had been hurled from the castle roof by the murderous hand of his brother Gaveston.

"The assassin had little pleasure from his ill-gotten wealth. A year after his brother's death he fell from his horse while following the chase, and was lamed for life.

"Twenty years afterwards he entered Clavering Abbey, carrying with him the wealth of the house of Piers, which on his death passed into the possession of the monks."

"Ah!" exclaimed Herman; "I begin to comprehend—this wealth——"

"This wealth still exists, and to-night will pass into the hands of the Society of the BLACK BAND. The reign of Henry the Eighth brought the hand of the spoiler upon the property of the Church, but the monks of Clavering were too wise to fall a prey to the robber; the whole of the wealth appertaining to the order was concealed in stone coffins in the vaults beneath the Abbey. Those vaults were walled up, and for all these years have remained unsuspected and undiscovered; they have never been opened till now."

"But how knew you all this?" asked Herman Griffiths.

A sardonic smile curved the thin lips of Colonel Oscar Bertrand.

"You look as if you thought I had dealings with the Evil One," he said. "No, Herman, I obtained my information from an old Latin manuscript which I found among the papers of the late Lucas Clavering, and which neither the miser nor his ancestors had ever taken the trouble to peruse."

"Strange," muttered the old butler.

"My star is in the ascendant, Herman; every day adds to the wealth of the marvellous association of which I am the head. But there is no time to be lost; get a lantern, and lead the way into the vaults. I long to reconnoitre the spot, and discover if I have been deceived by the crabbed Latin syllables upon this mouldering parchment."

Herman Griffiths obeyed, and the two men crept through the door of the oak sideboard, and lowered themselves into the vault beneath. A couple of pickaxes and a spade lay upon the ground, in the close vicinity of one of the stone coffins of which the Colonel had spoken. Herman Griffiths seized one of these pickaxes, and with a dozen vigorous strokes lifted the massive stone coffin-lid, which fell back with a clamour that resounded through the arched vault. Oscar Bertrand turned the light of the lantern full upon the contents of this coffin. The Latin manuscript had not deceived him. The light shone upon a heap of glittering gold.

CHAPTER XXXIX.

THE HIDDEN DAGGER

AN heir was born to Colonel Oscar Bertrand, of Clavering Abbey. The bells rang joyously from the village church, and the happy rustics assembled in the great oak-panelled hall, where Herman Griffiths feasted them with good old English cheer and strong old English ale.

But amidst all these rejoicings, a gloomy shadow seemed to hang over the luxurious chamber of the young mother.

Colonel Bertrand was seldom by the side of his wife's couch. A hurried visit in the early part of the day was all Ellen ever saw of her beloved husband.

He had business, he said, important business, which obliged him to run up to London; or he had visits to pay in the neighbourhood, or improvements to superintend on the estate.

Ellen was too well used to submission to venture one murmur at this; but she did not feel it the less deeply.

The heir of Clavering was a noble and a thriving baby; but the young mother lay for some weeks on a sick bed, while the bright June sunshine stole through the narrow crevices in

MIDNIGHT IN THE COLONEL'S CHAMBERS

the closed Venetian shutters, and the beeches in the park waved their verdant branches under the clear blue summer sky.

Throughout the illness of her mistress, Rosine Rousel never quitted the sick-chamber. In vain had Ellen implored her husband to dismiss the Frenchwoman. He had only laughed at her fears, and dismissed her arguments as childish and absurd.

Ellen had never forgotten the strange words uttered by this woman, and the scene of that lonely night, on which her heart had sunk within her at the sight of Rosine's vengeful face reflected in the glass, often returned to her in the long and monotonous hours of her illness.

She shuddered as she lifted her heavy eyelids to see the Frenchwoman seated, gloomy and silent, half hidden by the dark shadow of the

No. 12. [*Weekly, One Penny.*]

purple velvet bed-curtains, watching her mistress as Death himself might watch for his expected victim.

A month after the birth of the child Ellen Bertrand lay one evening in an uneasy slumber, while Rosine Rousel kept watch in an easy-chair at the head of the bed. The shaded lamp shed a dim light upon the pale face of the invalid, and left the rigid and stony countenance of the attendant in shadow. The nurse and child were sleeping in an inner room, separated from Ellen's apartment by a short corridor. Colonel Bertrand was in London.

The invalid's slumber had been disturbed by fearful dreams. Sometimes she had thought herself wandering alone at midnight in the dark avenues of Clavering Park, her baby in her arms, and her naked feet torn by the wild undergrowth and thorny briars growing in the narrow pathways. Neither moon nor stars illumined the gloomy sky—she could scarcely see the child clinging to her breast, but struggled blindly on, striving to reach a place of safety, yet for ever compelled to retrace her steps, and ever going backward instead of onward, till, in the midst of one of these dark pathways, she was arrested by a man whose face was masked, who snatched her infant from her, and as he turned to leave her raised his mask for one brief moment, and revealed the pale face and flashing black eyes of her husband, Oscar Bertrand.

This was the first dream.

In the second she was with her husband in some strange foreign city. The streets were crowded by an excited and noisy populace; eager faces looked from every window, from the roofs of ancient houses; even from the battlements and pinnacles of a vast cathedral; from the casements in the dizzy belfries of grey old churches. In the centre of all this expectant crowd, in the midst of a square of stone buildings, stood an elevated platform, on to which Oscar Bertrand was about to ascend, to be crowned, as he told his anxious wife, Archduke of his native Austrian city. But suddenly, as he mounted the wooden steps, a cloud obscured the bright noonday sky, sonorous peals of thunder roared in the distance, the city clocks struck the hour of twelve, the voices of the populace rose in one hoarse yell of execration, and the platform changed into a scaffold, while two masked executioners advanced, axe in hand, on either side of the pale Colonel.

This was the second dream.

The third brought a change to the sleeper's vision. She was alone once more—alone upon some mighty plain—some vast desert, far away in an unknown tropical clime. The wide expanse of smooth white sand stretched like the ocean before her feet. The midnight sky was lighted by a moon larger and brighter than she had ever seen before—a moon that shed a terrible blue lustre upon the hideous monotony of the desert scene. This time, again, the young mother carried her child in her arms, and this time again she had the same fear for her infant's safety which she had felt in her dream of the avenues in Clavering Park. And again her fears were not deceived. Suddenly a glittering serpent uncoiled its shining rings from the sand at her feet, and, rising slowly till it towered above her, looked down upon her with strange and evil eyes, the green light in which gradually died out, leaving them dull and lustreless as the pale grey orbs of the Frenchwoman, Rosine Rousel.

With a shriek of terror Ellen Bertrand awoke to behold her hated attendant standing over her with a slender blade of bright steel shining in her uplifted hand.

Another moment and she might have been stabbed to the heart as she slept.

Paralysed by terror, Ellen Bertrand lay for some few moments powerless either to speak or move.

With a wonderful presence of mind the Frenchwoman concealed the long and pointed blade of a peculiarly-shaped dagger in the sleeve of her black silk dress, and reseated herself quietly by the bedside.

Ellen caught the bell-rope hanging at the head of the bed within the folds of the velvet curtains, and pulled it violently.

It was past eleven o'clock, and the shrill peal of the bell vibrated through the quiet mansion.

Rosine Rousel bit her pale lips with a savage energy.

"If you want anything, my lady," she said, in a suppressed but steady voice, "why not ask me to procure it for you? The ringing of the bell may disturb the infant, and there is no one below at this hour but the old butler, Herman Griffiths."

Ellen Bertrand shuddered, but did not answer.

The Frenchwoman rose from her chair, and crossing the room, unlocked a cabinet of jet and Indian gold.

Ellen knew instinctively that the would-be-murderess was concealing her weapon.

The bell was answered by the nurse and Herman Griffiths.

"Is anything wrong, Madam?" the old man asked.

"I have been disturbed by fearful dreams, Griffiths," answered Ellen, who had by this time partly recovered her self-possession; "I was very foolish to ring and arouse you all, but as I have done so I will make a little change in my arrangements. Rosine, who has been watching two or three nights running, can retire to rest, and Mrs. Rignold will, I daresay, be good enough to sit up with me."

Mrs. Rignold was the nurse, a comfortable, motherly-looking woman, who had been hired from London to attend the invalid.

"Ah, that I will, ma'am," she said, "if it was six nights instead of one, for it's a right down pleasure to wait upon such a sweet lady, that it is. And when I fail in my dooty toward you, ma'am, why say that Sarah Jane Rignold, as has been a monthly nurse now these thirty years and more, ain't fit to be trusted and don't deserve a good word said of her."

"You are very kind, my good Mrs. Rignold," said Ellen. "I shall not give you much trouble, and you can take a comfortable nap in that easy-chair. You hear, Rosine!" she added, addressing the Frenchwoman, who stood perfectly still, staring straight before her with the fixed and stony gaze peculiar to her, " you hear, Rosine, you can go!"

The lady's-maid moved slowly to the door, but, pausing as she was about to leave the room, she turned round and addressed her mistress.

"You are not satisfied with me, Madam?" she said.

"I did not say so," answered Ellen, coldly.

"But you dismiss me from your bed-chamber?" said the Frenchwoman in the same tone of suppressed passion.

"I dismiss you because I consider you have watched long enough, and I do not choose you to remain any longer," answered Ellen, firmly.

Her courage had returned, for she felt that she had a friend in Sarah Rignold, the nurse, and one who, woman as she was, could defend her stoutly.

"Can't you take no for an answer, young woman?" said the nurse, as Rosine Rousel still hesitated; "you furriners seem uncommon hard of hearing. Your missus don't want you, and you can go about your business! That's plain English, ain't it? I should think if you can understand anything you can understand that."

The Frenchwoman did not condescend to notice this speech; she did not even appear to be aware that the portly nurse had spoken.

"I am to go, then, Madam?" she said, still addressing herself to Ellen.

"Yes."

"And you decline to say why you send me from your chamber?"

"To-night I do, but to-morrow morning I will tell you my reasons."

Rosine walked slowly from the room followed by the old butler. The door had scarcely closed upon them when Ellen beckoned the nurse to her, and exclaimed in an agitated whisper—

"Lock the door, Mrs. Rignold, double lock it if you can, and come and sit close by my side; I only look to you for protection for myself and my child. The lives of both of us are in danger while that terrible woman remains beneath this roof."

Meanwhile Rosine and the old butler walked slowly through the long corridors leading to the part of the Abbey which had been rendered habitable for the servants.

"So," said Herman Griffiths, "so, Mademoiselle Rousel, alias Lalouette, alias Merlan, alias Perelle, alias Babincourt, alias De la Grécy,

you are at your old games, are you, tiger-cat? You have some of the old venom left, have you, viper? You can sting yet, can you, wild cat! And even that poor dove up yonder is not safe from your claws."

"What is she to you?" asked the Frenchwoman, fiercely.

"She is a poor little helpless, innocent, loving creature, who has fallen into a nest of serpents; and I will not see her harmed."

"You!" exclaimed Rosine, with an expression of pitiless scorn. "Who are you, Monsieur Herman Griffiths, that you should dare to interfere? Are you not one of us?"

"One of the Black Band? yes, Mademoiselle. One of the society of clever men for the appropriation of the misapplied wealth of fools," added the old man, with a sardonic tone; "but there is no *red cross* against my name in the Grand Master's Register."

The Frenchwoman shivered involuntarily.

A red cross was inscribed against the name of any member who was known to be ready to shed blood, if necessary to secure success in his horrible calling. Two crosses for the name of him or her whose hands had been already dyed in human gore; and a fresh cross for every new murder.

* * * * * *

Early the next morning Colonel Bertrand returned to the Abbey. His first visit was to his wife's room.

He found the invalid in a high fever, but she was not delirious, and she was able to relate to him the whole of the events of the previous night.

But this time as before he treated her terrors as childish.

"My darling Ellen," he said, "this is very foolish. Your weak state of health, and nervous temperament, make you subject to terrible dreams. You wake from one of them and find your servant watching you, alarmed, no doubt, by your restless slumber. Blending your dream with reality, you fancy you behold a dagger in this poor girl's hand, and cry out that you are going to be murdered. If you were not an invalid, my dearest Ellen, I should really scold you for disturbing a whole household on account of such silly delusions."

Ellen Bertrand raised herself from her pillow and looked long and steadily into her husband's face. The piercing gaze of those burning black eyes did not flinch even beneath that earnest scrutiny. The soul within was too deeply steeped in crime, and had been too long familiar with guilt, not to have become a stranger to both remorse and terror.

"Oscar," said the young wife, "this is not

the first time you have laughed at my fears and ridiculed my instinctive terror of this woman. Do not, for pity's sake, give me reason to believe that the safety of my life is a matter of indifference to you; or, more terrible still, that some fatal link binds you to this French lady's-maid, and compels you to be blind to her actions. Be it as it may, I tell you that, sooner than stay another hour beneath the same roof as that which shelters Rosine Rousel, I will rise from my bed, ill as I am, and walk from this house, never again to re-enter it."

The Colonel shrugged his shoulders, looking at the excited speaker with a pitying smile. "It shall be as you wish, my poor Ellen," he said; "the woman shall go. What interest can I have in detaining her, beyond the wish that you should have a clever attendant?"

As he said this he rose from his seat by the bedside and rang a bell. It was answered by Mrs. Rignold.

"Send Mrs. Bertrand's maid here," he said.

Five minutes afterwards Rosine Rousel entered the room. The Frenchwoman was deadly pale: dark purple circles surrounded her dull grey eyes. Her thin lips were rigidly compressed above her shining white teeth—teeth that in their glittering whiteness reminded one of those of a wild animal.

"Mrs. Bertrand will dispense with your services henceforth, Mademoiselle Rousel," the Colonel said, ceremoniously. "You will receive a month's wages, as well as the amount already due to you, and your travelling expenses to town. You may, therefore, consider yourself free from this very hour."

"Has Madam assigned any reason for dismissing me?" asked the Frenchwoman.

"She has."

"And that reason is——"

"The caprice of an invalid. Mrs. Bertrand had a disagreeable dream."

"Was I connected with that dream, Monsieur?"

"Yes. My wife imagined that she saw you bending over her with a dagger in your hand."

The Frenchwoman laughed aloud, a hollow, mocking laugh, that rang sharply through the room.

"Madam must have had the fever very badly last night," she said, sneeringly. "She had very foolish dreams."

Ellen Bertrand raised herself from her pillow, pale with agitation, and her hazel eyes flashing with indignant lustre.

"So true were those dreams, murderess," she exclaimed, "that I can point out the very spot in which you afterwards concealed the dagger.

Oscar Bertrand, search yonder cabinet, and you will find the confirmation of my words."

The Colonel crossed the room, and threw open the doors of the Indian cabinet to which Ellen pointed.

It was a valuable and intricate piece of workmanship, with numerous drawers and shelves.

After one hasty glance at its contents, the Austrian officer wheeled the cabinet across the room to his wife's bedside. "Search for yourself, my dear Ellen," he said, quietly; "I can see no dagger there."

He was indeed right. Ellen examined drawer after drawer, but could find nothing but a few Indian shells and feathers.

The Colonel did not choose to inform her that the principal and most useful receptacle in this piece of furniture was a species of trap-door in the top, which opened with a spring, and let any object dropped into it fall through a narrow shaft communicating with the compartments below.

The architect and the bricklayers employed in the restoration of Clavering Abbey had, every one of them, been members of the Black Band. Every chamber in the old house communicated in some mysterious way with the apartments above, below, and surrounding it.

A sneer of triumph curled the thin upper lip of the Frenchwoman.

"You see that your dream was a false one, Madam," she said. "You will be more careful another time how you condemn an innocent person. Monsieur, Madam, I have the honour to bid you good morning."

She curtsied to the ground, and slowly left the room.

"Now, Ellen, are you convinced of the unfounded nature of your fears?" said Oscar Bertrand, when the lady's-maid had retired.

"No, Oscar. I still fear, I still tremble. That woman is more, even, than a murderess. She has the cunning of a fiend!"

CHAPTER XL.

THE SECRET INTERVIEW IN THE ALBANY

We must now change our scene to the luxurious set of bachelor apartments occupied by Colonel Oscar Bertrand in the Albany.

The events of the terrible night described in our last chapter had checked the progress of Ellen's recovery, and she still lay on a sick-bed, attended by the faithful and warm-hearted monthly nurse, Sarah Rignold, who was assisted in her duties by a young girl of about sixteen years of age, who had been hired in the village to take charge of the youthful heir of Clavering.

The helpless infant, unconscious of its mother's fears and sorrows, unconscious of the thousands and the broad acres to which it was the heir, slept the dreamless sleep of infancy, heedless of all that passed around, and happy in its young nurse's arms.

Meanwhile Oscar Bertrand mixed once more with the fashionable throng in the crowded saloons of the aristocratic world, while the meaner members of the association of which he was master did his bidding in the dark hours after midnight.

It was late one night when he returned to his chambers from a dinner-party at which he had been one of the most distinguished guests.

He had only one servant in the Albany, a confidential man, who went about his work with the silence and regularity of an automaton; who asked no questions, but who could almost guess his master's wishes from a look or a gesture.

The Colonel stopped in the hall to speak to this man.

"Has anybody called?" he asked.

"No one, sir."

"Any letters?"

"Only one, sir."

Colonel Bertrand entered the library, which was lighted by a shaded lamp, and exchanging his evening costume for a loose brocaded dressing-gown, flung himself on to the downy cushions of a morocco-cover couch.

A little table stood at his elbow, and upon this table lay the letter the servant had spoken of.

It was addressed in a cramped foreign-looking hand.

The Colonel shrugged his shoulders as he broke the seal.

"So, she will be here to-night, she says, at half-past eleven," he muttered, as he threw down the letter impatiently. "She knows of my engagement at Lord Willoughby's, and has chosen her time accordingly. So be it; the woman is clever, and is useful to us. I will see her."

He touched the spring of an ormolu bell on the table at his side, and his watchful servant appeared immediately in answer to the summons.

"A lady will call here at half-past eleven o'clock," said the Colonel. "Admit her."

The man bowed, and retired as softly as he had entered.

About ten minutes afterwards a low double knock sounded on the panel of the outer door.

The servant re-entered the room ushering in the expected visitor.

"The lady," he said, announcing her.

The lady lifted her veil and revealed the features of the Frenchwoman, Rosine Rousel.

But not Rosine Rousel as the reader has already seen her. No longer attired in her plain and tight-fitting dress of black silk, the French lady's-maid was now arrayed in the height of fashion. Costly silk flounces rustled about her as she moved; valuable bracelets adorned her wrists; her small hands were exquisitely gloved; her mantle trimmed with the richest lace; her bonnet such as a countess might have worn.

But it was not alone in costume that she was changed. Her sallow complexion was relieved by a faint blush of carmine, so skilfully applied as almost to escape detection; her dull grey eyes were lighted up by a slender line of black drawn through the lashes; her pearl-white teeth were contrasted by the artificial redness of her lips.

In manner, as well as in appearance, Rosine Rousel had undergone a complete transformation. No longer the subdued lady's-maid, with stiff and rigid movements and suppressed tone of voice, she was now a dashing and elegant Parisian, and as she glanced round the room and flung herself carelessly upon a sofa, it was evident that she felt more at her ease in the Albany than she had been at Clavering Abbey in her menial capacity.

"Are you alone, Oscar?" she said.

"Quite alone."

"You have denied yourself to me many times," she murmured, reproachfully.

"Yes; because I had nothing to say to you," he answered, coldly.

"But might not I have something to say to you?"

"Nothing that I had any wish to hear."

"Oscar, have you quite forgotten the past?"

"Forgotten!" cried the Austrian, with a bitter laugh; "do we ever forget the past? Does the criminal, listening in his condemned cell for the stroke of the clock that shall summon him to the knotted noose and the yawning drop—does he, even in that last horrible hour betwixt life and death, forget the past? No. The green fields in which he played as a boy; the rustic cottage beneath whose roof he was born; the face of his mother; the voices of his boyish playfellows; all, all are remembered! Every hillock on the greensward, every bird's-nest in the tangled hedge, every tree and flower, are more distinct to him than the events of yesterday. There is no such thing as the past. The recollections of our youth are ever present. We may kill remorse, we may smother conscience, stifle regret, pity, terror, despair; but MEMORY still remains—*that* we cannot destroy."

"Then you have not forgotten, Oscar?" asked the Frenchwoman.

"No, Rosine. But if you would not have me hate you, do not attempt to recall the events of ten years back."

An angry cloud passed over the woman's face.

"My devotion might have deserved a better return than this," she said, reproachfully.

"*Your* devotion!" he exclaimed, with a sneer; "the devotion of an accomplished trickster and cheat, who found a dupe and a tool in a young man of noble birth, and who taught him to become guilty as herself! Who guided the young officer's hand in his first forgery? Who planned the first slender elements of that terrible association which now overruns Europe with its depredations? Indeed, Rosine, I have ample reason to be grateful to you, since but for you I should not be—what I am!"

"But for me," said the Frenchwoman, scornfully, "you might still be a sub-lieutenant in an Austrian regiment, without enough money in your purse to buy yourself a new pair of gloves."

"But for you," answered the Colonel, "I might have been an honest man."

Rosine Rousel laughed aloud.

"*You* an honest man!" she said. "You! No, Oscar Bertrand; there are some men born to be kings, legislators, politicians, sages, poets; and there are others born to be great criminals. You are one of these. As a boy I recognised in you the undeveloped genius which would make you greater than Cartouche, greater than Lacenaire. The result has proved that I was not wrong,"

"Be it so, then," answered the Austrian; "I admit that I must follow my destiny, and I blame you no longer for the share you have had in shaping my pathway. Neither have you cause to reproach me."

"Have I not, Oscar? Does your own heart not reproach you for your forgetfulness of me, who would have died to serve you? Do you think when you chose me as your tool in this business, whose purport I can fathom, although you scorned to make me your confidante—do you think I did not suffer the tortures of jealousy and despair when I beheld you wedded to that pale-faced girl whom you have chosen to be your wife?"

"I had a motive for that choice," replied Colonel Bertrand; "you and I were never meant to mate, Rosine. We are too much alike; each has the spirit that would rule: it would have been a life struggle between us for the mastery. Ellen is beautiful, affectionate, gentle: as far as it is possible for such a man as I to love, I love her. More than this, she is rich."

"Very rich?"

"Very rich. Her father died possessed of an immense fortune—a fortune that had been hoarded through years of penury. This wealth, by the old man's will, is bequeathed to his daughter."

"And to her alone?" asked the Frenchwoman, with peculiar significance. "Has the will no other clause?"

"It has," replied the Colonel. "After her death the money is to go to her children. If she have a son, he is to assume the name of Clavering."

"And if she die childless?"

"The money is to go to her husband."

The Frenchwoman lifted her strongly-marked eyebrows with a puzzled expression, as if absorbed in deep thought; then, looking at the Austrian with a new light in her grey eyes, she said, with a sinister smile:

"I know now why you wanted me at Clavering Abbey, Oscar."

The Colonel shrugged his shoulders.

"I wanted some one on whom I could rely," he said, carelessly; "some one in whose courage and discretion I could alike confide. You have failed me. Your imprudent conduct towards my wife has ruined my scheme."

"You should have trusted me sooner, Oscar," answered Rosine. "Do you think that I could endure the hateful presence of the woman you love? No, my passion carried me out of myself. I was no longer the cold-blooded, calculating Rosine, whom you have known and trusted for years. I was a tigress—nay, I was something more terrible than a tigress—I was a jealous woman!"

"Your jealousy has spoiled my plan, Rosine. I must trust to meaner instruments to do my work."

"And your work is—death?" gasped the Frenchwoman, in an awful whisper.

Colonel Bertrand shook his head.

"The heir of Clavering will die!" said Rosine.

"He will take the chances of all other heirs of this mortal flesh," said the Austrian, "but neither I nor those who serve me will have any hand in his death."

"What, then, is your scheme?' asked his accomplice.

"He will disappear!"

Rosine Rousel drew a long breath,

"Bah!" muttered the Colonel, as he perceived her air of surprise. "Do you think these hands are ever stained, directly or indirectly, with unnecessary blood? It is only your vulgar villain who wades to the accomplishment of his purpose through gore. No; death is but the last fatal instrument of the accomplished criminal. I have little need to deal with the poison chalice or the knife. A word, a look, and the creature who stands in my pathway is removed for ever, to drag out life in some dim obscurity; to lose his own identity; to disappear from the ranks of his fellow-kind; so that his own brother, meeting him in the street, shall pass him by with a shudder of loathing; but still to live!"

"I see the drift of your scheme, Oscar," said Rosine, "and you may still trust me if you require my service. In the meantime, remember that I am poor, and have need of your assistance."

"Poor! with those gewgaws about you," retorted the Colonel, pointing to the gold bracelets upon her wrists.

"I live amongst people who believe me to be wealthy," answered the Frenchwoman; "it is necessary to my interests; nay, more—it is indispensable to the interests of the Society that they should continue so to think of me. Pshaw! Oscar, out of your wealth you will never refuse me a few poor hundreds?"

"A few poor hundreds!" echoed the Colonel, smiling; "the Countess de la Grécy has not forgotten her old ideas of splendour. No, my dear Rosine, I will not refuse you a cheque on my bankers," he added, rising from his seat and opening an *escritoire* opposite to the sofa on which Rosine was seated; "I will write you one for a hundred pounds to begin with, and in a few days you will hear further from me on the subject of which we have been speaking. I can trust you, can I not?"

"You can, Oscar."

"You will swear to me, Rosine, that no jealous feeling, no hatred of this unhappy girl, shall influence you in the matter?"

"It shall not, Oscar; I swear it!"

CHAPTER XLI.

DARK DEEDS BROUGHT TO LIGHT

LOLOTA VIZZINI had returned to London, and had resumed her old position as Star of the Ballet. In vain did the Spanish woman endeavour to persuade Clara Melville to resume her professional duties.

"No, dearest friend," said the young girl; "weary as may be the drudgery of the life of a morning governess, I can bear it better than the busy excitement of a theatre. My spirits fail amidst the noisy crowds and dazzling lights of the Opera House. I think of my poor father, pining it may be in some wretched solitude; or, with a fate more cruel still, perhaps hunted to death by his relentless enemies. No, Lolota, I am not fit to wear a simulated smile and charm a careless public."

The Spaniard laughed bitterly.

"Am I fit, then, to be the brilliant idol of an hour?" she said, mournfully. "Ah! Clara, if you only knew! But to me excitement is at at least temporary oblivion. There is an intoxication in the lights, the music, the hot-house flowers, the applause. For one brief hour I forget."

The children were delighted to be with their dear Madame Vizzini once more. In vain Clara begged her benefactress to allow them to remove to humbler lodgings. "No," said Lolota, "while I have a roof over my head in your English city we will share it together, sister—friend! If your proud spirit cannot brook dependence, and you insist on working yourself to death, it shall be to save money for these little ones; for mine is a precarious life, and I often think will not be a very long one."

But, generous as the fair Spaniard was, Clara Melville could not bear the weight of obligations which she had little future hope of repaying. She submitted quietly for a time, but never abandoned her determination of removing from Arlington Street at the earliest opportunity. That opportunity presented itself when she least expected it. She had long promised, as the reader knows, to pay a vist to the old house by the waterside in which Anthony Verner's uncle had breathed his last, and which was still occupied by the young man and his mother.

Clara's obligations to the tragedian since the fire in Morley Street were not of a nature to be disregarded, and the young girl felt that she should be indeed ungrateful did she hesitate to comply with his wishes.

One fine spring afternoon, then, beheld the two children, George and Jessie, perched at one of the windows in the drawing-room at Arlington Street, dressed in their best, and anxiously awaiting the cab which was to convey them to the house in Blackfriars.

While they were talking of the delights of a visit to Mr. Verner's house, Clara entered the room, and a few moments afterwards a double knock at the door below announced the arrival of Antony himself, who had come to escort them to his strange abode.

If possible Clara Melville looked prettier in her simple straw bonnet and black silk mantle than in the most brilliant stage costume. Hers was one of those fresh and innocent faces that need no adventitious aid of jewels or of gorgeous dress to make them lovely. Its very simplicity was its greatest charm.

"At last, dear Clara," said the young tragedian; "how delighted my mother will be to see and know her of whom she has heard so much; not as she has seen you on the stage, but in your own dear, simple character. Come, little ones, you'll go with uncle Anty, won't you?"

It pleased the young man to hear George and Jessie call him uncle Anty, a name the children had selected to express their regard for the kind friend who rarely visited Arlington Street without bringing them toys, or picture books, or some other pleasant token of his regard. With singular delicacy, Antony Verner had never once alluded to the conversation between Clara and himself the day after the fire in Morley Street. But the young girl had not forgotten that conversation, nor the promise then made by her; and she felt that if ever the time should come, she would be prepared at any sacrifice to keep her word.

The cabman drove through Piccadilly, the Strand, and Fleet Street, crossed Blackfriars Bridge, and then began to thread his way through the intricacies between that and the Borough, till suddenly turning into a narrow street, he emerged upon the bank of the Thames, and stopped at the house described in one of our early chapters. The exterior of the old mansion promised little. Gloomy and dark-looking, it appeared what indeed it was, the deserted habitation of some wealthy city merchant. But within it wore a far more cheerful aspect. Since the death of the old man, Mrs. Verner had worked the transformation which is always to be effected by cleanliness and order. The stone staircase was white as snow, the warehouses and offices on the ground-floor had been let off to a neighbouring manufacturer, and the rent of these alone produced a decent little income. The first floor was the only part of the roomy old house occupied by the mother and son; the massive old-fashioned furniture had been polished and repaired; the dusty carpets beaten and cleaned; the books carefully arranged upon their oaken shelves; the old pictures restored, by the simple use of soap and water, to something like their original brightness. A stand of geraniums in one of the windows bloomed as sweetly as though they had grown in the pure air of a country village, and a vase of freshly-cut flowers on the centre table whispered of distant gardens even amid the roar of busy London life.

George and Jessie were delighted with the gloomy old mansion. That intense love of novelty which seems natural to all children made the strangeness of the place its greatest attraction. Accustomed as they had grown to Madame Vizzini's luxurious West-end abode,

they were lost in admiration of this dark and dingy old-fashioned City dwelling.

"How nice to see the river and all the boats!" cried Jessie, as she and her brother climbed on the oaken window-seat and looked out on the murky waters of the Thames, crowded with barges, steam-packets, and almost every species of craft. "How I should like to live here! Wouldn't you, George?"

Mrs. Verner smiled at the children's enthusiasm.

"You would soon grow tired of this dull old place, my darlings," she said; "and your sister would find it impossible to attend to her pupils if she lived in the City."

"Yes, indeed!" cried George, eagerly; "I know that the little girls Clara teaches live somewhere in the City; don't they, Clara?" he added, appealing to his sister.

"Yes, dear," answered the young girl; "my pupils are the daughters of a rich tradesman on Ludgate Hill. A Mr. Smithers," she continued, addressing herself to Mrs. Verner. "A good, kind creature, who does not consider it any disgrace to live at his place of business, though he is, I believe, a rich man."

The mother and son exchanged glances as Clara said this.

"Ludgate Hill!" exclaimed Mrs. Verner; "you must find your residence in Arlington Street very inconvenient."

"I shall not stay there much longer," replied Clara; "though I should not leave on that account; for my dearest friend, Madame Vizzini, always insists on her brougham taking me backwards and forwards to my studies; but noble and generous as she is, I cannot much longer intrude upon her hospitality. I am more deeply indebted to her already than a life of gratitude could ever repay."

"My dear Miss Melville——"

"You will call me Clara, will you not?" murmured the young girl, taking Mrs. Verner's hand.

"Yes, darling, I will call you Clara, for I feel already that I shall love you as a daughter. My dear Clara, this is the very subject upon which I wished to speak to you. Your residence in Arlington Street is scarcely wise. My son tells me that you have powerful enemies, enemies who are ever on the watch. These wretches would be always able to find you and to place spies upon your actions in the house of Madame Vizzini. For your interest, therefore, and for the interest, perhaps, of your father, it would be better for you to reside in some obscure neighbourhood, whither your foes would be unlikely to track you. For that purpose, no place could be better than this very house."

"My dear Mrs. Verner!" exclaimed Clara.

"Now, my darling child, pray hear me out. The floor above this is entirely unoccupied. There are four rooms: three of them in excellent repair and very comfortably furnished; for my unhappy brother was not a poor man, and though he shut himself out from all human sympathy, he did not deprive himself of the comforts of life. The fourth apartment is a lumber room; but the three will be sufficient for you and the children. Come, then, dearest Clara, and take up your abode with us. You may have a home rent free, and yet be under no shadow of obligation to us, since we only offer you that which is useless to ourselves. Under this roof you will have the safeguard of a mother in myself, the protection of a brother in Antony, who, I know, would shed his last drop of blood, were it necessary, in your cause. Say that you will come, Clara?"

"Yes, yes, Clara," cried the children, simultaneously. "You will come—won't you? It will be so nice!"

"Have you forgotten Madame Vizzini, you ungrateful little creatures?" said Clara, reproachfully.

"No, no. Madame Vizzini will come and see us here; but it will be so nice to live in this big house and see the boats on the river every day."

"You will come, Clara?" repeated Mrs. Verner.

Antony was perfectly silent. He did not attempt to sway the young girl's decision.

"I will accept your generous offer, my dear Mrs. Verner," exclaimed Clara, after a few brief moments of hesitation. "This place seems a haven of refuge. This City neighbourhood is far from the haunts of my persecutor, Sir Frederick; that alone would make it dear to me."

A great deal more was said upon the subject in the course of the evening. Clara and the children accompanied Mrs. Verner to the second floor to see the apartments, which were handsome and roomy, and commanded a full view of the river.

Before the little party left it was arranged that Clara should come at the end of the week and take possession of her new abode.

Lolota Vizzini scolded her *protégée* heartily when she heard what she had done.

"My silly, noble, naughty, proud, tiresome Clara," she said; "I suppose you must have your own way; but I think it is very cruel of you to leave me in this gaudy house, surrounded with every senseless luxury that extravagance can buy, and with nothing but my own dreary thoughts to keep me company."

"You will not think me ungrateful, Lolota?" whispered Clara, tenderly. "You know how I love you."

"I do, my darling. I know that you love me far better than an impetuous, wayward, capricious creature like me can ever deserve to be loved. I appreciate your motive for running away from me. Silly little Clara! to be afraid of such a pitiful obligation, when if Antony Verner is right and justice is done you, you may be one day a young lady of fortune, and able to despise the poor ballet-dancer, Lolota Vizzini!"

"Despise you, Lolota! You, my benefactress!"

"No, no, Clara, not benefactress. That's an ugly word. Your friend, your elder sister, if you will."

The voices of the two children gave a sound of life and happiness to the old house by the Thames. George and Jessie were never tired of playing about the large and roomy apartments and the wide landing-place; but the spot which had for them greater attraction than any other was the lumber room.

This lumber room was situated at the back of the house, its one window looking out upon the yard and warehouses below. It was a large, ill-shaped room, with a low shelving ceiling, and it was completely filled with the accumulated rubbish of perhaps half a century.

Great wooden boxes were piled one upon the other, slowly rotting away, till the rusty locks dropped asunder under the decaying touch of time. An old guitar, broken and stringless, hung from a nail against the dusty wall. Heaven knows how it had come there, or to whom it had belonged! Perhaps to a fair young girl, whom Martin Beaumorris's guilty steward had married fifty years before, and who had pined and died within those darkening walls. Old newspapers, the edges of which were gnawed into festoon-like fringes by the sharp teeth of the mice, lay about the floor. An old birdcage, shattered into half a dozen pieces; piles of mouldering rags; old garments; ironware and broken crockery, all lay in hopeless confusion about the untenanted chamber.

"I once thought of setting all this in order," Mrs. Verner said, as she opened the door of the lumber room, and allowed Clara to take a hasty peep at its miscellaneous contents. "But the impossibility of ever getting rid of all this rubbish disheartened me. I shut up the room and left it as I first found it. Here is the key, Clara; you may as well keep it in case you should want to stow anything away here; and some of this rubbish may amuse the children."

The children were indeed amused with the

contents of the apartment, but the very first day they entered it they emerged so covered with dust, and with garments so very much disfigured by their exploring operations, that Clara most strictly forbade their entering it again.

In order more surely to enforce their obedience she locked the door and hid the key behind a looking-glass upon the mantelpiece in the sitting-room. Having done this she felt perfectly secure, and departed early the next morning to her pupils on Ludgate Hill, after having made both George and Jessie promise faithfully that they would "be good" in her absence.

Mr. Smithers' five children required a great deal of tuition. They had been half educated at a large boarding-school, where they had religiously forgotten, in the miscellaneous scraps of learning which had to be acquired every day, the lessons of the day before.

Clara did not pretend to teach every accomplishment under the sun, but what she professed to teach she taught well, and in such a manner as to ensure its not being easily forgotten by her pupils.

The little Smithers had had a dozen different teachers before, from all of whom they had barely learned to read and write; but they had never had any instructress whom they liked or respected as they did their new governess.

Young as she was, Clara's firm manner ensured the respect and obedience of her pupils, while her amiable nature obtained their affection. Mr. Smithers saw that his children were in good hands; he was one of those straightforward and liberal-minded men whose motto is, "If you require good services, you must give good pay for them," and he doubled Clara's salary immediately he perceived the improvement of her pupils. It was late in the afternoon when the young governess returned to her new home. She stopped for a few moments on her way to buy some cakes for the children's tea.

"Poor darlings," she murmured, as she hurried homewards with her purchase; "they will well deserve some little treat if they have kept their promise."

But, alas! for human nature, George and Jessie had not kept their promise. Clara found them standing at the window with very penitent faces, and dirty hands and pinafores, waiting for her return.

"Oh, Clara," cried George, as his sister entered the room; "we did not see you come in, and yet we have been watching such a long time, and we are so hungry. We took the dinner you left for us at one o'clock, and Mrs. Verner came up to see that we were comfortable, but that is a very long time ago."

Clara looked very grave.

"You have broken your promise, George," she said.

"Yes, Clara, we know we have been very naughty; but you will forgive us, please, won't you?" pleaded George. "The time was very long, and we learned our lessons, and wrote our copies, and did all you told us to do, and then at last—I couldn't help it—I took down the key, and Jessie and I went to play in the lumber room. And oh! it was such fun. Just look here."

The boy turned up the sleeve of his little frock, and showed his arm bruised black and blue about the elbow.

"I don't see how there could have been so very much fun in your hurting your arm, Georgy," said his sister, smiling.

"No; it's not that, Clara, but what do you think? we've found something!"

The little fellow's blue eyes sparkled with triumph, as he opened them to their widest extent.

"Found something?" exclaimed Clara.

"Yes," repeated George and Jessie, simultaneously; "we've found something."

"And what, pray, is this wonderful treasure?" asked Clara.

"A door," said both the children, with the same mysterious look of triumph.

Clara laughed aloud. "A door," she said; "I really don't see anything very remarkable in that discovery. Old-fashioned rooms have generally several doors in them. This mysterious door of yours belongs to some closet, I daresay."

"I don't know," answered the boy; "but I think whoever put the things into that room wanted to hide the door, for we should never, never have found it but for an accident."

"An accident! What accident?"

"Why, you know that big pile of boxes, piled up, oh, ever so high?"

"Yes."

"Well, Jessie and I were playing at sailors, and she was the Captain, and I was—I was—the head man; and she told me to go up into the maintop, and of course I wouldn't disobey orders, or I should have been hanged at the yard-arm; so I climbed up, and in climbing I dragged over the top box, and it fell and bruised my arm; but I didn't much mind that, for when it had fallen, Jessie and I could see the top of a door."

"A door behind the boxes?"

"Yes, will you come and look at it?"

"No, Georgy; we have no right to disturb the things in the lumber room, for even if they are but rubbish they belong to Mrs. Verner, and not to us. After tea we'll go downstairs and tell her of your wonderful discovery; though I daresay she knows all about this door, and will only laugh at us for our pains."

Antony Verner was just about setting out for the theatre when Clara and the children entered his mother's room, but he took off his hat and stopped to hear what they had to say.

George and Jessie were in such a hurry to tell their story that they would scarcely allow Clara to speak.

Mrs. Verner received the intelligence very quietly; but Antony seemed strangely impressed by it.

"Did you know of this door, mother?" he asked.

"No, Antony, indeed I did not. I never disturbed any of the things in the lumber room; those boxes were too heavy for me to lift. Your uncle told me, during his last illness, that they were only filled with rubbish."

"Strange," exclaimed Antony; "do you remember, mother, that when my uncle was endeavouring in his last moments to reveal some secret—some guilty secret, as he said—he spoke several times of a door, and tried to tell us where it was. A door which was evidently connected with this secret."

"I do remember," answered Mrs. Verner, thoughtfully.

"Shortly after his death," continued Antony, "I made a careful examination of every door in this house, every room, every closet, in hopes of throwing some light upon this mystery; but without any result, as you know. How strange if the innocent hands of these children should be the first to come upon a clue to this tangled skein of darkness and guilt!"

"Do you think it possible?" exclaimed Clara.

"It seems to me more than probable," answered Antony, "that this very door may be the one of which my unhappy uncle tried to speak. These boxes, piled almost to the ceiling, were evidently placed there to conceal it. I dare not stop a moment longer to investigate this matter now," he added, looking at his watch, "or they will have to perform the tragedy of *Hamlet* with the part of Hamlet omitted; but, the first thing to-morrow morning we will have the boxes cleared away and open this door, even though it should lead to some haunted chamber, and I have to encounter the ghost single-handed."

In spite of herself, Clara's mind dwelt much upon the mysterious doorway, and she was awake and at breakfast before six o'clock the following morning.

Antony Verner knocked at her door a little after seven.

"I hope I do not disturb you at too early an hour, Clara," he said, as she admitted him, "but I come armed for the attack. I have brought a locksmith with me, and we are prepared to defy bolts and bars."

The little party adjourned to the lumber room, the children in the highest spirits, Antony pale with excitement.

This matter was no careless jest with him; he knew by his uncle's confession that he had been mixed up in some wicked transaction, and he felt that he might soon perhaps discover the full extent of the old man's guilt.

The locksmith, a great brawny fellow, handled the wooden chests as if they had been made of pasteboard, and in a few minutes the doorway was clear. Antony Verner had not been wrong in bringing the man with him, for the lock of the door was a complicated one, and it was upwards of a quarter of an hour before the skilful workman succeeded in removing it.

This quarter of an hour seemed an age to the impatient Clara and Antony. At last the rusty lock dropped to the ground and the door fell open. It only communicated with a small closet filled with old papers.

Antony paid the locksmith and dismissed him.

The children were cruelly disappointed. Nothing but papers behind that mysterious door, which, they thought, might perhaps have led to Fairyland.

"Now, my darlings," said Antony, "you can go back to your play, and leave your sister and me to set all this rubbish to rights. You see there is nothing pretty here for you to look at."

The children submitted, and Clara and the tragedian were left alone.

"Now, Clara," said the young man, earnestly, "if, as I suspect, your fortune is involved in my uncle's secret, it is but just that you should witness my efforts to discover the truth. I firmly believe that some of the papers in that closet will reveal the secret. Come and assist me to examine them."

Clara merely bent her head in concurrence. She was too much agitated to make any reply.

She took up the papers one by one with a trembling hand, but her search was vain: old leases, old agreements between landlord and tenant, all kinds of deeds relating to the property of the late Martin Beaumorris, but nothing in any way concerning his nephew Arthur.

As she was beginning to despair of the issue of her investigation, she was arrested by an outcry from Antony. There was no mistaking the sound: it was a cry of triumph.

He was standing on a chair examining the upper shelves. She could not, therefore, see his face.

"Come," he said, springing to the ground; "come over to the window, Clara, and tell me what you think of this."

It was a dilapidated old parchment, which had been half torn asunder, as if by a hasty hand, which, in the very midst of the work of destruction, had stayed its purpose.

The ink was pale, the characters crabbed and faded, but the sense of the document was clear.

It was the last will and testament of Martin Beaumorris, executed within a week of his death, and it appointed his " beloved nephew, Arthur Beaumorris, and his children after him," sole heirs to the entire bulk of his fortune.

" I swore that your father's wrongs should be brought to the light of day, Clara," exclaimed Antony Verner, in an outburst of enthusiasm, " and I will keep my oath yet!"

CHAPTER XLII.

THE LAWYER'S HACK.

EARLY the next morning Mr. Weldon Hawdley, a lawyer of some eminence, attended by his confidential clerk, waited upon Clara Melville, and learned from her and Antony Verner the whole history of her father's abduction and the new-found will.

Mr. Hawdley looked grave when he was told that the sole proof of Clara's identity with the Beaumorris family consisted of her likeness to the portrait of Arthur, and in her own assertion that this very miniature was that of her father, who had been only known to her as Jasper Melville.

"This is a very peculiar case, Mr. Verner," said the lawyer, with a dubious shrug of the shoulders; " a case that very few men with my numerous and overwhelming engagements would care to handle. Indeed, I must tell you candidly, that unless Slythe here can help me, I cannot see my way a step."

Slythe was a little ferret-eyed, shabbily-dressed man, who had acceompanied the grave and aristocratic-looking Mr. Weldon Hawdley. He was one of the lawyer's numerous clerks; but he was by no means a common clerk. No one could exactly have told Joshua Slythe's actual position in Mr. Hawdley's office, and yet everybody was fully aware that he was one of the most useful men in that establishment.

He was rarely seen at a desk, his business consisting rather in out-of-door work. Sometimes he was absent for the whole day, only coming in just as the office was closing to make his report to the principal.

Sometimes he was running in and out every half-hour, always being admitted into his master's private room, whatever important business was in hand.

The junior clerks whispered among themselves that Joshua Slythe was a spy—an amateur detective police-officer. Be it as it might, the ferret-eyed little man was always employed in cases of a critical nature—dark cases, as they were called in the office.

"No," repeated the dignified Mr. Weldon Hawdley, elevating a double gold eye-glass to his cold blue eyes, and looking with lifted eyebrows at the torn parchment; " the case appears to me a very weak one. Who is to prove that this is the genuine will of Mr. Martin Beaumorris? Who is to eject Sir Frederick from the estate and deprive him of the fortune after thirty years' possession? Above all, who is to prove that this young lady is really the daughter of the baronet's younger brother, Arthur, when that brother is not forthcoming to swear to his own identity?"

"There is little doubt in my mind, Mr. Hawdley, that Arthur Beaumorris has been got out of the way, on this very account, by Sir Frederick or his agents," said the young tragedian.

The old clerk, whose sharp and restless eyes had been shifting hither and thither during the above conversation, looked earnestly at Antony as he spoke.

"May I ask *your* interest in this case, sir?" he said, in a dry, grating voice.

"I am simply interested as the friend of Miss Melville—of Miss Beaumorris, as she should rightly be called," replied Antony, coldly.

"Humph! You're a generous young man! No idea of securing a fortune for the young lady, and marrying her as soon as she gets it—eh? No idea of hatching a nice little case out of a sheet of waste paper you came across by chance, eh?" mumbled the old clerk, chuckling at his own wit.

Antony Verner grew pale with suppressed passion at this insult.

"Mr. Hawdley," he said, "will you tell your clerk to be silent, or shall I? I should be rather rougher than you, as I *might* feel tempted to throw him downstairs."

The lawyer waved his gold eye-glass deprecatingly.

"Slythe," he remonstrated, " my good Slythe, we really can't allow this."

"Beg pardon!" muttered Joshua Slythe, still chuckling. " Only an old man, sir; rather a sly old dog, perhaps. Eh, eh! Rather a cunning old fox, perhaps. Eh, eh! Don't mind me, sir," he added, turning to Antony. "Nobody ever minds me. No harm meant, you know; but Joshua Slythe likes to see what

MR. WELDON HAWDLEY IS INTRODUCED TO CLARA

mettle a man's made of before he gives his advice upon a case."

Antony bowed haughtily. "No further apologies, pray, Mr. Slythe," he said. Then turning his back upon the clerk, he added, addressing the lawyer, "Do you decide on undertaking our case, Mr. Hawdley?"

"Haw, hum, well, I think——" said the lawyer; and then withdrawing a few paces from the table, he beckoned to his clerk—"Eh, Slythe?"

"Yes," replied the old man, quietly.

Mr. Hawdley lifted his eye-glass once more, glanced at the will, then at Antony, then at Clara, and lastly at his clerk. He next frowned deliberately, dropped his eye-glass, shook his head, coughed once or twice doubtfully, and then, turning to Antony, said with considerable solemnity:

No. 13. [*Weekly, One Penny.*]

"After due consideration, Mr. Verner, I have decided on undertaking the management of this case. There are very few other men in my position who would have anything to do with such a hopeless-looking affair; but our house has become rather distinguished for the management of critical matters. Come, Slythe! Good morning, Mr. Verner. Good morning, Miss —— hum, ah, Beau-melville. I beg pardon— Mel-morris."

The lawyer retired with a stately bow, and Joshua Slythe shuffled after him, bestowing a familiar nod upon Antony and Clara as he left the room. Malicious people said that in spite of Mr. Weldon Hawdley's dignified manners, his double gold eye-glass, massive bald head, snowy shirt-front, stately walk, and splendid offices in Doctors' Commons, the distinguished lawyer was little more than a pompous fool, stuffed with legal knowledge that he had not the brains to use; that the shabby, ferret-eyed old man, Joshua Slythe, was the soul of the business, and that Mr. Hawdley dared scarcely say "Good morning" to a client without asking permission of his clerk.

Mr. Hawdley lived in a magnificent house at Putney, with sloping lawns, sheltered by weeping willows, whose branches dipped into the rippling bosom of the silvery Thames. The clerk inhabited a pitiful garret in an alley near Shoreditch; but for all that, Joshua Slythe's salary was twelve hundred a year.

The lawyer's carriage was waiting for Mr. Hawdley and his clerk. The principal flung himself back upon the downy cushions, the factotum sat on the extreme edge of the front seat, his legs screwed up into a kind of knot under him.

"Well, Slythe?" said Mr. Hawdley, as they drove across London Bridge.

"The first thing is to find the old man," answered the clerk.

"Arthur Beaumorris?"

"Yes."

"I don't see any hope of that," said Mr. Hawdley.

"Of course you don't, sir," replied the clerk, with rather a malicious chuckle. "But that's no reason other people shouldn't. As we're rather slack just now, I may as well run down into Yorkshire by the night mail and look about me. Arthur Beaumorris is in Yorkshire."

"How do you know that?"

"Why, the men who kidnapped him wanted to keep him out of the way, that's clear. For that purpose it was as well to keep him in Yorkshire as to bring him up to London; and less trouble. They were only another man's agents so of course they took the least trouble; agents always do. The children and the old man were parted in Hull, and it strikes me the old man isn't far off Hull. If he's alive I'll find him."

"But how are you to identify him, since you never saw him in your life?"

"I'll tell you how, sir. That farmer, John Atkinson, seems to be be an honest fellow, and a shrewd fellow, by what I can make out of the children's account. I shall put my hand upon him at once, and he'll assist in the search. You may depend, by the old man's going there, that this Atkinson knows something of his early life. He may assist us in establishing the identity of Jasper Melville with Arthur Beaumorris."

Mr. Weldon Hawdley stared admiringly at his clerk.

"Joshua Slythe," he said, "you're a wonderful creature."

"No, I'm not; no, I'm not!" chuckled the old man; "I ain't anything miraculous. A sly old dog, perhaps; a cunning old fox, perhaps; but nothing more, nothing more."

Early in the grey dawn of the following morning Joshua Slythe entered the town of Hull. The old clerk did not suffer much inconvenience in travelling from a superfluity of luggage, since all that he carried was a pocket-comb and a nightcap in one of the pockets of his threadbare coat.

Some malicious people said that Joshua carried even these two luxuries merely out of ceremony; for as he never combed his hair, he could scarcely want a comb; and as, while out on business, he very seldom went to bed, he might have managed without a nightcap; but for all this Joshua was very methodical, and whenever he went out of town the pocket-comb and nightcap went with him; much to the amusement of the impertinent junior clerks, who used to delight in watching the old man busy "packing up."

Joshua Slythe did not waste much time in Hull. He took the first train to the town of Beresford, and walked from the station across the fields to Mr. Atkinson's farm.

He found the farmer seated at a well-spread breakfast-table with his wife and children; and quietly taking his place at this hospitable board, Slythe managed to dispose of a tremendous cargo of ham and eggs while he told his business.

It was the clerk's habit to eat when and where he could. Sometimes for an entire day food never crossed his lips; sometimes he took a heavy meal; sometimes only a crust of bread and glass of water to sustain life.

Eating and drinking caused a great waste of time, he said; and you ought always to knock off the business when you could.

John Atkinson was up in arms when he heard of Clara Beaumorris's wrongs.

"I was but a child when the old man came here for a shooting-season," he said; "but I'm danged if I couldn't swear before a dozen juries that he's Arthur Beaumorris and no one else. And what's more, if I was to see the two chaps that were hanging about this place when he was took away, and as I think did the business, I could swear to them too: especially the one I chooked into the dook-pond. I shan't forget his oogly moog in a hurry," added the honest farmer, speaking very broad Yorkshire in his anger.

"Then you'll help me to find him, and to track these men?" asked the clerk.

"Darned if I don't!" cried John, slapping his hand upon the table till the breakfast-things rattled again. "Darned if I don't, if I go to the end of the world to do it."

THE BLACK BAND; OR, THE MYSTERIES OF MIDNIGHT

"You will be well paid for your trouble," added Joshua.

"Paid!" roared John, growing crimson with indignation; "lookye here, Mr. Londoner: I've heard my old father say, many a time, that Mr. Arthur Beaumorris had been a good friend to him when crops was bad and rich landlords hard upon a poor farmer. And before I'll take pay for doing him a service, I'll chuck you into the same pond where I chucked the rascal as come here after the old gentleman. *Pay!* Do you think there's anything in an honest York-shireman's phiz that says he's the chap to take pay for doing a service to the weak and help-less?"

"Don't mind me," chuckled Joshua Slythe, "don't mind me! Bless you, it's only my way. I'm a sly old dog, perhaps; a cunning old fox, perhaps, eh, eh; and when I want a man to help me, I like to find out the metal he's made of, that's all."

"That's all very well," answered John, rather sulkily, "but I wouldn't have you find out too much of my metal, unless you want to find yourself in the dook-pond."

"John Atkinson," exclaimed the old clerk, grasping the farmer's hand, "I'm an old de-ceiver, but you're a trump, a trump, sir, and—egad—with your help I'll find Arthur Beau-morris before the week's out."

CHAPTER XLIII.

THE STAR OF HOPE SHINES ON A DARK HORIZON

Let us return to the solitary mountains amidst whose granite-bound recesses the wretched wife of Robert Merton, the Manchester merchant, counted the lonely days and hours. In vain had she waited for the rescue promised by Oscar Bertrand. Despair had not long since succeeded hope, and she no longer thought of the Austrian Colonel, who had, as she imagined, basely de-ceived her.

Edith Merton little knew the gigantic schemes in which this man was involved, and which, with-out him, must fall in shattered ruins to the ground; she little thought of the sleepless nights, the weary watches, while the master-mind worked out its mighty problems of crime and fraud. She only knew that he had promised her freedom, and that she was still a prisoner.

She did not know that this man never *forgot*, and never broke his promise.

The condition of the Earl of Horton's daugh-ter had been much ameliorated since the reader last looked within the grey walls of Castle Mac-lomond. She was no longer a prisoner in the turret-chamber. Her husband had relented, and though he had never looked upon his wife's face since the night of her departure from Park Lane, he could not endure, would-be murderess as he knew her to be, to doom her to perpetual misery.

"Her own conscience must be a sufficient punishment," he said, little knowing that within some guilty breasts the voice of conscience is for ever still.

The best rooms in the castle had been fitted up for the merchant's wife, the luxurious furni-ture of her Park-lane apartments having been conveyed into the Highlands for that purpose.

Lady Edith Merton was still a prisoner, it is true. Martha and her two assistants still watched night and day over their so-called *patient;* but the vigilance of the mad-house nurses had been much relaxed by Robert Mer-ton's orders, and their chief care now was to prevent Lady Edith leaving the Castle.

Within its walls she was free to follow her own pleasure.

The discovery of his daughter's guilt, or mad-ness, had been too much for the declining years of Lord Horton. He never entirely recovered the fatal night in Park Lane, and in the January after her removal to Castle Maclomond, a black-bordered letter reached Lady Edith, telling her of her father's death.

The heartless woman shed no tear. Every thought, every feeling, was absorbed in one wild desire—escape from Castle Maclomond—union with Lionel, Marquis of Willoughby.

"I will wear that coronet before I die," she said. "I could not rest in my grave as the wife of a cotton-spinner."

Lady Edith's bed-chamber was the last of a long suite of apartments, all of which had been refitted with the furniture from Park Lane. The aspect of the place was entirely changed; the tall canopied bed, hung with curtains of amber satin damask; the skin of ermine spread at the side of the couch, over the rich carpet of velvet pile; the ivory dressing-table, and oval mirror framed in frosted silver; the perfume-bottles of crystal and gold; the soft light stealing through globes of pale rose-hued glass —all transformed the dreary Castle; but the old pictures still frowned from the wainscot, and the embers still burned upon the wide hearths of two centuries gone by.

Martha Crookman slept in a little dressing-room opening out of Lady Edith's apartment; she was therefore within hearing of her patient, but she no longer annoyed the haughty lady by her perpetual presence.

Early one morning in June Lady Edith awoke from long dreams of liberty and hope—

awoke to see the summer sunlight shining in upon her gilded prison.

"Alas!" exclaimed the haughty woman, as she glanced at the costly decorations of her apartment—" of what avail is all this wasted splendour?　The lowliest peasant-girl who treads her native heather is happier than I, for she at least is free."

As she murmured this complaint her glance wandered listlessly round the room, and rested by chance upon the toilette.

Her eye was arrested here by an object amidst the crystal perfume-bottles.

This object was simply a narrow slip of paper.

Strange that such a trifle should have brought the hot blood to the lady's cheek and brow!　Strange that her eyes dilated, and her breathing grew short and quick, at sight of this scrap of paper!

The reason of her agitation was this: She knew that last night no such paper lay upon the dressing-table.

It was evident, then, that some one had entered her apartment during the night.　Yet how could that be, since she had locked the only door of the chamber?　There must be some means of access unknown to herself—unknown to her gaolers.

She remembered the picture of the dark knight in the turret-chamber, and Colonel Oscar Bertrand's mysterious appearance.

With one bound Lady Edith sprang from the bed, rushed to the dressing-table, and snatched the paper.

It contained only two lines, written in a peculiar cramped hand.

These lines ran thus:—

"You have waited patiently, but you have not waited in vain.　The hour is at hand.　Hope! Watch! Be prepared.

　　　　　　　　　"O. B., G. M. B. B."

Lady Edith Merton knew that these mysterious letters were the initials of her deliverer's name and title—Oscar Bertrand, Grand Master of the Black Band.

She folded the oblong slip of paper, and opening a secret drawer in her jewel-case, carefully concealed her treasure.

"Good heavens!" she exclaimed, as she glanced at the diamonds, rubies, and emeralds lying on their snowy satin cushions, and flashing in the morning sunlight, "is it not strange that this one scrap of paper should be of more value to me than all these gems?"

Her agitation was so intense that it was some time before she could venture to summon Martha Crookman to assist at her toilette.

Even when she did so the hectic flush of emotion and excitement still burned upon her cheeks—the fire of new hope still sparkled in her eyes.

The attendant noticed this change in her patient's appearance.

"Lor' a mercy on me, my lady!" she said, "you look regular feverish this morning.　I hope you haven't been worritting of yourself tryin' to get out of the Castle?　It would be right down ungrateful if you did, seein' the liberty we let you have now."

Lady Edith Merton laughed bitterly.

"Except through your room, there is but one outlet from this chamber," she replied, pointing to the oriel window; " and the unhappy wretch who would attempt to escape that way would be dashed to atoms upon the stonework below. There is no fear of my attempting to quit my prison."

The loud beating of her own heart contradicted her words as she spoke; but suspicious as Martha Crookman was, she was reassured by her patient's manner.

But the long anguish of the past year had been too much for the delicate constitution of Edith Merton; the strain upon the mental system had been too great for her to endure.　In the very hour when she had abandoned herself to despair—when she had bid farewell to all hope of ever again beholding the outer world, and had resigned herself to the thought of slowly sinking into the gloomy depths of the grave, uncared for and forgotten by the man she had loved—at this very moment, in the darkest crisis of her life, the star of hope again shone upon her.

Her enfeebled spirit could not bear its lustre.

Throughout the day her manner continued to be restless and agitated.　She roamed from room to room.　If she took up a book, it was only to cast it from her with an impatient sigh.　If she opened the piano, it was only to strike a few brief chords.　She could not rest in one place nor occupy herself with any one thing.

This marvellous change in her manner, from the listlessness of resignation to the agitation of expectancy and hope, did not escape the sharp eyes of Martha Crookman.

The mad-house nurse had long since discovered that her patient was as sane as herself. She looked upon Lady Edith Merton as a very clever and determined woman, and she felt that her task was by no means an easy one.

But her wages were high, her perquisites enormous, and she was resolved on keeping so good a place.

She managed to watch her patient very

closely without awaking Lady Edith's suspicions.

The mental shock had been too great for the overwrought brain. That night Edith Merton was in a high fever.

The mad-house nurse watched by her through the long silent hours of the night, listening to every wandering word that fell from the delirious lips.

She heard only brief, disjointed sentences; broken and unintelligible words; but all hinted alike at one object—*escape.*

"Yes—yes!" cried the unconscious woman; "at last it comes—the hope—the liberty—the return to life and love."

Martha Crookman heard quite enough to assure her that something out of the common had happened on the preceding day—what she knew not; but prudence counselled immediate action. She sent Donald on a Highland pony across the mountains to the nearest village to summon the surgeon, whoever he might be; but before she did even this, she sent another messenger to the railway station with a telegram addressed to Robert Merton.

This telegram informed him of his wife's illness, and hinted at an intended escape. The merchant received the message in his library in Park Lane. He threw down his books and papers, and consulted his watch.

It was eleven o'clock in the day; but he knew that he should have to wait many hours for the mail to Scotland, which left King's Cross station in the evening. Had the telegram told of danger, the millionaire would have ordered a special engine to have conveyed him to the Highlands. But Martha Crookman had carefully worded her message, which distinctly stated that Lady Edith's illness was not alarming. The merchant therefore decided on quietly finishing his day's work, and patiently waiting for the evening mail.

CHAPTER XLIV.

THE STRANGE TRAVELLERS AT THE DUKE OF ATHOLL

TWELVE miles from Castle Maclomond, and half hidden amongst the rugged mountain-tops which overshadowed it, there was a humble hostelry, called the Duke of Atholl. It stood upon the rough and narrow high road leading from one village to another, and was chiefly frequented by drovers and shepherds, with now and then a travelling hawker, who gratified the simple villagers by bringing them the latest news from Aberdeen or Dundee. The railway, that mighty herald of civilisation, though it passed within a few miles of the spot, had as yet brought no change to the Highland inn. Four rude stone walls, a couple of chimneys, and half-a-dozen small square windows, which let in a great deal of wind and rain, while admitting very little light; these were the humble elements of architecture employed in building the Duke of Atholl. The house was kept by an old woman called Margery Dicks, a woman who, a hundred and fifty years before, would have been burnt for a witch, on the sole testimony of her withered face, bent form, bristling grey beard, and evil-looking eyes. But in these modern times Margery Dicks was much respected; for those who knew her said that she sold a mutchkin of very good whiskey, and, what was still more, always gave honest measure.

The very day succeeding that upon which the telegram from Maclomond Castle reached the merchant prince, Margery Dicks was rather surprised by the arrival of two travellers, who came to her hostelry at an hour when she rarely received customers; for the time when the shepherds and drovers dropped into the inn was generally when the sun was sinking behind the heather-fringed hills, and the stars beginning to peep from the calm blue arch above.

It was little past noon when the travellers arrived, and their first question was to ask if they could have dinner. They were told they could have nothing but a basin of barley broth and some oat cakes, and were forced to content themselves with this humble fare and a liberal allowance of whiskey. This refreshment despatched, the two men stretched their legs on a couple of rude benches that were placed on either side of the wide hearth, where, in spite of the June weather, blazed an excellent turf fire, and prepared themselves for a nap, very much after the manner of people who had been up all night.

There certainly was very little in the appearance of these two travellers either to attract admiration or to inspire confidence. Both were big men—both dressed in rough, coarse garments, which looked much as if their owners were in the habit of sleeping in them; both with faces that indicated rather a strong predilection for the bottle; both with a certain sinister expression lurking in the eyes and hovering about the mouth that told of evil deeds which had been done in the past or were to be done in the future.

Old Margery Dicks, who was almost purblind, could yet see clearly enough to perceive that these two unexpected visitors were rather queer customers. She determined, therefore,

OSCAR BERTRAND AT THE HIGHLAND INN

on keeping a sharp eye upon them. There was nothing they could rob her of within the four white-washed plaster walls of the common parlour of the inn, and Margery was a great deal too sharp to give them a chance of escaping without settling her score.

Perhaps, though, she had some deeper motive for being rather afraid of these strangers. People whispered that Margery had saved money during her tenancy of the Duke of Atholl, and that, being afraid to trust her hoard to any bank in Aberdeen, Edinburgh, or Glasgow, she made it quite secure by hiding it away in some nook or cranny known only to herself.

The afternoon wore on, however, and the men remained perfectly quiet. It was only when it grew nearly dark, and the regular customers began to make their appearance, that the two travellers awoke.

They both seemed surly fellows, and neither of them attempted to enter into conversation with the honest Highlanders, who stared rather suspiciously at these silent strangers.

After ordering another measure of whiskey, the two men drew aside into a corner of the room and conversed in an undertone, while the assembled company crowded round a rough deal table, on which burned a light in a metal candlestick, and abandoned themselves to rather boisterous good fellowship.

" Will he come, do you think ? " muttered one of the strange travellers to his companion.

" *Will he come!* " answered the other, contemptuously. " You must be new indeed amongst us, to ask that question. When did *he* ever fail to keep an appointment? If he had bade us meet him at the North Pole or the Torrid Zone, he would be there. Whenever he fails at the appointed time, be sure that something has happened—that all is discovered, and he is in the hands of justice."

It was night. There was no moon, but the stars shone coldly upon the distant summits of the mountains.

The corner of the room to which the two travellers had retired was close against an open casement.

The man who had spoken last put out his head and looked down the dark road before the house.

" What is the time? " he asked, still looking out.

His companion consulted an old-fashioned turnip-shaped silver watch.

" It wants three minutes of the half-hour after nine."

" Good ! " answered the other ; " in three minutes he will be here."

The man held his watch in his hand, gazing earnestly at the dial-plate. The minute hand marked the half-hour.

At that very moment the hoofs of a horse sounded on the mountain-road.

" I said so," exclaimed the man who had been looking out, withdrawing his head and glancing triumphantly at his companion. " The moment has come—and he comes with the moment."

" He has dealings with the devil," muttered the other, gruffly. " I don't like such gentry."

" Pshaw ! Simon ; the only devil he deals with is shut up in his own brains. All things are possible to genius."

" I don't know anything about genius," answered the other. " I only know he's a deal too clever for me. I'm afraid of him."

" Hush ! he is here."

The horse had stopped at the door of the Duke of Atholl, and the rider had dismounted and flung the reins to Margery, who acted as her own ostler.

The worthy hostess was not a little surprised to behold a traveller of such aristocratic appearance stop before her door.

" Will your lairdship rest here the nicht ? " she asked, curtsying.

" No, my good woman ; but if you'll let any honest Highland laddie you have about the place wash out my horse's mouth, and give him a handful of corn, while you get me a noggin of your best whiskey, I shall be obliged."

A sandy-headed lad who hung about the place came out of a shed in answer to Margery's summons, while the new arrival, who was no other than Oscar Bertrand, entered the common room of the hostelry.

The Austrian wore a travelling-coat with a velvet collar, buckskin breeches, and top-boots, and had evidently been riding some distance.

He removed his hat as he crossed the threshold of the inn, and bowed courteously to the group of Highlanders, who stared at him with open-mouthed astonishment, while a sheep-dog crept from beneath the table and sniffed suspiciously at the intruder. Neither of the travellers uttered a word to the Colonel, nor did they, by any sign whatever, acknowledge his presence or appear to recognise him.

Oscar Bertrand drank a small portion of the whiskey in silence, and then lighted a cigar and strolled out of the house into the road. Five minutes afterwards the two men also left the house.

The red spark glimmering at the end of the Colonel's cigar showed the direction he had taken. The two men followed him, and, when they had overtaken him, stopped respectfully, waiting for him to address them.

"Well," said the Austrian, "you have made inquiries?"

"We have," answered Simon's companion; "the Manchester merchant arrived at Maclomond Castle this very day. He travelled by the mail-train, but we only discovered that he was our fellow-passenger at Edinburgh, where one of the men in our carriage pointed him out as he stood on the platform."

"Robert Merton here!" exclaimed Oscar Bertrand. "This is unlucky."

"I feared so," answered the man; "it was too late to communicate with the office when we made this discovery, as I knew that, before a telegram could reach London, you would have started for Scotland. We had no course, therefore, but to push forward and obey orders."

"And you were perfectly right," answered Bertrand; "this Manchester cotton-spinner has checkmated me once. It shall go hard with him or with me if he tries to do so again. The game is never lost when the player has genius, courage, and experience on his side—no matter what the cards. Small trumps win big tricks in the hands of the skilful whist player, and, mark my words for it, we will baffle Mr. Merton yet. Can you sleep here to-night?"

"Yes; they can give us a garret and a flock bed."

"Good! never mind the roughness of your quarters, men, there is work to be done. Sleep here to-night, remain here all day to-morrow, and I will meet you at half-past nine in the evening. By to-morrow night Robert Merton will have returned to London."

"How, captain?"

"You are surprised! Nothing more easy. He will receive a telegram from Manchester informing him of another conflagration, and demanding his immediate presence on the spot. We have agents in Manchester."

He walked back to the door of the inn, mounted his horse, and rode off at a gallop.

The two men stood staring after him, mute with admiration.

CHAPTER XLV.

THE PLOTTERS AT WORK

ALL occurred exactly as Oscar Bertrand had prophesied.

On reaching Maclomond Castle, Robert Merton found that Lady Edith had recovered from the brief attack of fever that had so alarmed Martha Crookman. The physical system of the guilty woman had been in no way affected, and

the mind, by its innate power, recovered from the shock which had at first prostrated it.

The brief interview between himself and his wife was cruelly painful to the Manchester merchant. The wounds of the past were ripped open; memory, vivid and undying, brought back old feelings, and he looked with a passionate admiration, mingled with shuddering horror, upon the beauty which he knew was but the mask of a fiend-like soul.

Lady Edith received her husband in the boudoir which had been fitted up for her, and upon the black oak panelling of which gleamed the broad claymores, the two-handed swords, and sharp-edged battle-axes of the followers of Bruce and Wallace.

The unexpected arrival of her husband had filled her with rage and terror. What if the coming of Robert Merton should prove a hindrance to those mysterious friends who were, perhaps, at that very time planning her escape? But intense as was her vexation, Edith Merton was too accomplished a hypocrite to betray what she felt. No statue could have evinced less emotion than the merchant's wife when Martha Crookman informed her of Robert's arrival.

Lady Edith was, of course, ignorant of the fact that a telegram had summoned her husband to Maclomond Castle. She thought that he had, by some means or other, become informed of the intended rescue, and that he had hurried to the Highlands to prevent its success.

Inspired with this idea, Lady Edith Merton resolved upon a plan of action which would, perhaps, have occurred to none other than herself.

In order to convince Robert that she was unconcerned in any plot for escape, she resolved on affecting actual madness, and thus throwing the merchant completely off his guard.

Early on the day after his arrival at Maclomond Castle, Robert Merton entered his wife's apartment.

He found her seated at the open window, looking vacantly at the wide expanse of mountain and moorland that stretched before her dreary dwelling. The aspect of his wife touched the manly heart of the merchant.

"Lady Edith," he murmured, in a subdued and tremulous voice; "Lady Edith, I come to——" His emotion overpowered him, and he was unable to continue.

The skilful actress lifted her eyes and looked at him with the wild expression rarely seen in the countenance of any sane being.

"It is lonely here," she said; "the mountains are cold and dreary, even in the bright summer. The snow never melts upon the craggy summit of Ben Nevis; only the eagle lives upon the peak of Ben Lomond."

Her words had the cold, meaningless tone peculiar to the insane.

"The harebells and the heather are blooming on the hills," she continued, still gazing upon her terrified husband with a fixed, unrecognising stare; "but I may not gather them. It is cruel to keep me here—very, very cruel. If you are the madhouse doctor," she added, changing her tone to one of feverish eagerness, "tell them that I shall soon be better; tell them that I may be trusted—that I shall not harm them if they let me breathe the summer air upon those lonely hills."

Aghast with horror, Robert Merton retired from the apartment, to seek an explanation of the change in his wife from Martha Crookman.

"Merciful powers!" he murmured, as he hurried through the corridors of the castle, on his way to the room in which he had left the nurse; "is it possible that she is indeed mad, and that the hideous wickedness which I attributed to a perverted soul was in reality the criminal propensity of a maniac, whose vilest actions are blameless; or has the solitude of this place, acting on a restless and haughty spirit, reduced the unhappy woman to the state in which I find her?"

While Robert Merton, full of doubts like these, hastened to seek an interview with the madhouse nurse, Lady Edith laughed a soft, silvery peal of triumphant laughter in the solitude of her own apartment.

"Fool!" she said; "poor, weak, deluded, unseeing fool. I have thrown him completely off his guard and he will now consider me a harmless maniac, powerless to dream of escape from the chains he has cast around me! Robert Merton, we have a heavy account to settle, but the day may not be far distant when my first payment shall be made."

The merchant found Martha Crookman seated at needlework in the housekeeper's room. She rose and curtsied at the entrance of her employer, but could scarcely repress an exclamation of surprise upon beholding his pale face.

"You found her ladyship quite restored, I hope, sir?" she said.

"In body perhaps," answered Robert, "but not in mind. Lady Edith seems far worse than when she left London last year."

Martha Crookman looked at him with undisguised astonishment.

"We all thought her ladyship so much better," she said; "though, of course, by no means sufficiently restored to leave Maclomond," she added, hurriedly, lest her employer should think of dispensing with her services.

"You have, no doubt, become accustomed to your patient's manner," answered the merchant, "and do not, therefore, perceive its strangeness. My unhappy wife is very quiet, is she not?"

"Very quiet, sir."

"And she never betrays any violence?"

"Never."

"You were alarmed during her brief attack of fever by some words she dropped about escape; but it appears to me that her only desire is to go more into the open air. You have the landau which I sent from Park Lane; see that her ladyship has a drive every day that the weather permits. You need not either of you accompany her, as I wish her to feel herself free, and Jervis, my old coachman, is sufficiently trustworthy to keep guard upon her during her airing. Take care, too, that in all your attendance upon her you leave her as much liberty as may be consistent with her safety, and do not attempt to restrain her in any harmless whim or fancy."

The nurse curtsied, and promised to obey these directions.

"I shall only be able to spend a few days at Maclomond," said the merchant, as he left the room, "for the House is sitting, and I am wanted in London. As soon as I reach town I shall send an experienced physician to see Lady Edith, as a great change appears to have taken place in her state."

"What do you think of this?" said Martha to one of the under-servants when Robert had gone.

"Why, that she's been shammin', that's what I think. Mad, indeed! Why, she's no more mad than I am! But she's a precious deep 'un, and there's somethin' in the wind, depend upon it. But he can think her as mad as a March hare for aught I care. All we've got to do is to keep our places. Plenty to eat and nothin' to do—liberal wages and, perkesites. You don't get that sort of situation every day, Mrs. Crookman."

At three o'clock that afternoon Robert Merton received a telegram announcing the partial destruction of the largest of his factories, and summoning him immediately to Manchester. He ordered his horse, and rode to the railway-station in time to catch a train that passed at five o'clock in the afternoon.

Thus it was that when Colonel Bertrand met the two men at the "Duke of Atholl," at the same hour as on the previous night, he was able to announce to them the departure of the cotton-spinner.

It was rather a long conversation which Oscar Bertrand held this night with Goggle-eyed Simon and his more polished companion. The three men walked for some time upon the mountain road outside the humble hostelry, and when they separated Goggle-eyed Simon's turnip-shaped watch marked the lapse of upwards of three-quarters of an hour.

*   *   *   *   *   *

The weather was lovely on the morning succeeding this rendezvous at the "Duke of Atholl," and Martha Crookman, in obedience to the merchant's directions, ordered the landau to be got ready and the coachman in attendance at noon.

Lady Edith Merton evinced no surprise upon being requested to attire herself for an airing, but wrapped herself in a voluminous cloak of cream-coloured cashmere, and put on a large Leghorn hat, ornamented with long ostrich feathers.

She quietly seated herself in the carriage, to which Martha had attended her, and the coachman, having received some brief instructions from the nurse, drove away from Maclomond Castle.

The balmy air of heaven fanned the burning brow of the prisoner; the voices of a hundred birds, the perfume of a thousand flowers, rose in mingled music and sweetness on the summer air: but these bounteous gifts of an all-beneficent Providence could not move the hard heart of Lady Edith Merton. Her sole thought was escape—rescue from her stately prison-house, and revenge upon her husband.

Lost in a reverie like this, she took no heed of the road by which the carriage went, and scarcely perceived that, after driving some miles, the character of the scenery had changed, the roadway being sheltered by a few trees, and lying in a valley winding by the foot of the hills.

Here the coachman drove slowly, in order to rest his horses, which had gone through hard work in ascending and descending mountain roads. By this means two men were enabled to address Lady Edith with a petition for alms.

These men were stalwart-looking ruffians, whose hideous countenances were disfigured by the brand of vice and crime. Our readers will have little difficulty in recognising in these pretended beggars Goggle-eyed Simon and his companion. The two men had been lurking about the neighbourhood of Maclomond Castle all the morning; they had seen the departure of the carriage, and had contrived to meet it on its return homeward.

Goggle-eyed Simon fell back, and allowed his comrade to address Lady Edith.

"You won't refuse a poor man a sixpence to buy a loaf of bread, will you, beautiful lady?" he pleaded. "We are strangers in Scotland, and cannot get a stroke of work or a mouthful of food. Charity, beautiful lady!"

The heart of Lady Edith Merton was not wont to be softened by the accents of distress. She looked at the two men with a haughty frown.

"I have no sympathy with tramps and beggars," she said. "Drive on, Jervis."

The coachman was about to smack his whip, when the man laid his hand upon the door of the carriage.

"You may not have sympathy with common beggars, Lady Edith Merton," he said, "but, for all that, you won't refuse to listen to *me*. I *was not always a tramp and a beggar. I was once servant to a wealthy Austrian colonel, whom I think you know!*"

The man laid a particular emphasis on these last words. Lady Edith looked at him.

"In Heaven's name, what do you mean?" she exclaimed, dropping her voice almost to a whisper. "Is it possible that you come from *him*?"

"We do."

"Give me some proof of this."

"Your ladyship received a scrap of paper the other morning, on which were written words that told of hope. Shall I repeat those words? I have a duplicate of them in my pocket."

"It is needless," said Lady Edith; "I see that you are no impostor."

"Thanks, good lady," replied the man, raising his voice so as to be heard by the coachman.

"If your bountiful ladyship would only add to your kindness by driving to the wretched hut where my sick wife and starving children lie, you will see that I have not deceived you."

"Is the place far?"

"Within three-quarters of a mile."

Lady Edith consulted her watch; it was nearly three o'clock.

"Jervis," she said, "I wish you to drive me to this poor man's cottage. He will give you the necessary directions."

"Straight ahead," said the man; "you can't mistake the place; it lies right in this road. My comrade and I will be there almost as soon as your ladyship."

The coachman, Jervis, reflected for a moment before complying with Lady Edith's request. He had been told to look after her safety, it is true, and he knew that report called her mad, but, on the other hand, he had been desired to obey all her reasonable commands, and there appeared to him nothing unreasonable in a great lady's wishing to visit a starving woman on an errand of charity.

"If the two men mean any mischief," he muttered to himself, "I shall be there to see that they act on the square, and I give them full leave to get the better of John Jervis in a fair stand-up fight, big and ugly as they are."

They reached the hut in about a quarter of an hour. It was a lonely, half-ruined hovel, with a broken chimney and a narrow casement, which could not boast one entire pane of glass, but which was so stuffed with rags and paper as to preclude even a glimpse into the interior.

"Shall I get down and tell them your ladyship is here?" asked the coachman, preparing to descend from the box.

"No, Jervis; I know your horses have not been long in harness: it would be unsafe to leave them. I can open the carriage door myself."

Suiting the action to the word, Lady Edith opened the door of the landau, and sprang lightly to the ground. In another moment she had entered the hovel.

CHAPTER XLVI.

THE MIDNIGHT FLIGHT

IT was as Lady Edith expected. The sole inhabitant of the ruined hovel was the Master of the Black Band. He removed his hat as she entered, and taking her gloved hand in his, raised it to his lips.

"You expected to see me here, Lady Edith," he said; "you are not surprised?"

"No; for I have seen your messengers."

"You have expected me ever since last September?"

"At first I did so; but expectation died out at last. I thought you had forgotten me."

"Forgotten you, Lady Edith! No! Ask those who serve me if I ever forget a promise or break an oath."

"Thank Heaven, you are come! Bless you for remembering a wretched prisoner—bless and thank you!"

"Nay, Lady Edith, no thanks! You are but one thread the more in the many-coloured fabric of my life. You can never guess all I have achieved, the enemies I have baffled, the schemes I have thwarted, the victories I have won, since that night on which I last saw you. But I will not speak of this; we have more serious business in hand—your escape. Your husband has left Maclomond."

"How did you learn that?"

"As I learned his arrival here—as I learn all things which I wish to know. The coast is clear. Now, Lady Edith, for the plan of action. You received my brief scroll?"

"I did."

"But you could not guess by what means it had been placed where you found it?"

"Indeed, I could not."

"You had locked the only door of your apartment before retiring to rest?"

"I had," replied Lady Edith.

"Listen, then, and I will explain the mystery. You remember that, on my last visit to Maclomond, I informed you that I was intimately acquainted with the late noble owner of the castle. Hector Maclomond, who sold the place to your husband, was a ruined man; he lived in daily dread of his creditors, and shut himself up in his mountain stronghold, besieged by bailiffs. In order to avoid these gentry, he made frequent use of the secret passages, trap-doors, and sliding panels which abound in the castle, as they do in all buildings that date from the feudal age. It was thus that I, who was then on a visit to him, became acquainted with all the mysterious ins and outs of the edifice—amongst others, the passage communicating with the picture of the black knight in the turret-chamber; and also with another secret way, leading from the hall of the castle, and terminating in an iron doorway that opens into the fire-place of the very apartment occupied by your ladyship."

"But how did your messenger obtain access to the hall of the castle?" asked Lady Edith.

"By the simplest possible stratagem. One of the men whom you saw to-day, and who came to Scotland by my directions, contrived to penetrate into the hall on a begging errand. I had fully explained to him the mystery of the secret passage. He pleaded so piteously for help, that the old housekeeper left him, promising to bring him a few handsful of oatmeal. On her return the man had disappeared. He had contrived to enter the secret passage during Mrs. Macpherson's absence, and he there remained until all had retired to rest, when he penetrated to your ladyship's chamber, executed his commission, and discreetly retired."

"It is wonderful!" exclaimed the merchant's wife.

"You can understand, therefore, all that has to be done to-night. The mail train stops at the nearest railway station at two o'clock in the morning. At twelve one of the men you saw to-day will strike one faint tap upon the metal door at the back of the fire-place. If you are alone, and all is safe, you will reply by three similar taps; he will then open the door; you will creep through the aperture, and follow where he leads. I shall be waiting on horseback within a hundred yards of the castle, and the same horse will carry both of us to the station. There is no moon, and we are not likely to meet a creature on the mountain-road."

"My preserver! My only friend!"

"Nay, Lady Edith Merton; once more, no gratitude. I never act without a motive. The life of Oscar Bertrand has been one long calculation, based on the weakness and wickedness of men. One word more : you will be dressed in the plainest and darkest clothes you possess. A black dress, a thick veil, and a large woollen shawl; these will entirely disguise the elegant Lady Edith Merton. Collect all your jewels, and conceal them about your person. Remember, also, that you dismiss your attendants early; that you lock the door of your chamber, and that you do not reply to my agent's signal unless you know the coast to be clear above stairs. I will answer for the premises below, which I shall be caused to be closely watched from sunset."

*   *   *   *   *   *

This time no accident occurred to mar the scheme so well planned, even in its smallest detail.

As the hands of her watch pointed to the midnight hour, Lady Edith sat in her chamber, breathless and anxious, awaiting the expected signal. Martha Crookman had retired at a little before ten o'clock, when her mistress, after partly undressing, had dismissed the nurse. Martha had been in bed, therefore, two hours.

Five minutes before twelve, Lady Edith softly turned the handle of the door of communication between her own apartment and the little dressing-room occupied by her attendant. She peeped in upon the sleeping nurse. Martha Crookman snored with the regularity of a heavy sleeper. Tinges of crimson had begun to illuminate the nose of the madhouse nurse. Martha Crookman liked Scotland, and —Scotch whisky.

Lady Edith assumed the style of dress suggested by Colonel Bertrand. It was indeed difficult to recognise the proud daughter of the Earl of Horton in the homely costume suitable to a domestic servant, or the wife of a small tradesman.

As the principal turret vibrated with the strokes of the clock, the promised signal met Lady Edith's eager ears.

She knelt upon the wide hearth, which was large enough to admit half a dozen men, and struck three times upon the metal doorway.

It slowly revolved upon its hinges, and a hand—the coarse hand of a ruffian—grasped her wrist, as if to draw her through the aperture. For one horrible moment the cold drops of terror burst forth upon her forehead.

Who was this man? She knew not! It was midnight: all were sleeping in that lonely Highland fortress. He was about to lead her into the black darkness of a passage of whose windings she was ignorant. What if she was to be entrapped there only to be murdered for the sake, perhaps, of her jewels? What did she know of this Austrian, save that he was linked with dark deeds of crime—save that he had been the Mephistopheles who first taught her to think of murder?

These doubts occupied no longer than that brief moment between the opening of the secret door and the strong grasp of the agent fastening on her wrist.

That one instant decided all.

"Better to die in a trap like some venomous beast," she muttered, "than to rot day by day in this gilded gaol."

She crept through the aperture, the metal door once more revolved upon its hinges, and all was darkness.

The passage seemed interminable to Lady Edith; but she patiently followed her unseen guide, who still kept his hand upon her wrist until they had emerged into the Castle hall. Here, too, all was dark.

"We are saved!" exclaimed Lady Edith, as the sliding panel, which terminated this end of the passage, closed behind her.

"Hush!" whispered her companion; "not a murmur, not a breath. The shepherds sleep in the kitchen, only separated by a short corridor from this hall. They have their dogs with them. One of the men has a staghound of the Maclomond breed. Those dogs are superhuman in intelligence."

"A Maclomond deerhound!" said Lady Edith. "I thought that Sandy's dog was dead."

"Hush! He has purchased another with his hoarded savings. The man is half a maniac."

While this brief conversation was going forward, Oscar Bertrand's agent had been softly withdrawing the bolts of the castle door, which Mrs. Macpherson had securely fastened at dusk—about ten minutes after the agent had crept into the hall, and secreted himself in his hiding place.

The cold night air swept in upon Lady Edith's face; in another moment she had followed her conductor across the courtyard, out at the gates, and to the sheltered spot where Oscar Bertrand waited beneath the shadow of the castle wall. Another moment, and the horse was flying across the stunted grass upon the mountain side.

Colonel Bertrand disdained the beaten track, and took a short cut across country to the railway station.

THE TWO STRANGERS APPEAL TO LADY EDITH'S BENEVOLENCE

His horse was a thorough-bred, swift and sure-footed as a stag. In less than half an hour the Colonel drew rein before the little Scottish station; the faithful animal, with reeking sides, panting under his double burden. There was no one but a solitary clerk at the station.

"There's no train passes here till the 1·55 up," he said, sulkily.

"I know that as well as you do, my good friend," answered the Austrian; "but as my wife is going by that train, and I want to see her safely off, perhaps you'll allow us to sit in your office till the train stops. It is nearly one o'clock now."

At the same time he contrived to slip a half-sovereign into the clerk's hand.

The sulky functionary became immediately more obliging. He led the Colonel's horse into a shed adjoining the station, and secured the animal by the bridle. He then conducted the travellers into an office about ten feet square where there was a feeble sea-coal fire, a flickering oil lamp, a wooden bench, and the desk or counter at which all the business of the station was transacted.

Lady Edith and her preserver seated themselves, and the clerk retired once more to the room above the office, to take a brief nap before it was time to give the passengers their tickets.

"Now, Lady Edith," said Oscar Bertrand, "listen to me. You are free, but caution is still necessary. I shall not go to London by this train, but shall start from a station twenty miles from here by the next, which leaves six hours hence. We shall thus throw our pursuers off their guard, and render it impossible for them to track us. Your absence from the castle will not be discovered till to-morrow morning; you will by that time have travelled half your journey to London. Martha Crookman, on finding you fled, will immediately telegraph to London. Were your husband in town, all would be lost, as he would meet the train at King's Cross, and you would be a prisoner on alighting from the railway carriage."

"Oh, horror!" exclaimed Lady Edith.

"In order to guard against this unpleasant contingency, I have taken two precautions. First, in all probability your husband will be in Manchester when the telegram reaches London. Secondly, for still greater security, you will stop at Rugby, where my agents will await you with a carriage and post-horses that will take you to London."

"And your motive in taking all this trouble for a wretched and friendless woman——?"

"You will know that when we meet in town. I work with lofty instruments as well as humble ones, and *I want you*, Lady Edith Merton."

CHAPTER XLVII.

THE SECRETS OF THE DARKNESS

ALL occurred exactly as Colonel Oscar Bertrand had foretold Lady Edith. The Austrian himself placed his charge in a comfortable corner of a second-class carriage, choosing this humbler class as another method of averting suspicion.

"If anybody questions you," he whispered, as he took leave of her at the window of the carriage, "you will say that you are a lady's-maid, travelling to join your mistress in London. Farewell, till we next meet."

Lady Edith found a man in a dark livery waiting for her upon the platform at Rugby. He merely said that he had been sent to receive her ladyship, and conducted her immediately to a close carriage, which was in waiting at the station-gates.

The carriage travelled at a good pace, stopping often to obtain relays of horses.

It was long after the midnight following Lady Edith's escape from the Castle when they entered London, and drove through the now silent thoroughfare on the north of the city.

Once only in the course of this rapid posting-journey had Lady Edith taken any refreshment. Midway between Rugby and London she had consented to take a glass of sherry and water.

Her brain was dizzied with the excitement which she had undergone.

She had escaped from her hated prison-house; she was free—free to go whither she would.

But whither was she to go?"

Not to the London residence of her husband; that was no home for her. Her father was dead —the home of her youth for ever broken up. She had sisters, married and in lofty positions, but they had accepted Robert Merton's account of her health—they believed her mad. There had never been any sisterly love among these proud women; each, anxious to obtain the grandest position and the largest wealth, had only striven to eclipse the others.

The poorest wanderer in the streets of London was not more homeless than Lady Edith Merton, laden as she was with the magnificent jewels she had brought from Maclomond Castle. She must go to an hotel.

She was about to stop the carriage and order the coachman to drive to Claridge's, when the man stopped of his own accord, and the servant who had met her on the platform at Rugby, came to the window of the vehicle.

Lady Edith perceived with a shudder that this man now wore a mask. He carried a large black silk handkerchief in his hand.

"Will your ladyship be so kind as to remove your bonnet, and allow me to adjust this for you?" he asked respectfully.

"What is that?"

"A bandage, with which it is my duty to blindfold your ladyhip."

"To blindfold me! Why?"

"Because you are going where none ever go with their eyes uncovered."

A sickly faintness crept over Lady Edith's exhausted frame—the faintness of terror.

"Dare I trust you?" she asked, imploringly.

"Has our master ever deceived you, Madam?"

"Never."

"Then you may trust to him and follow us without fear. We are but instruments."

Edith Merton perceived that this man was no vulgar ruffian, like him whose rough grasp she had felt upon her wrist in the secret passage at Maclomond Castle. The hand which held the silken bandage was ungloved, and she could see that it was nearly as white as her own.

She removed her bonnet, and allowed the man to fasten the handkerchief across her eyes; but before she did so she looked out of the carriage window and saw that they were stationed in the centre of a great piece of waste ground, bordered by the backs of broken-down habitations.

"Where are we now?" she asked.

"In the neighbourhood of Smithfield."

When the handkerchief was tied she sank back on the cushions of the carriage and abandoned herself to her fate.

"They may murder me now," she thought: "I am at their mercy."

It was about a quarter of an hour before the carriage stopped : then the door was softly opened, and Lady Edith felt herself lifted on to the pavement in the arms of two men.

She heard a door open opposite to her. She was carried up some steps, and the same door closed behind her with a sonorous noise as of iron.

She felt that she was in a tomb or a prison, as it pleased her gaolers.

A soft and delicate hand was clasped upon her wrist, and she was led through several passages—passages that seemed to wind like the pathway of a maze.

The air, when she first entered this strange habitation, had seemed damp and chill, now it grew warmer with every step; and instead of the stony paving on which she had at first trodden, she felt that she was walking upon a thick carpet.

Presently the hand suddenly released her wrist. She felt that a door, hung on noiseless hinges, or else a sliding panel, closed behind her, and a voice, which seemed to proceed from somewhere above her head, exclaimed, "Remove the bandage from your eyes and look about you." She raised her hands and discovered that the bandage had been already loosened; in another moment it dropped from her eyes.

The blaze of light was almost too powerful for her dazzled gaze. She was in the inner chamber of the Central Office—that wonderful chamber which contained the books whose mysterious pages recorded the business of the society.

On her right hand there was the small morocco table, with the two lamps, all their light being directed upon her face, while behind them in the shadow sat a man wearing a velvet mask, a jet cross, and the running noose of crape, the ghostly badge of the Order, fastened upon his white and slender wrist.

Lady Edith Merton was too bewildered to cast more than a glance at this man.

Everything in this mysterious chamber filled her with amazement. She saw that in the plain surface of the walls there was no visible mode of egress or ingress, and yet she believed that she had heard a door close behind her.

Exactly opposite to her stood the cabinet, the secret of which is already known to the reader.

The masked man at the table remained perfectly silent. The voice overhead spoke again.

"Lady Edith Merton, you have been rescued from the living death of perpetual imprisonment."

"I have," faltered the trembling woman.

"For this you owe your preservers some gratitude."

"Indeed, indeed I do."

"You are required, therefore, as some return for the services rendered to you, to here accept the solemn oaths of the Order of the Black Band, the Companions of Midnight."

"I accept them."

"Beware how you accept them lightly," continued the voice; "those oaths are only dissolved by death, and death is the reward of those who break them. On every side the Companions of the Order are surrounded by invisible death."

She fell on her knees, clasping her hands in terror.

"You accept the oaths of the Order?"

"I do!"

"So be it; in the circles of which you are a member you are Lady Edith Merton; with us you are known as Number Two Hundred and Thirty seven."

All was silent; the man at the table rose, and removing his mask advanced into the centre of the room.

Lady Edith Merton uttered a shriek, and fell senseless to the ground.

This man was Lionel, Marquis of Willoughby.

CHAPTER XLVIII.

THE SECRET MISSION

WHEN Lady Edith recovered from her swoon, she found herself reclining upon a couch, with the Marquis of Willoughby watching by her side.

She was no longer in the mysterious chamber, with its secret instruments of death.

An atmosphere of perfume pervaded the apartment, which was a small, square chamber, hung with crimson silk and carpeted with velvet pile of the same glowing hue.

The subdued light which proceeded from a large globe of ground glass was softened by a shade of crimson silk.

To the o'erwrought brain of Lady Edith Merton it seemed as if every object in this chamber wore the hue of blood.

This apartment was the retiring-room, sacred to the Grand Master of the Black Band. Here, stretched upon the cushions of a divan, he wove the intricate schemes of guilt which were afterwards executed by his instruments.

"Where am I?" murmured Lady Edith, lifting her heavy eyelids, and gazing upon the face of her lover.

"Safe, dearest, safe with him who loves you!"

"Love me! Oh, Lionel, can you love a guilty wretch like me?"

"Guilty!" echoed the Marquis, with a hollow laugh. "Edith, do you remember that fatal twentieth of December, upon which you and I met at the masked ball? That meeting was the turning-point of our lives. From that hour to this I have been the slave of guilt—an unwilling slave, it is true, but powerless to extricate myself from my bonds; but across the dark sea of crime over which I have been driven, Love has still been my lode-star."

"Love, Lionel, and for me?"

"For none other, Edith. Long ere this I should have tried to save you, though I had risked my life in the effort; but he who is more powerful than I bade me wait. My oath compelled me to obey him, and I waited."

"Lionel, tell me, who is this man?"

"I know not. Hush!"

Lord Willoughby laid his finger on his lips, and at the same moment a door opened behind the silken hangings, and the Grand Master stood before them.

"I have left you long enough alone for the renewal of the vows of the past," he said; "I come now to speak to you of more serious business."

"We are listening," said the Marquis.

"You will leave England at daybreak."

"So soon?"

"Yes; your passports are already procured; they are made out in the names of the Marquis of Willoughby and his widowed sister, the Countess de Grancy. You, Lady Edith, will be known as the Countess de Grancy, the widow of a French nobleman."

"And our destination?" said the Marquis.

"You will go at once to Paris, thence to Marseilles, thence to Venice."

"Why Venice?"

"Because we have work for you to do there."

"Deeper guilt?" exclaimed Lord Willoughby.

"No, my lord; the business in which I require your aid is of a political nature."

The Marquis drew a long breath of heartfelt relief. He had yet to learn the crimes which are committed in the obscure intricacies of state policy—crimes which men dare to call *necessary*.

"Will the work I have to do be in the interests of England?" asked Lord Willoughby.

"No, it concerns the welfare of Austria."

"And Edith—"

"Lady Edith will also have her mission to perform—one for which her beauty and fascination eminently adapt her."

"When shall we receive our instructions?"

"On your arrival at your destination. But in the meantime, my dear Marquis, I may give you and your fair companion a brief outline of my motives in sending you to Venice."

"I am all attention," said Lord Willoughby, eagerly.

"Venice, as you are aware, is beneath the Austrian rule; but these pitiful Italians have a happy knack of hating their masters. With these fierce southern natures, hatred is no passive passion; it breathes its deadly fire in vengeful words—it whispers treason in obscure hints and dark suggestions. But words do not for ever suffice it; it has need of deeds, and it conspires. The dog grows weary of growling and gnawing at his chain—he tries to bite."

"And the master—"

"Laughs at the impotence of the animal's fury, and waits."

"For what?"

"For the proper hour to strike, to crush, to destroy—to kill."

"Hapless Italy!" exclaimed the Marquis.

"Ay, hapless indeed," echoed Colonel Bertrand, with a vengeful light glowing in his dark eyes; "hapless indeed, when she would revolt against the iron rule of Austria."

"But explain the mission upon which you would send me."

"It is very simple! At Venice, Naples, Milan, Turin, and Florence, there are different branches of one political society. That society is strongest in Venice. Austria requires information respecting the proceedings of this society. Such information can only be obtained from a member."

"Ah!" exclaimed Lord Willoughby, "a light dawns upon me."

"You will therefore become a member of that society," said the Austrian quietly.

"In order that I may betray it?"

"That you will learn hereafter. For the present you have heard enough. It is now six o'clock; at half-past six you will leave here, and at seven start from London Bridge for Dover. Robert Merton will receive a telegram apprising him of Lady Edith's escape; but when he does so, you and your lovely companion will have bidden adieu to the white cliffs of Old Albion and to Oscar Bertrand."

He extended his hand to Lady Edith as he spoke. The proud woman lifted her wondering eyes to his face, with an earnest and searching glance.

"Inexplicable being," she murmured; "you have rescued me from a captivity which was far worse than death. You have restored me to the only man I ever loved; and yet so mysterious is your every act that even now I scarcely know whether to look upon you with gratitude or hatred. Am I to thank you for that which you have done for me?"

"No!" exclaimed the Marquis, throwing his arm around her, and drawing her away from Oscar Bertrand, "Thank him not, Edith. The devil, to obtain possession of the souls of his victims, tempts them with fair gifts and with terms that seem to realise their wishes. So does he. Yes, better for both of us that we 'had never seen him—better that I had lived and died a penniless younger son—better that you had perished even within the dreary walls of Castle Maclomond."

The Austrian Colonel laughed a mocking laugh at the fiery words of the young man.

"My Lionel," he said, seating himself on the crimson cushions of the divan, and beginning deliberately to fill the meerschaum bowl of a long pipe, which reached from the lips of the smoker to the velvet pile beneath his feet; "My Lionel, it is such a pleasure to me to serve you, and yet you accept my services so ungraciously. There, go, foolish children, love and liberty are yours. Go, be happy!"

The Austrian touched a spring in the wall behind him, a door opened, and the man who had met Lady Edith at Rugby again appeared, still wearing a black mask.

"Blindfold these members of the Association, and conduct them to the entrance at which my carriage waits. Thence you will accompany them to the railway station, and you will not leave them till they start for Dover."

"We are prisoners, then?" exclaimed Lionel, indignantly. "We are to be followed — watched!"

"No, Marquis, you are to be *protected*. There, no more delay, go!"

In three minutes the Marquis and Lady Edith were seated in the Colonel's well-appointed brougham. The cool air of morning blew in upon them through the open windows of the vehicle and cooled their fevered brows.

They reached the station; the bandages were removed from their eyes; the man—who was no longer masked, but concealed his features by a hat slouched over his forehead and a thick handkerchief wrapped about his chin—handed them their tickets and conducted them to a first-class carriage. He remained on the platform watching this carriage until the departing whistle of the engine pealed through the station.

CHAPTER XLIX.

ANTONIO VECCHI REVEALS THE PLOT

ON arriving at Venice the Marquis and Lady Edith found a superb suite of apartments prepared for them in a palace-like building, situated in the Square of St. Mark. The identity of Robert Merton's wife was entirely lost—she was henceforth to be known only as the Countess de Grancy, the widow of a French nobleman, and the sister of Lord Willoughby.

Her only fear was that amongst the few English residents or visitors at Venice there might be some whom she had known in the fashionable world of London.

In order to be satisfied upon this matter, her first care was to send for a *valet de place*, and to ascertain from him the names of the English in Venice.

She breathed a sigh of relief as the man ran through a brief list of titles.

There was not one amongst them whose owner was known to her. She was therefore safe—for a time, at least.

Oscar Bertrand had, as the reader will remember, told Lord Willoughby and Lady Edith that they would receive their instructions at the end of their journey.

On arriving at Venice they waited anxiously for the person, whoever he might be, from whom they were to obtain those instructions.

They had not long to wait!

On the morning after their arrival, Lady Edith reclined on a couch in a small octagonal boudoir, the walls of which were adorned with paintings by the old Italian masters.

A small circular table was adorned with an elegant service of Dresden china and chiselled gold, a basket of hot-house peaches and grapes, a raised pie, and other costly delicacies.

This table was placed close to the couch on which Lady Edith reclined, and on the other side of it sat Lord Willoughby, his elbow resting upon the pale azure cushion of his arm-chair, his head leaning upon his hand.

The breakfast, which might have tempted the appetite of a Lucullus, was entirely untouched.

It is often in the hour of his triumph, in the culminating moment which crowns his proudest wishes, that man most bitterly regrets the crimes by which he has purchased success. Blest with wealth and rank, and with the love of her for whom he had stained his soul, Lionel, Marquis of Willoughby, was yet a wretched man.

He had not the power for evil of the woman whom he loved. Lady Edith Merton might have been a Borgia, a Medici, a Brinvilliers, for she could be deaf to the voice of conscience. He could not.

THE VOW OF THE FIVE

THE BLACK BAND; OR, THE MYSTERIES OF MIDNIGHT

Turn which way he would, the vision of his murdered brother ever rose before his eyes! Look where he would, between him and the sunlight appeared that frank and noble countenance—those mild, reproachful eyes!

Lady Edith perceived the traces of these mental agonies in the face of her lover.

"This folly in another would inspire in me nothing but scorn, Lionel," she said; "as it is, I pity you; and I would have you beware of a woman's pity for the man she loves. Pity may indeed be akin to love, but it is also allied to contempt."

"You have a soul of iron, Edith," answered the Marquis.

"I have that which you do not possess," she replied coldly; "I have the soul of a man. What avails this perpetual whining about the past? Would you be again poor, again obscure (for poverty is obscurity), again despised? No! Then if you had the power this moment you would not summon your brother back to life, though one word spoken by you might restore him from the tomb. He fell in a duel, that is all—a duel with another than yourself."

"Ay, Edith, we may mock the world by the seeming truth: the *real* truth, like a serpent, winds itself about the aching heart of the guilty man, and gnaws at its inmost core."

"Bah! Lionel, you are a coward. Hush, there is some one at the outer door. Compose yourself, and smooth that troubled brow, for pity's sake."

Lady Edith was right. A groom of the chambers entered the apartment furthest removed from the boudoir, and came with softly sounding footfall through the intermediate room. He carried a silver salver, upon which lay a visiting card.

Lord Willoughby took it in his hand with a careless gesture. It was inscribed thus:—

Signor Vecchi,

Accredited by COL. OSCAR BERTRAND.

"Admit this person," said the Marquis, handing the card to Lady Edith.

We have neither seen nor heard of Signor Antonio Vecchi since his escape from the prison in Coldbath Fields.

His outer man was much improved since last we beheld him. He now wore a well-made fashionable morning suit; but in spite of this change in his attire, there was a sinister expression in his dark, olive face, a cold and serpent glance in the one stony eye, which contrasted so strangely with its restless and shifting fellow—that stamped him a villain.

Lord Willoughby motioned to his visitor to be seated.

Signor Vecchi bowed, but declined the offered chair.

"I am but an humble member of the mighty association," he said, with a studied and hypocritical humility. "I have been employed only in the meaner work of the order. I would rather remain standing."

As the Italian spoke, the one restless eye glanced with a rapid but searching gaze from the Marquis to Lady Edith, from Lady Edith back to the Marquis, while the other eye remained fixed and stony as that of a corpse.

"You come from——!" Lord Willoughby began interrogatively.

"From the most powerful amongst us," answered Vecchi.

"You are charged with instructions, I believe?" Lady Edith said, haughtily. "Pray, let us have them without delay."

"I obey you, Madame!" answered the Italian. "You have been already informed that there exists in Venice a branch of a certain political society, which is spreading itself throughout Italy. Austria requires the secrets of this society; but its members are circumspect, and nothing is more difficult than to obtain admission to the inner circles of the association. I am not of sufficient importance to be elected a member. There may be other reasons also for my exclusion; enough that I am not trusted, or the secrets would long ere this have been in the possession of the Grand Master of the Black Band."

"But you—you, who are yourself an Italian—would you betray your own country?" exclaimed the Marquis.

"The poor have no country," answered Vecchi imperturbably; "they serve those who pay them best."

"You are at least candid, Signor Vecchi," said Lady Edith.

"Why should I be otherwise, Madame. I tell no lies save those which have a purpose. I have no purpose to serve here: I have but to deliver my instructions. You, my lord, are required to become one of the political society of which I have spoken. Its members call themselves the Mountaineers. A terrible excitement is now pervading Italy; for the grey-headed chief of this society—the admired and venerated Count di Novaglia—was assassinated three nights ago in the streets of Venice."

"Horrible!" exclaimed Lord Willoughby "but by whom was this vile deed committed?"

"Nay, my lord, it is not for me to say. The old man was found lying on the steps of a doorway in one of the darkest streets of Venice—his breast pierced with upwards of twenty stiletto wounds. The hilt of a small dagger remained buried in the heart when the corpse was found. To the hilt was attached a narrow strip of parchment, upon which these words were written : ' The bloodshed which policy prompts is not murder ; it is *necessity*. Let the Mountaineers remember this and beware ! '"

"The unhappy man was, doubtless, assassinated by some Austrian spy," said Lady Edith.

"The hand of Austria might guide the dagger, and yet not strike the blow, Signora," replied the Italian, with significance. "You, Lord Willoughby," he continued, "will not *offer* yourself as a member of this society ; but you will, this day, pay a visit to the Marquis Montebello, the present chief of the Mountaineers. You will declare yourself a devoted friend of trampled Italy ; you will proclaim also your hatred of Austrian tyranny—your adherence to the cause of liberty. I know the Marquis well enough to know that the bait will answer. He will fall into the trap—delighted by your sentiments, dazzled by your rank and wealth, he will ask you to join the Mountaineers."

"And I—?"

"You will obey the orders of the most powerful amongst us. You will become a member of this secret society. To-morrow is the day appointed for the funeral of the Count di Novaglia ; at that funeral will occur events of some importance. You, as a trusted member of the society, will be present. You will hear all, and you will repeat all to me."

"Oh, Heavens, this is too horrible !" exclaimed the Marquis.

"You, my lord, will be perfectly secure ; suspicion will never attach itself to *you*, for your rank will blindfold the keenest eyes. None will dare to breathe one doubt of the Marquis of Willoughby's honour. And now, my lord, I will bid you good morning."

Antonio Vecchi bowed and glided from the room. Lady Edith touched the spring of a bell, and the groom of the chambers appeared at the furthermost door to conduct the visitor down the grand staircase.

Lord Willoughby breathed more freely when the Italian was gone, but his heart sank at the contemplation of the act of treachery he was to commit.

CHAPTER L.

THE FUNERAL OF THE MURDERED CHIEF

THE funeral of the murdered Count di Novaglia was conducted with all the pomp and grandeur peculiar to the Roman Catholic Church. The interior of St. Mark's was brilliantly illuminated with the massive wax tapers which adorned the high altar and the smaller altars in the many chapels of the sacred edifice. The mighty tones of the organ reverberated through the solemn aisles as the mass for the dead was sung by the rich voices of the choir.

By the side of the Marquis Montebello, and near the velvet-covered catafalque upon which the coffin was placed, stood the English nobleman, Lord Willoughby.

He had that morning taken the oaths of the Society of Mountaineers.

He who became a member of this society swore to be faithful until the hour of death —he who betrayed his brothers was subject to a fearful penalty.

The arm of the traitor was branded with a red-hot iron, which stamped the sign of his infamy upon his quivering flesh.

The brand thus burnt upon the arm of the guilty brother was the initial T.

The initiated knew that this letter signified the word *Traditore*, or traitor.

Whenever a member of the society met a man thus branded, it was his business to destroy him.

The laws of the association knew no mercy. If a father had discovered a traitor in his only son, that father's duty would have been to assassinate that son.

Lord Willoughby was told all this, yet he repeated the fearful oaths dictated to him.

The mass was concluded, the priests retired from the altar, and the crowd slowly retreated from the church, until the vast edifice seemed almost entirely deserted.

The Marquis looked round with surprise. The ceremony was concluded, but nothing of peculiar significance had occurred.

"All is over, then?" he said to his companion.

"Not yet," answered the Marquis Montebello ; "wait and watch."

It was growing dusk within the church ; the tapers had been extinguished, except in one of the smaller chapels at the further end of the edifice.

Presently Lord Willoughby perceived, from the shadowy recesses of the church—from behind archways, pillars, statues, fonts, and tombs, dark figures, which slowly emerged from their hiding-places, and gathered round the Marquis de Montebello.

Rich and poor were alike to be found in that motley group ; old men and women, youth and childhood, all were there.

"You are ready, my children ?" said the Italian Marquis.

"We are," answered the crowd.

"And you are all faithful?"

"All! all! Excellenza."

"By yonder sacred symbol?" he asked, pointing to the jewelled cross upon the high altar.

"Yes! yes! Eccellenza."

"Then follow me," said the Marquis, taking a lighted torch from the hand of an attendant.

At these words, five men whom Lord Willoughby had not before observed emerged from the crowd, and approached the coffin.

These five men were masked.

They were Venetians of high rank, trusted members of the Society of Mountaineers.

With slow and solemn steps they approached the coffin, and, lifting it from the catafalque, carried it in the direction of the Novaglia chapel, the crowd following.

The five men bore the coffin into the chapel, and placed it on a bier which stood ready to receive its solemn burden.

At the bronze gates which separated the chapel from the body of the church of St. Mark the crowd paused respectfully.

The Marquis Montebello placed himself upon the threshold of the chapel.

"My children," he said, addressing the crowd, "you will enter one by one into the presence of your murdered chief, and each of you, as he passes through the gates, whisper in my ear the password of the association. You understand?"

"Yes, Eccellenza, yes," replied the crowd, simultaneously.

One by one the people entered the chapel, until they filled the edifice. When the last had entered, the Marquis Montebello closed the chapel gates, and locked them with a key which he carried attached to his belt.

"We are now secure," he said, when he had done this; "the might of Austria cannot touch us now, unless we have a traitor amongst us."

The noble Italian little dreamed that the English patrician by his side was there only to betray.

One by one the five masked men advanced to the coffin. The lid had been removed, and the rigid face of the corpse looked calmly upwards to the torchlight.

The five men stretched forth their hands over the chill form of clay, and in measured accents uttered a terrible vow. It was a vow of vengeance upon the murderers of the noble and generous patriot, Count Annibale di Novaglia.

It is not for us to repeat the awful terms of that oath. Enough that the blood of the bravest man amongst the crowd seemed to curdle in his veins, as he heard the measured accents of the five masked associates.

These men were the five remaining chiefs of the Mountaineers. The sixth was the Prince de C., absent amidst the heights of Calabria, the seventh the murdered man.

These seven men represented the heads of the association; without their consent no step could be taken, no member admitted.

The crowd slowly dispersed, and the five men, the Marquis Montebello, and Lord Willoughby, were left alone in the chapel. Alone with the dead!

"We meet to-night, my lord," said the Italian Marquis, "at the Palazzo Montebello. You will join us, will you not?"

"Willingly," answered Lionel.

"The present is a crisis in which English aid will be of inestimable service to us. We are in hopes that we have secured the help of the mighty power which is newly arisen in France; but we would have the aid of your free country also. Remember, we meet at eleven. Until then, farewell."

The warm-hearted Italian grasped Lord Willoughby's hand, and left the church followed by the five masked associates. That night, in the innermost saloon of the Palazzo Montebello—a secret apartment, whose existence was unknown to any save the Mountaineers—the business of the society was discussed in the presence of the English traitor.

Lord Willoughby left the palace with a whitened cheek to complete the work he had begun.

He wrote a concise account of all that had passed, folded the paper, and secured it in an envelope fastened with six immense seals.

In drawing up this document, the Marquis of Willoughby took care to disguise his hand. The seal he used, although a peculiar one, had never been used by him before.

Early the next morning he took a gondola, and leaving Venice some miles behind him, threw the seal into the waters of the Adriatic.

He knew the fearful penalties to which the traitor was subject, and he was eager to remove the traces of his crime. Antonio Vecchi received the packet from the hands of the Marquis, in the presence of Lady Edith Merton.

CHAPTER LI.

LOLOTA'S MIDNIGHT GUEST

On the same night upon which the meeting of the Mountaineers took place in the Palazzo Montebello, the pleasure-seekers of Venice flocked to the Opera House, to do honour to the first appearance of a favourite dancer, who had newly arrived from England.

That dancer was Lolota Vizzini.

Lovely as of old, she bounded upon the Venetian stage amid the plaudits of her admirers, who crowded the house from the orchestra to the ceiling.

If the poor glories of a dancer's life—if the triumphs of success could have satisfied the Spanish woman's proud heart, she might indeed have been happy.

But she was not so.

She had loved—once only in her life—and she had loved in vain. The crowd wooed and admired; but he—he for whom she would have thought life too poor a sacrifice—he loved her not.

She little dreamed that he was at that self-same hour in Venice.

Tired and worn out with the excitement of her first appearance in the queen city of the Adriatic, exhausted with her recent journey, she was only too glad to find herself alone in the comfortable apartments of her hotel at the close of the performance.

Her maid had brought home the bouquets and laurel wreaths which had been thrown to the favourite. She had heaped them on a table near her mistress. Lolota glanced at them with a smile of contempt.

"Take them away, Justine," she said; "their perfume oppresses me."

"But I thought Madame would like to look at them," remonstrated the girl; "they are very beautiful."

"Perhaps so, but they are all alike. Take them from the room, child; I don't care for them."

The lady's-maid shrugged her shoulders with a gesture of astonishment, and collecting the fragrant exotics, carried them from the apartment.

"My poor mistress gets worse and worse every day," she murmured. "I'm very much afraid she'll go melancholy mad before she dies. People who see her, all smiles and beauty upon the stage, little know what she is when alone."

Five minutes after this the servant re-entered the apartment, carrying a card upon a salver.

"A gentleman, Madame," she said, "who wishes to see you."

Lolota looked up with considerable vexation.

"Surely you told him that at such an hour I could receive no one," she exclaimed.

"I did, Madame; but he insisted upon my bringing you this card."

"Insisted? pshaw! you knew your duty, and should have refused."

"Why, so I should, Madame," faltered the girl; "but the truth is that there is something so strange in the gentleman's look that I—I thought he had what the people here call the evil eye!"

"The evil eye!"

"Yes, Madame, one of his eyes is glassy and still, like the eye of a corpse, the other——"

Lolota started from her sofa. "Can it be?" she said; "no, surely no! Give me the card."

She snatched the card from the salver, and read the name inscribed upon it.

"Alas, alas! why am I thus persecuted?" she murmured, and then recovering herself by an effort, she addressed the girl: "Admit this man," she said.

The girl left the apartment, and presently returned ushering in Antonio Vecchi.

With a careless nod to Lolota Vizzini, the Italian flung himself into one of the brocaded easy chairs which adorned the apartment.

His manner was here altogether different from the humble and almost servile demeanour he had adopted in the presence of Lady Edith and Lord Willoughby.

Here he was insolent, defiant, self-assured.

"The clock of St. Mark's is striking the hour of midnight," said Lolota, pointing to the spires visible in the purple atmosphere, through the large open window; "it is a late hour for your visit, Signior Vecchi."

The Italian laughed maliciously.

"There are some relationships, Madame," he said, "which justify a trifling breach of etiquette."

"Bah!" exclaimed Lolota, contemptuously. "Since you are here—you are doubtless here for one purpose. Speak, what do you require?"

"Money!"

"You have already impoverished me!"

"But Lolota Vizzini, the ballet-dancer, can earn more. Work, Madame, work. I must have money or——"

"What if I refuse?"

"Your admirers in Venice, Paris, Milan, Naples, and London, shall be told who you are!"

"Enough—enough!"

"Shall be told that the so-called Lolota Vizzini is the wife of a supposed murderer—an escaped criminal—a suspected traitor. They would treat you with little mercy in this city, Madame, did they know you to be the wife of Antonio Vecchi!"

———

CHAPTER LII.

THE WARNING

WITHIN a week of the despatch of Lord Willoughby's communication the following appeared in the list of deaths, in the principal English and Continental papers:

"On the 17th inst., in London, *suddenly*, Antonio Vecchi, aged 33. No. 69, G. M. B. B."

This advertisement was inserted in these papers in order that all the members of the association who were scattered about Europe might know that a traitor had met a traitor's doom. To the initiated this advertisement had a terrible meaning. The word *suddenly*, printed in italics, signified that the traitor had been assassinated. The mode of his death was known only to those who had witnessed it.

Amongst others who read this strange paragraph was Lolota Vizzini.

The newspaper dropped from her hand, and a dizziness came over her as she perused the brief line which told of her husband's death.

She was free! From her earliest youth she had been a bondwoman, a slave, tied to a wretch whose very name was loathsome to her. She had been toiling for him, lavishing on his low and degrading vices the gold won by her genius and beauty.

And now in one brief moment she had become free. The chain of iron which she had thought to wear until the grave released her from its cankering links was broken for ever. It had been broken by a stronger hand than hers—the hand of death.

"Oh, heaven!" she exclaimed, falling on her knees, in an agony of remorse. "Merciful heaven! forgive me if I cannot feel a Christian sorrow for the death of this guilty wretch. I am but human."

Then, unable to conquer her agitation, she rose from her knees and paced up and down the apartment, with her hands clasped, and her beautiful head bent upon her breast.

"If Lionel had but loved me!" she murmured, "if he had only loved me!"

*　　*　　*　　*　　*

The Marquis of Willoughby sought in the excitement of dissipation to banish those memories which made life intolerable.

His reputed sister, the widowed Countess de Grancy, was not loth to take her part in the brilliant existence for which alone she was fitted. In the gay world Lady Edith Merton shone, a star, a goddess. By the domestic hearth she was a proud and discontented woman; gloomy and silent.

In the palatial saloons of the Venetian nobility, the Marquis and Lady Edith were courted and caressed. Young, handsome, distinguished, wealthy—they were an acquisition to the society in which they moved.

Amongst others, the grave Marquis di Montebello was fascinated by the beauty of the pretended widow.

Past the meridian of life, the Italian Marquis was still a handsome man; his manners had all the grace and polish natural to those who descend from a race of princes. He was no mean conquest, therefore, and Lady Edith felt some pride in having subdued a heart long considered dead to the charms of beauty.

She therefore did all in her power to encourage the attentions of the Italian Marquis. She had another motive for this line of conduct.

She had for some time been piqued by the cold and abstracted manner of the Marquis of Willoughby, and she wished to make him suffer the pangs of jealousy. But her efforts were vain.

Lionel Montfort beheld her flirtation with the Marquis with the eye of indifference. He had ceased to love, and jealousy can only exist where Love holds his throne. The reader will marvel at the suddenness of this change, and will ask how it was that a soul-absorbing passion like that of the young Marquis could expire like the short-lived fancy of an hour?

For years Lady Edith had been the lodestar of his existence—the bright and wandering meteor leading him through seas of guilt, indifferent whither he went in pursuit of her he loved.

But during those past years he had only seen her at intervals. He had beheld her the queen of a ballroom, the idol of a crowd—he had beheld only her beauty and fascination, and for these he had alone worshipped her.

Within the last few weeks he had learnt to *know her!*

He had dwelt beneath the same roof—he had seen her day after day cast off the brilliant mask she wore to bewitch the world. His horror-stricken gaze had fathomed the black depths of that callous and guilty heart: he now knew her as she really was, and love had changed to loathing.

He remembered that for this woman he had steeped his soul in crime. For her sake he had procured the murder of his brother, and caused his mother's heart to break; for her sake he had occasioned the death of the innocent girl who loved Angus; for her sake he had joined an association of midnight robbers and assassins; had become the bond slave of a man, half fiend, half felon, and had betrayed the noble members of a grand political confederacy.

Despairing of peace or rest upon this weary earth, indifferent alike to every pleasure, he still tried to drown the torments of his soul in scenes of mirth and revelry.

Upon the evening of the very day on which Lolota Vizzini read her husband's death in an Austrian paper, the Marquis and Lady Edith for the first time visited the Opera House at Venice.

They were accompanied by the Marquis di Montebello, whose box they occupied. Devoted as the Italian nobleman was to the delights of music, it was to the melody of Lady Edith's voice that he listened rather than to the harmonious strains of the opera which was being performed.

The opera finished, the ballet commenced, and after two or three opening dances by inferior performers, the star of the night, Lolota Vizzini, bounded on to the stage.

Lord Willoughby had not looked at the programme of the night's performance, and he was utterly ignorant of Lolota's presence in Venice.

He started at the sight of that lovely face which had so often been uplifted to his own. He sighed as he remembered that noble heart, whose love had been so lavishly bestowed upon him, but bestowed in vain.

Neither the start nor the sigh escaped the falcon glance of Lady Edith Merton. Absorbed as she appeared in conversation with the Italian nobleman, no look nor action of Lord Willoughby was lost upon her.

She saw his start of surprise, and looking on to the stage beheld Lolota Vizzini in all her glorious southern beauty. She felt that this woman was a fitting rival even for herself, and a thrill of jealousy convulsed her soul.

For the rest of the evening she kept an unfailing watch upon Lord Willoughby, while with consummate artifice she appeared solely engrossed by the Marquis di Montebello. She saw that Lionel's eyes followed Lolota through every step of the undulating dance.

The Marquis di Montebello's box was on the grond tier and near the stage; so near that it was possible for the actors to recognise those seated in the box.

As Lolota Vizzini retired, curtseying to the ground, and laden with costly bouquets, she raised her eyes, and looking round the house suddenly met the eyes of Lionel Montfort.

Again Lady Edith Merton beheld the start, the glance of surprise; but this time gladness mingled with the surprise.

"This woman knows him," she thought; "they have met before—met, perhaps loved each other. Yes, yes, there was love in her eyes as she raised them to his."

She crushed the stems of the hothouse flowers which composed her bouquet till the fragile blossoms perished beneath the pressure of her clenched hand, but her face betrayed no emotion. She still smiled, still listened and replied to the gallant speeches of the Marquis.

"The dancer is very beautiful," she said presently in a careless tone.

"Lolota Vizzini?" replied the Italian; "yes, she is indeed lovely, and they say she is as good as she is beautiful."

"Has she ever been in London?" asked Lady Edith.

"Oh! yes, and in Paris also. She has been the star of the Opera House in both places. Is it possible you have never seen her, Madame?"

"Never."

Lady Edith relapsed into silence. She was thinking that doubtless while she was a prisoner in her husband's dreary Scottish home Lionel Montfort was at the feet of Lolota Vizzini.

"This accounts for his indifference," she thought; "this explains all. He loves another, and time has extinguished the old passion."

She knew not that her own infamy had alone changed the heart of her lover.

"Of course you have seen this Spanish dancer before to-night, Lionel?" she said, as they were rising to leave the box.

Lord Willoughby changed colour.

"Yes," he replied, "I have seen her often—that is—on the stage of course."

"And never off the stage?"

"Yes, sometimes—that is—"

"You forget, Lionel!" answered Edith, with chilling irony. "Why should I weary you with such trifling questions? Come, Marquis?" she said, taking the arm of the Italian nobleman.

At the door of the box they found servants awaiting them, carrying lanterns with which to light the way to the gondolas.

On the steps of the landing-place they paused to bid each other adieu. The night was dark and moonless, the place crowded.

As the Marquis was assisting Lady Edith into her gondola, a man stepped from amidst the crowd, and laid his hand upon the arm of the Italian nobleman, with the fingers placed in a peculiar position. This was one of the counter-signs of the Mountaineers. The man wore the ordinary working garb of the lower orders, and his face was concealed by his slouched hat.

"What is it, brother?" asked the Marquis.

"Danger! treason! Eccellenza! Do not return to your house to-night."

"Danger!"

THE DEAD HAND

"Yes," replied the man, "danger which menaces you, even as you stand here. Lose not a moment, Eccellenza, if you love us. Fly to some place of safety. We are betrayed—Venice is filled with Austrian spies—the Five have been arrested within the last half-hour."

"The Five arrested!"

"Yes, yes, my lord! I tell you we are lost! For the love of the brotherhood fly to some place of concealment without a moment's delay! While we linger here you may be arrested. You will have some chance of escaping amongst the crowd leaving the Opera House, but in a few moments more the quay will be nearly clear."

"Right, friend, right!" exclaimed the Marquis; "I will follow your advice, and seek a hiding-place! The brotherhood will know where to find me!"

No. 15. [*Weekly, One Penny.*]

"Ay, Eccellenza!"

"Good night, friend, and thank you for the warning."

"I need no thanks for doing my duty," replied the unknown, as he and the Marquis mingled with the crowd, and disappeared in the darkness.

Meanwhile the gondola occupied by Lady Edith and Lord Willoughby shot through the waters of the canal. They were both absorbed in thought.

"If this is indeed as I suspect," said the haughty woman, "if he has dared to love another, he shall pay dearly for his treachery. A terrible revenge is in my power, and I will not scruple to snatch it."

CHAPTER LIII.

THE FIRST ACT IN LADY EDITH'S REVENGE

BOTH Lady Edith Merton and Lord Willoughby had read the paragraph in the foreign newspapers which announced the death of the Italian, Antonio Vecchi, but neither of them knew its awful meaning.

Neither of them were aware of the hideous significance of that word, *suddenly*, printed in italics.

A thrill of hope vibrated through the heart of the Marquis, as he thought that perhaps the hand of Death had interposed to arrest the Italian ere he delivered the papers; but the next moment's reflection dispelled the thought. Was not the advertisement signed with those terrible initials, G. M. B. B.—Grand Master of the Black Band? The papers had, therefore, been safely lodged in the hands of Oscar Bertrand.

The noble Italian confederacy of the champions of liberty, whose generous members had so freely admitted him into their ranks—this glorious association was betrayed, and at any hour the blow might fall—the vengeful hand of Austria might be stretched forth to crush its foes.

Already he seemed to feel the burning brand upon his arm. Already he felt himself stamped as a traitor—an accursed wanderer upon the face of the earth; a wretch whom the brotherhood were sworn to destroy, meet him where they might!

The sleep of the Marquis was haunted by visions such as these, yet on the night of his visit to the Opera House the radiant face of Lolota Vizzini shone like a star through the darkness, and dispelled the blackest thoughts. He awoke with the morning light—awoke to think of her whose loveliness had haunted his sleep.

He could not refrain from comparing her with that haughty and ambitious woman whose evil influence had worked the destruction of his soul.

He wept bitter tears of rage and regret as he remembered the fatal passion which had been the one madness of his life.

He thought of the love of Lolota; pure, fervent, disinterested, generous, devoted!

This priceless jewel had been cast at his feet, as flowers are thrown before an idol's shrine—unheeded, to wither and decay.

He thought of Edith—Edith who had coldly told him that she loved him, yet that she would never be his till he had won rank and wealth.

He had sacrificed all for this one end and aim; and now, now that he saw her daily, hourly—now that he dwelt beneath the same roof with her—now he found the depth of his delusion. The goddess he had so long worshipped was an imperious and jealous-tempered woman, who demanded every thought, every glance of the man she loved, and was restless and unhappy save when surrounded by admiration and excitement.

But surely he might escape from the bondage of crime. Surely he might fly from this woman and from Colonel Oscar Bertrand. Superhuman and gigantic as were the operations of this man, surely there must be some corner of the earth where he might hide—some unfrequented spot in which he might lose all identity!

He determined on making an attempt to escape—even if he perished in the act; for to remain was to remain in the thrall of a demon, who might at any moment call upon him to commit some new crime.

"Lolota still loves me," he thought; "I could see that last night in the one thrilling glance of those dark eyes when they met my own. If she will join me in my flight, to her and to penitence I will devote the remainder of my days. We will seek some lonely spot, near enough to civilised life to enable us to enjoy all its blessings; yet, so unfrequented that none shall ever discover our retreat: and there, if Heaven's pity can lull the agonies of remorse, I may yet be happy."

He determined on seeing Lolota that very morning, and ascertaining from her own lips whether she still loved him.

Lady Edith and the Marquis met at the breakfast-table in the azure-curtained boudoir.

Lady Edith met him with her sweetest smile; conversed gaily on the performances of the previous evening, and on a dozen indifferent subjects. Determined to test him to the uttermost, she praised Lolota's beauty and genius; affected an interest in the lovely Spanish woman, and asked a great many questions about her previous career.

She gloated over the embarrassment of Lord Willoughby as he endeavoured to reply to these questions, until at last, determined to escape from further torture, he rose from the breakfast-table, and prepared to leave the room.

An angry light flashed from Lady Edith's eyes as she saw the Marquis prepare to depart. Every word, every action, only confirmed that which she suspected. He no longer loved her.

"Are you going out, Lionel?" she asked.

"Yes."

"May I ask whither?"

"I—I—have two or three visits to pay."

"To whom?"

"To the Marquis Montebello amongst others."

"Shall I accompany you?"

He smiled bitterly at this question.

"Scarcely, I think," he answered; "easy as Continental manners may be, it can scarcely be etiquette for a lady to visit a gentleman who has no ladies in his household. You already display a sufficiently marked preference for the Marquis."

This was the first allusion Lord Willoughby had ever made to Lady Edith's flirtation with the noble Italian.

"The Marquis of Montebello amuses me," she said, wearily; "he is handsome, noble, accomplished—nay, more—he is sincere. Should you think it strange, Lionel, if I were by-and-by tempted to return his affections?"

The young man started. Himself unskilled in hypocrisy, he dreamt not of the hidden purpose of these words.

"Lorenzo Montebello is indeed all that you say, Edith," he replied. "His affection for you seems earnest and intense. Better, perhaps, that you returned it—better, perhaps, that you and I had never met."

Without waiting her reply he hurried from the room. His last words had revealed all which the designing woman sought to discover, and she was not long in deciding on her course of action.

"So," she murmured, "this is the end of all! He no longer loves me, and his visit of to-day is doubtless to this Spanish woman. He shall pay dearly for his treachery."

Lady Edith rang a bell, and ordered the servant who answered it to send her own maid.

This maid was a Frenchwoman, who had been recommended to her by the Grand Master of the Black Band. She was no other than Rosine Rousel.

The reader knows the system of Colonel Oscar Bertrand. It was to surround those who served him with spies, so that should they attempt to betray him he would be the first to hear of their intention.

Three days after Lady Edith's arrival at Venice, Rosine Rousel had presented herself, with a brief note of introduction from the Colonel.

This note was rather a command than a recommendation. It was worded thus :

"The bearer of this is worthy of your confidence. Employ her as your maid.—G. M. B. B."

Edith Merton and Rosine Rousel had but to look into each other's eyes to understand each other fully.

That which had filled Ellen Bertrand with a shuddering horror and loathing was welcome to the designing and guilty Edith. She felt that the Frenchwoman might be useful to her. She had as yet had no occasion for her services, but the time had now come for her to demand them.

Rosine Rousel entered the room and, after curtsying almost to the ground, awaited the orders of her mistress.

For some moments Lady Edith remained silently abstracted, as if she had forgotten the motive for which she had summoned her attendant.

Rosine Rousel made no attempt to arouse her from this abstraction.

With her cold grey eyes fixed upon Lady Edith's gloomy face, she remained watching her mistress; presently the lady lifted her eyes and met the steadfast gaze of Rosine Rousel.

She saw in that one glance she had to deal with one whom no fine words could cajole, no falsehood deceive.

"Rosine," she said, "I think we understand each other."

"If Madame means that I am willing to do my duty as her servant she is right," answered the Frenchwoman.

Lady Edith laughed contemptuously.

"You are very cautious, Mademoiselle Rousel," she said, "and since you will not speak plainly I must. When I say that we understand each other, I mean that we are both women upon whom hypocrisy would be wasted. We know each other. I know that you are treacherous, ambitious, unscrupulous, determined; and that you are a member of a certain brotherhood of criminals which we will not name. You know the same of me."

"Perhaps, Madame."

"You are too cautious even to say yes; no matter. I am wronged, and would be avenged on those who have wronged me. Will you assist me to gain that end?"

"Nay, Madame, that depends——"

"Upon whether I can make it answer your purpose to do so?"

"Precisely, Madame."

"Look here, Rosine Rousel," said Lady Edith, throwing back the wide open sleeve of her loose morning robe, and displaying an arm as white as alabaster, and perfect as that of the Florentine Venus. Upon this arm glittered a bracelet of emeralds; a serpent entirely formed of these precious stones, and bearing upon its head a crest of diamonds.

It was a gem which many a duchess had coveted, and which had been purchased for Lady Edith by her adoring husband, the merchant prince.

"This," she said, pointing to the bracelet, "shall be yours an hour after the destruction of those I hate. On these terms you will serve me?"

Rosine hesitated for a moment, her cold grey eyes fixed on the bracelet with the eager glance of avarice.

"One word, Madame," she replied, "before I answer that question. Is your enemy Oscar Bertrand?"

"No."

"And the service you demand of me involves no treachery to the association?"

"It does not."

"Then I am yours, Madame."

"Good!" said Lady Edith. Now listen to me. That which I want you to do to-day is simple. There is a certain Spanish dancer in this place called Lolota Vizzini. You must contrive to obtain admission into the house in which she lives within half an hour from this time, and ascertain if she receives any visitor this morning.

"Yes, Madame."

"And you will further do your best to discover what conversation may pass between Madame Vizzini and this visitor."

"But, Madame, how am I to do this?"

"That I leave you to find out," answered Lady Edith, opening a casket and taking from it a purse filled with notes and gold. "Money can do much, and you need not spare that. Intellect can do much, and I know you are not deficient in that. Go, lose no time. That which you have to do to-day is the first step towards your reward. The rest will soon follow, and you will win the prize easily. Go!"

The Frenchwoman curtsied and departed. Her manner betrayed neither surprise nor emotion. She seemed as if about to execute some ordinary commission.

Rosine Rousel was thoroughly accomplished in every species of treachery, and knew how to set about her business.

She had no difficulty in finding the house in which Lolota lodged, and at once proceeded to the porter and wormed herself into his confidence. She spoke Italian with fluency, and had therefore no trouble in making herself understood.

She told the porter that she was a lady of rank staying at Venice with her husband; that she had been to the opera every night to see Lolota Vizzini dance, and that she had now but one wish, and that was to behold her off the stage.

As she said this she dropped a piece of gold into the outstretched palm of the porter.

The Italian chuckled, and told her that if she would be so gracious as to condescend to sit in his lodge till Madame Vizzini went out in her gondola she would obtain a full view of her.

Rosine appeared to accept this offer with delight, and, seating herself in the chair offered by the old man, talked to him about the dancer.

He spoke in raptures of Lolota's beauty and generosity. "She is lovelier off the stage than on, Madame," he said, "but you will see for yourself if you will please to wait; she always goes out for her airing at two o'clock."

"Two o'clock!" exclaimed Rosine, looking at her watch, "and it is now only half-past twelve. An hour and a half to wait! I fear I cannot waste so much time upon this silly caprice of mine. I must abandon the hope of seeing Madame Vizzini to-day." She rose with a sigh as she spoke and looked at the porter. The old man scratched his bearded chin meditatively.

"It is distressing—it is desolating, Madame," he said. "I have an idea, it is true, but I am almost afraid to speak of it."

"Oh, pray tell me what it is!" exclaimed Rosine.

"Why," replied the porter, "Madame must know that this house is very large; there are forty rooms at least—and, what is more, there are three staircases. That one yonder, which Madame may observe, is the principal; then there is a second at the back of the house, and a third, a small private staircase communicating with the street by a little wooden door, and leading directly past the door of the apartment occupied by Madame Vizzini."

"Ah!" cried Rosine, "I begin to understand; nothing could be better."

"Now I was thinking that Madame and I could creep softly up this staircase without any one being the wiser, until we reach Madame Vizzini's apartments. The door of the boudoir opens on to the stairs, and inside the door hang thick damask curtains, in order to exclude the draught, for the house is old and draughty. We might therefore venture so far as to open the door, and standing behind the curtains Madame might safely behold Madame Vizzini. Yes!" exclaimed the old man, with enthusiasm, "and even hear her speak."

"If you can do this for me," said Rosine, "I will double the little present I made you just now."

"Madame is a princess. Come, then! Yet, stay, there is one objection."

"What is that?"

"There is a visitor now with Madame Vizzini."

"A visitor?"

"Yes, an English gentleman."

"A gentleman of rank?" asked Rosine.

"Yes, of the highest rank. A Marquis. An English Marquis. I forget his name."

"So," thought Rosine, "it is as I expected. I came to play the spy upon Lord Willoughby."

The Frenchwoman easily overruled the old porter's objection by the gift of another piece of gold. He led her round to the little wooden door in a side street, and up the narrow winding stone staircase which was squeezed into an angle of the building, and had been no doubt used in darker ages for many a deed of crime.

The old man softly opened the door communicating with Lolota's boudoir, which was the inner apartment of a suite of rooms leading on to the grand staircase.

Between the door and the curtains there was a deep recess, and in this Rosine placed herself, motioning to the porter to keep silent.

The dialogue which was going forward within the chamber was spoken in English. The porter had therefore no idea of its meaning, nor of the act of treachery in which he was playing the part of accomplice.

We have no occasion to repeat the conversation overheard by Rosine Rousel. Enough that she discovered that Lolota had told the Marquis of the death which had so lately freed her from a hateful bondage, and that he won her consent to meet him at Naples, and there become his wife.

"From Naples," he said, "we will fly to a securer retreat, dearest! In the recesses of the Black Forest there are spots of unrivalled loveliness, whither the foot of man rarely penetrates. In one of these I will build a villa, where we may live far from all those who have a horrible power over him who loves you. Say, my Lolota, could you endure a life of solitude with me?"

"Solitude with you, Lionel!" murmured the Spanish woman, "you who are all the world to me could make an Eden in a desert."

Arrangements were made for the meeting at Naples. Lolota was to leave Venice after that evening's performance at the Opera House, attended only by her maid, Justine. Lord Willoughby was to leave upon the following night.

"You will wonder, my beloved," said the Marquis, "at all this caution and concealment; but I know that for my sake you will consent, and will not question me as to its fatal cause."

"No, Lionel; blest by your love, I am more than happy. You tell me that I indeed possess this. I neither seek nor wish to know more."

Rosine Rousel found Lady Edith awaiting her return in her own apartment.

"So," she said, when the Frenchwoman had told her story, "I did not overrate your abilities.

The first part of your work is done; the second is perhaps even more critical, but I think that you will be able to accomplish it. There are two to be destroyed, and the blows that crush both, to be fatal, must be struck simultaneously. As for *him*, the traitor, the renegade, *I* will undertake his doom. I must trust you with hers."

"Is it to be murder, Madmae?" whispered Rosine, in an awe-struck tone, but yet without a shudder.

"No," answered Lady Edith; "diplomacy!"

She was silent for some minutes, absorbed in thought. Then taking a newspaper from a table near her, she searched its pages for some particular paragraph.

"You say that this Spanish woman is to start for Naples to-night, and she is there to await Lord Willoughby?"

"Yes, Madame."

"Read this," said Lady Edith, placing her finger upon a passage in the paper.

This passage contained only the following lines :—

"We are grieved to state that the fever which was so fatal last summer has again broken out in the lower part of the city, where several entire families have already fallen victims to its ravages. It is a disease of a fearfully contagious nature."

Rosine Rousel read this passage twice over, and then looked inquiringly at her mistress.

"You understand?" said Lady Edith.

"Scarcely, Madame."

"Bah!" murmured her mistress, "then you are not as clever as I thought you. Listen!"

Rosine bent her head, and Lady Edith whispered a few words into her ear. This time the Frenchwoman, hardened as she was in crime, recoiled with an exclamation of horror.

"Do you not consider the plan a good one?" asked Lady Edith.

"Yes, yes—Madame—only—I—I——"

"You were horrified at first. A few moments' reflection will convince you that nothing could be more simple. She will perish, and the cause of her death will be an accident—a mistake. Will you do this for me, Rosine? Remember, the bracelet is worth three thousand pounds."

"I will do it, Madame."

"Good. There is only one steamer that goes to Naples. You must travel therefore in the same boat with Madame Vizzini; and you must form your plans so as to execute them the moment you land. It is a difficult task, but to a determined mind nothing is impossible. Meanwhile my work is to be done in Venice."

THE MEETING AT NAPLES

CHAPTER LIV.

THE LEGEND OF THE DEAD HAND

The Marquis of Willoughby and Lady Edith were in the habit of dining together at seven o'clock, but upon this occasion the lady sent a message by Rosine Rousel to say that, as she felt slightly indisposed, she should dine alone in her apartment. Lord Willoughby was much relieved by this arrangement; he felt that he could never look into the face of the woman whom, guilty as she was, he had sworn to love. He consoled himself by thinking that Lady Edith was herself inconstant; that she no longer loved him, and had bestowed her affections upon the Marquis Montebello.

While Lord Willoughby sat at the solitary dinner-table, Edith Merton was not unemployed. She wrote a brief note to the Marquis Montebello, requesting to see him without delay, and gave it to Rosine Rousel to carry to the palace of the Italian nobleman. Rosine returned to tell her mistress that the Marquis had not been home since the preceding evening, but that the letter would be conveyed to him, as he sent a special messenger for his letters every two or three hours.

"Strange," said Lady Edith; "there must be some mystery in this. The Marquis evidently has been warned of his danger."

Eight, nine, and ten o'clock struck from the clock of the church of St. Mark. The steamer by which Rosine Rousel was to go to Naples did not start till twelve. At a quarter past ten a messenger delivered a note for the Countess de Grancy.

Lady Edith tore it open, and read these words:

"Dear Signorina,

"The letter in which you express a wish to see me reaches me in a place of concealment known only to a faithful few. A noble society has been betrayed by a villain—who that villain is, we know not, but time will reveal his infamy. If you would indeed see one who would give his life to serve you, follow the bearer of this whither he will lead you. He is faithful, and you may trust him.

"Yours till death,

"Lorenzo Montebello."

"Tell the messenger that I will accompany him," said Lady Edith.

She wrapped herself in a large cloak, and took from her dressing-case a black velvet mask with which she concealed her features.

Attired thus, in the obscurity of the night it was impossible for her to be recognised.

At the foot of the staircase she found a man waiting for her with a lantern.

It was the same man who had given the timely warning to the Italian nobleman the previous night.

"I am prepared to follow you," she said.

The man bent his head in silence, and led the way to the nearest landing-place, where a gondola awaited them.

Lady Edith took her seat in a curtained recess, and the boat shot rapidly away beneath the darkness. She knew not which way they went, but they seemed to be long in reaching their destination. It was half-past eleven when the gondola stopped at a dark landing-place, in a street so narrow that the roofs of the houses nearly touched each other, leaving only a ribbon-like streak of sky between.

Edith Merton had never been in that part of Venice before.

The peasant assisted her out of the gondola, and taking her hand in his, opened a low, arched wooden door, and led her up a narrow stone stair, the steps of which were worn and slippery with age.

After ascending several flights of stairs the man stopped and knocked at a door.

"Eccellenza," he said; "the Signora."

The door was opened from within, the man fell back, and Lady Edith entered a small circular chamber, and found herself face to face with Lorenzo de Montebello.

"This is indeed kind, Madame," he said; "I never dared to dream that you would do me this honour."

"Nay," replied Edith, with her sweetest smile, "what honour can be too great for the patriot who has risked all for his country's freedom, and—has been betrayed?"

A dark frown obscured the handsome face of the Italian.

"Aye, lady," he said, "betrayed—but by whom? By whom?"

"You do not know the traitor, then?"

"Know him, Signora! If we knew him, think you that he would live to pollute the air of heaven with his traitor-breath?"

"You would destroy him?"

"He would meet the traitor's doom," answered the Marquis, with gloomy meaning.

"Yes, you would destroy him, if he were some obscure wretch about whose fate none would care to inquire," replied Lady Edith. "But what if his rank protected him?"

"No rank, however exalted, could protect him, Signora. Were he the highest in the land, he should meet the vengeance of the Mountaineers. Have you never heard the legend of the house of Montebello?"

"Never."

"It is called the legend of the Dead Hand Shall I tell it to you, Signora?"

"Yes, yes."

"You will judge then if I come of a race that forgives its enemies."

"Speak, Marquis, speak."

"In the first half of the sixteenth century the Montebellos were princes in the city of Florence. There was no more powerful family in Italy after the Medicis, and the heads of that haughty house nourished a deadly jealousy towards my ancestors. Those were the days of the dagger and the poison-cup; and the chief of the Medicis was not long in finding an instrument mean enough to serve his purpose. Prince Michael de Montebello was young, handsome, generous—newly-wedded to a lovely girl, of a race scarcely less haughty than his own. Victoria de Montebello adored her husband, and when an heir was born to the princely house, it seemed as if mortal felicity could go no further than that shared by Michael and his wife.

"They little knew of the serpent lurking beneath the flowers which adorned their path.

"A certain poor relation, a distant kinsman of Prince Michael's, lived in the Palace de Montebello, and fattened on the bounty of his generous cousin.

"This was the instrument chosen by the Medici to serve his vile purpose. Failing all other heirs to the title and estates of the prince, this man would succeed to them. He had, therefore, a double motive for his guilty work."

"He murdered the Prince!"

"Ay, Signora! poisoned him at a festival given in honour of the Medici; and Michael de Montebello fell a corpse, clasping in his hand the jewelled goblet which he had drained to the health of the wretch who had prompted his murder."

"And the Princess?"

"They said that she died of a broken heart; but there were those within the mansion who knew better, though they dared not speak. An old servant left a written record of the truth, hidden in a niche of the palace-wall. Victoria de Montebello was poisoned."

"And the child!—the heir?"

"You shall hear, Signora. It was the intention of the murderer to destroy the child; but, lest public suspicion should be aroused, he resolved to wait until the excitement caused by the death of the Prince and Princess had subsided before he struck the fatal blow."

"He was prudent."

"Not always, Signora. I have told you that he was a mean villain. Avarice was his besetting sin, and when on the eve of obtaining an enormous fortune, he could not resist the temptation of a smaller gain. Amongst the costly jewellery possesssed by the Princess de Montebello was a miniature of her husband, encircled by two rows of diamonds of immense size and purest water. With her dying breath she gave orders that this miniature should be buried with her; and there were faithful servants round her bed who took care to fulfil her wishes."

"And the murderer—did he not interfere?"

"He dared not oppose the behest of the dying woman. The Princess was to lie in state for two nights in the chapel of the Montebellos. The bier on which she lay was draped with purple velvet, emblazoned with the escutcheon of the princely house, worked in massive embroideries of gold. To this chapel the murderer stole in the dead of the night, and, admitting himself by a key which was in his possession, approached the bier upon which Victoria lay."

"He went to steal the miniature?"

"Yes, Signora. For the sake of the diamonds he desecrated the sanctity of death. He took the locket from the icy breast of the corpse, and thrust it into his own bosom. He then turned to leave the chapel; but, as he turned from the bier, the hand of the corpse was slowly lifted, and the icy fingers of the dead grasped him by the wrist. In vain he tried to extricate himself from that grasp of death. A band of iron seemed to hold him to the spot. He shrieked aloud, but the echoes mocked the murderer's cry of despair. He was found the next morning lying by the side of the bier, the fingers of the corpse still twined about his wrist."

"He was dead?"

"No, lady; but he was a raving maniac, and he perished years afterwards in the cell of a madhouse.

"The infant heir was carefully tended by those about him, and lived to perpetuate the race of Montebello."

"It is a horrible story," said Lady Edith, with a shudder.

"Yes, Signora, I have but told it to you to prove that even after death the Montebellos can avenge themselves upon a traitor!"

"Would you learn who has betrayed the Mountaineers to the Austrian tyrant?"

"Can you ask me, Signora?"

Lady Edith laughed bitterly.

"I will tell you, then," she said; "the traitor is no other than the Englishman you trusted so implicitly. The nobleman whose truth and honour you never dreamed of doubting. The traitor is called Lionel Montfort, Marquis of Willoughby!"

————

CHAPTER LV.

THE FEVER-STRICKEN CITY

LOLOTA VIZZINI and her maid Justine left Venice by the steamer which departed at midnight. As the dancer took her place in the cabin, she noticed that the berth next her own was occupied by a woman so muffled in the thick and heavy garments she wore that it was impossible to distinguish either face or form.

But in the course of the voyage this woman contrived to enter into conversation with Lolota. She talked much of Naples, with which place she appeared perfectly familiar, and offered her services to Lolota, who had never been there.

"But although a stranger to the place, you will no doubt have friends who will meet you when the steamer arrives?" she said.

"No, indeed," answered Lolota; "I know no one in Naples. I have a friend who will join me to-morrow or the next day. In the meantime I must go to an hotel."

"Then allow me to be of service to you, Madame," said the stranger. "Naples is terribly crowded just at present; you may therefore have considerable difficulty in finding a lodging, and the people you will have to encounter are terrible cheats—they will take you anywhere for the sake of a reward."

Need we inform the reader that this woman was Rosine Rousel, the agent of Lady Edith Merton?

Lolota Vizzini fell an easy victim into the trap prepared for her. Confiding and truthful, she placed implicit confidence in the words of this stranger, who seemed only anxious to serve her, and when they reached Naples she placed herself entirely in the hands of Rosine Rousel.

The Frenchwoman wished for nothing better than this. She begged Lolota to remain on board, while she herself landed and made the necessary inquiries. The dancer readily assented, and in about ten minutes Rosine returned to inform her that there was not a lodging to be had for love or money in the better part of Naples, but that in the humblest quarter of the town she had heard of a place where Lolota and her maid could be accommodated.

Lolota, who was sinking with fatigue, declared that she cared little where she went, so long as she was with clean and honest people.

"That I will take care of," answered the Frenchwoman. "I know the people to whom I have recommended you; they are poor, but as honest as—I am."

She called a coach, and when Lolota and Justine had taken their seats in the vehicle, she gave some directions to the coachman.

These directions were given in an undertone, and were evidently of considerable length; for Rosine was upwards of ten minutes in giving her instructions to the man. Had Lolota been seated where she could have perceived the actions of the two, she might have seen the Frenchwoman slip some money into the driver's hand. But the dancer suspected nothing, and when Rosine came to the door of the vehicle she overwhelmed her with thanks for the trouble she had taken.

"Adieu, Madame," said the Frenchwoman. "We shall meet again ere long, I hope."

Lolota was about to ask the name of the person who had been so kind to her, but before she could do so the driver cracked his whip and the horses trotted off.

He drove through the principal streets of the city, and then plunged into the more obscure quarters, amongst narrow and winding streets, which seemed to lead only round to the place he had left.

In this manner they had been driving about for nearly an hour when Lolota let down the window and remonstrated with the man.

He apologised, saying that he had lost his way, but that he would make inquiries for the place he was in search of.

He dismounted from the box, and leaving the vehicle in charge of an idle little ragamuffin, ran off, and turning a corner very near, disappeared from sight.

Five, ten, fifteen minutes elapsed, and still he did not return. Meanwhile Lolota looked from the window of the carriage into the narrow street. She observed that in almost all the houses on either side of the way there were blinds lowered and shutters closed. No children were at play upon the door-steps—no lazy peasants lay upon the pavement basking in the sun. While she was observing these things a humble funeral procession started from the door of a house at a little distance, and passed the carriage.

Lolota perceived to her surprise that in this funeral procession there were three coffins.

Three deaths in one house! Crowded as were these dwellings of the lower orders, there seemed something terrible in the thought.

She called the boy to her, and asked him the reason so many blinds and shutters were closed in the street.

The lad shook his head mournfully.

"Alas! kind Signora," he replied, "it is for the dead."

"For the dead?"

"Yes; in each of these houses there are people lying dead of the plague."

"Oh, heavens! What plague?"

"A fever, gracious Signora. A fever which has stricken the inhabitants of this quarter."

Lolota was about to question the lad further, when the driver returned, and saying that he had obtained the necessary directions, mounted into his seat and drove rapidly off.

They traversed several narrow streets and alleys, which Lolota recognised as those through which they had driven before, and at last stopped before the door of a house in a street very little wider or better than any of the others.

"This is the house, Signora," said the driver, opening the door of the vehicle.

Lolota alighted, and, as she entered this house, glanced back at the windows on the other side of the way. She perceived that in almost all of them the blinds were closely drawn. This street, then, like the other, was chiefly tenanted by the dead.

Horrified at the thought, she drew back from the threshold of the door, and asked the driver of the coach whether the fever had not raged terribly in this quarter.

The man stared as if unable to comprehend her.

"The fever, Signora!" he repeated.

"Yes, the fever which is devastating Naples. Does it not most prevail in this quarter of the town?"

The man hesitated for a moment, and then shrugging his shoulders replied, "Alas! no, Signora, it is everywhere alike."

Lolota still recoiled from the threshold. "It is like entering a charnel-house," she said; "I wish we had never left Venice; but there is no help for us, Justine; we must remain here for to-night, and to-morrow we will remove to the suburbs."

Lolota was welcomed by an old woman of respectable appearance, who led her into an apartment very poorly furnished, but apparently clean.

It was by this time nearly two hours since Lolota and Rosine had parted at the landing-place. There had been, therefore, sufficient time for the carrying out of the hideous and diabolical scheme plotted by the subtle brain of Lady Edith Merton.

Lolota Vizzini had been decoyed into the plague-stricken quarter of Naples.

The driver had received his orders, and had been richly bribed to execute them. Those orders were, to waste all the time he could in driving backwards and forwards through the streets of Naples, and when he could no longer do this with safety, he was to cause a further delay by leaving the carriage to make pretended inquiries.

Meanwhile Rosine Rousel drove with all possible speed into the plague-stricken quarter. Here she had little difficulty in finding a lodging or the intended victim. Death had been busy in almost every chamber; the rooms were tenantless and deserted. She therefore speedily found a place which suited her purpose, and engaged the apartments for Lolota, imposing secrecy upon the woman who occupied them. This done, she despatched a messenger to an appointed spot, where he was to meet the driver, and inform him whither to bring the Spanish woman and her maid.

The foul plot had been concocted and carried out with consummate art. Death had not long been absent from that very chamber. But a few short hours previously a corpse had lain upon the couch on which the unconscious Lolota was to rest.

CHAPTER LVI.

IS HE TOO LATE?

LATE upon the night succeeding that on which Lolota Vizzini quitted Venice the Marquis of Willoughby, for the first time since her departure, prepared to leave the house. During the whole of the day he had kept his room, never once stirring outside the door.

This disconcerted the plans of vengeance which had been formed against him.

Lady Edith Merton trembled lest one of her victims should escape.

She knew that the assassin, armed with his fatal dagger, lurked in the corners of the streets, awaiting the coming of the traitor; and so terrible was her fury against the man who had deceived her, that every hour of delay was to her an hour of suffering.

In the meanwhile Lionel Montfort was busied in making preparations for his flight. He wrote to his lawyers, ordering them to draw up a deed, by which he should make over half his income to Oscar Bertrand for his natural life. The Austrian Colonel had hitherto received half that princely income, but he had received it by no legal agreement: he had taken it as the master might take from the slave. Henceforth he would hold it by a lawful bond, and the compact between him and the Marquis would be carried out. The Grand Master of the Black Band would, therefore, have no motive for pursuing his victim; he would then, surely, suffer him to rest in peace. To Oscar Bertrand himself the Marquis addressed the following brief epistle:—

"From this hour until my death it is scarcely likely that either you or the world will ever hear of me again.

I have carried out our agreement to the letter. As soon as possible after the receipt of this you will receive from my solicitors a deed of gift making over to you the half of my income. Riot in the wealth which has been won by crime, but leave me unmolested, to repent of my sins, and, if possible for one so guilty, to win the forgiveness of an offended Heaven. It is your trade to ensnare souls to perdition, amongst so many you can surely afford to lose one.

"LIONEL MONTFORT."

This done, the next care was to provide for the guilty woman whom he was about to abandon for ever.

He collected the best part of the ready money in his possession, which amounted to a considerable sum, in circular notes, and placed these notes in a sealed packet, with a slip of paper, on which he wrote the following words:—

"EDITH,—Farewell for ever. Better for us that we never had met; better to part now than plunge still deeper into a boundless abyss of infamy."

This was his last task before leaving his apartment.

He placed the two letters for his solicitors and Oscar Bertrand in his pocket, in order to post them before quitting Venice. The packet addressed to Lady Edith he laid upon his desk, where she could not fail to find it. The clocks were striking ten as he left his chamber, and quietly departed from the house without encountering any of the servants.

He proceeded at once to the post-office, where he despatched his letters.

On his way thither he was too much absorbed in thought to perceive a circumstance which might otherwise have aroused his suspicions. The gondola in which he was seated was followed by another gondola, which kept close to it wherever it went.

As he was returning from the post-office to his boat he was seized by two men, who threw a cord over his shoulders, and thus bound, flung him into a gondola.

But they had to deal with no coward. The Marquis was armed to the teeth. He carried a pair of revolvers concealed in the bosom of his waistcoat, and a dagger hidden in his belt.

Before the men who had seized him were aware of his intention, he extricated his left hand, drew the dagger from his belt, and cut the cord with which they had bound him.

Then firing one of his revolvers at the men, he sprang from the gondola into the canal, and swam rapidly towards the quay.

The men in the gondola pursued him to the landing-place, which they reached just as he had clambered ashore.

But they were too late. An Austrian soldier, alarmed by the report of fire-arms, had hurried to the spot to ascertain the cause of the explosion.

The Marquis placed himself under the protection of this man; but base as Lionel Montfort had been under the coercion of Colonel Oscar Bertrand, he felt himself now a free agent, and he was too generous to betray the men who had attacked him.

He knew that these men had acted by the directions of the chiefs of that noble society which he had assisted to betray. He felt that he deserved the worst at the hands of those who had so freely trusted him.

Instead, therefore, of delivering his assailants into the hands of justice, he told some rambling and unintelligible story of an attack by some assassin, who had shot at him from the bank of the canal. This afforded the two men time for escape. Their gondola glided away in silence, and quickly disappeared upon the inky waters.

Lord Willoughby then requested the Austrian soldier to accompany him to the steamer, and, thus protected, he embarked in perfect safety.

At twelve o'clock that night the Mountaineer who had before conducted Lady Edith to the hiding-place of the Marquis de Montebello, came again to the palace with a note, requesting her once more to entrust herself to his guidance. She obeyed; and disguising herself in a cloak and mask, as on the previous occasion, she accompanied the man to the same dark door, and up the same staircase, into the obscure chamber occupied by the Italian Marquis.

Lorenzo de Montebello was pacing up and down the apartment in a state of intense agitation.

"What has happened?" exclaimed Lady Edith.

"We have been foiled, Signora; the traitor has escaped us, and by this time has doubtless fled from Venice."

"Fled from Venice!" cried Edith Merton; "fled to join her!"

For a moment the thought filled her with a terrible despair; then, recovering herself, she burst into a mocking laugh.

"Let him go as swiftly as the waters can carry him," she thought; "if Rosine has been but faithful, he will only find a corpse to welcome him."

* * * * * *

Lord Willoughby was no stranger to Naples; he had been there in early youth, when travelling with his brother Angus and his tutor.

His first proceeding on landing was to hasten to the principal hotel, where he fully expected to find Lolota. It was an establishment much frequented by English visitors, and he had begged her, if possible, to obtain apartments there. To his surprise he discovered that she had not even applied for them. He then drove to every hotel in the city; but at none could he obtain any tidings of her he sought. He knew that she had started for Naples, because he himself had accompanied her on board the boat, and he knew also that the boat had safely arrived.

Where, then, was he to seek her?

He inquired at every private lodging to which she would have been likely to go, but with no success. So far from being crowded, the hotels were almost empty, for the pestilence had terrified all visitors, who had fled to Portici and the suburbs.

This was the first time that Lord Willoughby had heard of the fever. Filled with alarm for her he loved, he made anxious inquiries as to its dangers.

He was told that the disease was only prevalent in one quarter of the city, namely, that occupied by the poorest class, and scarcely ever visited by foreigners.

Lolota Vizzini could therefore have no possible motive for penetrating to the neighbourhood of the pestilence.

But he Marquis could no longer control his alarm at not finding her. He hurried to the head-quarters of the police, and stated his case, offering a princely reward for the information he desired.

On entering Naples he had taken care to disguise himself by the aid of a long cloak, and a black wig which overshadowed his face and gave him a foreign appearance. He spoke Italian like a native, and therefore was not afraid of betraying himself by an English accent.

He knew that he was a marked man, and that, so long as he remained upon Italian ground, he was in danger of being seized upon by the Society of Mountaineers.

In six hours the police succeeded in their task, and conducted the Marquis to the almost deserted street into which Lolota had been decoyed.

The murderers had well nigh triumphed in their horrible work; the fatal pestilence, speedy as it was terrible, had not been slow to seize upon its victims.

Lolota lay upon her lowly couch, unconscious, helpless, to all appearance dying. Upon a mattress near her lay her maid, Justine, in the agonies of delirium.

The old woman who kept the house had died that morning. There had been, therefore, no one to tend the sick woman; no one to soothe or comfort; no one to summon medical assistance. Lolota Vizzini had been left to die.

Lord Willoughby's first care was to despatch the members of the police to seek for the best medical aid and the most skilful sick-nurse to be found in Naples, and, at the same time, to order a carriage from the principal hotel to bo spread with cushions and mattresses, to convey the stricken women from the infected quarter into the purer air of the outskirts of Naples.

Alas! Death seemed already to have laid his withering touch upon his lovely victim; all human care seemed worse than hopeless. When the messengers had departed upon their several errands, Lionel Montfort fell upon his knees by the bed of the unconscious woman and prayed the prayer of the penitent and remorseful man.

CHAPTER LVII.

THE SECOND MARRIAGE

LIONEL MONTFORT watched by the bed of her whose worth he had so lately learned to know. He had awakened from the feverish dream of passion for a cruel and wicked enchantress to find that he was still capable of a pure attachment.

It was like emerging from the lurid light of a volcano into the sunny atmosphere of day.

But the icy hand of Death was raised as if to separate the lovers.

The Marquis prayed long and earnestly in that fever-haunted chamber. He had no fear of the infection which had stricken her he loved. He watched every faint flutter of that bosom; he counted every feeble beat of the heart which had throbbed with love for him alone. He knew that the beloved one hovered between life and death, and he thought that he beheld in this calamity the punishment of his own sins.

The physicians summoned by the Marquis forbade the removal of the invalid beyond the healthy quarter of the city.

In vain Lord Willoughby endeavoured to obtain from these men some word of hope or comfort. They shook their heads gravely, and told him that time alone could determine the issue.

Lolota and the faithful girl who had attended her were removed to one of the principal hotels. Here airy apartments had been prepared for the invalid, and here the Marquis watched with untiring vigilance in the sick-chamber.

But the recovery was as slow as the attack

THE GRAND MASTER MEETS THE MARCHIONESS DE MONTEBELLO

had been rapid. Instantaneous as was the fever-stroke that had prostrated the two women, it was not the less crushing in its effect, and the hope of recovery was but a slender one.

Rosine Rousel remained in Naples to watch the effect of her infamous work. She contrived to obtain information of all that occurred in the lodging to which she had caused Lolota to be conducted.

The reader may imagine her surprise on hearing of the arrival of Lord Willoughby.

The Frenchwoman was too well versed in the workings of a guilty mind to have been deceived in Lady Edith Merton. She knew that a woman who could plan the hideous scheme by which

Lolota Vizzini was to have been sacrificed would hesitate at no means by which the tortures of her vengeful and jealous heart might be appeased.

She knew therefore that Lord Willoughby was never to have left Venice alive. His arrival at Naples convinced her that a part of Lady Edith's plot had failed.

If that scheme was altogether a failure, Rosine knew that she would lose the emerald and diamond bracelet—the costly gem for which she had been ready to steep her soul in guilt. She determined to have recourse to falsehood to obtain the promised reward, and then to escape from the anger of her employer by a flight to Paris, where she knew herself able to elude pursuit.

She returned to Venice, and went at once to the palace in the square of St. Mark.

Three days had elapsed since the French-woman and her victims had left Venice—three days of anguish to the guilty soul of Lady Edith Merton. The merchant's wife was seated alone in her luxurious bed-chamber when Rosine arrived.

"At last—at last," she said; "this fever of suspense must now be ended. Speak, girl, speak—your mission——"

"Has been successful, Madame," answered Rosine, her measured tones contrasting strangely with the wild impetuosity of her questioner.

"The Spanish woman—is she dead?"

"She is."

Lady Edith drew a long breath. Her lips were locked together with the rigidity of iron. In that moment she suffered—suffered from the intensity of the mental effort by which she suppressed all evidence of the demoniac joy she felt.

Rosine Rousel could read this silent struggle.

"Tell me," exclaimed Lady Edith, "tell me all!"

The Frenchwoman related the manner in which the guilty work had been carried out; but she told her dupe that the fever had been fatal to Madame Vizzini.

"And when the Marquis reached Naples he found her——?"

"Dead!" answered Rosine.

Again Lady Edith was silent; but a hellish triumph lighted up her dark eyes.

"And, now, Madame, have I won the bracelet?" asked the Frenchwoman.

"You have, Rosine," replied Lady Edith. "Give me the golden casket yonder. The reward is yours."

The Frenchwoman placed a casket of chased gold before Lady Edith. She opened it with a tiny jewelled key attached to her watch-chain, and took out a morocco case containing the emerald bracelet.

"Take it, Rosine: it is yours," she said, placing the gem in the eager hands of the traitress; "take it, and leave me. I shall ring for you by-and-by. For the present I shall not want you. The suspense I have undergone has almost turned my brain, and I have need of rest. Go!"

Rosine Rousel curtsied and left the room.

An hour afterwards she had departed from Venice in a steamer bound for Marseilles. She knew that the bracelet was worth three thousand pounds, and that with such a sum she might lead a life of splendour in Paris until the produce of some new crime should replenish her coffers.

Meanwhile the five chiefs of the secret society had been released from prison. The information obtained by Lionel Montfort, and sold by Colonel Bertrand to Austria, enabled that government to fix upon the conspirators, but had afforded no clue to their designs. The crafty policy of the Austrian government had therefore decided upon the release of the five prisoners.

This seeming clemency veiled a deep design. The five men would be henceforth surrounded by an invisible circle of spies; their every act, their lightest word, would be recorded to the supreme masters of Venice.

The Marquis de Montebello emerged from his retreat after the release of the five prisoners.

He was a constant visitor at the palace occupied by Lady Edith, whom he only knew as the Countess de Grancy.

In the very prime of manhood, he found himself for the first time in love—deeply and sincerely in love with this beautiful Englishwoman.

Encouraged by Lady Edith's smiles, and by the pleasure which she seemed to take in his society, he made her an offer of his hand and fortune.

That offer was promptly accepted.

He little knew the terrible situation in which the pretended widow found herself. With no longer any claim upon her wealthy husband, and deserted by Lord Willoughby, what was to be her fate when the money left her by Lionel should be exhausted?

She accepted the hand of the Italian Marquis, reckless of the crime involved in this second marriage. As the Countess de Grancy, the widow of a French nobleman, she thought that she had entirely lost her identity, and that none would discover the wife of Robert Merton, the merchant prince, in the Italian Marchioness de Montebello.

If by evil chance she could ever encounter any of those who had known her in England, she trusted to her own assurance to extricate her from the dilemma.

She would defy recognition, and those who had known her most intimately would only believe themselves deceived by a striking likeness—such a likeness as has sometimes existed between two people unconnected by any tie of relationship.

The Marquis de Montebello was delighted at the happy issue of his suit. He loaded his promised bride with presents, and lavished upon her the boundless devotion of a generous heart.

Within a month of Lord Willoughby's departure from Venice the marriage of the Marquis and Constance de Grancy (it was thus that Lady Edith called herself) was solemnized with great pomp and splendour in the church of St. Mark.

Lady Edith had declared herself to be a Roman Catholic.

The vows were spoken which united Constance de Grancy and Lorenzo de Montebello in the holy bonds of matrimony.

The would-be-murderess added the guilt of bigamy to her list of crimes.

CHAPTER LVII.

THE MARCHIONESS DE MONTEBELLO

A BRILLIANT crowd is assembled at the Palace of the Marquis de Montebello. The festival of the night is given in honour of her whom we know as Edith Merton, but who is admired in Venice as the newly-married Marchioness de Montebello, the reigning queen of Venetian society.

She has not long been the wife of the proud and generous Marquis, and as yet he is happy. He knows not the serpent he has taken to his breast.

To-night the capricious beauty has chosen to attire herself in the most simple costume. She wears a dress of unsullied white silk, unrelieved by ornament or jewellery. No diadem encircles her haughty forehead, no bracelets are clasped upon her slender wrists. Her heavy raven hair is simply parted from her forehead. Her only adornment is a necklace of classical design.

She knows that in this simple costume she outshines the handsomest woman at her assembly, and she glories in her power.

The rooms are crowded with aristocratic guests; political ties unite many of the male visitors to the Marquis. The most distinguished of those present belong to the society of Mountaineers.

The evening passes gaily. Amongst the joyous and light-hearted the Marchioness is queen. Her silvery laughter echoes through the lofty saloons, her radiant smiles shine alike upon all.

Yet had any very close observer kept watch upon that beautiful face, he might have seen an uneasiness which no smiles could conceal, a restless anxiety no effort of will could entirely subdue. The brilliant Marchioness was wretched.

She had committed a crime—a crime which placed her within the fell grip of the laws of her native country; and she knew not when the hour of discovery might come. Daring and determined though she was, this thought poisoned every moment of pleasure.

Her chief terror was that amongst some of the English visitors to Venice she should be recognised at the wife of Robert Merton.

She listened eagerly to every name that was announced, lest one familiar to her in her past life should strike upon her ear.

She did not listen in vain.

Late in the evening a tall elegant-looking man entered the principal saloon, while the powdered lacqueys announced Colonel Bertrand.

A cold perspiration bedewed the forehead of the Marchioness. This man of all others was the last she wished to meet. She had hoped that she had escaped from his toils. She had hoped that her very identity would be lost to him for ever.

She awaited with fear and trembling the effect of his appearance. Would he betray her?

To her surprise the Austrian affected not to recognise her. She saw him introduced to the Marquis by a busy little German Baron, who presently approached with the Colonel towards the spot where she herself was seated.

"Allow me, Signorina, to present to you Colonel Bertrand, one of the most distinguished of my countrymen!" said the German, introducing Oscar.

The Colonel bowed with as much ceremony as if he had never before beheld his fair hostess.

"Believe me, Signora," he said, with emphasis, "there is no happiness I more ardently desired than to make the acquaintance of the beautiful Marchioness de Montebello."

CHAPTER LVIII.

THE COMPACT

LADY EDITH felt that the net was closing round her.

As she recoiled involuntarily beneath the burning eyes of Oscar Bertrand she felt and knew that discovery and ruin had overtaken her.

The German Baron withdrew, and left the Colonel and Edith alone together. Oscar was the first to speak.

"Your welcome is scarcely so cordial, Marchioness, as I had hoped. Do not tell me I am unwelcome."

"Bah," replied Lady Edith, in a cold hard voice, "why mock me with these courtly speeches, the exact value of which is as well known to me as to yourself? I am in your power, and had hoped never to see you more. You come, therefore, as an enemy, and as an enemy you are unwelcome."

"You are cruel, my dear Marchioness. Granted that you are in my power: there you speak the truth, and I am not hypocrite enough to contradict you—but what if I come as your friend—your ally?"

"*You* my friend!" echoed Lady Edith, with the bitterest scorn; "you, the most merciless of men!"

"Nay, dear Madame, I am only merciless to those who oppose me. I can be generous to those who serve me. Have you not reason to remember me with gratitude? but for me you might still be an inmate of your lonely Scottish dungeon — despised — forgotten — as the mad Lady Edith Merton. Through my agency you were restored to liberty, reunited to the lover of your choice. Is it my fault if Lionel Montfort proved false?"

Edith Merton felt the sting in these words. A dark and angry cloud obscured her face.

"You know that, then?" she said.

"I know all. But once more I ask you, Lady Edith—pardon me, Madame de Montebello—whether I have not some claim upon your gratitude?"

"No!" she cried, with a sudden but suppressed vehemence. "No, Oscar Bertrand, you have none. Gratitude! What gratitude can the master-fiend ask from his slaves? Let him be content if they do his bidding."

The face of the Grand Master darkened as Lady Edith spoke, but a sardonic smile curved his pointed moustache.

"Good!" he exclaimed. "I see we shall understand each other. I have no weak silly woman to deal with, and shall have no sickly sentimentality to contend against. If you will do me the honour to accept my arm, I will conduct you to yonder balcony, where we can pursue our conversation in the balmy atmosphere of the Italian night, and where we shall not run the risk of being overheard."

He offered her his arm as he spoke. She rose and obeyed him—obeyed him as submissively as if she had acted under the influence of a spell.

The marble balcony was untenanted. Above them was the starry night, beneath them the blue waters of the canal. All around told of peace and beauty; the storm and the darkness were in the bosoms of the guilty.

Edith Merton seated herself upon a low couch that had been placed in the balcony; Oscar Bertrand lounged upon the balustrade of polished marble.

"Lady Edith Merton," said the Colonel, "for by whatever name you choose to call yourself here, I will call call you by that to which alone you have a right—Lady Edith, you spoke the truth just now when you said that I am the most merciless of men. I am merciless to those who refuse to serve me. I hold them my foes, and I crush them as I would crush a noxious reptile beneath my feet. Do not place yourself amongst their number. So far, you will own I have been your friend?"

"Friend," she repeated, in a mocking tone.

"At least I have served you?"

"Oh, yes!" she answered coldly; "I admit that you have served me."

"Enough," said Oscar Bertrand; "you recognise no claim of mine to your gratitude, because you think that I have served you for purposes of my own. So be it. I had powerful motives, for you are the kind of woman whose aid my schemes required. You were a treasure, to be secured at any price—I spared no effort to make you mine, my colleague, my slave—and now I call upon you to serve me."

"In what manner?"

"You shall hear. It has pleased you to take a very desperate step—to commit a crime which places you in a position of imminent peril. You have committed bigamy in becoming the bride of the Marquis de Montebello, but in doing so you have unconsciously done me a service."

"A service—to you!"

"Yes, and a service for which I, the master, thank you, the slave. There are certain important political secrets, priceless almost in their pecuniary value, the key to which can be only got at through seven men. The Marquis, your husband, is one of the seven. Now there are few secrets which a wife cannot wring from her husband. It must be your task, therefore, to obtain that which I require. Do you understand?"

"It is some new treachery which you ask," said Lady Edith.

"Why call it by so ugly a name? Let us say, rather, it is a piece of diplomacy which I require to be carried out, and which none can execute so well as a woman."

"I scarcely understand you, yet."

"Then I will put the matter more plainly," replied the Colonel. "You have committed bigamy. The man you have married is one of the chiefs of a political society called the Mountaineers; I require to know the plans of that society—their secret places of meeting—the hours at which they meet, their schemes, their dreams, their hopes—all these you must extort from your husband. Fool him as a woman can fool the man who loves her. Fool him with false smiles and lying caresses, and win from him the inmost secrets of his soul. If at the end of a week from to-night you have not procured for me the information I require, I shall consider you my enemy and the enemy of the Association to which I belong, and I shall denounce you as a bigamist. Choose, therefore, whether you will serve me or oppose me."

"The secret shall be yours," answered Lady Edith, after a brief pause.

"At the week's end?"

"At the week's end."

The Colonel offered her his arm, and they returned to the ball-room. He felt that the hand which rested on his arm trembled convulsively, but her face was perfectly calm.

"She is a wonderful woman," he muttered to himself, as he watched her rejoin her guests, "and she will succeed in the task. My tenth and last fortune will be made before the month is out, and after that one lucky stroke I will retire from business for ever. The Association is in danger, and its chief would be the first to fall."

CHAPTER LIX.

THE CLUE TO THE SECRET

SIX nights after that upon which the above interview took place between Lady Edith Merton and the Grand Master of the Black Band, a man, dressed in the garb of an Italian peasant, moored his gondola near a low doorway in one of the most obscure quarters of Venice.

This peasant was the same man who had conducted Lady Edith to the hiding-place of the Marquis de Montebello, and the doorway at which he now stopped communicated with the very building in which that hiding-place was situated. The society of Mountaineers numbered the noblest of the land amongst its ranks, but it was also open to the humblest. Love of Italy and of Freedom were the only qualifications demanded from the members of the Association.

This man, commonly known as Black Carlo, was one of the most devoted of these humble members. Rough, daring, impetuous, unscrupulous, it was well known that he would have willingly given his life in the interest of the Society. It was also known that he would have thought little of taking the life of any traitor to the Association.

He was half-brigand, half-peasant; his nature almost that of a savage. He cared little for the laws of civilisation, and his hatred was as powerful as his love.

It was past eleven o'clock at night when he approached the low wooden door which we have before described. He did not knock, but pressed his clumsy forefinger upon an iron ring in the panel. The door slowly and silently opened. Black Carlo entered the small stone hall, but, instead of ascending the circular staircase leading to the hiding-place of the Marquis, he descended a narrow flight of steps which conducted him to a stone chamber, built upon a level with the canal which flowed past the house.

This chamber was lighted by an oil lamp hanging from the ceiling. The furniture of the apartment was heavy and cumbrous; in the centre of the chamber, exactly below the lamp, stood a massive oaken table covered with papers. Before the table was a piece of furniture the singularity of which was the first thing that attracted the eye of the stranger entering the apartment.

This object was a large covered chair, such as those used by the porters in the halls of great houses. It was made of ebony ornamented with brass, and before the front of it hung curtains of dark green silk in such a manner as entirely to conceal the face and figure of the person seated within, but so contrived [as not to obscure that person's view of others, for as Black Carlo entered the apartment a long thin hand was stretched forth between the folds of the curtains, and a voice within the chair said—

"Is it you, Carlo?"

"Yes, my Prince."

"That is well. You are faithful to your appointment, and you are ready to serve us?"

"To the death, my Prince."

"Approach, then, and I will tell you what is required."

The peasant obeyed, and drew nearer to the curtained chair, in which was seated the mysterious being of whose name he was ignorant, but whom he knew to be one of the chiefs of the Association.

"You see those papers," continued the voice: "they contain directions for speedy action—they contain the particulars of a great blow which is to be struck for the freedom of Italy. Those papers are to be distributed among the members of the Association, but the work must be done secretly. It must, therefore, be done by one whose humble station will entirely remove him from suspicion. Will you undertake the task, Carlo?"

"Willingly, my Prince."

"And you will carry it out faithfully?"

"With the last breath of my life if need be."

"That is brave. Take the papers. Caution is all that is needful. These documents must be delivered to every member of the Mountaineers resident in Venice before twelve o'clock to-morrow night. You understand?"

"Perfectly," replied Carlo, gathering together the papers indicated by the long thin hand which emerged from the silken curtains.

"Is there no more, my Prince?"

"No more."

CARLO AND THE INVISIBLE CHIEF

The peasant bowed, and was about to retire, when he was checked by the occupant of the curtained chair.

"Stay," exclaimed the voice, "there is one more service that you can render us."

"Name it, my Prince."

"The Marquis de Montebello; he must be watched."

The Italian started.

"Surely he is faithful, my Prince."

"*He* is faithful, but he has lately married. Women are dangerous. Watch the Marquis and his wife."

"I hear only to obey," answered Carlo, humbly; but it was evident that he considered the orders of his chief unnecessary.

"Enough. I have no more to say."

The peasant retired, returning as quietly as he went.

*   *   *   *   *   *

Six nights had gone by since Lady Edith's interview with the man whose terrible power had subdued even her haughty soul. On the seventh she had sworn to deliver up to him the secrets of the Mountaineers, or abide the alternative—exposure and disgrace.

One day and night only remained, and she had all yet to accomplish. Hitherto she had failed signally in her endeavours to wring the secret from her husband. Passionately as the Marquis de Montebello loved his bride, his honour was still dearer to him. He might have sacrificed his life for her, but he could not sacrifice his word.

All her efforts were therefore in vain. Skilful actress as she was, in this she utterly failed. She affected an intense love for Italy, and implored her husband to win for her admission into the ranks of the Mountaineers.

"Woman as I am," she said, half-playfully, yet with serious meaning, "I might be of use to you, for at least I should be earnest—my whole soul would be in the work. Surely you and your colleagues could trust me?"

The Marquis smiled at what he thought the ardour of an enthusiast.

"Nay, dearest," he replied, "the oaths that we take are too fearful to be spoken by such lips as thine. The task we have to accomplish involves danger and death. It is not for woman even to know of our struggles, much less to share them."

Defeated on every side, Lady Edith's despair became terrible, as the days and nights flew by, and she was still no nearer success.

She felt assured that Oscar Bertrand would keep his word.

Throughout those six weary nights she had not slept. Lying in a feigned slumber, she had listened, hoping that her husband might betray himself and his associates by some chance words dropped in sleep.

But she had listened in vain.

The seventh morning dawned. Lady Edith had grown haggard with care and watching. Her husband noticed the change in his beautiful bride; but she laughed at his anxiety, telling him that she was only exhausted with the dissipations of Venice.

While they were seated at breakfast, a servant entered, and told the Marquis that a peasant was below who requested an audience, if only for a few moments.

Lady Edith's intellect was intensified by despair. No word, no look, no act of her husband's, however insignificant, escaped her.

"I will see him," said the Marquis, rising and following the servant from the room.

"So," murmured Lady Edith, when she found herself alone, "he consents immediately to see this peasant. There is something out of the common in this. What if I succeed in the eleventh hour in gaining a clue to the secret?"

Her face flushed crimson at the thought. She descended the staircase, and on her way met the servant who had announced the humble visitor of the Marquis.

She asked the man in which room he had left his master and the peasant, and was informed that the Marquis had himself led his visitor to his own dressing-room.

Lady Edith lost no time in hurrying to this apartment. She felt now convinced that this peasant was a member of the Association, and that his visit was one of political importance.

She determined to go suddenly into the Marquis' dressing-room on the chance of surprising the man in the utterance of some words that might enlighten her. She was prepared with plenty of excuses for entering the apartment.

But, on trying the door, she found herself foiled. It was locked on the inside.

She drew back silently, pale with rage.

"I will wait," she muttered. "They did not hear me try the door. They will come out engaged in conversation. I may yet overhear something."

The dressing-room of the Marquis opened upon a picture-gallery. Nothing was more natural than that Lady Edith should be lounging in this picture-gallery.

She took a book from a stand near by, and, seating herself in one of the windows, waited patiently.

In a quarter of an hour her patience was rewarded; the Marquis opened his door and came out, followed by the peasant.

The Marquis held a paper in his hand.

He started at the sight of Lady Edith, and thrust this document hurriedly into his bosom.

"I will attend to this paper, Carlo," he said. "I will do my best in attending to the petition of your fellow-fishermen."

Carlo bowed and withdrew; but as he left the gallery he gazed with a protracted scrutiny upon Lady Edith.

"So," she thought, as she watched her husband's confusion, "they would deceive me; but, in spite of them, I have obtained the clue I want. That paper contains the secrets of the Association. *It must be mine.*"

CHAPTER LX.

THE PERFUME IN THE GOLDEN BOTTLE

"THAT paper must be mine," thought Lady Edith; and in that moment her resolution was taken.

She knew that the first care of the Marquis would be to place the document under lock and key; that once done, it would be beyond her power to discover the secrets contained in the paper. Her object was, therefore, to prevent this; and, in order to do so, she resolved on a desperate course.

She approached the Marquis, and, twining her arm lovingly in his, she led him towards her own apartments.

"How weary you must be, dearest Lorenzo," she said, "of such interviews as these! What, in mercy's name, did that tiresome peasant want with his fishermen's petition? But, stay," she added, as she watched the Marquis's confusion, "do not fatigue yourself in explaining the stupid business; give me the petition to read—it will save you the trouble of reading it yourself."

She stretched her hand towards his breast, as if about to take the paper from him. He caught her wrist in his powerful grasp, and arrested the movement.

"I have read it," he said.

"My kind Lorenzo, how good you are to these people!" murmured Lady Edith, admiringly. "But come, I know the morning's work must have wearied you. Come to my room, and let me read you to sleep with a page of your favourite, Petrarch."

"By-and-by, dearest. I have some business to transact which——"

"Which you shall transact after you have rested half an hour. Come, Lorenzo, come."

He could not resist her winning smile—her soft, entreating tones; and, besides, he feared to arouse her suspicions respecting the nature of the paper in his breast. He determined, therefore, on complying with her request and awaiting a better opportunity of removing the document to a place of safety.

Seated on the luxurious cushions of a couch in his wife's apartment, the Marquis abandoned himself to the music of her voice, as she sat at his feet reading to him from the pages of his favourite poet.

The morning was sultry and oppressive, but the atmosphere of the apartment was cool and soothing—strangely conducive to slumber.

In spite of himself the Marquis felt his eyes closing—the sounds of his wife's voice growing every moment less distinct in his ears.

He made an effort to arouse himself, but with no effect. Lady Edith appeared to perceive this.

"Come," she said, "Lorenzo! you must not pay my reading so poor a compliment as to fall asleep immediately. Stay, I have some perfume here which is sure to revive you."

She rose from her seat, took a small bottle of ruby glass from her dressing-table, and, removing the stopper, sprinkled the perfume upon a cambric handkerchief, which she handed to the Marquis.

He inhaled the essence. It was a strange and rather sickly perfume—not exactly disagreeable, but terribly overpowering.

Lorenzo de Montebello's eyelids sank heavily over his eyes, and he fell back in a stupor.

The pretended perfume given to him by Lady Edith was CHLOROFORM.

She sprinkled the handkerchief a second time, and, holding it before the face of the unconscious man, she knelt down and took the paper from his breast.

The document was brief; but the information it contained was of the utmost importance. It described the whereabouts of a mountain stronghold in Calabria at which the associates were to meet. It also named the date and hour of the meeting.

Lady Edith possessed herself of the contents of the paper with wonderful rapidity. There was no fear of her memory failing her in a matter which to her was one of life and death.

In less than five minutes she had refolded the document and replaced it in the bosom of the Marquis.

Then, taking a bottle of eau-de-Cologne from her dressing-case, she sprinkled the fragrant liquid about his face until his eyes slowly opened, and he looked wonderingly about him.

"Where am I?" he murmured.

"In my dressing-room, dearest, where you were so very foolish as to faint away not five minutes since," replied Lady Edith. "I must insist, my dear Lorenzo, that you take more care of your health in future."

The Marquis clutched involuntarily at the paper in his breast.

"Oh, your fishermen's petition is perfectly safe, I assure you," said Lady Edith, laughing. "Upon my word, if you display so much anxiety about that document, I shall begin to think that it is some love-letter you are concealing from me."

The Marquis smiled gravely.

"Ah, dearest," he murmured, "you have good reason to know that there is but one woman upon earth whose love I prize."

Late that evening the name of Colonel Bertrand was once more announced in the brilliant saloons of the Marquis. The assemblage of guests was upon this occasion a small one, and the entrance of the Austrian officer attracted more attention than upon the former evening; but after conversing with the Marquis and two or three of his most distinguished visitors, Oscar Bertrand contrived to withdraw to the balcony, accompanied by Lady Edith Merton.

The sky was dark and cloudy, and the canal below the balcony was wrapped in obscurity, save where the reflection of some lighted window glimmered redly upon the bosom of the water.

"Well, Lady Edith," said the Colonel, in an impassible voice, "what is your decision? Are we to be friends or foes?"

"Friends," replied the lady, with a sneer.

"Good—then you have succeeded?"

"I have."

"You have accomplished all I asked?"

"All, and perhaps more."

"Then you are as wonderful a woman as—as I always believed you to be. Hush, what was that?"

The Austrian and his companion started, for both had fancied they heard a splashing noise, as of the dipping of an oar in the water beneath them; yet on leaning over the balcony neither boat nor boatman was to be seen.

"My ears must have deceived me," muttered the Colonel; "there is no one there."

Oscar Bertrand knew not of the existence of a narrow archway immediately below the balcony. A man seated in a small gondola had shot his barque into this archway at the moment the Austrian's attention was attracted by the sound of the oar.

Three minutes afterwards, the same man emerged from the archway, and raising himself from the gondola, clambered upon the stonework below the balcony in such a manner as to be able to overhear every word spoken by those above him.

Lady Edith repeated the contents of the paper; she named the appointed place of meeting at the stronghold in Calabria; she named also the date and the hour at which the associates were to meet. The date was at the expiration of ten days from that night.

"You have indeed succeeded wonderfully," exclaimed the Austrian, as he wrote the information he had just obtained in a leaf of his memorandum-book; "but tell me, did the Marquis turn traitor—did you extort this from his own lips?"

The man clinging to the stonework below listened, if possible, more intently than before.

"No," answered Lady Edith, "all my artifices could not wring one word from Lorenzo de Montebello; you owe your information to woman's wit and not to man's weakness."

He questioned her further, and she told him the story of the golden bottle, and the so-called perfume which it contained.

"Bravo!" exclaimed the Colonel. "I myself could not have done better. You have served me nobly, *Madame de Montebello;* henceforth I am ready to forget that there is such a person in the world as Lady Edith Merton, the millionaire's runaway wife."

Soon after the termination of this conversation Colonel Bertrand left the saloons of the Marquis. Three hours afterwards he was on his way to Vienna.

The man who had hung to the stonework below the balcony throughout the brief dialogue between the Colonel and Lady Edith dropped back into his gondola as they retired, and rowed away in the direction of the low doorway communicating with the house in which was the apartment occupied by the hidden chief in the curtained chair.

CHAPTER LXI.

THE ROCK OF TERROR

THE night approached upon which the Mountaineers were to meet together in their Calabrian stronghold.

It is needless to inform our readers that the mountainous country in the neighbourhood of Naples is thickly infested with brigands. Even now it is unsafe to go alone and unarmed upon the country roads. Children and lads are carried off to the mountains; men and women are robbed, and all kinds of outrages are committed by these Italian ruffians.

It was in a rocky pass inhabited by these brigands that the Mountaineers were to assemble. But every one of the robbers was also a member of the Association, for even a brigand may sigh for the freedom of his native land, and revolt against the oppressor, whose iron rule has perhaps driven him to a life of crime.

The meeting was to be held at midnight upon the 30th July—exactly ten days after that upon which Lady Edith had given Oscar Bertrand the information he desired. The Austrian Colonel had therefore ample time to visit Vienna and to return to Naples before the assembly of the conspirators took place.

Oscar Bertrand firmly believed that the hour and place of this meeting were known only to the conspirators, Lady Edith, and himself. So far he was right. But *he did not* know that the interview between himself and the traitress had been overheard, and that the associates knew themselves to be betrayed. He was received with open arms by the Austrian Minister of Police, and was promised an enormous price for his information should it result in the arrest of the five chiefs.

A week before the night appointed for the meeting all the conspirators residing in Venice met in the underground chamber in which Black Carlo had communicated with the hidden chief in the curtained chair. This time the chair was removed; the five chiefs assembled wore black masks.

Amongst these chiefs was Lorenzo de Montebello.

The Marquis heard with surprise and horror that the Association had been betrayed, and that the time and place of meeting were known to one who would not fail to sell his information to the Court of Austria.

"Good heavens!" exclaimed the Marquis, "how can it be that, in spite of all our precautions, we are betrayed at every point? Who is the traitor who has denounced us?"

"I cannot tell you," answered the chief who had communicated with Black Carlo.

"What, do you not know the name of the traitor?"

"Yes, Marquis, I do know the name of the person who has betrayed us."

"And you decline to communicate it?"

"Pardon me, my dear Marquis, but I am compelled to do so."

"Do I know the name of the person?"

"To the best of my belief you have never heard the *real* name of our betrayer."

"Indeed! The villain is some person of the lowest grade, then—some paid spy, who disguises his odious name."

"No one can be more infamous than this person; but you will know all soon enough, my dear friend," said the masked chief, gravely.

The Marquis turned away without making any reply to this speech. He was offended by what he considered a want of confidence in his associate, and withdrew in silence to another part of the chamber.

It is unnecessary for us to relate the conversation which was held between the masked chiefs at this meeting; let us therefore at once shift the scene of our life drama to Naples, upon the evening of the 30th of July.

The orb of day was sinking behind the purple waters as a party of men whose dress and manners proclaimed them to be brigands marched slowly upwards to the summit of a mountainous ridge in Calabria. The ground over which they were walking was wild in its aspect, dark, gloomy, and terrible, yet scarcely more so than the men themselves, who, roughly dressed and armed to the teeth, looked like the harbingers of death and murder.

Amongst the foremost of these men was Black Carlo.

"We are nearing our destination," said one of the men. "Yonder frowns the Rock of Terror.

The brigand stronghold had been called by the Calabrians the "Rock of Terror" from the horrible deeds which were said to have been committed in this mountain fastness.

"Ay, comrade," answered Black Carlo; "we're very near the end of our journey, and I'm not sorry for it, for time is short, the sun is sinking, and the Austrian dogs will be stealing a march upon us under cover of the darkness if we're not careful."

The footpath along which the brigands were now passing bordered a precipice. The traveller, gazing over the edge of this pathway, saw nothing but a black vault, for the bottom of the abyss was lost in darkness. Black Carlo paused, and, looking round at his comrades with a demoniac smile, pointed to the abyss below.

"We may have a burial on hand to-morrow," he said, "but we have no need to dig a grave. The Austrian dogs will sleep soundly enough at the bottom of yonder gulf."

The brigands gave a fierce yell of assent. Tyranny had transformed these men into demons.

"It's too good a grave for a traitor," muttered one of the men; "let them rot upon the rocks till the vultures have fed upon their vile carcases."

The grey shadows of the evening veiled the lower ground as the brigands reached the end of their journey, but on the craggy summit of the mountain it was still light enough to enable the eye to distinguish every object around.

The stronghold which had been christened the Rock of Terror was a stony ledge, upon which thirty men could have found standing room. This ledge was covered with a mass of rock, in a hollow of which a cavern had been formed, which had often served as a hiding-place for the band in times of danger.

This cavern was capable of containing about twenty men. Opposite to the Rock of Terror there was a second mass of stone almost similar in shape to it from the first, but divided from it by a frightful precipice. It was as if the mountain had been split asunder in the throes of an earthquake. The two rocks reared their awful heads like twin giants frowning upon the world beneath.

One of the brigands entered the cavern in the Rock of Terror, and drew out a long deal plank which he carried to the brink of the precipice and threw across the gulf which separated the two peaks. The whole of the party then crossed the chasm, and the plank was withdrawn from the abyss. The Rock of Terror was thus left in dismal solitude.

It was night by the time this had been done. The skies were dimly illuminated by the stars which glimmered here and there in the heavens, but the moon had not yet risen.

The brigands withdrew behind the shelter of the rock, and watched silently for the coming of the expected foe.

"The meeting of the brotherhood is appointed for twelve o'clock," said Black Carlo; "these Austrian dogs will doubtless come early, thinking to be on the spot before any of our band arrive. Hark!"

The men were silent, listening intently to an approaching sound which broke the stillness of the summer's night. The sound was the measured tramp of a small body of men.

"They come, the Austrian dogs!" whispered Black Carlo, as if fearful that his voice should penetrate the stillness, and reach the ears of those approaching men. "They come, the wolves of the tyrant, little dreaming that those they seek to destroy are here before them. Silence, comrades, watch and listen!"

The soldiers ascended the mountain. The little detachment consisted of only twenty men, marshalled by an officer who spoke every now and then, directing them which path to take. The place was evidently familiar to this officer, for he led his party straight to the Rock of Terror.

"Santa Maria!" he muttered, as they reached the summit, "what a weary journey! Examine the ground carefully, and see that none of these scoundrels are concealed behind the rocks."

The men obeyed, and dispersed themselves about the crags, inspecting every crevice.

"That will do," cried the officer at last; "men are not mice, they can't creep into a crevice no broader than my little finger. But, by our gracious lady," he exclaimed, suddenly dropping on his knees before the entrance to the cavern, "here is a hiding-place big enough to hold a dozen of them."

One of the men was about to enter the cavern when the officer pulled him suddenly backwards.

"Hist!" he whispered; "the place may be a trap, swarming with brigands. Fire your carbine into it before you go yourself, man."

The Austrian obeyed, and a bullet whistled into the black recess. There was no sound in reply to this challenge.

"All right!" cried the officer: "this place will serve us admirably: let us see what it is like."

One of the men produced a torch, which was quickly lighted, and by its red glare the officer examined the interior of the cavern.

"Now, listen," he said to the men who had gathered eagerly round him; "the conspirators are to assemble at midnight, and the signal which is to announce their arrival is the striking of a gong. It is now close upon eleven o'clock. Some of the brotherhood may chance to arrive before their time; we must therefore be upon our guard. The cavern will serve us for concealment; small as it is, we can contrive to creep into it, and by close packing it will hold every one of us. You understand?"

"We do, Captain."

"Our business will be to lie quietly in that cavern until the gong strikes. As the gong strikes we shall creep out, one by one, keeping silence, and coming suddenly upon the conspirators. The men we are to arrest are the five chiefs; these are marked men, and are to be secured alive or dead."

"We will not fail, Captain."

The men slowly crept into the narrow mouth of the cavern, and lying close together waited patiently for the appointed signal.

Black Carlo and his comrades had watched all these proceedings from the opposite rock.

"Huzzah!" he whispered, with a fiendish laugh, as the men disappeared in the cavern; "the rats have fallen into the trap. If the vultures knew what a feast there is in store for them, we should have a score of the hungry birds flapping their black wings above our heads."

The moon had slowly risen, and was high in the heavens, but there were dark clouds in the sky, and the thunder rolled hoarsely in the valley below.

"It is nearly midnight," said Black Carlo, after a long interval, during which some of the band had slept; "have you the gong ready, Pietro?"

"Yes, it is here."

"Keep it in readiness for the signal," answered his comrade, consulting a watch which he carried concealed in his belt, no doubt part of some recent plunder; "and now, Matteo Falcone, it is time to strip and prepare for the work."

Black Carlo suited the action to the word, and removed his scarlet shirt, leaving his chest, arms, and shoulders bare. His comrade did the same.

The aspect of the two brigands was now doubly terrible. Their long sinewy arms and broad chests seemed made for deeds of violence. Their wild hair and bristling beards gave them a savage appearance which harmonised well with their words and gestures.

"The swords, Matteo Falcone," exclaimed Black Carlo, "are they ready?"

"They are, comrade."

Matteo Falcone threw the plank once more across the chasm which divided the two rocks.

Pietro stood in readiness, with the gong in his hand, waiting to give the signal.

"Stay!" said Carlo, suddenly; "you take your dagger, Matteo Falcone. I will use the sword."

The two brigands crossed the plank to the Rock of Terror. The other men remained behind ready to rush across to the assistance of their comrades the moment their aid was necessary.

Carlo and Matteo placed themselves on each side of the mouth of the cavern.

Pietro struck the gong, and the signal reverberated through the air.

The Austrian Captain crept cautiously from the cavern.

Then followed a scene almost too horrible for description.

The sword held by Black Carlo swung through the air and descended upon the neck of the unhappy officer, severing his head at one blow.

The soldier who followed him met the same fate—the next also fell; and the rocky platform was scattered with gory human heads—the ghastly trophies of the triumph of the conspirators.

This horrible scene took place in solemn silence. The moon was hidden by a cloud. The hindermost soldiers having no warning given from their slaughtered comrades, knew nothing of the carnage which was going forward. One by one they crept from the cavern, and one by one their reeking heads were severed from their bodies. In little more than ten minutes the twenty men had been slaughtered. Twenty headless corpses, twenty gory heads lay in hideous confusion upon the stony ledge of that mountain summit, only too truly called the Rock of Terror.

"Come hither, comrades," cried Black Carlo, calling to the other brigands. "Behold the fate of the tyrants."

This ignorant man naturally forgot that the murdered soldiers were innocent of the wrongs of ill-used Italy.

The corpses were thrown hastily over into the abyss, but the arms of the Austrians were carefully collected by one of the brigands and carried off to a place of security. When this had been done Black Carlo resumed his garments, and prepared to descend the mountain.

"Whither are you going, Carlo?" asked one of the men.

"I go to my chiefs," answered the brigand, proudly; "I go to tell them that the cause of freedom has triumphed."

Where, while this frightful scene was going forward, was the prime mover of all, the arch-demon—the schemer—traitor—plotter—thief, Oscar Bertrand? Seated in an easy-chair in one of the best hotels of Naples, smoking his cigar and gazing calmly over the purple waters of the bay. As the hour of twelve approached, the Colonel looked up at the enamel dial of a Parisian clock over the mantelpiece and watched the progress of the hands.

"So," he exclaimed, as the silvery-toned chimes rang out the hour, "by this time my lord Marquis and the brotherhood are assembled, in five minutes more they will be my prisoners, and to-morrow I shall be on my way to Vienna to claim my reward from the Austrian Cabinet. My propitious star is in the ascendant!"

Is it so, Oscar Bertrand? What if that blood-red planet—that star of evil omen, should be rapidly going down! What if the hour of retribution should be near at hand?

CHAPTER LXII.

THE DARK JOURNEY

LADY EDITH MERTON sat alone in her boudoir upon the night on which the blood of the murdered Austrian soldiers dyed the stony ledge of the Rock of Terror.

She had obeyed the master-fiend whose slave her guilt had made her, and she felt secure in the triumph of her treachery. Utterly heartless—dead to the still small voice of an accusing

THE UNSEEN WATCHER

conscience, she thought of nothing but her own prosperity. She knew not at what hour her noble husband, the Marquis de Montebello, might be dragged to an Austrian prison, to waste his years in chains and darkness. She knew that in that case it would be easy for her to make friends with the authorities in Vienna, and that a princely income would be the reward of her treachery.

As the clocks of Venice struck one Lady Edith rose from her low easy-chair, and taking a candle from the table by her side, lifted a heavy silken curtain which hung across the arched doorway of her chamber, and passed into the adjoining apartment.

This was the bed-chamber of the Marquis de Montebello.

No. 17. [*Weekly, One Penny.*]

Lady Edith paused upon the threshold and listened. There was no sound in the chamber save the monotonous ticking of a timepiece and the regular breathing of the Marquis, who lay stretched upon the silken counterpane in the dress in which he usually travelled.

Lady Edith was surprised to see that he wore this costume, but she was still more astonished to perceive that he had steel spurs upon the heels of his high-polished leather boots.

He was evidently about to leave Venice, for in Venice he could have no possible need of riding boots and spurs.

But whither could he be going, and why did he lie down thus prepared for a journey?

Lady Edith sank into the chair by the bedside, and, leaning her head upon her hand, abandoned herself to reflection. Her cheeks blanched at the thought that the Marquis had, perhaps, discovered her treachery.

But how could that be possible? Oscar Bertrand alone was in the secret, and he, of all others, would be the last to reveal it.

She rose, and leaning over the sleeping man, contemplated his noble countenance.

It was as serene as the face of a slumbering infant.

Lady Edith was about to withdraw from the bed-side, when her eye was arrested by the glitter of some object half concealed under the Marquis' waistcoat. She bent over the sleeper, and looking more closely at this glittering object, perceived that it was the hilt of a dagger, and perceived also that the Marquis carried a pair of pocket pistols in the bosom of his coat.

He was evidently prepared for a journey, and he was also prepared to encounter danger of some kind. He must therefore have received some warning. But from whom?

While these thoughts were agitating the mind of Lady Edith, her eyes wandered to the hand of the Marquis, which was thrown above the pillow upon which his head reposed.

In this hand the sleeper loosely held a scrap of paper. So loose was the grasp of the sleeper, that Lady Edith was able to remove this paper without arousing him.

She then placed her taper upon a table near the bed, and reseating herself in the massive arm-chair, she unfolded and examined the scrap of paper.

The writing upon this paper was in a hand which she did not know. It was written in Italian.

"A WARNING TO THE BRAVE AND TRUE, FROM ONE OF THE WATCHERS.

"Sleep lightly, and sleep in your travelling dress. Wear spurs on your boots, and be ready for a long and perilous journey. Whatever fortune you wish to keep must be carried upon your person; and if you would go in safety, arm yourself to the teeth."

"Who can have written this?" murmured Lady Edith. "Who can it be who thus warns him of a danger which is known only to myself and Oscar Bertrand? The writer of this tells him to carry his fortune upon his person. I wonder whether he has obeyed that injunction as well as the others."

The Marquis lay upon his right side, and the left pocket of his loose riding-coat hung over the edge of the coverlet.

Lady Edith perceived that this pocket was unusually bulky. With a stealthy hand she drew out a small morocco casket, fastened with a massive steel lock.

This casket was of considerable weight.

"This doubtless contains bank notes and jewels," murmured the traitress. "The diamonds of the Montebellos are celebrated for their beauty and value; he has allowed me to wear them, but he has never left them in my possession. I remember this casket as that in which he kept the gems. What if I were to secure these and fly this night from Venice? I feel a mysterious dread of approaching danger, and a foreboding instinct tells me that there is no safety for me in this city."

She took the taper from the table, and was about to return to her own apartment, carrying with her the casket of diamonds, when her cautious footsteps were arrested by a rustling sound at the other end of the room.

This rustling sound was occasioned by the parting of the velvet curtains which hung before the panelled walls.

Lady Edith turned suddenly round, and with difficulty repressed a shriek of terror as she perceived the cause of this sound.

At the end of the chamber facing the bed upon which the Marquis lay, the green velvet hangings had been thrown aside, revealing an opening in the wall, through which was to be seen a secret staircase, dimly lighted by two lanterns.

Upon the threshold of this opening in the wall stood two men, both dressed in black cloaks which concealed their figures, and both masked.

Lady Edith recoiled in mute terror as she beheld these two men. For a moment she believed them to be members of the horrible association to which she herself belonged—emissaries of the Master of the Black Band; but an instant's reflection assured her of her mistake.

In her confusion she laid the casket of diamonds upon the table by the bed-side.

The two masked men advanced towards the sleeper, but at a few paces from the bed one of them paused. The other approached close to the pillow of the Marquis, and quietly laid his hand upon the sleeper's shoulder.

The Marquis started, and, lifting his head from the pillow, looked inquiringly at the mask.

"I received your warning," he said, "and, as you may perceive, have obeyed it."

The mask bent his head with a gesture of assent.

"Who is that?" he asked, pointing to Lady Edith, who stood horror-stricken.

"My wife," exclaimed the Marquis. "Do not fear to speak; she may be trusted."

The second mask had withdrawn to the other end of the room, and was standing near the open panel. As the Marquis de Montebello said these words this second mask laughed aloud,

The first mask answered—

"We do not fear her power to betray us," he said, slowly. "Rise, Marquis de Montebello, the hour of peril has come. The Mountaineers have been betrayed."

"By whom?" asked the Marquis.

"That you will know when you have crossed the Italian frontier on our way to England," answered the mask.

"And you have come to conduct me to a place of safety?"

"I have."

"My wife, too?"

"She, too, will be—safe," answered the mask. "Our business is to see her to a place of perfect safety."

Lady Edith Merton breathed more freely.

"They know nothing," she thought.

The Marquis rose from his bed, and took a hat and riding-whip from a table near him.

"I am ready," he said.

"Stay!" exclaimed the mask; "there is a casket upon yonder table which perhaps contains something of value."

The Marquis started as his eyes followed the hand with which the mask pointed to the morocco casket.

"Good heavens!" he cried, "this must be witchcraft. I placed that casket in the pocket of my coat before I lay down to rest."

Lady Edith smiled incredulously.

"You have been dreaming, my dear Lorenzo," she murmured.

"No matter, dearest," answered the Marquis; "the casket is safe, and will buy us a happy home in a free country, if danger forces us to fly from this. Wrap yourself in a cloak, dearest, for the night air will be cold."

Lady Edith retired into the adjoining chamber, and returned in a few moments enveloped in a voluminous velvet mantle, the hood of which covered her head.

"I am ready," she said.

"Is my wife to accompany me?" asked the Marquis.

"No, Signor," answered the mask, "the journey which you are to take is too long and fatiguing for a lady. We shall conduct the Signora to a place of safety at a shorter distance from Venice."

"And she will be able to rejoin me in England?" asked the Marquis.

"She will do whatever is most in accordance with the interests of the Society," replied the mask; "as the wife of a patriot she can do no less. Come, Signor, we are ready, and there is no time to lose."

The mask led the way to the secret outlet; the Marquis followed, conducting his wife.

As Lady Edith approached the narrow winding staircase, whose existence she had been ignorant of until that night, she perceived to her surprise that it was lined with ten masked men, two of whom held the lanterns which shed their light upon the steep steps.

"Why are all these men here?" she asked, anxiously.

"To conduct you to a place of safety, Signora," answered the mask, who had carried on the dialogue which we have just related.

The Marquis and Lady Edith descended the staircase, guarded by the masks, who kept close to them as if they had been prisoners of state. The staircase led to a small octagonal chamber, which Lady Edith had never entered during her residence in the Palace of the Marquis.

"Here," said the mask, "you and the lady must part, Eccellenza. You will be conducted in a gondola to the island of Torcello, where you will be picked up at daybreak by a steamer which will carry you to Marseilles. The captain is one of us. You will therefore be asked no questions."

"And my wife?" exclaimed the Marquis, anxiously.

"She will accompany us to Naples, where she will be placed in perfect safety."

"But why to Naples?"

"The Association have decreed it," replied the mask, sternly. "All that is done to-night is done for the interests of the Association. A good Mountaineer asks no questions—he trusts!"

"And I will trust," cried the Marquis, with enthusiasm. "I will trust in the honour and truth of a noble body of men, even though I leave that which is dearer to me than my life in their keeping. Farewell, beloved; Heaven bless and guard you."

He took the traitress in his arms, and pressed his lips to her icy brow. A deathly chill came over her as she saw him depart with the first mask by a flight of steps which led down to the water, where two gondolas, a large and a small one, were waiting.

The Marquis and his masked companion took the smaller gondola. The ten other masked men descended the steps and placed themselves in the larger one. The remaining mask gave his hand to Lady Edith, and conducted her to a seat in this larger gondola.

The small boat shot rapidly down the canal, and away into the open expanse of water.

This was the last that Lady Edith Merton ever saw of the Marquis de Montebello.

"Why are there so many men with me and only one with him?" asked Lady Edith of the mask at her side, as the small gondola disappeared.

"Because we are anxious for your safety, Signora," he answered.

The large gondola followed for a little time in the wake of the smaller upon the open expanse of waters, but the smaller boat soon shot away in the darkness, Lady Edith knew not whither.

They had been on the open water nearly an hour when the masked rowers plied their oars more slowly, and Lady Edith perceived that they were approaching a small steamer. One of the masks hailed this steamer. A rope was thrown out, and the gondola was drawn to the side of the vessel.

A few minutes after this Lady Edith found herself in a small cabin, scantily furnished, and lighted with a lantern like those carried by the masks.

Nine of the masks had come on board the steamer, the other two had remained in the gondola.

Lady Edith felt considerable relief at this change in her position.

"It is evident they have no hidden design against me," she thought, "or they would not place me on board this steamer, where it would of course be easy for me to communicate with my fellow-passengers."

She placed her hand upon the latch of the cabin-door as she spoke. It was locked and bolted on the outside.

There was a little window in one side of the cabin, but on examination she found that this window was of the thickest glass, and that inside the glass there was an iron grating.

It was impossible for the person within that cabin either to open the window, or to make his voice heard outside.

Lady Edith groaned aloud in an agony of terror.

"It is too clear," she murmured; "they know all, and they have separated me from my husband in order to wreak some terrible vengeance upon me. Yet they cannot mean to kill me, or they would scarcely have brought me here. It would have been so easy for them to have flung me from the gondola into the dark waters of the Adriatic."

She knocked at the cabin door, and shook the frail panel with her hand. A voice from without asked her what she wanted.

"I wish to see the stewardess," she said.

The person without laughed mockingly.

"We have no stewardess on board this boat," he answered.

"My fellow-passengers, then. Let me see them."

"You have no fellow-passengers,"

"Why am I here?" asked Lady Edith, unable to control her terror.

"You are here in order to be conveyed to a place of safety."

"To be murdered, perhaps."

"No."

"You do not mean to murder me?"

"I give you my honour that not one drop of your blood will be shed by the brotherhood of the Mountaineers," answered the man.

A few moments afterwards Lady Edith heard his measured step sounding upon the deck.

The wretched woman breathed more freely.

It was broad daylight when they came within sight of Naples, but instead of steaming into the bay, the captain of the vessel dropped his anchor at some distance from the shore, and the steamer remained stationary throughout the long and tedious day, until darkness hid the shore from Lady Edith's weary eyes.

She had tasted nothing throughout that almost interminable day, except a mouthful of bread and a glass of wine which had been handed to her through an opening in the cabin door.

In vain she had implored the mask to allow her to breathe the fresh air upon the deck of the vessel. He had turned a deaf ear to her prayers.

It was a moonless night, and the sailors could scarcely see the shore towards which the steamer was carrying them when they drew near to their destination.

Lady Edith was conducted on shore between two of the nine masks. The other seven ranged themselves round her as a guard, three walking before and three walking behind; one apparently superintending all.

Environed thus, all thought of escape was hopeless.

A few hundred yards from the pier at which they had landed they found a close carriage, drawn by two roughly-groomed horses, waiting for them.

One of the masks handed Lady Edith into this vehicle. The guilty woman shuddered as she remembered that it was in this very city that she had plotted the destruction of her guiltless rival, Lolota Vizzini.

After driving for about ten minutes, the little procession stopped by a high wall, in which there was a narrow wooden door.

One of the masks uttered a low bird-like cry, which was evidently a signal, for the door was opened, and two strange men, also masked, appeared upon the threshold.

Lady Edith recoiled with horror at perceiving that these two men carried a burden—a burden which resembled a dead body in shape and appearance.

The two men brought this ghastly load to the door of the coach, and laid it upon the seat opposite to Lady Edith.

"Is he dead?" she exclaimed, in a tone of disgust.

"No, Signora," answered one of the masks, "he is not dead, but he is silent. Now, comrades," he added, taking his place by the side of the vehicle, "march; and you, driver, see that your horses go slowly. You know the road. To the base of the mountain path which leads to the Rock of Terror."

CHAPTER LXIII.

THE BURIAL OF THE LIVING

THE dismal vehicle in which Lady Edith Merton was seated, closely guarded by one of the masked men who sat by her side, drove slowly onward, she knew not whither, through the darkness.

On each side of the vehicle marched four of the masked guards. Lady Edith looked from the window of the carriage, but she could discover nothing but the dusky shadows of these masked men, who looked like phantoms in the dark obscurity.

She gazed earnestly at the burden upon the carriage seat. It was as still as death.

"It is the body of a man!" she murmured to her masked companion.

"It is," answered the mask.

"And he is dead?"

"No," replied the mask; "I told you just now he is not dead; he is only silent."

"He is gagged, then?"

"No, he is silenced more surely. He will never speak again."

"Why not?"

"Because he is a traitor, Signora."

"A traitor!" exclaimed the shuddering woman.

"Yes, a traitor. A traitor to the cause of the champions of free and regenerated Italy. A traitor to the Brotherhood of the Mountaineers. You think, perhaps, that we are triflers, Signora —that we are children; and that our dreams of liberty are as shadowy as the fairy visions which haunt the sleep of childhood. But you are mistaken, Signora; we are no children, and our vengeance is no child's play."

Lady Edith tried to answer, but her parched tongue clove to the roof of her mouth, and she was unable to utter a word.

"Shall I tell you, Signora," asked the mask,

in measured accents, "how the Association of the Mountaineers have avenged themselves upon that man?"

He pointed as he spoke to the muffled burden upon the opposite seat.

Lady Edith bent her head. She was powerless to give any other reply.

"When the sun rose yesterday," resumed the mask, "that man was possessed of the intellect which can make a mighty ruler or a master fiend. He had chosen to pervert the gift, and had debased himself to the level of the fiends of hell. Remorseless, unscrupulous, and guilty, he trod the dark pathway which he had made for himself, reckless of the end to which that path was leading him. The plotting brain, the murderous hand, both were his. He rose yesterday morning in full possession of every power. Last night he was invited to a banquet by one whom he thought his dupe. That man was one of our brotherhood."

There was a pause. Lady Edith remained in the speechless terror to which she had been stricken.

"At the banquet to which the traitor was invited," continued the mask, "there were many costly and generous wines; but there was one flask of rock crystal, mounted with gold, which contained a crimson liquid, brilliant in its hues as molten rubies. The traitor's hawk-like glance was attracted by the beauty of this vessel and by the hue of the liquid which it contained, and he asked the name of the wine. His host smiled. 'It is a nameless wine,' he answered, 'and it is very powerful in its effect upon those who drink it. I would advise you to beware how you taste it.' The traitor laughed aloud at this warning. 'I have drank of too many vintages to be afraid of any wine which you can offer me, my dear friend,' he said, with contemptuous carelessness. As he spoke he took a goblet from the table and filled it with the brilliant fluid in the crystal flask. He looked round at the assembled guests with a smile of proud defiance, mockingly saluted his host, and drained the goblet. When he lifted that goblet he was possessed of the highest intellectual powers which Heaven can give to man; when he set it down——"

The mask paused for a moment.

"What then?" gasped Lady Edith.

"He was a drivelling idiot."

"Oh, horror!" murmured the wretched traitress.

"He had drunk of a draught, the secret of which is known only to three men—the three greatest chemists of the age. One of these men is a member of the brotherhood, and he it was who prepared the ruby-tinted fluid which, in its

THE ROCK OF TERROR

appearance, resembles the rarest wine. That draught has power to transform, in one brief moment, the intellect of a ruler of nations into the fatuity of an idiot. The plotting brain, which could weave the intricate web of a thousand schemes, is blotted out, and a blank alone remains. Memory, love, hate, all melt away beneath the force of that liquid fire, which consumes the brain without impairing the strength of the body. The traitor lying opposite to us heeds not our words, hears not our voices, knows not that we are here. To him earth is empty and the heavens a blank. The most terrible death which cruelty could inflict upon him would be an act of charity, for it would release him from a life of hopeless darkness and silence—darker than the darkness of the blind—more silent than the silence of the dumb."

A shivering motion agitated the folds of the cloak, and a low gurgling moan broke from the lips of the man lying upon the carriage seat.

Lady Edith started.

"Surely he must have heard!" she exclaimed.

"No," answered the mask. "He hears nothing. He has a dull sense of pain in his weary head. For the drug which he has drunk slowly rots away the brain of him who tastes it; and the process is not painless. Now, Signora, tell me if you think the vengeance of the Mountaineers is child's play?"

"No!" cried Lady Edith, with a sudden burst of energy. "It is not child's play; it is sport, perhaps; but it is the sport of fiends."

"There is no punishment too terrible for those who betray the cause of a struggling nation," answered the mask.

Lady Edith made no reply. She sat silent and motionless, her whole being absorbed in one dreadful thought—What was to be her fate?

"Listen to me," she exclaimed suddenly. "It is useless to pretend ignorance of your purpose in bringing me hither; you would be revenged on me for some wrong which you fancy I have done towards your Association. Guilty or innocent, I am in your power, and you can do with me as you will. I have but one request to make to you."

"I listen," answered the mask.

"Do with me what you will, but spare my reason. Let me die if you will, but do not leave me to wander with besotted brain upon the darkened face of a weary earth. Promise me that."

"I promise," said the mask.

"You will not rob me of my intelligence?"

"Nothing shall be done to cast one shadow upon the brightness of your intellect, Signora," answered the mask. "No violent hand shall assail you. No murderous knife shall shed one drop of your aristocratic blood. No poisonous compound shall be offered to you. No rough arm shall fling you to a watery death."

"You would not kill me, then?" exclaimed Lady Edith.

"No, Signora."

"What, then, would you do to me?"

"That is a secret now, Signora; but it will be no secret three hours hence."

Once more there was silence. Half an hour afterwards the voice of one of the masked guards called "Halt!"

The vehicle stopped. One of the guards lighted a torch, while another opened the carriage door.

"Dismount, Signora," said Lady Edith's masked companion.

She descended from the vehicle, and, looking eagerly round her in the red glare of the torch-light, she beheld a mountainous district, wild and lonely in its character.

Six of the masked guards formed themselves into a little procession, and marched towards a narrow mountain-path with Lady Edith between them.

"Stop!" cried the mask who had ridden with her in the carriage. "Stop, Signora; before you leave this place, it will be well for you to see the traitor upon whom the vengeance of the brotherhood has fallen."

Lady Edith paused; indifferent to all but the thought of her own peril.

"You do not ask the traitor's name, Signora," said the mask.

"I do not care to know it," she answered, coldly.

"It will be best for you to discover it from the face of the traitor himself," said the mask; "it will help the lesson you will learn to-night. Bring hither your burden."

Two men lifted the recumbent figure from the carriage seat.

They placed the man upon his feet. He staggered forward a few paces, still wrapt from head to foot in the cloak which concealed alike his face and figure, and then sank in a crouching attitude upon a block of stone which lay upon the mountain road.

Every now and then he uttered the dreary moaning noise which Lady Edith had heard in the carriage.

"Bring your torch, Luigi," said the mask, "and you, Donato, lift the cloak."

One of the masked guards advanced with a torch in his hand. His comrade bent over the idiot, and lifted the cloak from his head and face.

Lady Edith Merton looked at the face, which stared with a dull expressionless glare at the lurid light of the torch.

Then with one prolonged shriek of horror, whose echoes resounded along the mountains, she staggered back several paces, clasping her hands before her eyes.

The idiot was Colonel Oscar Bertrand.

The handsome face of the Austrian was now a ghastly spectacle. Every spark of intelligence had fled from his once brilliant eyes. His chin fell forward upon his breast, and his under lip hung powerless upon his chin, while a white foam oozed slowly from his open mouth. His head, which, four-and-twenty hours before, had been carried with the haughty grace of an emperor, now trembled like that of some wretched being in the last stage of palsy. His hands hung loosely from his wrists, as if every sinew had been withered.

This was the man who had defied justice and and laughed at danger. This was the man whose powerful intellect had ruled the souls of his fellow-men. This was the Mephistopheles who had led the weak and the guilty from petty crimes to deeds of horror and bloodshed.

"Leave him!" said the mask. "We have done with him. Let him go."

The man who had been addressed as Luigi untied the cords with which the Austrian had been bound.

Oscar Bertrand rose from his sitting posture and staggered away along a winding mountain path. Lady Edith Merton heard his idiotic laugh grow fainter in the distance as he disappeared.

"Now, Signora," said the mask, who was evidently the leader of the little band, "come with me."

He placed himself upon her right hand. The man called Luigi took his place on the left. The other masks walked in the same order as that in which they had gone from the steamer to the carriage.

In this order they slowly marched along the mountain pathway by which the brigand associates of the brotherhood had gone to the Rock of Terror.

The first pale glimmer of the morning light peeped over the summit of the mountain as the little party approached the Rock of Terror. Every object was distinctly visible in the cold grey light, when the dismal procession halted upon the stony ledge before the cavern in which the Austrian soldiers had hidden.

This stony platform was disfigured by a spreading stain of a blackish hue.

The masked captain pointed to this stain.

"Can you guess what that is, Signora?" he asked.

"No," said Lady Edith, indifferently.

"It is the blood of the enemies of Italy."

The terrified woman looked eagerly round her. She thought that her masked companion had deceived her, and that she had been brought into this mountain stronghold to be murdered. But, in looking searchingly at her masked guards, she perceived that they carried no weapons whatever, nor was there any appearance of intended violence in any object near.

Worn out as she was by long watching and lasting, her senses seemed unnaturally clear, as if every faculty had been intensified by terror, and no feature in the rugged scene was lost upon her scrutinising gaze.

One object attracted her attention, and filled her with wonder.

This was a niche in the rock; a niche which had evidently been newly hewn out of the solid stone, for the fragments which had been hacked out of the rock were strewn upon the stony ledge.

This niche, or recess, measured about three feet and a half in breadth, and six feet in height

By the side of this recess lay a heap of new bricks, a pile of wet mortar, and a mason's trowel.

As Lady Edith looked at these things a stalwart figure emerged from the opening in the rock, and Black Carlo appeared before the masked leader.

"We have done our work, captain," he said.

"Ay," answered the mask, "and you have done it quickly and well. The niche is neatly made, and we have brought the statue."

One of the masked guards laughed.

"Come, Signora," said the captain, "can you guess now why we have brought you here?"

"To murder me!" exclaimed Lady Edith.

"No," answered the mask, with horrible deliberation; "*to bury you alive!*"

The wretched woman uttered a piercing shriek, and flew towards the edge of the rock, from which she would have hurled herself to the abyss below, had not the masked captain grasped her wrist in his strong hand.

"No, Signora," he exclaimed, "you do not escape us thus. A rapid death for the brave and noble. A lingering fate for the traitor. Yonder niche has been hewn on purpose for so fair a statue. Come, lady!"

He clasped her slender waist in his encircling arm. Black Carlo threw a cloak over her head, and in another moment they placed her in a standing position in the stony recess.

Her wild shrieks of despair rang through the mountain air, but there were none to respond to those cries of anguish.

One of the masked guards took the trowel, and, with a rapid and unerring hand, fitted the bricks into the square opening in the rock.

Rapidly and surely the wall arose which was to shut Lady Edith Merton from a world for whose glories she had sacrificed her soul.

When this wall had been built on a level with the face of the traitress, the masked captain held up his hand.

"Stop!" he exclaimed, "let your work end here. We will leave the fair lady with power to see the skies and the mountain-tops. She will live the longer, and will have more time for repentance. Give her this."

He handed a crucifix to the mask, who hung it upon a craggy point of the rock, in such a position that it could be easily seen by his victim.

Lady Edith had now lost all power to shriek. A deathly faintness benumbed her senses. Her wild eyes gazed straight before her at the grey morning sky.

"March, comrades," cried the masked captain. "The work is done. The brotherhood is revenged upon those who would have betrayed it."

With a slow and steady tramp the masked company descended the circuitous pathway by which they had mounted to the Rock of Terror.

Black Carlo and his comrades disappeared in another direction.

Alone amid the silence and solitude of Nature—alone in the presence of the Almighty Power whose laws she had forgotten and whose justice she had defied, Lady Edith Merton waited for death.

CHAPTER LXIV.

THE MEETING IN THE VALLEY

WE left Lolota Vizzini and the Marquis of Willoughby at the very moment when the life of the lovely Spanish woman trembled in the balance, and when it seemed as if nothing short of a miracle could save her from the cruel fate which Lady Edith Merton had designed for her innocent rival.

It pleased Providence, however, to spare the generous-hearted Lolota. The hour in which Lionel Montfort reached the bed of the fever-stricken patient was the turning-point of the disease. The prayer of the penitent man was heard; and Lolota reached in safety a small village, within a few miles of Naples, to which

the first physicians of the Italian city advised Lord Willoughby to convey his charge.

The young nobleman rented a small villa half-hidden in a grove of orange-trees, and sheltered by the mountains which screened it on every side save one, before which stretched the sea.

The French girl who had attended Lolota, and who had also suffered from the infamous plot against the life of her mistress, was likewise conveyed to this retired villa, and placed under the care of the same skilful physician who was attending Madame Vizzini.

Lolota Vizzini was the first to recover. When she awoke to consciousness upon the evening of her removal from Naples, she opened her eyes upon a scene which was strange to her.

The bed upon which she lay was situated opposite a wide casement, which was opened to its fullest extent. Festoons of dark green foliage clustered round the framework of this casement.

Through the open space between these leafy festoons the purple sea, gilded by the last rays of the setting sun, greeted the gaze of the invalid, while the low plashing murmur of the waves sounded like the lullaby which a mother sings to her sleeping infant.

Lolota Vizzini closed her eyes, almost overpowered by her sense of the tranquil loveliness of Nature.

It was some time before she reopened her eyes. When she did so she perceived that she was not alone. A young man was seated near her pillow, but his face was shrouded from her view by the white curtains of the bed.

A little way from him sat a woman in the garments worn by the sisters of a religious order, whose members devote themselves to the nursing of the sick.

Although Lolota Vizzini could not see the face of the male watcher by her sick couch, she felt that he was no stranger to her.

"Lionel!" she exclaimed; "is it indeed you?"

Lord Willoughby threw himself on his knees by the bed-side.

"My dearest love," he murmured. "Heaven has heard my prayers; you will be restored to me."

The Sister of Mercy laid her hand upon the shoulder of the Marquis.

"Pray, Signor, do not forget the physician's orders," she whispered; "the Signora is to be guarded from every agitation, every excitement. Let me implore you to leave the room. While the Signora was sleeping you might watch over her without endangering her recovery; now that she has awakened, I must beg of you to leave us."

The Marquis rose from his knees.

"You are right, Madame," he said. "I will obey you to the letter. Let me but speak one word to your patient, and then I will leave her under your watchful care."

He bent over the couch, and taking the feeble and burning hand in his own, lifted it to his lips.

"Sleep in peace, dearest; but even in your dreams remember that I am near you."

The large dark eyes of the Spanish woman were suffused with tears as she lifted them to the face of her affianced husband.

She tried to speak, but her trembling lips refused to utter the words which her heart prompted.

Long after midnight, when her nurse was sleeping peacefully in an easy-chair by the bed, Lolota rose from her couch, weak as she was, and knelt to offer gratitude and praise to Heaven for happiness that seemed almost overwhelming.

Little did she suspect that an unseen watcher marked that suppliant attitude, that fervent prayer.

Lionel Montfort had found himself unable to rest, under the agitation of his thoughts, and had spent the silent hours between midnight and morning wandering in the garden, and pausing every now and then to peep through the casement of the sick room.

He saw his betrothed on her knees, heard her offering up her thanks to Heaven for the blessings of his love, all unworthy as he was.

Three days after this, Lolota Vizzini was pronounced by the physician to be out of danger.

Her recovery was rapid; for he whom she loved was near her, and his presence seemed to inspire her with new life and strength.

"I am too happy, Lionel," she murmured; "and I sometimes fear all this happiness must be some dream which will melt away and leave me to despair."

Three weeks after their removal to the villa, Lolota Vizzini was entirely recovered, and it was about this time that an event occurred which had considerable influence upon the lives of the two lovers.

Early one morning the Marquis of Willoughby walked out alone upon the mountain road which wound around the lovely spot upon which the villa was situated. His object in taking this solitary walk was to procure his letters from the post-office at a small village three miles from the villa.

He reached the village, called at the post-office, received the only letter which awaited him—the epistle of one of those few confidential friends whom he had ventured to entrust with a knowledge of his whereabouts—and set out on his return home.

In his eagerness to get back to the villa, he determined upon taking an intricate pathway, which skirted a ravine, and wound round a portion of the base of the mountain.

The way was gloomy and solitary; but he cared for nothing so long as it led him more quickly to the point which he was so impatient to reach.

He had walked about a mile and a half from the village when, to his annoyance, he discovered that he had lost his way.

The steep side of the mountain shut out the surrounding country, and he was therefore unable to discover where he had strayed.

He looked for some chance pedestrian who might be able to direct him in the right pathway, but for some time he looked in vain; by and by, however, he perceived in the distance the figure of a man walking along the narrow pathway before him.

This man appeared to be of advanced age; his form was bent nearly double, and his legs tottered under him as he crept along.

He was not dressed like the peasants of the surrounding villages. His clothes, though tattered and mud-stained, were those of an English gentleman.

Lord Willoughby had no difficulty in overtaking this man, whose pace was slow as it was feeble.

"Will you be good enough to direct me to the Villa Valdino?" he said, addressing the stranger in English.

There was no reply, the man still tottered onwards, taking no notice whatever of the question.

Lord Willoughby repeated his inquiry in Italian.

Again there was no answer, save a harsh idiotic laugh, whose discordant tones startled the Marquis.

He laid his hand upon the shoulder of the stranger.

The man turned, and raising himself from his stooping attitude, scowled with a wolfish glare at the young nobleman.

The stranger was Oscar Bertrand.

Lord Willoughby drew back speechless with astonishment.

His old enemy, the destroyer of his peace, the prompter of his brother's murder, stood before him.

But that guilty teacher was no longer worthy even of revenge. Helpless, feeble, decrepit, idiotic, he had sunk lower than the animals that grazed in the valley below.

The wretched creature burst into a loud peal of shrill laughter, and tottered away, gibbering and mouthing as he went.

The Marquis forgot even his eagerness to return home, in the astonishment which this unlooked-for meeting had inspired. He wandered slowly onwards, and half an hour afterwards met a peasant lad who conducted him into the right pathway.

He was pale as death when he re-entered the cheerful saloon in which his beloved Lolota awaited him.

Madame Vizzini was alarmed by the altered aspect of her lover.

"Something has happened, Lionel," she murmured, anxiously.

"Yes, dearest," he answered; "the vengeance of offended Heaven has fallen upon a guilty wretch—I have no longer an enemy. We can return to England as soon as you are strong enough to bear the fatigue of the journey."

"And that will be to-morrow, Lionel, if you wish it," replied Lolota.

"Dearest one," whispered Lionel, "I have arranged everything with Francisco, the good old priest at Marenna, and to-morrow he will marry us according to the rites of the Catholic Church. When we return to England the marriage ceremony can be repeated by a Protestant minister."

Early the next morning the lovers drove to the little village of Marenna, and accompanied the old priest to the humble chapel which devotion had raised even in that solitary district.

The marriage ceremony was performed with no witnesses but the physician, Lolota's faithful maid, and a few wondering villagers, who looked with considerable curiosity at the lovely but tearful bride.

As the Marquis and his beautiful companion were leaving the holy edifice, accompanied by the priest, they were startled by the appearance of a crowd stationed about the door of the village inn.

The members of the crowd saluted the priest with a respectful eagerness as he approached.

"Ah, Padre mio," said one of the men, " you are much wanted here; a poor creature has just been carried into the inn. She seems at the point of death, she can neither speak, nor move; but she still breathes, and she seems still conscious."

The priest hurried through the crowd. Lolota and Lord Willoughby followed, impelled by mingled curiosity and sympathy.

A strange and extremely painful sight met their gaze.

Upon a rough litter of green branches held by two men lay the dying woman.

Her face was of a leaden hue; her large black eyes were half starting from her head, and had the glassy lustre of approaching death. Her faint breath came in stifling gasps, each gasp more painful to her than the last. The priest knelt by her side, with the holy emblem of Christianity in his hand. He whispered words of comfort to the expiring woman, but was too late.

At the very moment that the good old priest uttered the first syllable of the prayer for the passing soul, the dying woman's eyes met the face of Lord Willoughby, who had just crossed the threshold of the room.

As she beheld that once familiar face, a prolonged shriek of agony burst suddenly from her throat, and at almost the same moment a crimson torrent gushed from her bedabbled lips.

She had burst a blood-vessel.

In the next instant she fell back dead !

This woman was the once brilliant and beautiful Lady Edith Merton.

A wandering goatherd, who had followed a stray member of his flock to the summit of the Rock of Terror, had been attracted by the extraordinary apparition of a human face looking out of a newly-built wall in the solid stone.

He had been still more bewildered on perceiving that the face was that of a living being.

With the aid of two of his comrades, he had succeeded in removing the bricks, the mortar having scarcely dried since the burial of the living.

For four-and-twenty hours Lady Edith Merton had remained in this horrible position when she was rescued by the goatherds.

But it was too late. Life was well-nigh spent. She survived long enough to be conveyed upon a roughly constructed litter to the humble inn at Marenna, which was within a mile of the base of the Rock of Terror, but she expired on beholding him whom she had once loved.

An inquiry was held by the Italian authorities upon the body of Lady Edith, and it was the Marquis of Willoughby who bore witness to the identity of the dead woman. A purse bearing the arms of the Vandeleur family, and containing a letter addressed to Lady Edith Merton, served to confirm his evidence, and an account of the English lady's terrible death was published in all the Italian papers.

*   *   *   *   *   *

Little more remains to be told.

Lionel and his wife live a retired but happy life at the country seat of the young nobleman. By deeds of benevolence, Lionel endeavours to atone for the sins of his youth; while in Lolota he has ever a ministering angel, eager to lead him into the golden pathway whose end is peace.

The foreign newspapers conveyed to Robert Merton the first tidings he received of the strange and terrible death of his once idolised wife.

Guilty as she had been, the noble-hearted husband could not read that ghastly story without a pang of pitying anguish. He hastened to Naples and made his way to the village of Marenna, where he ascertained the truth of the story.

By his directions a simple stone tablet was erected in the little Italian chapel, recording only the name and age of the deceased.

* * * * * *

We have followed the innocent and the guilty alike impartially through the intricate labyrinth of life. We have seen the innocent for a time oppressed—the guilty for a time triumphant; but we have also seen that the wondrous balance of good and evil will infallibly adjust itself in the end; and that a dire and unlooked-for vengeance will alight upon the heads of those who defy the Power which rules this universe, or laugh to scorn the just laws of an All-Wise Providence.

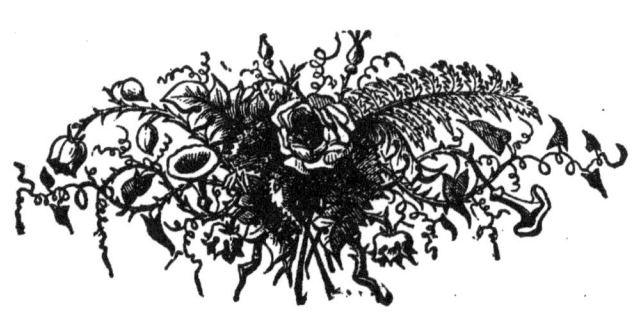